T0379013

BLACK TIE
AND TAILS

BAEN BOOKS by WEN SPENCER

BLACK WOLVES OF BOSTON
The Black Wolves of Boston
Black Tie and Tails

THE ELFHOME SERIES
Tinker
Wolf Who Rules
Elfhome
Wood Sprites
Project Elfhome
Harbinger
Storm Furies

ALSO BY WEN SPENCER
Endless Blue
Eight Million Gods

To purchase any of these titles in e-book form,
please go to www.baen.com.

BLACK TIE AND TAILS

WEN SPENCER

Copyright © 2025 by Wen Spencer

A Baen Books Original

Baen Publishing Enterprises
P.O. Box 1403
Riverdale, NY 10471
www.baen.com

ISBN: 978-1-6680-7284-4

Cover art by Dominic Harman

First printing, September 2025

Distributed by Simon & Schuster
1230 Avenue of the Americas
New York, NY 10020

Library of Congress Cataloging-in-Publication Data

Names: Spencer, Wen author
Title: Black tie and tails / Wen Spencer.
Description: Riverdale, NY : Baen Publishing Enterprises, 2025. | Series:
    Black wolves of Boston ; 2
Identifiers: LCCN 2025018630 (print) | LCCN 2025018631 (ebook) | ISBN
    9781668072844 hardcover | ISBN 9781964856346 ebook
Subjects: BISAC: FICTION / Fantasy / Action & Adventure | FICTION / Fantasy
    / Urban | LCGFT: Fiction | Fantasy fiction | Novels
Classification: LCC PS3619.P4665 B57 2025 (print) | LCC PS3619.P4665
    (ebook) | DDC 813/.6—dc23/eng/20250613
LC record available at https://lccn.loc.gov/2025018630
LC ebook record available at https://lccn.loc.gov/2025018631

10 9 8 7 6 5 4 3 2 1

Printed in the United States of America

This book is dedicated to my wonderful patrons on Patreon.
It is through their support that I am able to do what I do.

Special thanks to

Marti Garner
Roger A. Josephson
Andrew Riley Prest
Torsten Steinert
Elisabeth Waters

And

Kathy Brann
Michael Carter
Andrew Hart
Jacquelyn Jacobs
Richard Jamison
Alice Ma
Anders Ljungquist
Robert Williamson

And Extra Special Thank-You to

Ellen McMicking
Mary Carter Johnson
Joseph Merkling

BLACK TIE
AND TAILS

1: JOSHUA

"Pssst, hey, kid, over here," someone whispered from among the flock of sleeping penguins.

Joshua knew he was dreaming because he couldn't read the sign in front of him; the letters kept crawling about, refusing to let him understand the message before him. It had been a night full of nightmares, obviously brought on by the fact that in the morning he was going to a new high school.

His earlier dreams had started at the Tatterskeins' private school, Blackridge. In one he'd listened to the statues at the front gate talk about his real mother and father. Later, he ran through the hallways naked, late for a test in a class he'd forgotten to attend. But then his nightmares progressed to old familiar landscapes. The halls of his old high school. The barn where the prom committee gathered to hold a haunted house fundraiser. The cornfield where his classmates had died, and he'd become a werewolf.

Joshua had had a very bad senior year so far. There was little wonder why he was worried about the six months that were left until he graduated from his new school.

In the weird omniscient dream way, he knew that he was on a school field trip at an aquarium. There were other students scattered throughout the building, but currently he was alone in the vast dim space in front of the exhibit, trying to figure out what type of penguins were huddled on the bare rocks on the other side of the pool of water.

"Hey! Wolf boy!" the voice said louder.

"Hello?" Joshua looked around.

All the details deepened. He was in a big room with spotlights aiming light onto a fake rock island up against a wall painted black. At its foot was a deep tank of water with a gleaming blue floor. A dozen penguins stood on the rocks, seemingly asleep on their feet.

"Over here." One of the penguins waved a wing at him. "Are you blind or deaf or both?"

"You?" Joshua pointed at it. "You...you...you're a penguin."

"You—you..." The bird mimicked him. "You're Captain Obvious!"

"Wait. Penguins can't talk. What are you?"

The penguin hopped up and down as it shouted at him. "I'm a penguin! A penguin! You are a wolf. Penguin. Wolf. Can we just move on here?"

"Okay, okay, I'm coping here," Joshua said. "What do you want?"

"You're the new puppy, right?"

"How—how do you know that?"

"Oh, freaking hell." The penguin hopped up and down angrily. "There are only three black wolves on the planet and you're too short to be the Thane. It means you're either the prince or his brother. Everyone knows that the prince is still in New York City. It stands to reason that you're the one that she told me about. The new one."

"Not everyone knows—none of the teachers at school knows I'm a were...Who told you—you're a penguin..."

"We covered that!" the penguin shouted. "You're the new puppy, right?"

"Yeah."

"Good! I want to hire you."

"Wh-Wh-Wh-What?" Joshua stammered in surprise.

"Hire! Employ. Engage. Retain." The penguin listed synonyms. "Geez, were you dropped on your head as a kid?"

"Hire me?"

The penguin lapsed into Spanish, squawking out what might have been curse words. *"No te hagas el pelotudo! Sos un bolundo!"*

Joshua had taken Spanish as a foreign language but those were words he'd never been taught. "Hey, cut me some slack. Until a month ago, I didn't know anything about any of this weirdness. In my old boring world, werewolves and vampires were horror stories—and penguins couldn't talk!"

"He will cover you with his feathers," someone called out from the darkness. The voice echoed weirdly, as if the person was shouting from the bottom of a well.

Joshua jerked around to scan the dark aquarium behind him. "Hello?"

"Under his wings you will find refuge!" the person shouted, still hidden from Joshua's sight by the dark. It was a distinctive deep voice of a large man hoarse from shouting. "His faithfulness will be your shield and rampart."

Joshua glanced back at the penguin. It stood watching him with evil red eyes. Its "wings" were stubby little things. There was no way that Joshua was going to fit under them. There were two ways to interpret "cover you with his feathers." He had enough problems dealing with being covered with fur. Besides, he had the odd feeling that the speaker was in more need of protection than Joshua.

It was probably better not to get involved with flightless birds that could talk. His life had been weird enough since Halloween. Joshua headed away from the exhibit, trying to ignore the quiet *"Sos un boludo"* muttered behind him.

2: DECKER

Silas Decker needed Joshua to live with him.

In the middle of the last century, his housemaid's jealous suitor had burned down Decker's home in Philadelphia. The poor girl had died trying to rescue him from the fire. It prompted his move to Boston, fleeing anyone who might know that he was a vampire who was dead to the world during the daylight hours. He thought the change of city meant little since he'd been a monster when he first arrived at Philadelphia. He had rarely ventured out of his home. Rarely, though, was not "never." He had had frangible relationships scattered through the families of the gifted that he'd abandoned wholesale.

After the move, Saul Grigori and then later his daughter, Lauretta, had been his only associates.

Decker had fallen into a cold, dark emptiness after Lauretta had been killed. It was a darkness that her daughter couldn't banish. Unlike Lauretta, who'd come to Boston as an adult, Elise had grown up underfoot. She was more an estranged stepdaughter than a possible lover. She kept her distance, as if she blamed him for the death of her mother. Her visits were limited to when she needed his help to track down dangerous monsters.

Joshua was a bright star to guide him out of that soul-crushing darkness. Their cohabitation, though, came with a price. Decker used to know all the noises that his house made at night and what they meant. There had been the gentle rumble of the gas

5

furnace as it fired up. The soft purr of its blower, forcing heated air through three stories of ductwork. The creaking of the metal ducts as they heated up and then cooled down. Beyond that, there had only been the wind and the rain and the occasional creak of settling timbers.

The addition of a hyperactive ginger kitten and dozens of new mechanical devices—refrigerator, washing machine, dryer, rice cooker, computers—filled the house with all sorts of random noises.

The ice maker unleashed a load of ice cubes at random times; the noise totally mystified Decker until Joshua explained it. The new fancy washing machine would finish by playing a cheerful tune and clunking open the lock on its door. Even the rice cooker had a song that it played. Decker wouldn't call the noises frightening—but they often startled him after decades of silence.

The ice machine could be ignored. Decker was slowly mastering the new laundry machines. The dryer currently was rumbling softly. At some point—probably soon—it would stop and play a song to indicate that his bed linens within it were dry. There was something in the kitchen that occasionally ran water which Decker hadn't identified yet. (The mysterious running water always stopped before he got to the kitchen.)

The kitten—aptly named Trouble—was the problem. It was determined to live up to its name. The kitten would suddenly—unpredictably—decide to zoom about the house as if monsters were after it. Its claws skittered on the hardwood floors, sounding like breach-borne creatures that Decker had hunted down and killed in sewers. Sometimes the kitten would fearlessly attack Decker's ankles. Other times it made random—vaguely alarming—noises in some far corner of the house.

Like tonight.

The kitten was doing something in the kitchen. Somehow it was making a surprising amount of noise as it rattled and thumped whatever it was playing with. How did two pounds of fur make so much commotion?

Decker was in his library, organizing his books. His collection had overflowed his shelf space decades ago. Some of it had to go. It had been so long ago since he'd read most of the volumes, though, he no longer remembered if he liked them or not. Tucked between the pages of many of the books were poignant reminders of Saul. The man always used whatever was at hand as bookmarks. A torn piece of newspaper. An envelope. A playing card. They served as a reminder of the peaceful winter nights they used to spend, sitting and reading. Decker sorted through the books, trying to ignore the emotional pains triggered by the random bookmarks and the weird sounds from the kitchen of the kitten playing with something.

The noise became very unsettling when Decker realized two things: the first was that the refrigerator door had just been opened; the second was that Trouble was in the chair beside him, sleeping.

What was in the kitchen, raiding the refrigerator?

Decker's house was magically warded against everything but a narrow spectrum of creatures that included angelic beings, normal humans, werewolves, and himself. Joshua was the only werewolf in Boston. Elise was the only Virtue, and she always used the front door. (The backdoor had been unusable due to clutter until recently.) Decker could see the foyer from where he stood.

"Joshua" was the obvious answer to the question of "what is raiding the refrigerator," but the bottom of the stairs was even with the door into the library. There was no way Joshua could have come down from his bedroom without Decker noticing.

There was a loud, wet noise like something large slurping up a liquid. That really sounded like a very big wolf.

"Joshua?" Decker called softly as he drifted into the hallway. "Is that you?"

The living room and kitchen had been what the real estate agent called "an open-concept floor plan." The two had been merged to created one large space with only changes in flooring to mark where one ended and the other started. Decker could see perfectly well in the dark; he had turned off all the lights out of habit. Most of the room was cave dark but in the very back, a shaft of light poured out of the open refrigerator. A human—not a wolf—was leaning halfway into the appliance, eating.

Decker was fairly sure it was Joshua but equally sure that it wasn't the boy digging through the food stored inside the refrigerator.

"Joshua?" Decker half sang the name as he edged closer. "Are you awake?"

The answer was a mix of grunts, slurps, and whines.

No, the boy wasn't awake. It was the wolf half of Joshua who was currently awake and at the helm.

How did the wolf get past Decker? Joshua normally slept with his bedroom door closed. Between the soft rattle of the loose doorknob, the click of the old latch, and the quiet squeak of the hinge, Decker could tell when Joshua opened his door. Half the steps creaked loudly when Joshua went up or down the stairs. Even if the wolf managed to open the door and walk downstairs without hitting any of the normal noisemakers, he would have come within five feet of where Decker had been standing. How did Decker miss a large magical creature coming within arm's reach of him?

"Joshua?" Decker half sang again. He wasn't afraid of the wolf hurting him; it seemed to like him. He feared that the wolf might take Joshua out into the night. A single bite from the werewolf could spawn an entire pack of feral wolves. "Wakey. Wakey."

The werewolf turned to look at him. Its face was human, but its eyes gleamed in the dark kitchen.

"Joshua?" Decker tried again, carefully extending his hand. Because it was funny, he couldn't resist adding, "Who's a good boy?"

That got him an armful of squirming furry wolf puppy and a face covered with puppy licks.

"Yes, yes, what a good boy!" He carried the puppy to the couch, still murmuring praises. The danger of the wolf escaping in the night was most likely over. Probably. He just needed to keep the wolf distracted until Joshua woke up. "We should watch television. What should we watch?"

Decker settled on the couch, picked up the remote, and tried to remember which of the many buttons turned the television on. Once upon a time, he was smugly proud that he'd kept pace with the advances of technology. All the new appliances in the house made him realize how simplistic the machines of the last century had been. You turned on his old television with a button that was much like a light switch and manually turned a dial to change stations. Channel 2 was two. Channel 11 was eleven. There were no numbers on the "universal remote" to the new television, just arrows and stars and "OK" as if he should just *understand* what would happen when he pushed the button. "OK" to what?

This was another reason he needed Joshua in his life. He was losing knowledge of the world around him. He was already hopelessly confused by something as simple as turning on the device that he'd used for half a century.

Decker was randomly pushing buttons when Trouble suddenly tackled the puppy on Decker's lap.

Puppy and kitten tumbled to the floor, landing with a thump.

"Ow!" the puppy muttered sleepily. "What the hell?"

The puppy shook itself and became normal-sized Joshua wearing a T-shirt and boxer shorts. Trouble seemed unperturbed that his victim had changed size; the kitten maintained his death grip on Joshua's head.

"Decker?" Joshua peered around the living room. "Where's the penguin?"

"The what?"

Joshua rubbed at his eyes. "Oh. Never mind. I must have been dreaming. That was so weird. What am I doing downstairs?"

"Fighting with the cat," Decker said.

The kitten bit down on Joshua's ear.

"Ow. Ow. Ow. Trouble!" Joshua disengaged Trouble from his head. "Seriously. I have school tomorrow. Why am I down here at—" he paused to squint at the clock "—five-thirty in the morning?"

"You were raiding the fridge," Deckard said.

"Oh, that stupid wolf!" Joshua shouted and headed for the kitchen. "Oh, geez. What a mess. He better not have gotten into my lunch meat. I need it for sandwiches!"

"I can clean that up," Decker offered. "Why don't you go back to bed?"

"No, I don't want to go back to bed. I might have another bad dream. A real dream."

"Real dream?" Decker echoed, feeling a mix of confusion and fear. Did Joshua mean what Decker thought he meant?

"Do you remember that weird nightmare I had about the Wickers in the Frog Pond? How I *saw* the Boston Commons and the frog statues and everything when I'd never been there before?"

"Yes," Decker said carefully. He knew very little about werewolves. Prophetic dreams might be one of their normal powers. Joshua, though, had become a werewolf by a very abnormal route and seemed to have odd powers compared to his younger half brother.

"Well, I had this dream about a penguin. It felt very weird—as in 'might be real' kind of weird. Anyhow, I was on a field trip to an aquarium, and I was looking at these penguins when one of them started to talk to me."

There were lots of words in that last sentence that Decker didn't know. Field trip? Aquarium? He decided to focus on the one that seemed most important. "What's a penguin?"

"A penguin. You know. *The Penguins of Madagascar*? Skipper, Kowalski, Rico..." Joshua stopped and looked at Decker closely. "You're three hundred years old. How can you not know what a penguin is?"

"I'm not sure. Is it a tribe of natives like the Iroquois?"

"No!" Joshua wiped off his hands and picked up his impossibly slim electronic device that he called an iPad. He tapped on it a moment before holding the device to Decker. "Here. This is a penguin."

The iPad played a video of some very odd-looking creatures that seemed a weird cross between a seal and a bird. Four of the animals stood on a rock in what appeared to be some kind of exhibit, perhaps in a zoo. (Decker had never actually been to a zoo. The first one in America opened long after he became a vampire.)

The stoutest of the black-and-white creatures turned and said "Just smile and wave, boys. Just smile and wave."

"I've never seen anything like these—these birds?" Decker wasn't sure that they were actually birds.

"Never?" Joshua echoed with surprise.

"I'm assuming that they're not native to New England."

"No. They're from the South Pole. I guess it makes sense you've never seen one before."

"What exactly are they? They look like they might be birds. They have beaks but they can't possibly fly. Not with those limbs."

"They're flightless birds."

"Do they have fur or feathers? It looks like fur in the video."

Joshua gave him an odd, panicked look. "I have no idea. Here. Let me check." He put his hand out for his iPad. "I've never seen a real one in person, but I know that they're birds, so they should have feathers. Right?"

"There are platypuses," Decker said. "They're animals but they have duckbills and lay eggs."

Joshua paused, confused. "How do you know about platypuses and not penguins?"

"*Blinky Bill*."

"Who?"

"It's a children's book from before your time."

Joshua tilted his head as he read what he found on his iPad. "It says penguins have black-and-white plumage...so...feathers. I think. Plumage is feathers, right?"

One mystery solved.

Joshua had returned the screen to the video of the four penguins in the zoo.

Decker pointed at it. "This suggests that penguins talk."

"No, they don't. At least I don't think they do. These aren't real penguin—they're a cartoon, like...like...Mickey Mouse. You do know Mickey Mouse—right?"

"Yes." Somewhere he'd picked up that knowledge, although he wasn't sure where anymore.

"Parrots talk but that's just...parroting," Joshua said. "It's not really talking-talking. Although there is that one video where the parrot tells Alexa to turn the lights on and off."

Decker wondered who Alexa was. He didn't want to derail the conversation more than it already had been. Why were they discussing the communication skills of penguins again? Oh, yes, Joshua had had a possibly prophetic dream.

Joshua tapped on his iPad some more, murmuring "Do. Penguins. Talk?" He squinted at the screen before tapping again and reading aloud, "Penguins can produce loud, noisy, or shrilling sounds. Ah, there's a recording." Joshua made odd honking noises come from his iPad. "It doesn't seem like they do more than...whatever you call that."

"They sound slightly like a swan or a goose," Decker said.

"I guess. I'm not real familiar with geese."

All of Decker's firsthand knowledge was hundreds of years old, based on shadowy memories of a childhood long gone.

The iPad honked some more, sounding more gooselike.

"You're right." Joshua held up the slick rectangle of metal and glass. "They do kind of sound like a goose."

It showed a picture of a goose. No wonder the second honking sounded more gooselike.

"Tell me more about this dream." Decker tried not to sound worried. He no longer dreamed. When the sun rose, he lost all semblance of life, which included dreaming. Considering the truth hidden within Joshua's last "real" dream, though, Decker could not dismiss it lightly.

Joshua snorted. "There wasn't much to tell. I was on a field trip to an aquarium and there was a penguin that talked to me."

At least this time, Decker knew what "penguin" meant. "What exactly is a field trip? Is it a trip to an actual field or are you going afield as in going aboard?" Did this mean that Joshua was leaving?

Joshua tapped at the iPad some more. "It's a thing you do in school. You go to someplace educational for the day instead of having classes. At my old school we would go to the Hudson River Maritime Museum or the Henry Hudson Planetarium or the Utica Zoo. You take a bus to wherever, and generally get set loose to do whatever you want for a few hours. In my dream, I knew that there were other students at the aquarium, but I was alone. Huh. Boston does have an aquarium—although its official name is the New England Aquarium. Where is that? Boston looks like a bunch of jigsaw puzzle pieces that don't actually fit together."

Joshua was looking at the map of the harbor, which did kind of look like puzzle pieces on a blue tablecloth. He zoomed in and out, frowning. "Where are we on this thing?"

Decker leaned over to peer at it. The streets had changed so much over the half century, it took him a minute to get his bearings on the shifting map. There was a marker on the Inner Harbor, down by the ferry docks. "We're over here in Cambridge..." He started to point and accidently tapped the screen, making the map zoom in tight on the Hawaiian restaurant at the end of their street. "There's our house and over here is your school."

"Stupid map!" Joshua growled softly as the marker had vanished when Decker tapped the screen. He swiped more at the iPad, trying to get it to a scale where he could see where the aquarium was in relationship to the house. "I *think* that I didn't know about the aquarium before my dream. Maybe I saw a commercial and forgot."

It was unsettling, but there wasn't much Decker could do. He felt that first creeping numbness that signaled the rising of the sun. In a half hour or so, he'd be literally dead to the world. So far, he had avoided the subject as much as possible with Joshua. Usually, the boy was safely asleep so Decker could go unseen through the secret door that led down to his hidden bedroom.

"It's after six," Decker said pointing to the clock that he didn't need to look at to know what time it was. "You need to get ready for school and I need to go to bed."

Joshua swore softly. "I need to shave, take a shower, get dressed, and pack a lunch."

"We'll talk this evening," Decker said because it was all that he could do. He needed to get to his bedroom and locked safely in his coffin before the sun rose.

3: JOSHUA

Blackridge had a lone wolf statue standing guard to the right of its front gate.

Joshua eyed the bronze wolf in confusion. He'd thought that there were a pair of statues flanking the wrought iron gate. He'd dreamed there were two—but there was only one.

As he stared at the black wolf in confusion, he remembered that his cousin, Jack Cabot, had told him that there once had been matching statues. Joshua's birth mother, though, had smashed the one to the left when she flung it at his father. Cabot had mentioned the story in a constant flood of anecdotes and useless information like: *if a girl gives you a condom, that means she wants to have sex with you.* (Had Cabot actually looked at Joshua? Girls were not into short, hairy nerds with odd nervous ticks.)

Cabot's story about the statues had washed over Joshua and was gone, seemingly forgotten. It must have made a deeper impression than he realized. In his dream, the two wolves guarding the gate in the past had not been a matched set. The one to the right of the gate was the same as it stood in front of him now: large, black, its right haunch worn smooth. The missing wolf on the left had been red with a little gold *Star Trek* insignia on its chest.

In his dream, the two wolves had carried on light banter while staying frozen in place, not even their mouths moving.

"He's going to get it right," the red wolf said.

"No. No," the black wolf said. "He's hopeless. We're all clue-less in things like that. I think it goes with our coloration. Black for dense."

"It's been every day for a month," the red wolf said. "He's not that stupid."

"Shh! Here they come!" the black wolf said.

"They" were a teenage girl and a little boy in Blackridge uniforms. The girl's tight sweater vest said that she had already hit puberty, but she was only a head taller than the kindergar-tener that she led by the hand. The two were ambling toward the wolves, slowed by the boy's short legs. They swung their hands back and forth, singing in Russian. In a way that was only logi-cal in dreams, Joshua knew the song was a grim lullaby warning a baby that if it slept too close to the edge of the bed, a wolf would drag it off into the forest. Joshua had also known that this was his birth mother, Anastasia, and the kindergartener was his cousin, Jack Cabot.

The pair stopped before the gate to rub the worn shoulder of the black wolf.

"*Udachi!*" the girl said in Russian and then repeated it in thickly accented English. "Good luck."

"There he is!" the black wolf cried.

"He" was a lanky teenage boy in Blackridge uniform jog-ging down the street. Joshua knew this was his father, Gerald Tatterskein. In the school principal's office, there was a pic-ture of his father, painted shortly before he was killed. In the painting, Gerald seemed like a tall, regal prince. In the flesh, Gerald seemed like a younger, dorkier version of Joshua's half brother, Seth.

"Get it right," the red wolf whispered. "Get it right. Get it right. Get it right."

"Hey!" the boy called. "Hi, Jack! Hi, Annie!"

The girl snapped around. "What did you say?"

"Oh, boy," the black wolf whispered.

"Hi, Annie," Gerald repeated, sounding slightly confused.

She snatched up the red wolf statue. "My name is Anastasia!"

"No!" The hapless statue wailed as it went flying toward Ger-ald. It plowed through the teenage boy, taking him with it as it sailed another dozen feet down the sidewalk before shattering into a dozen bloody pieces.

Gerald lay dead still for a moment, and then groaned out a curse, "Are you mad? That could have killed me!"

"Clueless," the black wolf sighed. "Oh, I'm going to miss you, my dear, dear, friend. My soulmate."

The wolf wept as the gray skies poured down rain.

The dream had left Joshua uneasy. Why was he having these weird dreams? Was the dream about the wolf statues a normal nightmare fueled by what Cabot told him, or like his weird Frog Pond dream, somehow real? If it was real, what was it trying to tell him?

His mom—the woman who raised him—always said that there was a person for everyone. She meant that he would get a girlfriend—someday—if he was lucky. That was when he was just short, hairy, and dorky. Now he was also a werewolf. He doubted very much that his social life would improve.

Joshua had known nothing about Boston when he left home in New York State, yet he had "seen" the very real statues around the Frog Pond in his nightmare. In hindsight, it was easy to see that dream had been a warning that the Wickers had set up camp in the parking garage under Boston Commons. Joshua had gone to the park, waded through Frog Pond, and never found any clues that the Wickers were literally right under his feet. Because he didn't know how to decode the prophetic vision, it had been an utterly useless exercise.

Were the wolf statues another important nightmare that he couldn't decode?

The only reason the wolf-statue dream seemed so "true" to him was because he could recall it with such detail. He knew that both wolves probably had been black. The red wolf with the *Star Trek* insignia was an obvious reference to security officers in red shirts being killed in the original TV show. He knew that Anastasia had lived with Jack Cabot's family, so it was reasonable to imagine that she'd walked to school with Cabot. Had Joshua "seen" some version of the truth, or had the dream just been something his imagination knitted together from whole cloth?

And what about the talking penguin?

According to Wikipedia, there were around twenty different species of penguins. The one in his dream matched up to pictures of southern rockhoppers. They were one of the two types that the New England Aquarium claimed that they had. The webcam from the aquarium's official webpage showed the same rocky island that he dreamed.

What's more, southern rockhoppers could be found on the coast of Argentina. The internet said that the curse that the penguin muttered at him, "*Sos un boludo*," was a phrase commonly used by Argentinians that roughly meant "dumbass."

Joshua had known none of this when he'd gone to bed. Not the Argentinian insult, the breeding grounds of rockhoppers, nor the existence of an aquarium just a few subway stations away. How could he "know" all of that if his dream wasn't—in some way—true?

The aquarium's webcam showed only normal-looking penguins doing normal penguin stuff. But in the dream, the penguin that talked to him looked like all the others.

Was there an Argentinian were-penguin—or some weird monster that just looked like a rockhopper—at the aquarium? Did it want to hire him? To do what?

And should he be even thinking about it right now? He was about to start his first day at a new school—as a werewolf!

At his old high school, Joshua was the target of every bully. It was as if he had a huge flashing sign over his head saying *Tease Me* that offered a free prize for anyone who scored a hit. Joshua used to imagine that the prize was a giant stuffed animal that the winner could give their girlfriend to carry around as a status symbol. "I'm dating a stud" the toy would proclaim to all. It would explain why the bullies ignored the fact that Joshua had a brown belt in judo. He could and would wipe the floor with them. He had been able to since he was nine. He routinely proved that he wasn't an easy target—and yet the bullies continued to pick fights with him.

It was that illogical compulsion of bullies to pick on Joshua that made him worry. He was a werewolf now. He wasn't always the person at the helm of his shared body. His wolf was inhumanly strong with no impulse control.

"There's a school legend about that statue." A black Asian girl stood just inside the gate. She wore a school uniform with dark blue blazer, white sweater over a blouse, plaid skirt, and knee-high socks. She couldn't have been standing there long, as it was near freezing out. Her long black hair was up in pigtails. She wore black fingernail polish, lipstick, and eyeshadow. "They say a wealthy couple met here as students, fell in love, and got married. They picked out two wolves to guard the gate that they used to walk through together. The statues were to be a lasting symbol of their love. Shortly after the couple got married, though, the girl was killed. They say that the male wolf went off to find her killer."

That was ... romantic? Joshua wasn't sure. If what Cabot had told him was true, the left-hand statue had been smashed before his parents fell in love.

His face must have shown his disbelief in the story because the girl shrugged.

"Yeah, the story isn't completely accurate," she said. "But oral histories are like that. Everything grows and changes and evolves in the telling, but at the very heart of it is a seed of truth. Two young lovers. One missing wolf. They're tied together with one tangled red thread." She reached into her pocket and held out a piece of bright red Twizzlers licorice. "Candy?"

His mom and dad—the parents who raised him without bashing each other with statues—told him never to take candy from strangers. The girl seemed very strange. His wolf had the licorice in Joshua's mouth, however, before he could say no.

A second piece and then a third followed. The fourth she kept and nibbled on. The red was vivid against her black lipstick.

"I'm sorry," Joshua said once his mouth wasn't filled with candy. "Who exactly are you?"

"Ji Su Wise."

"She's so wise?"

"No, if I was truly wise, someone else would be standing here, talking to the—to you." She held out another piece of candy to distract the wolf from whatever she almost said. "Ji Su." She said it again, even slower. "Jeeee Suuu."

The wolf growled with annoyance.

"Close enough." She handed him the rest of the bag. "Moving on. It went through the grapevine that you'd been enrolled and would be starting this morning. Everyone thought that someone should welcome you to Blackridge and make sure you had what you needed."

"Everyone?" Joshua glanced toward a knot of girls about his age walking past, not even giving him a second look.

"The Goths. Or at least, that's what the normal kids call us. Some of us embrace the image. Some don't. As a black Korean,

I've learned that you don't get to pick your labels. People just stick them on you. To the Koreans, I'm black. To the blacks, I'm Korean. Frankly, I'm glad to have a group that no one can debate whether I'm part of it or not."

"And by Goths, you are...?"

"We're the gifted."

In his old school, the "gifted" were the honor roll students. They were called mostly geeks, nerds, and teachers' pets. They were the ones who secretly ran the school in terms of AV, theater, and the after-school clubs that didn't involve chasing balls.

"Who told you about me?" The penguin had known all about him. That Joshua was Seth's brother. That he was the new puppy. That he lived with Decker.

"Spirits talk," Ji Su said.

"Who?" Joshua said.

"Spirits. They know things that you don't expect them to know. It's like they're all connected up to a supernatural internet and have nothing better to do than to share memes."

"Memes? Wait. By 'gifted' do you mean..." He wasn't sure how to finish that sentence. He fiddled his fingers and went "oooOOOooo" to mean spooky horror movie stuff.

Ji Su huffed and rolled her eyes. "Yes, we have certain powers. You've met Winnie Whitebrow. I'm a medium like her."

Joshua glanced around. Winnie's spirit guide towered over her like some ghost tree. There weren't any weird towering shadows around them.

Ji Su cleared her throat and pointed downward. A snakelike shadow hid behind Ji Su's ankles even as Joshua glanced down. It looked like a rat snake with a head and eyes that indicated it wasn't poisonous. It had a blotchy brown-and-tan pattern on its scales like camouflage.

"This is Nam-gi," Ji Su said. "He is a very young *imugi*."

"A what?" Joshua shifted to the side in an attempt to look at it closer, but the ghost snake ducked back out of sight behind Ji Su's legs.

"They're dragons...well, almost dragons," Ji Su said. "They can become a true dragon if they catch a *yeouiju* which has fallen from heaven."

"A what?" Joshua had the feeling he was going to be saying that a lot today.

She gave him a "come on" wave. "It would be best that you're not late for homeroom on your first day."

Joshua had only a few scattered memories of grade school. They were like snapshots: isolated moments with no clear order to them. He wasn't sure if this was normal or something to do with being a werewolf.

He remembered being excited about the prospect of starting kindergarten. His older adoptive sister Bethy went to school every day; he wanted to do whatever she was doing. Judging by the artwork she brought home, there would be lots of crayons and clay involved. He loved Play-Doh. His mom stopped buying it because he ate it all. (When he was little, he had a bad habit of chewing on anything that he got his hands on.) He was sure that grade school would be the most wonderful place on Earth.

He could remember part of the first day of kindergarten. They sat in a circle, each kid introducing themselves. It had been going fairly smoothly until the boy sitting beside him said, "My name is Timmy Tinkles."

"Tinkles?" someone on the other side of the circle cried. "Your name is Timmy Goes Pee?"

The room erupted into cries of "Timmy Tinkles!" and laughter.

Joshua laughed until he realized that Timmy was crying. He felt guilty. The teacher got the class quieted down to soft giggles and then asked Joshua, "What's your name?"

He said it loudly to drown out the whispers of laughter. He said it without fear because he never had considered what his surname sounded like. Maybe if Timmy Tinkles hadn't been in his class, no one would have made the leap because it wasn't something your mother said in innocence. He couldn't remember who shouted his name and made it clear how it could be twisted into something cruel. He couldn't remember deciding to attack the boy (it was a boy, that much he could remember). He could remember leaping across the circle with a snarl of anger worthy of his wolf.

Everything else after that was blank. He knew he graduated from kindergarten because first grade followed.

He had a handful of good memories from grade school. At some point, the dorks and nerds and social outcasts drifted together and became friends. He couldn't remember the first tentative hello, or the decision to play together, or how it came to be that they all sat together at lunch. Their friendship just *was* from a very early time. The kids who were his fellow outcasts in first grade were his only friends in twelfth grade with the exception of Chris and D.J., who had drifted off and somehow become popular. They also ended up dead at the haunted house with the prom committee, the football team, and one teenage witch.

He couldn't remember how he made friends in his old school. How did it work? Did you just slowly fall together until it became a forgone conclusion? Had he forgotten some mysterious rite that made them friends?

Were those kids really his "friends" or just fellow residents of the country of Unpopular? It was not so terrible a place. They huddled together at lunch, talking about their shared obsessions with science fiction and fantasy books, television shows and movies. They'd spend the hour fighting over who was the better Star Trek captain or which Avenger was strongest or comparing Easter eggs they'd found in the newest video game. They shared the dream of escaping their backwater existence for high-paying tech jobs in a big city.

After Joshua learned judo, though, it seemed like he'd become the standing army of Unpopular. As such, he was expected to defend the nerds and geeks who sought asylum within Unpopular's safe borders. Again, and again, he'd been drawn into disputes between one of the citizens of Unpopular and one or more of the various bullies who lived in Popular Country. Usually the bullies started it, but not always. Having a standing army sometimes made the most cowardly geek cocky.

Decker was inhumanely resilient and had a powerful regenerative ability. He took no lasting harm every time he startled Joshua into judo-throwing him. (The vampire was far too quiet for his own good.) A normal high school bully, however, wouldn't survive being tossed across the room . . . through a wall . . . out a window. Joshua needed to get through half a year at Blackridge without killing anyone. It meant that he needed to make friends—and not with the inhabitants of Unpopular. He didn't have enough control over his wolf to be the standing army at a new school.

Was Ji Su meeting him at the gate a preemptive strike? Were the Goths claiming him as their champion? Nothing trumped a werewolf at the lunch table.

Seth had been proud and wistful showing off his—their—family's school. He claimed that all of the teachers and most of the students had no clue that werewolves existed. Joshua wasn't sure how they could be so clueless as there were pictures and statues of wolves everywhere. The school's mascot was a black wolf wearing a gold crown.

Seth explained that the original school structures had been clapboard but those had been replaced a hundred years later with the present-day stone buildings. As ruthless businessmen who could heal from almost every type of wound and were immune to all diseases, their forefathers had flourished in the new world. The Tatterskeins had gained an unsavory reputation that they wanted to shield their children from. If the blue bloods of Europe sent their kids to fancy cathedrallike schools, so would they. No money had been spared building Blackridge and it showed. That it was designed by werewolves for werewolves also showed. There were massive trunklike columns scattered everywhere. Some were for structural support, but most were there merely to make the wide hallways seem like a forest. Wooden ceiling beams stretched out like tree limbs. Light filtered through green-and-gold-stained glass, creating a dappled sunlight-through-leaves effect.

His wolf liked it. It wanted Joshua to like it too. It was giving little pleading whines.

Ji Su ignored the whining.

It seemed as if everyone else noticed Joshua's uneasiness—at least at some unconscious level. Joshua's progress down the hall was like a wolf plowing through a herd of sheep. Everyone in the hallways scuttled into rooms, fleeing the conflicted werewolf. In Joshua's wake, doors slammed shut.

"Exactly how many people here are Goth?" Joshua asked. Maybe the population of Unpopular was so large that it ruled the school.

Ji Su snorted. "Normal people can pick up that something is wrong if you run around dialed up to eleven. You need to calm down."

She led him to his locker and walked him through opening the combination lock. He had brought everything that he thought he might need. His backpack was stuffed with notebooks, pens, calculators, and his laptop. He also had a massive, insulated lunch bag and a gym bag with a change of exercise clothes. (Yes, his gym class was on Wednesday, but he wanted to be prepared for anything just in case that "naked at school" nightmare was a prophetic dream.) He was glad that the lockers were roomier than those of his last school. He left the gym bag, lunch bag, and coat in the locker but took his backpack with him.

"Okay, one more thing before homeroom." Ji Su led Joshua to a boy standing at his open locker, hanging up his heavy winter coat. "This is Ajax Ayres."

Ajax glanced over his shoulder. "Hi, Jiji."

"This is the new transfer student that I told you about." Ji Su flicked her hand toward Joshua. "Ajax will be your study partner on Thursday during sixth-period study hall for AP Comparative Government. You'll be meeting in the library."

"What?" Joshua said. "Study partner?"

Ajax was surprisingly short—one of the few guys that Joshua had ever met that he could look straight in the eye. While they were both in the same school uniform, the other boy was clean and neat in a way that made Joshua feel like a scruffy mutt. He could smell the product in the boy's stylish short brown hair. Did the other guys do that? Joshua glanced beyond Ajax to the boy at the next locker down. Ajax's neighbor was taller with broader shoulders, but he too was using some kind of product to guarantee a sleek, combed-back hairstyle.

"We have class together right after lunch on Thursday, so I can catch you up to speed afterward with it all fresh in your mind," Ajax said.

Ajax didn't look Goth. He was cute in a boy-band way—the innocent baby-faced one—and stylishly groomed. Maybe he was one of the "Goths" that didn't embrace being different.

Joshua pointed at the boy. "Is Ajax one of you?"

Ajax shot a hurt and angry look at Ji Su. "That's so not cool."

"I didn't say anything." Ji Su fended off the look with upraised hands.

"It doesn't matter what my birth certificate says," Ajax said. "I'm just as much a normal American boy as you are."

"What? Is he . . . a . . . a . . . you know?" Joshua twiddled his fingers in the air to mime what Winnie did to send Fred off to fetch dead spirits.

"Transgendered!" Ji Su said loudly.

"Oh! So...he doesn't have a..." Joshua trailed off while pointing down at the shadow that was Ji Su's spirit animal.

"That—that's private information," Ajax said firmly.

Ji Su pressed her hand to her forehead. "Ajax is the valedictorian for your class and your class president. He volunteered to tutor you. *That is all.*"

Not Goth. Normal. "Transgendered" finally sunk in. "Wait." A hard look from Ji Su warned Joshua not to probe. He scrambled to insert a reasonable question. "Where's the library?"

"I'll tell you later. Come on. Homeroom bell is going to ring." Ji Su backed away, gesturing for Joshua to follow. Once they were out of hearing range, Ji Su added, "I'll let you know when someone is a 'Goth' like me. There's only a handful of us per grade. The trustees have never demanded Blackridge be a profit generator, so it can afford to refuse someone with deep pockets and little social graces."

"What?" Joshua said.

"They don't admit bullies. There's a screening process that winnows out idiots that would try to go toe to toe with werewolves. The trustees saw no reason to lower their standards after the massacre. We Goths are given high school scholarships to tie our loyalty to your family. We get to have a quality education at a school where bullies are banned. You have no idea how hellish a public school can be when you have 'an invisible friend that talks to you.' We're even given opportunities to qualify for a college scholarship. It matters a lot to us."

In other words, Ji Su saw herself in debt to his family. She was determined to pay them back by taking Joshua under her wing—even if he scared her silly.

A bell rang. It made Joshua jump and Ji Su curse.

"That's the library." She pointed at a set of closed double doors. She turned to point at an open doorway across the hall. "That's your homeroom. You're with Mr. Williams. I'm a junior. I'm upstairs."

Quiet started to fall as the classroom doors were closed.

"You have two Goths in your homeroom." Ji Su held up two fingers. "Allie and Tal. Allie went home for Thanksgiving, and she got stuck in Albany because of the blizzard. I don't think she knows what's been going on. If you have any question, ask Tal."

A second bell rang. Ji Su winced. "Stay chill. You've got this." She gave a wave and dashed off.

Joshua stared after her, feeling lost. Was he going to be able to tell which girl was Allie? Was Tal a girl or a boy?

The forest motif continued inside the classrooms. The arched leaded-glass windows had wooden frames carved to look like trees. The cherry wainscoting was capped with a carved frieze molding of running oak leaves and acorns. The walls were painted a rich green. His wolf liked it. Joshua clenched his jaw against the pleading whine.

I like it, he told his wolf despite his misgivings. *You don't need to whimper!*

His old school had had steel chairs with built-in desktops. They had been little islands of safety. He could subtly shift them away from a bully's reach under the guise of dropping his books onto the desk or slinging his backpack onto the chair.

Blackridge had long oak tables and wooden chairs. There were seats for twenty students. Only a dozen had been taken but the remaining seats all put Joshua shoulder to shoulder with a stranger. The boys—with their uniforms and hair product—all looked weird to him. Too polished. The boys at his old school never looked like Hollywood stars. None of the six girls looked "Goth." Which one was Allie? The girl with glasses and braces? The girl with purple streaked hair? The Asian girl staring at him with open curiosity? How could everyone seem to be able to tell that he was a werewolf at first glance, but he couldn't pick out the "gifted" from normal students?

Mr. Williams was a young African American man who looked more like a student than a teacher. The man was attempting to grow a beard to separate him from his charges, but it merely looked like he'd forgotten to shave for a week. "Yes, I was told to expect a . . . special . . . transfer student."

The man sounded annoyed but that might have been because of his slight accent. Joshua guessed that it might be British or perhaps something more exotic, like Jamaican. Joshua had only heard both on television, so he wasn't sure. What did "special" mean in terms of "transfer student"?

"Listen up!" Mr. Williams called to the classroom. It quieted instantly, a huge difference from Joshua's public school experience.

"We've got a new student." He waved to Joshua. "Introduce yourself."

"What?" Joshua had a sudden flash to kindergarten.

Mr. Williams indicated that Joshua was to address the class. "Introduce yourself."

Everyone in the room looked at Joshua.

The wolf's enthusiasm for the classroom vanished into annoyance. It didn't like everyone staring at him.

Joshua swallowed down the urge to growl. "Hi." He waved until he realized how stupid it looked. "I'm Joshua."

"Joshua what?" Mr. Williams said. "You need to give your full name when you introduce yourself."

"I'm Joshua . . ." He almost said his old name but caught himself in time. "I'm Joshua Tatterskein."

"All the Tatterskeins are dead!" a girl in the back of the room stated loudly. Everyone turned in their seats to look at her. She sat at the last table glaring at Joshua like he was lying. Her brown hair was cut in an asymmetrical shaved bob and streaked with purple. She'd picked the version of the school uniform with slacks, blazer, and tie that gave her a very boyish look.

"All the Tatterskeins were killed three years ago," the girl continued. "Everyone knows that. Seth was the only one that survived the massa—" The girl caught herself before finishing the word "massacre." She swapped in the official story. "Seth was the only one that survived the fire at their house. He was in New York City when . . . when . . . when the fire broke out."

The Tatterskeins weren't killed in a fire. A breach had opened in the subway tunnels under Boston. Magic had flooded out of the tear in reality. It transformed every living creature in its path into monsters. Mice. Rats. People. Only magical creatures were immune to the effect, protected by their link to their source of power. Decker and the Grigori had joined forces with the wolves to try and contain the monsters while the Prince closed the breach. The fighting had spilled into the connected basements of the town houses where the werewolves lived. Seth's mother, elderly grandmother, and all his little brothers had been torn to pieces before their father managed to close the breach. The Wolf King and his Thane arrived shortly afterward to mop up the remaining monsters. By then, all the werewolves and half the Grigori were dead. Since the town houses had taken heavy structural damage, the Wolf King had decided to burn the Court down to cover the otherwise unexplainable deaths of the entire Tatterskein family. In the matter of hours, Seth had lost his parents, his little brothers, his entire extended family, and his ancestral home.

"Allie," the boy on the other end of her table murmured in warning. "Look closely. You'll see. He's a Tatterskein."

Joshua guessed that meant that the boy was Tal.

"I can see what he is but that doesn't mean he's a Tatterskein," Allie complained.

"Miss Thompson, this is not debate class," Mr. Williams said.

"I'm Seth's older half brother," Joshua said. "My mother was Anastasia. Originally my name was Ilya but it... it got changed. I'm Joshua now."

"O. M. G. they *found* you?" Allie cried. "The... The... The kidnappers didn't kill you?"

The word "kidnappers" made everyone turn and stare at Joshua. He put his hand over his mouth to keep from growling. Mr. Williams gave Joshua a surprised glance. Apparently, no one had warned him about Joshua's past.

"Miss Thompson." The teacher's tone warned her to be quiet or face consequences. "Our private lives are that: private. We do not push people on their religious view, their sexual preferences, or their economic background."

"But this is different," Allie said.

"We do not force people to talk about things they consider private," Mr. Williams said firmly.

The girl huffed but stopped asking questions.

"Mr. Tatterskein, will you please find a seat?" Mr. Williams waved, indicating that Joshua was to take any free chair.

The wolf didn't want to sit anywhere near Allie. Joshua didn't trust it not to snap. He sat down in the front row in the chair closest to the window. It was snowing again outside. He ate the rest of the candy, trying to think of calming thoughts.

Mr. Williams tapped on his desk. "Today was the last day to turn in your permission slips for the field trip. I'm missing two."

"Field trip?" Joshua echoed. In his penguin dream, he had been on a field trip.

"I have yours," Mr. William said as if that explained everything. "Your guardian signed it when you were enrolled."

Who was his guardian? The Wolf King? Jack Cabot? Seth?

Surely, they didn't let a sixteen-year-old sign the permission slip for his older brother.

Mr. Williams considered a list on his desk. "Miss Hatcher?"

"I've got an orthodontist appointment," the girl with braces said. "They're finally coming off. There's no way I'm missing it. I will snowshoe to my doctors if I have to."

"Considering the weather report, you might have to," Mr. Williams said. "Mr. Palfrey?"

"Yeah?" Mr. Palfrey was Tal, sitting in the back of the room with his fellow Goth.

"Permission slip?" Mr. Williams said.

"It's signed but I'm not going," Tal said.

Mr. Williams snapped his fingers together, demanding the paper.

Tal stood up. He wore something made of thin black plastic instead of pants. It hung from his waist like a skirt. Everyone stared in surprise.

"What are you wearing?" Mr. Williams asked.

"It's a Hefty thirty-gallon garbage bag in black." Tal lifted his shirt to show off that he'd used the bag's plastic pull tie like a belt. "It features a fashionable neon blue drawstring and a regulation at-the-knee hemline."

Tal modeled the garment as if it had been handmade in Paris. The class erupted into laughter.

"Why are you wearing that?" Mr. Williams indicated that Tal was to bring him the paper.

"A truck splashed me." Tal lazed his way up to the front of the room. The garbage bag crinkled as he walked. "I thought it was just slush and I could ignore it. There was something mixed into the snow. Sour milk and rotting flesh. It smelled awful once I got indoors. My mom is bringing me some pants to wear. I'm supposed to pick them up at the office at the end of second period."

"You didn't have gym shorts or something?" Mr. Williams said.

"Really, Mr. Williams?" Tal held out his signed permission slip. "If I had shorts to put on, do you really think I'd be wearing this?"

"I have found it best not to form expectations when you are involved, Mr. Palfrey." Mr. Williams took the offered slip. "You always surprise me. Why aren't you going to the aquarium?"

"Because I hate the aquarium," Tal said. "My mom says if the roads are bad, I can stay home."

Aquarium? Joshua flinched at the word. *We're going on a field trip to the aquarium?*

"What is wrong with the aquarium?" Mr. Williams added the permission slip to a folder. "It's world class with sharks and sea turtles and penguins. It's more interesting than the Paul Revere House."

There was a groan from the class in response of "Paul Revere House." Apparently, the class was well familiar with the Revolutionary war hero's home.

Tal lazed his way back to his chair while explaining. "When I was little, my dad took us there on the weekends that he had custody. Every trip was the same. He waited until his time was almost over to go to the aquarium. My sister would have meltdowns when we hit the penguins the second time because it meant we wouldn't see him for another two weeks. It made me hate penguins."

"The MFA, Sturbridge, the Paul Revere House, Plymouth Rock, and the aquarium," another boy listed. "They're the only places we go to. There are other places in New England."

"Six Flags!" someone suggested.

"Your field trips are for educational reasons, not your amusement," Mr. Williams said. "You are seniors. I know that most of you believe you have college acceptance in the bag. You've done the SATs and ACTs, the glowing letters of recommendation, and all the grunt work of applying. You think that you can kick back and relax. But these next few months are like an exit on a highway. If you mess up, it's hard to get turned around and get back on track. You might get hopelessly lost. Trust me. You want to get this right the first time. Keep focused."

Joshua snorted. When he focused, the wolf snuck out. It filled up the shopping cart with junk food, took candy from strangers, and tried to pee on nearby fire hydrants. Staying focused was bad. As Mr. Williams pointed out, he was done with all the grunt work of applying for college. He had a four-point-zero grade point average, extremely high scores on his college placement tests, and top scores for the Advanced Placement classes that he'd taken in his sophomore and junior years. He'd even joined a lot of clubs to make his submission package look better. Seth implied that Joshua's acceptance to Harvard was a done deal. Joshua only needed to get through the rest of his senior year without losing control of the wolf.

Morning announcements started. The principal greeted the students, gave the day's date, and quoted Yeats with "Do not wait to strike till the iron is hot; but make it hot by striking." Announcements were then read regarding team practices, club activities, and upcoming special events. It reminded Joshua of when he graduated from middle school and started high school. The bell had sounded different. The smells of the room had been strange. But the order and nature of the announcements remained the same. It had a comforting cadence despite the names and activities being unfamiliar.

The school had a crew team, which seemed to be some type of rowing. They also had lacrosse, tennis, and archery teams but seem to be lacking in football. They had the normal Math Club and Chess Club. They also had ones that sounded more highbrow than his old school with "Mock Trial" and "Model United Nations." Several of the clubs were raising money via the sale of candy.

The familiar cadence of the morning announcements and his deep breathing exercises from judo helped calm the wolf.

Then the bell ending homeroom rang and everyone bolted from their chairs, heading out the door in a controlled scramble to get to first period.

His wolf whimpered.

"I can do this," Joshua whispered. Then, reflecting that his problem was that he wasn't truly alone in this mess, added, "We can do this."

The hallway was filled with a flood of students, all moving in cross patterns with each other. His wolf laid back its ears and balked at the idea of going into the hall.

"Joshua!" Ji Su called from a quiet nook under the grand staircase. She flicked her black-painted fingernails at him, summoning him to her side. Her spirit guide, the little snake called Nam-gi, was wrapped around her wrist like a bracelet.

Joshua's wolf cooperated—either because of Ji Su's quiet haven or because it was hoping she had more candy.

Ji Su's breath still smelled of cherry licorice as she leaned close to whisper, "You do know that not all witches are evil? Right?"

"Who is a witch?" Joshua's voice was suddenly deeper than normal. It was full of dark menace. He coughed, trying to clear his throat. *Stupid wolf.*

"Easy," Ji Su pulled out an unopened bag of licorice. She ripped

open the bag and took one red strip for herself. As she handed
the bag to Joshua, Nam-gi crawled up under her sleeve to hide.

Once Joshua had his mouth full of candy, Ji Su stated firmly,
"Not all witches are evil."

In other words: he was going to cross paths with a witch
shortly. Considering his dangerous-sounding voice, he couldn't
trust his wolf not to attack someone if he was surprised.

"Who is a witch?" Joshua repeated. When Ji Su just glared at
him, he added. "Look, things go badly when I'm surprised. The
wolf steps in and takes control while I'm standing around going
'derp.' I need to know. Who is the witch and in which class?"

"I don't know everyone's class schedule," Ji Su said. "I didn't
have time to plan that far ahead. People don't choose to be a
witch; they're born with their powers."

"Like mutants?"

"Yes. Maybe. I don't know! It is genetic somewhat in that it runs
in families. There's an old legend that the first witches were actually
members of the Grigori tribes, although the legend doesn't say if
they were lost or exiled. Some people think that the Grigori 'angel'
forefathers might have been breach monsters. They could have been
Neanderthals that were transformed into super beings that then
crossbred with 'humans.' But don't ever repeat that to a Grigori."

"Doh!"

"But if you follow that line of logic, then Grigori children
are like werewolf younglings. Even prior to receiving a magical
wound that allows them to freely access their source, they are
strongly influenced by it. They're born linked to it in some way."

"Ooookay," Joshua said. Was that why he always had trouble
making friends? Could other people tell he was linked to his wolf
long before it could step in and take him over?

"It's possible that each witch bloodline can trace back to
magic-warped ancestors like the angels or the werewolves," Ji Su
said. "Where did the Wolf King come from? How did he get so
many wolves without having them massively inbred?"

His wolf growled.

"Sorry!" Ji Su raised her hands to fend off attack. "I'm trying to
explain weirdly complicated stuff shrouded by time and mystery.
I've gone to Blackridge since kindergarten. I knew all your half
brothers and cousins. I know that the Wolf King has never told
them squat. Maybe Alexander doesn't remember. Maybe he had the

worst case of alpha amnesia in recorded history. Maybe he wants to keep it secret so no one can use the information to build their own little army of unstoppable monsters. Sorry!"

This was because his wolf growled again.

"Not all witches are evil?" Joshua tried to put the conversation back on track.

"Witch"—Ji Su made air quotes around the word—"is a term used to describe a particular range of supernatural abilities. The Grigori consider some gifts as 'divine' in nature. Dowsing. Psychometry. Precognition. Postcognition."

"What is psychometry?"

"It's the ability to discover facts about a person or an event by touching an object associated with them. Some people refer to them as 'touch witches' but not the Grigori. They believe that divine gifts recognize the underlying pattern in the world which the Grigori see as God's blueprint. The Grigori believe that only people who are somewhat divine in nature can possess divine gifts."

"Okay," Joshua said slowly as he processed the information. He had wondered why Elise's family allowed Decker to live. Decker's dowsing ability apparently was the difference between being monster or non-monster. "That . . . kind of . . . makes sense."

"No, it doesn't. Far as I can tell, the Grigori might all be descended from angels but some of them are infamous pricks. Considering what their angelic ancestors did—basically flipping the bird to God—you can't even consider true angels as 'inherently good' based on their actions. The people who are witches are labeled as such because they were born with a certain range of gifts, not because of their nature or their actions. Very few witches are evil, despite their name."

"So, you're saying that these 'gifts' are like magical handguns? It's not having the ability that makes people evil, but what they do with it."

Ji Su squinted at him for moment in silence, phrasing through the sentence. "Yes. Basically."

"How many witches are there at Blackridge?"

"Half the Goths."

"What?"

"Like I said, 'witch' is a broad term! The only reason I'm not a 'witch' is because no one slapped that label on me when I was born. I volunteered to be your intermediary because you're already friends with Winnie Whitebrow. I thought I would be safe with you. I'm not sure why a medium isn't considered a witch when an inverse empath is."

"A what?"

"Inverse empath. You know what an empath is, right?"

"Deanna Troi on *Star Trek: The Next Generation.* 'I sense confusion.' Like that?"

It surprised him that Ji Su actually had to think a moment to get the reference. The Blackridge Goths weren't nerds. Maybe they were also popular. Now that he was over his initial paranoia and looked past the black makeup, he saw that Ji Su was actually cheerleader pretty.

"Yes," Ji Su said. "Empaths can tell what other people are feeling; for reasons I don't understand, it's considered divine in nature. Inverse empaths are the opposite—they can make people feel something. Persuasion is a type of inverse empathy, which is probably why both are considered witchcraft."

"Persuasion?"

"It's what allows witches to bend people to their will. Make them puppets. Persuasion can implant a script for the puppet to follow even after the witch stops focusing on them. It's also the ability that allows Wickers to create constructs by using blood magic to animate them."

The wolf started to growl.

"There's no one in school that has Persuasion!" Ji Su said. "Even if the wolves allowed a witch of that caliber to enroll, the Grigori would probably kill them."

"Why are we even talking about inverse empaths, then?"

"Because..." Ji Su paused to frown at him. "You realize that Thanes have already screened all the Goths and deemed them harmless, right?"

"There's an inverse empath at school?"

"Yes. They're harmless. You'll probably like them."

Ji Su was carefully avoiding pronouns. Maybe there was more than one inverse empath in his upcoming classes.

Joshua pushed on, following suit. "How do I know that I'll actually 'like' like them and it's not them making me feel things?"

"Inverse empathy only allows someone to know what the witch is feeling—be it fear or anger or happiness. It's useful in that it transcends language but that's it. While it lets you know what the witch is feeling—and thinking in strong witches—it doesn't change how you feel. If you're sad and they're happy, you'll know how they're happy, but you won't stop being sad. See—it's totally different from Persuasion."

The wolf rumbled with unhappiness.

"Werewolves are immune to Persuasion," Ji Su said. "The only reason why werewolves historically kill witches—or more accurately Wickers—is because they can use people as puppets. A trusted human—a teacher, a crossing guard, a vet, a butcher—can be turned into a time bomb. There's no one in school that can do that. You're the only dangerous one."

Joshua pointed toward the door of his first-period classroom. "There's a witch in there?"

"If one uses appropriate terms, yes. Scared out of their mind. There is nothing they can do to hurt you. Your wolf can rip them apart before you could stop him. You're the only one that can stop you in this whole school."

Joshua closed his eyes and focused on taking deep calming breaths. "I promise..." Promise what? He couldn't keep his wolf from doing anything. Even when he was deep asleep, it was down raiding the fridge. "I need to know what to expect so I can keep ahead of my wolf."

Ji Su pursed her black-painted lips. She didn't like trusting him. "Maisy Carter is an inverse empath. She's in the front row. She doesn't talk. Well...she can talk...but she doesn't. I don't remember her saying anything aloud in the last..." Ji Su paused to think. "I think she said something in seventh grade—or was that sixth grade? Seventh. She used to talk a lot more in grade school, but her powers got stronger, she stopped needing to say anything aloud."

Deep cleansing breaths.

"You'll probably like her," Ji Su repeated. "Your cousin Alyssa was her best friend."

"I had a cousin Alyssa?"

Sadness rushed over Ji Su's face. "Yeah." Her voice cracked with emotion. "She was one of my best friends. She was the youngest daughter of your aunt Enid."

Youngest daughter—meaning that there were a lot more cousins that he knew nothing about.

Seth and he had talked mostly about being a werewolf and

how to keep control of his wolf and the current political situation in New York City. They never talked about dead relatives. Joshua needed to start a list of questions to ask his brother.

Before he had the thought completed, the wolf had his notebook out and was scribbling.

"Not now," Joshua whispered.

The "questions" were a series of stick figures. Ji Su was identifiable by her almond-shaped eyes. Candy floated around her like a sugar halo.

The real Ji Su looked seriously worried.

A second bell rang loudly in the empty hall.

"I need to go in." Joshua headed toward the closed door to his next class.

"Oh, please, be careful," Ji Su said.

"I'll try."

"There is no try," Yoda had told Luke Skywalker. There was only "do or do not."

But Yoda didn't have to share his body with a thousand-pound wolf.

Maisy Carter was a small, frightened rabbit of a girl with huge brown eyes and a very cute pixie haircut. She was sitting in front by the window. She stared in alarm as Joshua went through the entire "introduce yourself to the class" ritual.

The teacher then added an unexpected twist. "Everyone, introduce yourself. Maisy, you start."

Maisy pressed a trembling hand to her chest, as if to say "Me?" She begged Joshua with her eyes not to sit in the empty seat beside her.

"I'm John Dana," the boy behind Maisy stated as if she had answered aloud and was done with her turn. The rest of the class followed suit.

"We're having a pop quiz," the teacher announced, picking up a stack of quiz papers from his desk. "Grab a seat, Joshua, and get out a pencil. Calculators are allowed."

A pop quiz? On his first day? Joshua hadn't been in a classroom for over a month. He'd crammed all weekend but there was no way he was up to speed. This was going to kill his grade point average. Joshua headed for the second row, hunting through his backpack. Had he remembered his calculator? Yes. There it was.

He took the paper and scanned the questions. The first few seemed very basic. Perhaps the teacher had designed the test solely to find out what Joshua knew. Joshua was writing his name on his paper when he realized that the wolf had detoured to the front row and sat in the chair next to Maisy.

He glanced at her.

Maisy stared at him in surprise and dismay.

"Stupid wolf!" Joshua whispered. He glanced behind him, thinking of moving.

Maisy shook her head, giving a meaningful look toward the teacher.

He leaned toward her, intending to whisper "I'm sorry" or "I didn't mean to sit here" or "the stupid wolf picked this seat" or simply "I'm an idiot." He wasn't sure. He didn't get to say anything. As he got in range of her face, the wolf licked her on the cheek.

Her eyes went wider. She covered her cheek with her hand and stared.

Joshua felt embarrassment go through him like a forest fire. It was so hot and burning that he was sure that black fur would follow. He slapped both hands over his face, taking deep breaths, willing to stay human. *Deep breath. Stay calm. Don't wolf out!* He sunk down under the table just in case.

He felt Maisy pat him on the head. He spread his fingers to peer out at her.

She grinned, her nose wrinkling. Joshua suddenly *knew* what she was thinking as if she'd spoken out loud.

It's okay, she thought, *I understand how hard pretending to be normal is. I like you too.*

And with the words came a flood of warm affection like sunshine spilling into a dark room. The knowledge of her fondness washed away much of his anxiety.

Wow, Joshua thought. *So that's what inverse empathy is like? How cool!*

The wolf wagged its currently nonexistent (*let's keep it that way*) tail.

"Mr. Tatterskein?" the teacher called hesitantly.

"Dropped my pencil!" Joshua cried. He slid back up into his chair. "Here it is! Everything is fine!"

Nothing to see! (Oh, thank God.)

4: SETH

Seth frowned at the pink slip of paper that Jack had handed him. It was a sheet from the "While You were Out" message pad kept by the main landline telephone of the Wolf King's castle. His name was written in the "To" section of the form. The "Date" and "Time" had been left blank. The caller's name was given only as "your wife." A phone number, starting with the area code 858, had been written on the line reserved for company name. "Telephoned," "Please Call," and "Urgent" were all checked. There was no indication who took the phone call or when or why his wife had called or even what her name was.

That was a problem because, at the moment, he was blanking on her name. He couldn't remember anything about her except her bloodline.

He hadn't seen her since their wedding when they were both thirteen. The ceremony was held three days after Seth's family was massacred. Seth had inherited the Boston's alpha seconds after his father died. It hit Seth with the force of a tsunami, washing out everything that was Seth. It nearly made him feral. Only the Wolf King's constant presence protected him from losing his humanity. The alpha amnesia lasted for weeks.

Seth only had random snapshots of memories from that time period. He remembered staring at his hands and feet, wondering why they looked so odd to him. He remembered Jack crying at the memorial for their family and not understanding why. He couldn't keep the names or faces of the Thanes locked down; each encounter had been like he was meeting them for the first time. He recognized only Jack, but everyone knew Seth's name. He alternated between being mystified and frustrated as to why. Everything else was lost in darkness, washed away by the power of the Boston alpha flooding through him.

Seth didn't have a single memory of his wife. Jack told him about the wedding later, after Seth recovered. The Wolf King chose Seth's bride within minutes of Seth becoming the Prince of Boston. His bride's father was the Marquis of San Diego but her mother, both of her grandmothers, and all four of her great-grandmothers were daughters of princes. Alexander had been breeding her bloodline for generations. She was born to be the mate of someone like Seth.

Seth's in-laws were ordered to fly to New York City on a red-eye commercial flight. They arrived at the Castle eight hours after the Wolf King informed them of his decision. Everyone was focused on saving Boston, cremating the remains of Seth's family, and making sure Seth didn't kill anyone while lost in the haze of alpha amnesia.

Jack told him it was a simple affair, officiated by the Wolf King, witnessed by her family and the king's Thanes. Werewolves didn't wear rings; their hands changed too much during trans-formation. His bride had brought her white first communion dress to wear as a wedding gown. Jack dressed Seth in one of his suits; Seth looked like a little boy, lost in his father's clothes. No one thought to hire a photographer. The only photograph of the ceremony that Seth had ever seen was taken by Jack on his cell phone.

The photo suggested that his bride wasn't completely happy with the arrangements. While Seth stared vacantly at the cam-era, lost in the haze of the Boston alpha, she glared as if she wanted to kill everyone, starting with Jack as he snapped the picture. Her dress was torn. She was missing a shoe. Her nose was bleeding. It looked as if she'd been dragged kicking and screaming to the altar.

They exchanged vows. Jack said that she had growled throughout the ceremony. At the end, the Wolf King joined them together using the Boston alpha. It shifted his bride from her father's pack into Seth's. She stormed out afterward to break every piece of furniture in her guest room and put holes in the walls. Her family left abruptly the next day, probably embarrassed by the damage she had done.

"What's her name?" Seth asked Jack.

"Bethy?" Jack misunderstood because a moment before they'd been talking about Joshua's foster sister. Christmas was coming and Seth hadn't been sure if he needed to buy Bethy a present. They were only connected through Joshua. It would be awkward if she showed up at Decker's and Seth had nothing for her. "Probably Elizabeth since she wants to be called Liz now."

"No." Seth held out the pink paper. "My wife. What was her name?"

"Kate. Katrina María Marrón, but she went by Kate."

Seth read over the form again. "Why do you think she called? Do you think she fell in love with someone? That she wants an annulment?"

"What? No. I don't think so." Jack considered a moment longer. "Maybe. She did seem extremely angry about something at the wedding."

"I better call her." Seth took out his phone. "See what she wants."

"Yeah, but not right now," Jack said.

"Why not?"

"Because it's six in the morning here. She's West Coast. It would be..." Jack made a noise as he tried to remember if San Diego was three or four hours behind New York City.

"Three a.m.," Seth said.

Jack yawned deeply. He was still recovering from being shot multiple times with silver bullets. "Yeah. I don't know when she called but it wasn't last night."

Seth growled. He'd have to wait until at least noon. "I'll call her later. I need to grab something to eat and then get to school."

He'd skip breakfast altogether, but a hungry wolf was a dangerous wolf.

He currently attended the fifth best private high school in New York City as he'd been kicked out of the first through the fourth best. It took only one slip in his control and everyone within a dozen feet of him realized—subconsciously—that they were in extreme danger. No amount of money or power could keep him enrolled at a high school where he'd let his temper flare.

He needed to keep his wolf under control, which meant

eating a full breakfast. He also needed to be at his school when the homeroom bell rang, which meant he needed to get out the door within the next half hour to catch his train.

He locked the door to his bedroom suite, trying not to be annoyed—again—that he and Jack were the only people in the entire building who needed to do so.

It was another point of contention with the Wolf King's son, Isaiah. The king had housed Seth in one of the suites meant for a visiting prince. It was a recently remodeled spacious room with big windows and a large private bath. Isaiah was down three floors with the other members of the New York pack. The Thanes had small dormitory-style bedrooms that shared a large communal bathroom. Wolves liked to be in close physical contact with their pack. The Castle provided plenty of space for the Thanes to gather together in large social groups. There were also many small private areas if for some odd reason one of them wanted to be alone.

Isaiah hated that Seth had a large bedroom suite one floor down from the king while he was given one of the dorm rooms, no different from the other Thanes. He wanted to be elevated and set apart, awarded the status that he thought should go to the future Prince of New York. What he ignored was that he hadn't gone a day without being at the heart of his pack with all the constant emotional ramifications that it implied.

Seth had learned by experience that Isaiah, and his followers, would use "the door wasn't locked" as an excuse to steal his personal items. Since the floor was otherwise empty between visits of werewolf nobility, the elder Thanes couldn't keep an eye on Seth's quarters while he was in school. It was Isaiah's way to use the room's location against Seth.

Seth needed to stay calm to remain enrolled in school. He'd missed all eighteen days that the state of New York allowed and had already triggered an "educational neglect" flag from the Board of Education. The only thing saving him from having to repeat the entire year was the fact that he was an honor roll student, had a perfect attendance since he was thirteen, and had a myriad of excuses—from a real death in his family to a made-up illness. He could still graduate from high school this year but only if he kept his head down and his wolf under control.

Graduating would get him one step closer to moving back

to Boston. He'd hoped that he could go to college at Harvard, but the Wolf King had already stated that Seth would attend a New York City college.

"I sent you an email," Seth said as he and Jack trotted down the steps together. There was an elevator, but he avoided the ancient device when he could. The Wolf Castle had been built with the belief that stairs were things to be well used. All nine floors of the staircase were wide, well lit, and carpeted to reduce echoes. "I want to proceed with moving back to Boston."

"The king isn't going to allow that," Jack said.

"I realize that." Seth wished everything wasn't colluding against him keeping his temper. "But there's a lot of groundwork that needs to be put in place. I realized that while babysitting the new Marquis of Albany. The paperwork alone was insane…"

"We can't do the paperwork until you're eighteen and a legal adult," Jack pointed out.

Patience. "Yes. I know. That wasn't where I was going. Albany needs to shuffle around everyone that had been living with the old marquis—two of Ewan's aunts and four female cousins—and deep-clean the alpha quarters before Ewan can move in. Ewan is living in the Court of Albany's bachelor house until they can finish cleaning. It made me realize that we don't have a place for adult wolves. We need someplace other than Decker's to stay when we're in Boston. I'm sure Decker doesn't mind now. If we're going to recruit wolves to fill out our pack, then we'll need someplace for them. I don't want them camping on top of Joshua without me to oversee dominance issues. We need a bachelor house, like what Albany has. I don't know why we didn't have one."

"Ah! Yeah," Jack said. "We had one—we just weren't using it as a bachelor house. We didn't need the space after the mauling."

One of the pack's newborn wolves had accidently bitten his younger sister, who was still wholly human. Without an alpha overseeing her transformation, she'd became a feral wolf. The pack lost an entire generation as she mowed through all the other children except Seth's grandfather.

"Our place was the old bachelor house." Jack meant the town house that he grew up in. The Cabots' home, though, had shared walls with the rest of the Court. None of the buildings were still standing.

"I want to start on whatever we need to do to get the Court

rebuilt," Seth said. "Hire an architect. Draw up plans. Find out what the city requires. That area is a historic district, so there's going to be a lot of red tape involved. Yadayadayada. It could take years before we're allowed by the city to start rebuilding. We should start the process now."

"Should I be taking notes?" Jack asked as they hit the second-floor landing and exited out of the stairwell just beside the grand foyer staircase down to the first floor.

"It's all in my email but I wanted to talk to you before I headed out to school. There's stuff I might have missed. I should have been thinking about this for years, but I've focused only on getting myself back to Boston."

"Your schooling is important," Jack said. "You're going to be making all the business decisions for the pack."

Seth waved that aside. Yes, his father and grandfather had been very hands on, and he hoped to follow their lead, but he'd seen how the king ran his worldwide organization. Alexander let his brightest wolves handle the day-to-day operations. The king limited himself to the big picture decisions. Of course, there was the problem that the Boston pack only had three members. Four, if Seth's wife hadn't bailed on him. Unless Kate skipped years like Seth had, she was a junior in high school or maybe even a sophomore, if her birthday was in the fall. She might have even failed out a year, considering the trauma of getting married at thirteen could have put her through.

"What I want to do—as soon as possible—is establish a bachelor house," Seth said. "Elise has a condo in Cambridge. If the Grigori can use normal apartment buildings, so can we."

"Rent a place?" Jack said slowly as he rolled the thought around in his head. "I guess it is just tradition to own the places we live in. I guess it would be faster to find someplace to rent. We will need a place to stay while we're overseeing Court being rebuilt."

"Rent or buy something," Seth said. "I looked at some real estate websites for Boston. Most rental places seem to have just one bedroom."

They were all disappointingly tiny, far too small for their needs. Wolves needed private bedrooms because of dominance issues and a large communal space to strengthen social ties. The Castle had multiple rooms where all thirty-six Thanes could gather.

Seth listed out points he'd picked up while staying with the

Albany pack. "We would need three bedrooms at minimum, a full kitchen with a dishwasher, a real dining room, a large living room, and private laundry facilities. I would love a big house like what the Albany pack has."

Decker's place ticked all the boxes, but they couldn't turn Decker's place into Wolf Central and still keep the vampire's location a secret. Seth had to consider a hundred years or more with any decision that might impact Decker.

"We could buy a house," Jack said.

"I'm not sure that's an option until I turn eighteen and have access to my inheritance." Seth had thought that a pack's property and businesses was an estate that the entire pack shared. His experience with Albany taught him otherwise. When people said that Boston was Seth's, they literally meant everything that the pack owned.

"Rent a house?" Jack said. "I can sign a lease and pay the rent with my allowance."

"A house locks us into a set amount of space. We need three bedrooms just for you, me, and my wife. Even if we find one house with three bedrooms, we might not be able to find another on the same block to accommodate a fourth or fifth person. I'm hoping we can quickly recruit young wolves from other packs. If we rented an apartment in a large complex, we could rent additional units as needed."

Jack growled softly at the idea of living with humans so close by. "I suppose it's just until we can get Court built. I don't know anything about renting condos. I could ask Elise how her people found her place."

Seth wasn't sure what to feel about Jack's relationship with the beautiful Virtue. The woman had saved Jack's life more than once and was a useful ally. The Boston pack, though, needed Jack to marry and have children. Like Seth, he was a black wolf, one of only three left in the world.

Seth focused back on the problem he could easily solve. "We won't know what we can get until we start looking. Certainly, we can be flexible. The most important thing is location. We want to be near Harvard and Court. I want to be able to walk to both points." It would also put them close to Decker, but Seth expected Jack to repeat the information to the king. Alexander wouldn't be swayed by anything that included the vampire.

"So ideally Cambridge," Jack said. "Or Back Bay."

Seth nodded. Harvard was in Cambridge. Back Bay was across the Charles River, near Court's construction site. "I watched some videos on renting apartments in Boston. They were aimed at college students. Most of the details like getting roommates lined up don't apply to us, but it did indicate that we're probably going to need to get some kind of agency to show us the apartments. If you want to get into a nice building, there's also some kind of application and interview process, like getting a job. I included a link to the videos in my email. I'm passing you the ball."

"I'll get on it," Jack promised as they walked into the dining room. "I think you're right. The king won't let you move back to Boston, but he understands the need for logistics. We need a safe base of operations. A hotel doesn't cut it, not with anyone who is on staff being able to get into our rooms."

Breakfast at the Wolf Castle was served buffet-style in the dining room. It allowed the Thanes to keep flexible schedules. It also kept the king's wolves out of the kitchen and under Cook's feet.

Despite living in America most of his adult life, Cook kept to his cuisine of his birth with a few nods toward the Wolf King's ancient past. It meant that the buffet was Danish in favor. Seth had grown accustomed to the thin porridge called *Øllebrød*, which was really just rye bread soup topped with whipped cream. Despite their odd names of *franskbrød, boller, birkes, rundstykker*, and *håndværkere*, the various types of bread weren't very exotic in nature. Seth didn't like the pickled herring, liver pâté, or cooked tongue, and was iffy on the smoked eel. (He would eat them—his wolf liked everything even if he didn't—but he avoided them when he could.)

He loaded up on bread, soft cheese, and three soft-boiled eggs. He had a moment of homesickness, remembering his chaotic family breakfast with English sausages and baked beans for his father and his mother's huevos rancheros with tomatillo sauce or chiles rellenos. English Breakfast tea with milk and sugar for his father and grandparents. Café Bustelo coffee for his mother.

He must have been broadcasting his unease. Half a dozen of the Thanes had been sitting and eating. As he turned away from the buffet, the room was empty except for Jack.

"I need to watch that." Seth sat down beside Jack.

Jack shrugged. "It was Hoffman, and Silva, and Russo. They would have left anyhow."

They were supporters of Isaiah. They had let Jack lie dying in New York.

"I'm more than happy to do the legwork for finding a bachelor house," Jack said. "You're going to have to get permission, though, for us to act on what I find."

"I know," Seth said unhappily. "I'll talk to the king after school."

"And call your wife."

5: JOSHUA

Joshua sat at the Goths' table at lunchtime. He had no choice in the matter.

He'd been distracted by a giant Christmas tree in the center of the cafeteria. It reminded him that the holiday was barreling down on him like a freight train. He needed to buy presents for everyone on his list. He needed to create a list.

Who did he need to buy for?

His sister Bethy, their mom and dad, Decker and Seth went without question.

Cabot? When Joshua was growing up, he never had to buy presents for his "cousins" even though they would see his dad's family on Boxing Day. (They had to be the only American family that even celebrated Boxing Day.) Cabot was more like a big brother than a cousin; so yes, Joshua needed to get something for him.

Elise? If she didn't have family in Boston to eat Thanksgiving dinner with, then she had no one to celebrate Christmas with. She was Decker's godchild and Cabot's girlfriend all wrapped up in one. Joshua had no idea what to get her, but he should have something for her to open on Christmas morning. It would be awkward if everyone got a present from him except her. What did you get a beautiful older woman without being creepy? Jewelry was out—that was a boyfriend-only kind of gift. A warm scarf? That seemed as uncool as getting underwear and socks from your parents.

Decker might know of a perfect gift for Elise. He'd ask him when he got home.

With that decision made, he realized that the wolf had taken advantage of Joshua's distracted state. It had found Maisy in the chaotic cafeteria, sat down beside her, and leaned uncomfortably close to be petted.

"Stupid wolf," Joshua muttered as Maisy patted his head.

All activity had stopped at the table as the Goths—and Ji Su's snakelike spirit guide, Nam-gi—stared at him in nervous surprise. Ji Su, Allie, and Maisy took up three of the eight seats. The spirit guide had been wrapped around Ji Su's neck like a choker, but it slithered down into her lap. There was evidence that other Goths were in line getting food; books and bags were stacked on the table, saving an unknown number of chairs.

"Was this seat taken?" he asked. Maybe he could escape if he'd just stolen someone's seat.

The Goths looked surprised and then glanced behind Joshua.

"He can sit there," a female voice said behind him. "There's other seats."

One of the most beautiful girls that Joshua had ever seen claimed the chair at the far end of the table. She was prettier than any cheerleader at his old school, but her beauty seemed effortless. She wore no makeup, her black hair fell in stunning natural waves, and all her clothes seemed effortlessly elegant. She seemed a little young to be in high school. Based on all the disappointed looks from the tables around them, she was extremely popular, at least with the male population of the school.

Without comment, the Goths shifted a pile of books from beside Joshua down to the girl. She ignored Joshua and focused on the food on her tray.

Maisy patted Joshua on the hand. With a wash of warm affection, Maisy let him know with her inverse empathy that the pretty girl wasn't really ignoring him, that she was too shy to introduce herself.

Tal sat down beside Ji Su. "Hey, cool, welcome to Gothland! You probably caught my name in homeroom, but if you didn't, I'm Tal Palfrey."

He no longer wore the black garbage bag. Tal had on instead orange-and-taupe camo pants. He seemed no more embarrassed by the outlandish pants as he had been by the plastic skirt. "I'm a senior—obviously. Honor roll student. President of the Drama Club and the French Club. One-quarter Choctaw. One-quarter Cajun. The other two quarters... we're not sure of. Originally from Hugo, Oklahoma, now hailing from Watertown. Palfrey means 'horse' because one half of my family is a long, long line of mediums. The other half is an equally long line of circus performers."

"Circus performers?" Joshua echoed. "Like clowns and ring-masters?"

"*C'est moi!*" Tal grinned. "After I graduate, I'm going to college for either acting or film studies. I like acting but I also like telling people how to put on a cool show."

The orange-and-taupe camo pants made sense now.

"Alisha Thompson. Allie—please." Allie introduced herself. "I only use Alisha for school forms. I'm sorry about this morning. I'm a boarding student and I went home for the holidays. I missed..." She waved vaguely to indicate all the insanity that happened to Joshua. She blushed, glanced at Tal, and seemed to decide to borrow his introduction format. "I'm a senior. Honor roll student. I want to get a degree in Forensic Science. The University of New Haven is my first choice, but I'll consider anyplace that offers me a scholarship. If I can't get a full ride, I'll probably go to Excelsior College in Albany and commute from home. I'm the secretary for the Asian Studies Club. We mostly watch anime, read light novels, and celebrate Japanese and Korean culture. We're looking for members... if you like that stuff."

Maisy radiated unease. As if she had whispered her fears aloud, Joshua knew that she wasn't sure what she was going to do after she graduated. Her inverse empathy had no practical uses. She was envious that the others had such clear goals. She touched Allie's hand and indicated the pretty girl studiously ignoring Joshua.

Allie took the clue and introduced the pretty girl. "That's Ottilie. She's a freshman." Which would make her only fourteen or fifteen compared to Joshua's seventeen. Allie thought for a moment and then added, "She's a Grigori."

"She's a Virtue?" Joshua said in surprise.

Everyone at the table flinched. Great, he'd obviously said the worst thing possible.

Ottilie frowned at him and then ducked her head. "Virtues are not the be all and end all of being a Grigori, despite what my parents might think. Dominions are just as important, if not more so. Dominions do the real grunt work of running a monster-hunting organization that spans the world. They gather information and analyze it so that they can make the best of our resources. Virtues are just glorified executors."

"Elise is the only Grigori that I know," Joshua said in his defense. "I don't really know much about her—your family."

"We're not related," Ottilie said. "The Grigori is a race descended from angels. We are from the same tribe, but her family traces down from the first elder of the East Coast Tribe. Her people are in Philadelphia running Central Office. I'm from a less exalted branch centered in North Carolina. No one even remembers we exist."

That would explain why Elise thought she was the only Grigori in the city. Her grandfather Saul had to move Decker out of Philadelphia because his sister disliked the vampire.

"What are you doing in Boston?" Joshua said. There was a moment of surprised silence at the table.

Joshua blushed as he realized he'd followed up with the second worst possible thing to say. "I mean, there are other private schools that you could go to closer to home—isn't there?"

"You really don't know anything," Allie said. "I would have thought Seth would have told you something about your family history."

"Seth and Thane Cabot were busy fighting Wickers and whatnot," Tal reminded the others. He leaned closer to Joshua so that he could lower his voice. "There was an accident during your great-grandfather's reign. For some reason, all the little kids except your grandfather had been left alone with the teenage puppies to watch them. No one survived to explain exactly what happened, but apparently one of the puppies bit a youngling. She went feral. Things cascaded out of control from that. Everyone under the age of eighteen was either torn apart or went feral and had to be put down."

"In terms of Blackridge," Ji Su said, taking up the narrative, "the accident meant that the school was going to be mostly empty for a couple decades—at least until your grandfather had kids of his own. Your great-grandfather decided to open the school to non-werewolf children. The locals felt that it was in their best interest to step forward and make sure that your grandfather—who was just a youngling—was safe from all dangers. They enrolled their kids here at Blackridge. It worked so well that your great-grandfather established a scholarship program to ensure that we could attend, no matter what."

"Not all packs have the wherewithal to build a school like Blackridge," Tal said. "My family used to live down the street from the Oklahoma Court. They have always homeschooled their kids."

"The Albany pack has their own private school," Allie said, "but they don't give out scholarships. To be fair, Albany isn't as well to do as the Boston one. Their school is closer to my family, but we couldn't afford the tuition."

"Blackridge is the only school run by wolves that will allow a Grigori to attend," Ottilie said "We don't have our own private schools—that would make too much sense. Most families do homeschooling until we're thirteen. We learn the basics: reading, writing, and stabbing things. Then most of us go to Greece to try and become Virtues. Over eighty percent of people wash out and become Dominions. Utterly pointless in my opinion—why train for something you can't possibly become? I didn't want to waste my time. Blackridge was the only real option for me."

"Why?" Joshua asked, mystified. "What about public school?"

"You don't know about angelic glamour?" Allie asked.

Joshua shook his head. They all looked surprised and dismayed.

"He doesn't know anything," Allie whispered, a mix of surprise and horror.

"We could tutor him," Tal said. "Like during study halls and stuff, fill him in on how the world really works."

Ji Su shook her head. She took out a piece of paper and slid it out for the others to look at. "He's going need all the help he can get just to keep up with his classwork. I already have Ajax helping him with AP Comparative Government."

Tal's eyes widened as he read the paper. "Dude, why so many Advanced Placement courses? Normally people only take one or two a year."

They were looking at Joshua's class schedule.

"The Wolf King said I had to take them." Joshua said. "I was taking AP Physics C and AP Chemistry at my old school. I don't want to drop them after putting so much effort into them, especially the physics. The king added AP European History, and AP Comparative Government and Politics."

"Oh, that is brutal," Tal said. "Does he want you to fail?"

"I don't think so," Joshua said. "Seth says that I don't have to take the placement test for European History and Comparative Government, I just have to take the classes."

"That doesn't make sense," Allie muttered.

"Welcome to Ancient Child Rearing Logic 101," Ottilie said. "The king probably considers Joshua to be Seth's heir and thus wants him to have the education of a prince. Politics and history are fundamental in dealing with wolf packs. The king is thousands of years old, he doesn't care about test scores, GPA, or college applications."

"Well, I can help catch you up to speed on European History," Tal said. "It will help me to go over it again in detail."

Allie nodded. "I can help with the Chemistry."

Maisy looked sad. Joshua sensed that she wanted to help. She silently let him know that she hadn't taken any Advanced Placement courses as she hadn't decided on a career path. She wasn't sure what to do with her abilities, which sometimes felt like a handicap. The future vaguely frightened her.

Ji Su spread her hands. "I've focused on economics, psychology, and English Composition."

Ottilie, head down in embarrassment, quietly blew raspberries. Since she was a freshman, she wouldn't be able to help Joshua with his coursework even if she wanted to. She looked unhappy with the fact.

"I don't understand why you all want to help me," Joshua said. Even when he was the standing army of Unpopular, no one ever offered to help him with his classes.

"Your cousins and brothers were our friends," Ji Su said. "Your family died protecting us. Just last week, you nearly died saving this city. Of course we would want to help you."

Joshua was surprised that they knew about the events of last week, but Ji Su was a medium with a spirit guide. (Said ghostly snake was peering over the edge of the table from Ji Su's lap to watch Joshua closely.) Winnie had known weird things. Winnie had helped Joshua because of her unrequited crush on Cabot. She hadn't been afraid of his wolf because she had attended Blackridge.

"Your family opened up their school even to me—daughter of their long-standing enemy," Ottilie said. "To be a sanctuary against those who would make our life unbearable."

"Who would hate us for being different," Allie said.

He slowly nodded. "Okay."

"I think Vijay is taking Physics," Tal said. "He can help out with the AP courses. I'm sure he'll be happy to have someone else geeking out over hard science."

"Vijay didn't come to school today," Allie said. "Has anyone seen or heard from him lately?"

This prompted the others to take out their phones and check.

"He wasn't here for play practice Friday afternoon either," Tal said.

Maisy gazed anxiously at Allie.

"No, I haven't heard from him," Allie said as if Maisy had asked her a question. "That's why I asked; our club is working on a scanlation, and he was supposed to bring his translated section in for our meeting this afternoon. He might have gotten taken by something. We might have to track him down and do an intervention again."

His wolf distracted Joshua by cramming a huge sandwich into his mouth. It forced his attention back onto his lunch. To his dismay, he discovered that his wolf had plowed through all of the food he'd brought from home. Without noticing, Joshua had already eaten his banana, drunk his thermos of hot tomato soup, stripped the meat off the three large drumsticks of fried chicken, eaten his apple pie, and slurped down his chocolate pudding. There were only bones, banana skin, and empty containers to show that the food had even been in his bag. Even distracted, though, Joshua couldn't miss the fact that he was eating a monster-sized sandwich. He could barely chew, his mouth was so full.

What in the world?

Joshua had made a normal roast beef sandwich that morning. Or at least, he thought he had. Sometime while he was distracted, the wolf must have piled the entire package of sliced beef onto the long crusty hoagie roll. Seth had introduced Joshua to the joy of cheese beyond plain American. The wolf had added a slice of every type that Joshua had bought to sample. Munster. Havarti. Sharp Cheddar. Pepper Jack. It had also used an entire refrigerator-worth of condiments. The resulting sandwich was a half-foot tall and rained mystery toppings as Joshua struggled to bite into it. He tasted two types of peppers and olives, mayo and mustard and horseradish and BBQ sauce and maybe honey. There were tomatoes, lettuce, spinach, cucumbers, and possibly cabbage.

The discussion about Vijay paused as the Goths eyed Joshua's sandwich with surprise and dismay.

"You know…" Tal recovered first. He pointed at a giant piece of lasagna on his plate with his fork. "The food here is really good. Restaurant level."

Ju Si backhanded Tal without even looking at him. "Leave the wolf alone."

"There's a line," Joshua managed to say before the wolf took a second bite.

They all eyed the students lined up with trays on the other side of the cafeteria. It wasn't a long line, but it was slow moving.

"Yeah, maybe packing your lunch is a good idea," Tal conceded.

"With his class load?" Allie said. "He doesn't have time to pack a lunch like that every day." Allie meant the five-course meal followed by a sandwich piled high with the entire contents of his refrigerator. "Maybe he could have a snack until the line goes down. Or maybe we could get a lunch for him, so he doesn't have to stand in line."

"We'll work it out," Ji Su said.

Joshua's mouth was too full to answer. Nor did he know what to say. He didn't want the Goths buying him food. It ran close to the borderline of a bully beating up wimpy kids for their lunch money. Yet it might be a good idea to enlist their help; they were volunteering. He wasn't sure what was left in his fridge. He probably needed to go food shopping after school. He'd only gotten a few hours of sleep because he'd been so nervous that he had lain awake half the night. He felt a little blurry around the edges. (Although that could be the wolf pushing to be let out.) Maybe he should take a nap after getting home. He had thought it would get easier to handle the wolf. Seth implied it would. It felt like the wolf was slipping out of his control more and more.

He focused on chewing and backtracked through the conversation. Everyone had been concerned about Vijay until the wolf distracted them. He swallowed and asked, "What do you mean Vijay got taken? Like by Wickers?"

Ji Su shook her head. "Vijay is a medium."

"Like you and Winnie?" Joshua said.

"Yes and no." Ji Su pointed down to the ghost snake in her lap. "Winnie and I have spirit guides. Vijay doesn't have one."

"Why not?" Joshua asked.

"It's not a matter of choice," Ottilie said. "It's more of a bloodline thing. Either you get one at birth or you don't."

Joshua remembered that Winnie's father had the spirit guide called Dorothy. After he died, Dorothy continued to protect the book that had been his life's work to restore. Sioux Zee didn't have a spirit guide, but she was the Wise Woman, so maybe she wasn't a medium. He didn't ask the Goths as he didn't want to derail the conversations—more—from what might have happened to Vijay.

"I'm from a long line of mediums but no one in my family ever had a spirit guide." Tal waved at the empty space around him to indicate a lack of weird ghostly companion. "It was easier to act normal growing up without an 'invisible friend' but it really limits my career paths."

"Career paths?" Joshua echoed, confused.

"A medium with a guide can make the big bucks," Tal said. "You make money by holding a successful séance where you talk to a ghost that can provide the information that the client wants to know. You can milk the gullible by going through the motions and awing them with theatrics—which is my family's fallback—but it's a lot of risk for little reward. There's a reason my grandma ended up with the circus. It's not a career path that I personally want to take."

"Spirit guides are exactly that," Ji Su explained. "They guide spirits. They can either guide specific spirits to a medium or act as a guard, shooing away unwanted ones. They can also sense ripples in the spiritual wavelengths. So, if there's a crazy knock-down fight between the Prince of Boston, a Thane, a Virtue, Silas Decker, and a bunch of Wickers—you get a heads-up that leaving the city for a while might be a good idea."

Her ghostly snake nodded its head as if it was following the conversation and agreed with the assessment about fleeing. It explained how Ji Su knew about the fight.

"A medium without a guide needs to run a crapshoot of which ghost they contact during the séance." Tal continued on the economics of being a practicing psychic. "The biggest bucks come from families trying to find missing loved ones. With a guide, you can get a spirit that actually knows something. Uncle John might be living with a rich widow in Florida or lost control of his car, went into the Charles River and drowned, or was killed by the next-door neighbors and buried under their rose bushes. Without a guide, you're pissing into the wind. You might get a spirit that knows what happened to Uncle John but you're more likely to get some little old lady who is only worried about what happened to her cats after she died."

"Or worse," Ji Su said darkly.

Tal nodded unhappily at the possibility. "Much worse."

There was a moment of silence as they considered Vijay's possible fate.

"What's worse?" Joshua said.

"Doing a séance is like opening up all the windows and doors of your soul, then turning on an 'Open' sign composed of hundred-foot-tall letters," Tal said. "You get everything in the neighborhood trying to move in and set up shop. You can use protective measures to limit what can gain access to you—but the more you need to fish about for the right ghost, the greater the danger."

"There are some things that you can't classify as ghosts that can possess us," Ji Su explained. "We use the general term of 'spirits.' Catholics would call them demons—but the church is generally clueless and slaps that term on anything that they don't understand…"

"Like everyone with an ability is a 'witch' to them," Allie muttered angerly.

Ji Su plowed on. "Demons are a certain range of spirits from a very specific layer which has been quiet for a long time."

"Like it lost its hold," Tal said cryptically.

"Spirits are monsters without form." Ottilie took up the explanation torch. "Without a body, they're harmless whispers on the wind but with a body, they can be extremely powerful and dangerous. They are said to have abilities beyond what the host has—which can make them deadly. Some are mindless as breach-borne but others are more rational. Some are benign but those usually don't set up house in a medium without a general disaster looming on the horizon. Exorcism is the only way to drive a spirit out of a human—which is the preferred method. Push comes to shove with my people, though, killing the medium is often an easy solution to the problem."

This got all the Goths staring at Ottilie, who blushed.

"It's just a warning how my people think," she said in defense.

"Not that I agree with the practice. Most of my people operate in a bubble without any contact with anyone outside of their tribe. Beyond the local butcher, I don't think my mother has ever talked to a normal human, let alone a medium."

"I texted Vijay on Saturday to see if he got his translation done," Allie said. "When he didn't get back to me by Sunday, I started to worry. I tried to check his location then, but his phone is off."

"Last time I saw him was at lunch on Thursday," Ji Su said, and then added for Joshua's sake, "Vijay doesn't live in the dorms. I think his parent's house is warded—they're very traditional."

"Wait, there's dorms?" Joshua said with surprise. Seth had never mentioned dormitories.

"They're more like a group home than a dorm," Ji Su said. "One for girls and one for boys. We share rooms and have a house mother that makes sure we get a decent dinner and go to bed at a decent hour."

It turned out that all the girls lived at the school dorms but none of the boys did.

"We don't meet the 'need' scale. Either our parents make too money—like Vijay's—or live too close to the school, like my mom does." Tal slid his pumpkin pie toward Joshua as the wolf had finished the massive sandwich.

Joshua ate the pie as the Goths conferred on Vijay's last known whereabouts.

The Wickers had tried to kidnap Winnie, but the ghost of Marie Antoinette and Winnie's spirit guide, Fred, foiled their plans. While Marie possessed Winnie's body, Fred had sought out Joshua. Winnie hadn't been the Wickers' only victim: they had kidnapped, enslaved, and killed a multitude of people. Memories of the college student pleading for his life before the Wickers killed him flashed through Joshua's mind. He shuddered.

At least Vijay seemed to have gone missing after all the Wickers were dead.

"Can I help?" Joshua said.

"No!" the Goths all said together.

"Ghosts and wolves are a bad mix," Ji Su added. "Ghosts know that wolves can't hurt them directly, so they don't watch what they say or do. Wolves can hurt the medium when they lose their temper."

That sounded about right, based on how snarky the ghost Wonder Woman Alvarado had gotten during the séance that Sioux Zee and Winnie had held.

"I meant not me directly," Joshua said. "I could call Seth and he could do his 'Prince Peeping Tom' thing." Seth checked in on Joshua every few hours using the ability. It would be annoying if Joshua hadn't been kidnapped by witches and nearly killed the week before.

Allie and Tal looked to Ji Su. She shook her head. "The prince could find Vijay if he had a spirit guide. Without one, though, Vijay would feel like every other human in the city."

"Even with a ghost riding Vijay?" Tal asked.

Ji Su spread her hands. "What can I say? While wolves can sense spirit guides—at least some of them can—ghosts are invisible to all of them. I think it has to do with how much ghosts project into our reality. Spirit guides operate much more on our plane of existence. Wolves can't perceive the ghosts until they mount a horse and then the wolves can only perceive the horse, not the ghost."

"Ghosts ride horses?" Joshua asked.

It got him another surprised and dismayed look from all the Goths.

"A 'horse' is a medium," Tal said. "That's why my surname is Palfrey. We're from a long line of horses that ghosts can ride."

Ottilie added, "The name highlights the fact that the spirit is responsible for any crime that the body commits while the spirit possesses the medium, not the medium themselves."

"In Wild West terms, the posse should head out for Billy the Kid, not his stallion," Tal said.

Joshua nodded even though he only vaguely understood the problem. Seth had explained his powers when they were searching for the Wickers. With over four million normal humans within the confines of the Boston metro area, Seth couldn't pinpoint individuals unless there was something unique about them. Younglings—children born to werewolves but not yet a werewolf themselves—and Grigori were different enough from regular humans that they could be spotted during a search. Dr. Huff wore a signet ring to identify her as the royal vet. Seth could vaguely sense Winnie because of her spirit guide, Fred. Witches were too close to being a normal human to be picked out unless they were casting a spell.

Joshua had known Winnie was in danger because her spirit guide had come to him for help. He found her not by following Fred, who he could barely see, but by using an app on his phone that located his friends. Judging by the way that the Goths had frowned at their phones, they'd already tried that trick.

"What about Nam-gi? Couldn't you send him to find Vijay?" Joshua said. Everyone made another face as if he had said something stupid—again. "What?"

"I probably will but not here in school," Ji Su said quietly.

Tal expounded on the plan. "She needs to set up protections before sending out Nam-gi. It might seem like we're just 'talking' to the supernatural and they're drifting around 'listening.' What we're actually doing is projecting into the spirit's realm—meeting them halfway, so to speak. While we're in their territory, we're vulnerable to anything that might be nearby, looking for a horse."

Was that why the ghost of Wonder Woman couldn't hear Joshua during the séance?

Maisy patted him on the head. She added that Joshua couldn't have known since he'd grown up with normal people.

"It wasn't like this while we were growing up," Ji Su said. "Wolves somehow block a lot of the bad from happening. Either they burn up excess power or by their very nature make supernational wards against evil, or because they're very scary things to piss off..."

"Or all three," Tal said.

"Whatever the reason, while your family was alive, we were safe," Ji Su said.

"Another reason we're actually happy to have you here at school with us," Tal said. "Why we're willing to help you."

Happy? Tal was happy that the wolf had taken advantage of the newest distraction to eat the rest of his lasagna?

"Trust us to take care of it," Ji Su reassured Joshua. "We've done this before."

"Lots of times," Allie added.

"Laissez les bons temps rouler," Tal murmured.

"Hopefully with you in town," Ji Su said, "we'll have to do it less often."

He didn't want to be the standing army of the Unpopular, but he knew—firsthand—how dangerous some of the spooky things in Boston could be. The Goths would be utterly helpless to the

Wickers' constructs like the huntsman, its hounds and the fetch that had been sent to kidnap Winnie.

"Tal, let's exchange phone numbers." Joshua took out his phone and held it out so they could do a quick electronic swap. "That way you can call me—you know, if something really bad grabbed Vijay."

He picked Tal out of the Goths because he didn't have the nerve to ask the girls for their phone numbers.

"Good idea." Tal tapped his phone to Joshua's and hit SHARE. "You don't know anyone else in the city. That way you could call one of us if you need help."

"Oh, yes, that is a good idea," Ji Su agreed and held out her phone too. The other three girls shifted toward him, phones ready.

It wasn't exactly what Joshua was thinking. Technically, he'd never traded numbers with a girl before. Bethy didn't count as a girl—she was his sister. He had Elise's and Winnie's contact information but again, they weren't really "girls." Winnie was nearly thirty and he'd copied Elise's info from Decker's phone. He quietly tapped his phone to the girls', gathering numbers. He felt a blush start to creep up his cheeks.

6: SETH

By the sixth ring, Seth wasn't sure if his wife was going to answer. What time was it on the West Coast? He did the math. Kate should be home from school. Probably.

His call might go to voicemail. What the hell was he going to say? "This is your husband returning your call. What do you want?" No, that sounded weird. He didn't know if the number he dialed was her private number or her pack's landline number. Seth should have checked. The king required all packs to maintain a landline for emergencies. That number, though, would be manned at all times. The phone number probably was Kate's cell phone.

A woman answered on the eighth ring with an angry, "Who the hell is this?"

"Seth. Seth Tatterskein."

There was a long, stunned silence. "If this is some kind of prank, I will find you, grab your tonsils, and yank them out of your throat."

Oookay. "This isn't a prank."

"You're really Seth Tatterskein?" She didn't sound convinced.

"Yes," he said.

"Prove it."

Seth stared at his phone. How could he prove that it was him? Alexander had joined them together, but Seth had never actually explored their connection. It seemed too creepy stalker-ish to do with a girl he couldn't remember. It was weirdly unsettling lately to do it to Jack now that Jack had a girlfriend.

He closed his eyes and focused on Kate. She wasn't in his territory, so all he could sense was her. Nothing of her surroundings. She wore her black hair extremely short even though her next transformation would make it long again. She also had a dozen piercings, which was odd for their people. Such wounds healed the moment that the jewelry was removed. Judging by the sunlight warming her skin and the soft traffic noise he could hear over the phone, she was outside. It was December. It might not snow in San Diego, but most of the population would be bundling up as if it did. Kate was a werewolf. She only needed warm clothes to fit in with everyone else. She wore a tank top and blue jeans and sandals as if she couldn't care less about fitting in.

She half turned to face the East, gasping in surprise. "Holy shit. Is that you?"

He felt her focus on their connection. It was as if she had reached out her hand to him. He focused tighter on her. It felt like he'd taken her hand and pulled her close. It felt good.

She gave a breathless laugh. "I guess it is you."

Seth reluctantly dropped his focus on her. If she had bad news to give to him, he didn't want to hear it while feeling how they could be. "You called me. Left a message. You said you needed to talk to me."

"A week ago!" she shouted. "Dude, what the hell happened? I was sitting in class, and all hell broke loose in Boston! I freaked out so bad that I nearly got kicked out of school! The idiots in my class are still putting me on blast because of it. They're pushing for Darwin Awards. It's almost laughable how they think teasing me is safe to do."

As the Princess of Boston, Kate could wipe the floor with just about anything on the planet short of a Power. It was a testament to her control over her wolf that her classmates weren't aware that she was a large scary predator. When Seth lost his temper, everyone within a hundred-foot radius knew it unless they were total psychic nulls.

"Who shot Jack?" Kate asked. "Wickers? Were those Wicker constructs? Whatever they were, they were gnarly. Why the hell did you stick your hand into a breach? Are you insane? What were those things fighting with you? One of them felt like a Grigori but the other was the weird creepy thing that lives in Cambridge. Who is the new puppy in our pack? How is he getting so small? Why is he living with that thing in Cambridge? What the hell is it?"

Kate had a stronger connection to their alpha than he gave her credit for. He realized it was because his mother's bond had been weak. His parents rarely talked about this aspect of their marriage. Everyone compared his mother to his father's first wife and found her lacking. It had been a constant sore spot—so one rarely broached.

By the hierarchical nature of the Source, Seth was the primary connection. Kate shared the load. She had been insurance against Seth being overwhelmed by the alpha, hence the need for their rushed marriage. Seth buffered her from the flood of magic, which was why she hadn't suffered alpha amnesia. It meant that she probably remembered the entire wedding in painful detail. She would also have had a harder time controlling her wolf immediately after the ceremony, hence all the broken furniture at the Castle.

The king had shifted Jack back to the Boston pack within minutes of Seth's father dying. If Jack and Kate hadn't been enough to keep Seth from being overwhelmed, the king could have transferred in some of his Thanes. Seth was glad he hadn't been stuck with Isaiah's lackeys as his pack mates.

Kate's connection, however, meant that she had a ringside seat to the chaos of November.

"Oh," Seth said. "You saw all that."

"Yes! I called the Castle to tell them. The Thane that answered the phone said that the king was on his way to Boston. I skipped the rest of the day at school; there was no way I could have stayed calm until I was sure that you and Jack and our new puppy was safe."

Our new puppy. That made Seth smile.

"The puppy is Joshua," Seth said. "He's my older half brother from my father's first wife. The one that was murdered."

"I thought his name was Ilya."

"Yes. And no. Not anymore. It's—it's complicated. We fought the same coven of Wickers that kidnapped Joshua as an infant. They had some big, crazy plan to take control of the Boston alpha. I'm not sure I understood all of it. It might have worked if they raised Joshua like one of their twisted homicidal children. Luckily, they had lost control over one of their puppets when my dad killed their leader. The puppet took my brother when she bolted. She sold Joshua to a family totally unconnected to the coven. They thought Joshua was her son and that the money that they were giving her was to cover hospital bills. They had no idea the mess they bought into. They'd raised Joshua as their own, so he's had a nice normal childhood. His adoptive sister drove through a blizzard to cook him Thanksgiving dinner. It makes me happy that there's so much love there."

Kate snorted. "I wouldn't do that for my brother. He's a total jerk face."

Seth suddenly remembered that Jack complained about Kate's twin throwing a series of hissy fits during the visit. Jack suspected it was because her brother was used to being the center of attention. Since the daughters of alphas were usually married out of the pack long before their father died, the firstborn sons were considered the heir apparent. Seth knew how that worked. He'd been a spoiled brat when he arrived at the Castle. His father's death erased that character defect.

"Joshua is nothing like that," Seth said. "He's fun to be around. I think you'll like him. Maybe you can fly to Boston and meet us. Him."

"Send me money," Kate said.

"What?"

"My dad is being a total jerk about money. He gave my brother a car when we turned sixteen but he's like 'get one from your husband' when I complained that it wasn't fair."

The one thing Seth learned from his parents was never bitch about your in-laws, no matter how crazy they drove you. The news made him angry at his father-in-law and at himself. He should have made sure that she had what she needed.

"I'll send you money," Seth promised. "I'll pay for anything you need."

There was a long silence in reply. As he waited for her to reply, he made a note to get her a car. Something he discovered while fighting the Wickers was that the freedom that cars provided got very important fast. He added a note to get a car for Joshua too so that he wouldn't be limited by public transit.

"I want you to agree to some ground rules first," Kate said cautiously. "We're married but I don't know you. No sex. Not until I'm sure I'm ready. That I actually like you. I want to date like normal people do. You know—like what they do in rom-coms. Dinner. Dancing. Bowling. Maybe not bowling. Whatever. I want the right to say when we do the dirty."

"Okay." Seth realized that he'd wasted time by not contacting Kate earlier. They could have spent the last three years becoming friends. He wouldn't have felt so alone at the Castle if he had had someone other than Jack to talk to. He was supposed to spend the rest of his life together with Kate and he didn't know anything about her. Why did she cut her hair so short? Why did she have so many piercings? Why had she been so angry when she answered the phone? Why had she been so angry during their wedding? It didn't sound like she wanted an annulment. She sounded cautious. He thought it was a good trait to have.

"I mean like a year or maybe more," Kate said. "I'm not a baby machine. I'm not coming to Boston to get knocked up."

"I think dating is a good idea," Seth said. "We have so much stuff to do before even thinking of having kids. I want to go to college, so I'll know what I'm doing when I take over our businesses. We need to build a Court and a real bachelor house and gather more wolves to our territory. If there's anyone there that wants to come with you from San Diego, that would be great. We need more people that we can trust."

There was silence on Kate's side and then a quiet confession of, "I've been burning all my bridges for the last three years. It's hard. Everyone knows that I'm going to leave and not come back. There's no reason for them to get along with me."

Seth felt a stab of guilt. He'd spent the last three years assuming that Kate was "safe with her family." His mother had stayed close with her parents, but his mother had left home the day she came into her power. His grandfather's funeral made him realize that visits between his grandparents and mother had been deliberately few and far between. It was the nature of wolves to be territorial. Daughters married out of their family packs instantly became interlopers. Human love kept wolf instinct in check—but not completely.

It was a large part of his problems with the king's Thanes. They belonged to the New York City pack. Seth was a strong wolf at the heart of their territory. It grated unconsciously on their nerves to have him sleeping so close. Worse, the Thanes knew that Seth's presence at the Castle was temporary. Isaiah was the most dominant of the Thanes. Whether or not Isaiah became the Prince of New York was moot; the king would never move his son to another pack. Many of the Thanes had no desire to ruin their relationship with the strongest wolf of their pack for a puppy that would leave in a few years.

Seth hadn't considered that Kate would be in the same position.

"I'll make sure you can fly to Boston whenever and as often as you want," he promised. The need for the bachelor house and other wolves just went up a notch. "I plan to move forward on rebuilding the Court of Boston soon. I'm not sure how fast I'll be able to push it through, but I would like your input on our future home."

"Wow. That's—that's scary and exciting at the same time. I've seen every single movie and television show ever set in Boston. I collect pictures of the city. I dream about walking through the streets. I really, really want to see it for myself."

She didn't define what was scary about what he said. She really didn't need to. He was asking her to trust him, a complete stranger who had ignored her for three years. To fly to the other side of the country alone. To restart life in a war-torn city. It made him scared for her.

"I look forward to getting to show you Boston." He was reminding both of them that she wouldn't be alone. "I'm looking forward to getting to know you better."

Hanging up felt like he was letting go of something warm and wonderful. He had to set things right with Kate, which meant he'd have to talk to the king even sooner than he planned.

The throne room at the Wolf King's Castle had been built to hold large numbers of people. It was the only room that could take all the Thanes and the upper ranks of two packs in disagreement over territory and business deals. Only the dining room came close in size. Unlike the dining room, here the occupants could launch themselves into battle without breaking chandeliers or furniture. Over the years, Seth had seen a dozen different such fights. Wolves weren't known for their decorum.

The architect decided that he would use the space to impress. Maybe he foresaw the angry groups of wolves descending on the place and wanted to batter them into submission with gold and stone. The floors were polished marble, and the vaulted ceiling coffered and edged with gilded molding. The crystal chandeliers were all high overhead, struggling to light up the floor without endangering themselves from flying bodies.

The only window was high over the raised dais. During the day, its arched sunburst design spilled light down over the king like God's blessing. It was an illusion; the Wolf King gleamed from his own inner power.

Between the high chandeliers, the lack of windows, and its overall design, the room was much like a cave. It seemed sometimes that the Wolf King was a wild thing lying at the mouth of its den. Rarely was he a man in the throne room. Most of the times—like now—he was a massive white wolf lying on a couch strewn with dark bearskins.

Two of his oldest Thanes lay at the foot of the dais. Another king, another culture, they would be guards. Here, they attended Alexander merely for companionship; wolves were most comfortable when surrounded by their pack. Coming and going were the rest of the Thanes, reporting on their duties as the king's voice and presence to scattered points of the globe. Ichirou Nakano had just returned from Japan, where he settled disputes between warring packs. Felix Leung was being sent to Vancouver on the king's private jet to deal with a border dispute between Canada and the barons of White Rock, British Columbia, and Blaine, Washington. Edward Bishop was discussing how newly elected politicians in United States might influence the wolves' businesses. The Wolf King lay on the furs, listening with his eyes closed. It would be a mistake to think he was asleep.

Seth walked toward the king, his stomach doing somersaults. He would have preferred facing Alexander alone. The king could be more readily swayed when he didn't have an audience. While the king was in New York, though, he was rarely unattended.

When Seth was a little boy, he had hated having to sit quietly through his father's business meetings, listening to debates that he wasn't allowed to partake in. His father said it was part of learning how to be a prince. Back then, he used to yearn for Ilya to be found and fill the "eldest son" slot so he could be out playing with his friends.

He was grateful now for the experience. He had learned a lot, even while he was bored senseless. His father always said that the strongest argument was the one that was focused and easy to understand. Sometimes it was best to aim for the easiest goal to achieve in order to leverage the more difficult one.

As Seth neared the dais, he realized that the king had turned his focus onto Joshua. The king's power felt like a hand resting on top of Seth's hold on his territory. In Boston, Joshua had been sitting at the island in Decker's kitchen, apparently doing his homework. He went still, raising his head, as if he was suddenly aware of the scrutiny.

"He's safe," Seth voice echoed through the room. The Thanes turned to look at him as if he was a bored, spoiled brat, interrupting the adults' important business. Seth struggled to ignore the judging looks. "I've come to you about the Boston estate."

Seth had chosen his words carefully to cover his two major projects and yet raise the least number of objections.

"What about it?" The Wolf King's voice was deep and rich in a way Seth hoped that someday he could sound like. It would make being the prince so much easier if he could sound so regal.

"I need to care for my wolves without being hopelessly fettered," Seth said.

"Your businesses are being cared for."

"The businesses are not my wolves. I trust that Thane Levine's office has them well in hand. They do not need my oversight to run. It is my wife that I'm concerned about."

"Last I heard," Alexander said, "you have never contacted her."

Seth gritted his teeth. He'd earned that criticism. He could only hope his neglect didn't doom this conversation. "I rectified that earlier today. She reported that her father is providing only basic Shelter and Assistance as due her status as an outsider within his territory. I have made the mistake of assuming that he would continue to see her as his daughter, not the child of another pack."

"Boston is an older territory with more resources. You should not assume that other territories have pockets as deep as yours."

Seth nodded, keeping hold of his temper. Did Alexander know the truth this whole time and never said anything to him? S&A was taken out of a pack's tribute before submitting it to the king. The shortage was then charged to the traveler's home pack. It was set up as an incentive for alphas to freely help any wolf that stumbled into their territory. The alpha would not have to worry about being out funds since the Wolf King would be balancing the books. There were thousands of packs scattered across the planet; it was Levine's office that kept the records straight. Had Levine brought the accounting to the king's attention or simply juggled the money?

And what would a proper response be to the king's statement?

"I'm attempting to be the prince that Boston needs." Seth struggled to pick out words without seeming to think deeply. A slow answer, his father taught him, sounded like a lie. "I have neglected my wife. I want to ensure that we have a strong relationship for the good of Boston."

"That would be wise." The king tone sounded like he might be teasing Seth. It was hard to tell with Alexander. His wit was dry and sharp, when he chose to tease, which was rarely.

"My wife is still under her father's guardianship. It means that all funds for her—and any decision on how to spend those funds—funnel through him."

"She is in his territory," the king said.

Seth paused, searching for a way to steer the argument in Boston's favor. Alexander was merely stating facts without giving a clue as to how he felt. Did it mean that he saw no problem with the situation or was this some kind of test? His father said never to weaken his stance by pleading. *State it as if it was your right.*

"I want her guardianship to be reassigned to someone on the East Coast, be it you, Thane Bishop, or Jack. She'll be an adult within two years. At that point, she can take over her own finances. I would like her to receive a car as soon as possible. She should have the freedom that a vehicle would provide. I want her to be able to visit Boston—get to know the city; get to know me." Because he thought it would strengthen his demands, he added, "I don't remember our wedding. She is a complete stranger to me."

"You've had three years," Alexander said.

"You have not allowed me out of your sight for three years," Seth said. "I was a child—"

"You are still a child."

"A few hundred days and I will not be a child anymore."

"That is debatable." The king's words were cutting, but still, it felt as if he was teasing Seth. It was hard to tell when he was a man, let alone a wolf.

Where was I in my argument? Seth had lost track. The most

important point was that the king allow Kate to visit Boston. Alexander hadn't said no. Yet. Seth would assume that the answer was yes and push on to the related needs. "I want to rent or purchase some housing in Cambridge. Something close to Harvard, MIT, and Boston University. That would make it attractive to any wolf that wants to shift packs for a better education. Two neighboring units of three or four bedrooms each would be ideal. That would allow a bachelor and bachelorette house."

"You plan to recruit all puppies?"

Seth didn't want to rebuild his pack with older wolves already forced out of one pack. In the three years that Seth had drifted in the Wolf King's wake, he'd learned that most older wolves left their packs only when they had behavioral problems. They were addicted to something undesirable: drugs, gambling, sex, or violence. Often it was three out of four at once. Other times, they had inflated egos and were dangerously petty, seeing any slight as cause to strike out. Seth would rather have no wolves in his pack than to gather a horde of monstrous problems.

Seth couldn't say that out loud, not in front of the Thanes. A good quarter of them were the wolves that the king couldn't place safely in another pack. "Not puppies. Young wolves. They would need to be adults. They're the ones who would be most willing to shift packs for what Boston has to offer. A bigger city. Better access to top universities. A stronger job market. More cultural resources. Theaters. Museums. Historic sites like Plymouth Rock, North Church, and Paul Revere's house. And—and places like the aquarium..." He realized that he was listing field trips for Blackridge. That was stupid. He'd better make a better list for his recruitment pitch. "A lot of young people are frustrated by the lack of potential mates. Some packs have an overabundance of females. Some have too many males. Most packs are in danger of inbreeding. You only set up marriages for the children of the alpha. It leaves the more rural packs without options."

At the king's feet, Armand Mandeville grunted in disgust. "You can't raise families with just puppies. You need seasoned fighters."

"They're not puppies," Seth repeated. "They've been trained to fight their entire lives. If they remained in their home pack, they would be given the most tiresome patrols and expect to deal with any problems that arose."

"Puppies or not," the king said, "you have no wolves now that need to be housed."

"I can't recruit wolves without a place for them to live. The Court of Boston will need to be rebuilt from the ground up. The empty lot is on a street deemed 'historic' so we will not be able to build anything we want..."

The king snorted. "It was a mud path through a cow pasture when I first visited it."

The king had visited his family's home back before history was made. It was fifty or sixty years between the king's coming to North America and the American Revolution.

"I'll have to deal with considerable red tape in order for construction to start," Seth said. "The new buildings will have to keep to the original footprint and exterior details. Plans will need to be filed with the city and approved. The city might request an archeological dig on the site before allowing us to start work. Someone will need to be in the city to oversee every step, be it Jack or one of your Thanes."

Seth preferred Jack, even though he hated the thought of being in New York without him. If Jack was in Boston, though, Isaiah couldn't harm him.

"A bachelor house would give whoever is working on the construction project a home base. Also, I want some place safe where my wife can stay while visiting the East Coast. I don't want her here in New York because of Isaiah. Since you haven't chosen a wife for him, Isaiah resents the fact that I was given one at thirteen. He is ignoring the fact that I needed help to bear the Boston alpha."

"He wouldn't dare hurt her," Mandeville said.

Seth gritted his teeth. Why did everyone defend the man when the proof that he was dangerously jealous was in plain sight? "He would dare. Just as he dared to attack me when I was thirteen. As he dared to ignore my phone calls from Mexico, saying that Jack and Samuels were in danger. He was willing to let a Thane on King's business die."

He shouldn't have taken this path. He shouldn't be criticizing the king in front of his Thanes. Not when he wanted something from Alexander. Yet he had to be sure that Alexander didn't insist that Kate come to the Castle.

"Your law states that no adult wolf should attack a puppy.

You have not punished him once for all his petty attacks on me. Why would he not dare attack my wife? While he would attempt it, he wouldn't succeed. She's the Princess of Boston and well chosen as such. She would destroy him. I do not want to start my marriage, though, by forcing her into that confrontation. I don't want to deprive New York of its prince."

Actually, Seth would do it cheerfully. The more people he had to protect, the more willing he was to kill Isaiah. The king could remarry and have another son. New York had waited three hundred years for a prince. It could wait another twenty.

"Kate deserves a chance to actually see the territory that she's part of," Seth pushed on. "I want her input on building our home. She needs a safe place to stay in Boston. At the moment, the only refuge for her is Silas Decker's home."

Seth knew that Joshua would happily host Kate, but he also knew that none of the Thanes were comfortable with the notion of puppies sleeping in a vampire's lair. Add "female" to "puppy" and the Thanes visibly flinched.

"Hm, yes, the Grigoris' pet monster," Alexander said. He fell quiet but his focus went to Joshua again. This time Joshua was asleep, head down on the kitchen island, homework scattered around him.

Seth clenched his fists. The other thing that his father taught him was not to press the attack until your position was known. He waited for Alexander to say something.

The king sighed deeply and stood up. "Belgrade took much out of me. I grow weary. Do the groundwork on establishing a bachelor house. We will talk about this again later."

Seth watched the king walk slowly to the door as if the weight of the world rested on him. What? Did he win? Was that a yes? Or just a "maybe"?

7: DECKER

Werewolves walked in their sleep.

Or something...

Normally Decker woke slowly with the setting sun. He gradually became aware as the light fled the land, becoming fully awake only when full dark had cloaked the land.

The evening that he learned that werewolves walked in their sleep, he had snapped suddenly, fully, awake.

There was *something* in his casket with him.

He jerked back in fear even as he realized it was some*one*, not a rat. The hairy thing that brushed across his face, waking him, was a head of hair. Who in the world was in his coffin with him? He could only think of one likely person.

"Joshua?" Decker measured off the intruder with blind fumbling. Strong shoulders encased in a fleece shirt. A short torso. Equally short legs tangling with his. Yes, correct size for his housemate, but what was Joshua doing in his coffin? The boy lay like a lead weight on Decker's chest, breathing deeply. "Are you asleep?"

The only answer was a sleepy whimper followed by a deep growl.

Decker had a wolf in his casket. Still in human form, true, but Joshua wasn't awake at the helm. Nor, technically, was the wolf. It was some gray area of joint slumber.

Joshua was in the loungewear that he called "sweats." The teenager must have changed out of his school uniform, pulled

75

on the comfortable clothes, and fallen asleep—someplace. Perhaps his bed or maybe the couch or even the kitchen island. Decker had found him asleep in several odd places in the last few days. Obviously, the wolf had taken advantage of Joshua being asleep to pick a new sleeping place. The question was, how had the wolf found its way down into Decker's secret bedroom and climbed into the locked coffin with the vampire?

More importantly, how did Decker wake up *just* the boy?

"Joshua." Decker sang the name. He had a fifty-fifty chance of ending up with a startled wolf who knew judo. Decker would rather not have a wrestling match with an insanely strong werewolf inside his coffin. It would most likely be very painful. Worse, it was also very difficult to custom-order superwide coffins and have them delivered to private houses. It made people curious. Curiosity killed the vampire.

"Jaaah-shuuu-ahh." Decker sang the name a little louder.

It got him sloppy puppy kisses all over his face. The wolf snuggled closer and huffed into Decker's armpit as it buried its head under his arm.

Decker could lie here until the boy woke up. It was pleasant. He always woke at room temperature and would spend the first hour awake freezing cold. Joshua was a little furnace of warmth. There was also something calming about listening to Joshua's deep breathing.

No, the longer he put it off, the more embarrassed Joshua would be. He should wake the boy.

Or maybe carry him back to his own bed . . .

If Joshua was that deeply asleep, Decker might be able to sneak him back to his own bedroom without the teenager being any the wiser. Yes, that seemed the best course of action since Joshua might be sound asleep for another hour or two.

Decker freed an arm to push up his casket's lid.

It was locked. Decker pushed on it a few more times to verify it. No. Locked.

His custom-built casket had a deadbolt lock on the lid. The throw latch was inside with him. Outside there was a keyhole for someone like Elise to unlock the casket with a key in case of emergencies.

The very literal part of "dead to the world" unnerved Saul even after a lifetime of association. Decker wanted to put off

Joshua having to deal with it as long as possible. They had only recently come to a compromise on Decker's need to feed on magical essence. If Decker carefully "sipped" power from Joshua's connection to the werewolves' Source, the act remained safely controlled—and more important from Joshua's perspective—non-sexual. It meant that Decker didn't need to hunt monsters daily to stay in control of his hunger.

Sooner or later, he would have to broach the whole undead aspect, but so far, he hadn't. He hadn't given Joshua a key to his coffin. He hadn't even shown the secret stairs down into his bedroom to the boy. The lid hadn't been forced open.

How did Joshua get into his casket?

Decker tapped the sides, checking them for large holes that the boy could wriggle through. No. None.

Maybe this wasn't Joshua.

The casket *was* pitch dark.

Decker ran hands over the body snuggled up against him. It felt like Joshua. It was his wolf scent of sunlight through green foliage with the hint of dried leaves underneath. Decker focused his magical "finding" ability.

Where was Joshua? In his coffin.

It was definitely Joshua, but it looped back to the mystery of how he had gotten into Decker's casket.

Decker tried the lid again. Locked.

Maybe Elise gave Joshua a key.

Probably not, once Decker considered it. Elise saw the werewolves as allies, but she didn't completely trust them. She wouldn't have surrendered a key without discussing it with Decker first. Nor would Joshua steal her keyring and duplicate the keys in secret. The boy had a great deal of respect for private property; he asked for permission before making any changes or rearranging to the house. (Besides, even trying to steal Elise's keys would get him knifed.)

How did Joshua even find his way past the secret doors? There was a trick to unlocking them. Did the wolf smash them open? He hadn't broken the casket's lid.

First things first. Get Joshua back to his room. Assess damage to doors later.

There was the small problem that the latch was currently under Joshua's tailbone.

Decker was trying to slip his hand between Joshua's butt and the pillowed silk side when the boy woke up.

"Hm?" Joshua sleepily prodded Decker's chest. "Why is my pillow so lumpy? What the hell?" He sniffed, taking in Decker's scent. "Decker? What are you doing—" he yawned deeply "—in my bed?"

Decker laughed. "I'm not in your bed. You're in mine—so to speak."

"Huh?" Joshua attempted to sit up and hit his head on the casket's lid. "Ow! What the hell?"

Decker found himself crushed against the side as Joshua shifted into a large wolf.

"What? What?" The wolf flailed in the small space of the coffin. "What's going on?"

Decker felt for the lock. "It's okay, Joshua! It's okay! Please don't break my bed!"

"You sleep in a casket?"

"Yes. I thought I told you." Decker might have avoided the subject.

Joshua became a boy again but hit his head again on the lid. "Ow! Why won't it open? Are we stuck?"

"No. We're not stuck. Just give me a moment. Be calm."

It was harder to find the lock in the dark with a squirming body in the way.

"What are you wearing?" Joshua whispered.

"My nightshirt." Decker wondered why he was whispering.

"Why is it so soft?" Joshua continued to whisper. Perhaps it because it was pitch dark.

"It's cashmere."

"Decker!" Joshua shouted when Decker misjudged where Joshua started and ended and accidently groped him. Abruptly there was a puppy burrowing into the space around Decker's feet.

"I'm sorry! I'm just trying—there!" Decker flipped the latch and flung open the lid. Elise had set timers on the nightstand lamp, so it was always on when he woke up. It always made him feel like a reverse refrigerator.

"Where the hell are we?" The puppy leapt out of the casket.

"This is my bedroom." Decker stepped out of the casket and closed the lid. There weren't even scratch marks by the lock. The door across the room looked intact, the deadbolt thrown.

"What the hell?" Joshua said again. "Did you carry me down here?"

"No." Decker pointed out the clock by his bed, planning to point out that he just woke up. The time surprised him. It was too early for him to be actually awake. "I went to bed first and I—I—shouldn't be awake. Why am I awake?"

Joshua frowned at the clock. "It's sunset, isn't it?"

"Not for another few minutes. Normally I don't wake up until the sun is totally down. It's daylight..."

He hadn't seen actual sunlight for nearly three hundred years. He started for the door.

"Decker!" Joshua transformed into a massive wolf and leapt between Decker and the door. "No. No. You can't go out during the day. Bad things happen to you in sunlight. Right?"

"If I stay inside, away from the windows, I'm fine." The first few months of life as a vampire had taught Decker the limits. At dawn, he'd collapsed where he stood until he came to recognize the signs. He'd awakened badly burned and dangerously hungry. The memory of the pain and near uncontrollable hunger kept him from growing careless. "Please."

"Oookay." Joshua sounded as if he thought it was horrible idea but moved aside. "Be careful."

Decker got as far as the front hallway before needing to stop. Sunlight poured through the lead glass of the front door. It shimmered and danced on the polished wood floor. It was the most beautiful thing he'd ever seen.

The massive wolf sat down behind him. It wrapped paws the size of dinner plates around him, keeping him back from the deadly beauty. Together they watched the sunlight die into darkness.

"How was school?" Decker asked once the house was dark.

"I'm not sure," the wolf muttered.

"Not sure?" Decker repeated, mystified.

"It was weird." The wolf pressed its face against Decker's back. "Everything was so different from my old school that I felt really lost. The food was amazing at the cafeteria. It was like going out to eat at someplace nice in Utica."

"I thought you packed a large lunch."

"My wolf kept trying everyone else's food to see what it tasted like," Joshua said in disgust. "Everyone was like 'let the wolf try it' like it was no big deal."

Decker doubted that Joshua actually fully transformed into the wolf, but it certainly sounded like it. "They knew...?"

"Yes, they all knew. Well, not everyone, just the Goths. The citizens of Unpopular. Although they didn't seem like they were all that unpopular. Everyone seemed nice to the Goths. Maybe it's because the school will always side with the nerds instead of the jocks, unlike what they did at my old school. They don't turn a blind eye to the football team acting like they're untouchable gods..."

Joshua trailed off. The Wickers had used the football team of his last school as puppets, setting up a situation where one of the Wolf King's Thanes would have to transform Joshua into a werewolf to save his life. None of the team had survived being used as tools; their lifetime of being petty bullies had ended in a massacre.

It was the main reason that Joshua hadn't contacted his parents. He knew that they would insist that he return home and finish his senior year at his old high school. (Bethy confirmed this, so it wasn't just Joshua being fearful.) As a minor—and as a good son—he couldn't say no. Barely able to control his wolf at the best of times, he wouldn't be able to deal with any petty resentment the students at his old school might have that Joshua survived the massacre.

Decker searched for something safe to say. "It sounds like you had a good day—all things considered. The people were understanding, and the wolf was well-fed."

Joshua snorted. "Too well-fed. All I seem to do is eat. I'm not sure if the wolf is actually hungry or if it's just eating to eat. I'm not even sure where all the food is going to. I'm not putting on any weight. If anything, I'm about five pounds lighter than just before Halloween."

That didn't seem possible. Joshua had been inhaling food since they'd met. Decker only had a Virtue's normal appetite to compare it to, but it seemed like an excessive amount. Yes, the Thane had eaten a great deal while visiting over the holiday weekend, but Cabot had been recovering from wounds inflicted by silver knives. Cabot was also a foot taller and a hundred pounds heavier than Joshua. More than once, Seth had lain on the floor, too full to eat more, while his brother and cousin continued eating.

Joshua made an impatient noise. "I wonder if there's anything to even pack for lunch tomorrow. My lunch seemed to be everything in the refrigerator."

The wolf let Decker go in order to check the contents of the refrigerator—and probably eat something. All the talk about food probably was making it hungry. Joshua made annoyed grumbling noises as he realized that the wolf had taken control of the body. "Oh geez, what a mess! What did you do while I was asleep?" Joshua howled at his other half when he reached the kitchen. "Did you eat everything? Dude, what did you do with the eggs? Did you swallow them raw? Oh, gross!"

"Do we need to go shopping?" Decker called as he stood up.

"Yes," Joshua called back. "He cleaned out the fridge! Stupid wolf! There's nothing in here but empty food wrappers. But not now, I have a ton of homework."

Homework? That was a term that Decker didn't know.

Decker drifted into the kitchen. Joshua was still a very large wolf, grumbling loudly about the mess that his other half made. He was picking up torn packaging with his teeth and dropping them in the trash can. The inside of the refrigerator was indeed remarkably bare considering how full it had been just days ago.

Joshua's backpack and textbooks were scattered across the island. It appeared that he'd fallen asleep while trying to study. He'd spent the whole weekend reading over the schoolwork that he'd missed since he'd fled his hometown. This seemed much more like marshalling for war than what he was doing before. His laptop and his iPad were both present. Calculator, pens, pencils, and paper were all gathered and strategically positioned.

"It's going to take me hours to get everything done," Joshua grumbled, head in the refrigerator. "I might not have to take the final tests for the AP classes but there's a ton of homework involved to keep up with the class."

"What is homework?" Decker asked since it was going to be an important part of Joshua's life going forward.

The wolf turned to stare at him. After a minute of silence, it asked, "You didn't have to do homework when you went to school?"

"Schools were very different back in those days," Decker said. "When I was first taught my letters, we would practice them on sand tables—which were trays of sand so high that you could stand and draw with your fingers or a little stick. Later we were given slate tablets—squares of stone about the size of your iPad, surrounded with a wood frame. We had little slate pencils—which were like chalk but not quite. You could write on the stone and then use a damp cloth to wipe the words away."

The wolf stared at Decker more. "Are you making that up?"

Decker laughed. The world was so different now that even he could barely grasp it. "No. Paper was much too dear to be used by children. Books too were very rare and expensive. I owned just one book as a child, and I loved it well."

"Just one? That had to suck. What was it?"

"*The Faerie Queen.*" The title obviously meant nothing to the boy, which wasn't surprising considering the book had been written over four hundred years ago. Decker had lost his beloved original in the Philadelphia house fire. He might have bought a newer copy when Saul moved him to this house. He wasn't sure; he hadn't seen it while digging through the overflowing stacks in his library. "It's all about knights fighting monsters and righting wrongs and finding their one true love. My favorite part was the third section, which is all about this lady knight, Britomart, who wins jousts while disguised as a man."

"So, it's like *Lord of the Rings*?"

Decker considered the movie that they'd watched recently. "I remember there being more armor involved but basically of that vein." Something buzzed in the kitchen. Decker thought he'd learned all the odd sounds that life with Joshua generated. This was a new buzzing. It bothered him more than it should. It had an odd quality, as if it wanted to be noticed. "What is that?"

"Ah, sorry, I left my phone on vibrate; we're not allowed to use our phones in class." Joshua shook off the massive wolf form like a dog shaking off muddy water. He always seemed very short when he returned to human. He pulled from his backpack the impossibly small, magical square of metal and glass that the phones were now. "It's Seth. He wants to know how school went. Oh geez, he's texted me like thirty times since the end of school. Something has him excited."

Joshua cocked his head as he scrolled down through the texts his brother had sent him.

"Is something wrong?" Decker said.

"Seth wants to rent a condo as a temporary base until the

Court is rebuilt." Joshua's voice inflected both on "condo" and "the Court," making them questions in the middle of his statement.

Decker knew that Elise lived in an apartment that she sometimes called "my condo" and other times "my loft," but he didn't know why she used those terms to describe it. The bed area—he would not call it a room—did remind him of a hayloft.

Decker addressed the unspoken question that he knew the answer to. "Court is the name that werewolves use to indicate homes that are either connected or very close in proximity that make up the pack's main living space. The Boston Court was a set of brownstone town houses near the Commons. I'm told that originally the pack had a cluster of log cabins on the site, back when Boston was founded. The town houses were partially destroyed when your father was killed, so the king set them on fire to act as a funeral pyre."

Joshua scrolled down the texts from his brother, shaking his head. "Oh! Yeah! Winnie said something like that when we were at the Frog Pond. I was distracted by the whole talking frogs being real statues thing." He made an odd noise. "Seth wants to know if I need more money. He gave me four thousand dollars in cash last Friday. Why would I need more money?"

"It's possible that Seth does not know the true worth of money." Decker certainly didn't. The official currency when he was a child in the British colony of New York was the English pennies, shillings, and pounds. They were, however, rare as hen's teeth as England didn't supply sufficient coin to its colonies nor would it allow them to create their own. The area had once belonged to the Dutch as New Amsterdam, so there were still some pennings, duits, stuivers, and guilders floating around. The most common coins were Spanish dollars, which could be broken into pieces of eight to make change. Any transaction was a complicated affair, especially when it involved paying for a service like dowsing. Then Decker became a vampire, and the colonies became a newborn country with currency problems that took decades to solve. At some point, Decker gave up trying to keep track of money and let the Grigori deal with it. It wasn't hard to guess that the young wolf prince was in the same boat. "Seth moved from Boston Court to Wolf Castle. His needs have always been met without touching a single dollar."

"Oh my god!" Joshua shouted. "Seth's wife is coming for a visit!"

"When?" Decker asked the most important question.

Joshua frowned, scrolling up and down. "He doesn't say. He just says it's one of the reasons he's looking for a condo is so that she has a place to stay while she's visiting. Huh. Visiting. That's weird. You never hear of a wife *visiting* her husband, but I guess she's just fifteen or sixteen. Oh! He wants to know if she can stay with us if they don't find anyplace before she shows up."

"Yes," Decker said instantly. If the wolves camped elsewhere, chances were good that Joshua would go and stay with them. "She is your sister-in-law. She's more than welcome to stay."

Joshua cursed.

"What's wrong?" Decker was afraid that he'd been too transparent with his instant acceptance.

"He wants to give me a car!" Joshua shouted. "He wants to know what kind of car I would like! What the hell am I supposed to give him for Christmas?" Joshua picked up a handwritten list and held it out to Decker. "I was going to get him *Caddyshack*. *Caddyshack*! And he's getting me a car!"

Indeed, next to Seth's name was written "Caddyshack" but Decker didn't know what it was or how much it cost. Next to Cabot's name "Exploding Kittens" had been crossed out and "drone" replaced it. Decker wasn't sure what a drone was, but it seemed much more appealing than cat bombs. He wasn't even sure why Joshua thought that his cousin wanted kittens that exploded. Certainly, Cabot didn't seem to get on with Trouble well—but perhaps that was the point. Bethy had "text and ask her" written next to her name.

"Shit! Don't look at that!" Joshua jerked away the list before Decker scanned down to his own present. Joshua buried the paper under his schoolbooks and returned his attention to his phone. "I think its freaking weird. Seth never mentioned his wife once when he was here for Thanksgiving. I don't even know what her name is. The vet told us about her. I think she lives in California someplace. Oh! Seth is planning to drive up from New York with Cabot on Friday night to look at condos Saturday afternoon. He wants to stay here. He says he can stay at a hotel if it's not okay. He would like it if we could pick out a Christmas tree first thing in the morning at Bog Hollow Farm. He says it's a Tatterskein tradition. I still say the place sounds like the site of a horror movie."

The name did sound vaguely familiar. Perhaps it was one of

the businesses that the werewolves owned, which would explain why they always got their Christmas tree from it.

"It is fine if he stays here." Decker tackled the easiest of the problems. "Tree and all. When he is here, you can sound him out about a present. It is possible he has all that he needs and will treasure anything you give him as long as it's given with good intentions. If not, perhaps that is why he's giving you more money. Perhaps he wants something that the king will only allow him to keep if it's gifted to him—like a kitten. One that doesn't explode."

Joshua didn't seem to be paying attention. He was swiping at the surface of his phone. "I probably should pick up lights and ornaments and such before they drive up—that way we can decorate the tree Saturday night. I think Seth is really excited about this whole 'family' Christmas thing."

Joshua paused to look up at Decker expectantly, as if he wanted an answer to some question that Decker hadn't caught. They were talking about Christmas trees—maybe. What did Decker know about Christmas trees? Not much. They didn't become popular until *Godey's Magazine* published the picture of Queen Victoria with her tree in the 1850s. When he lived in Philadelphia, he'd let his servants put up decorations. Surely after a hundred and fifty years, Decker had learned something useful about them.

"Yes, I think getting some lights and ornaments beforehand would be good," Decker said cautiously. "We'll need some kind of stand and perhaps a sharp wood saw—just in case the trunk needs to be evened out."

Joshua blew out his breath. "But I'm not going to have time to shop, not with all the homework I have to do. Not with my stupid wolf eating everything in sight."

"I don't suppose there's time to do a Sears and Roebuck order."

"A what?"

"It's a catalog. A book with things you can order..." Come to think of it, Decker hadn't seen a Sears and Roebuck catalog for years. It was such a staple for nearly a hundred years. It was surprising that it had vanished without him noticing. "It's a bigger version of the magazine-looking clothing catalogs. I still get those. It had all sorts of things from toys to dishes."

"It sounds like Amazon. Oh!" Joshua leapt toward his laptop. "Seth gave me a credit card! Maybe I can order groceries to be delivered!"

It seemed like something out of a fairy tale, a cornucopia of food summoned out of thin air. The most amazing thing was that Joshua seemed to know exactly what was needed to be done. Decker could only sit and marvel as Joshua found the correct "website"—or was that "web sight" since they were seeing it? Joshua set up an account using something called email. He then searched through seemingly endless menus for the things that he wanted. Beef? Joshua scrolled down through a long list to pick off a "family pack" of ribeye steaks. Deli meat? He changed the "quantity" indicator on the sliced roast beef to five pounds. Fruit? A bag of oranges and another of apples were searched out and selected. Desserts? "Bakery" was ignored in favor of "frozen desserts." A half dozen pies were selected while Joshua muttered darkly, "Maybe he won't eat them if they're raw and frozen."

There was so much Decker needed to learn.

The total cost seemed extremely high but anything over a penny for a loaf of bread seemed high to Decker.

"This is another reason I can't move back home," Joshua said as he entered his credit card number. "It would bankrupt my folks trying to keep my wolf fed. Nor would they let Seth pay for my food. My dad thinks of himself as the great provider. Probably because his parents are so sure that he's not. He's not a lawyer. He doesn't make the big lawyer bucks. We're not poor—or at least I never thought of us as poor."

Joshua paused to eye the credit card. "Suddenly being able to buy anything I want makes me realize that we were probably on the low end of middle class. My mom always made food shopping like a video game: how cheaply can you put food on the table? What's on sale? What's the special of the week? Never steaks. Always things made with ground beef. Meatloaf. Tacos. Sloppy Joes. Chili. Spaghetti and meatballs. I liked her cooking, so I never thought about the fact that we never had anything more expensive."

He put the credit card back into his wallet. "The thing is that my entire family is weird about money. Period. I don't think we've ever had a family holiday that didn't end with a fight over money. Who had it. Who didn't. Lease or own. BMW versus Ford. It always starts out sane and ends crazy. I'm sure it would begin with 'we can't take money from a poor orphan who probably isn't really your half brother,' but then it would end up someplace crazy even before they found out about the werewolf angle. Probably they would end up convinced that the king got all his money from drugs and prostitution. Rich man living in New York City with a bunch of enforcers? Mafia. Definitely Mafia. You wouldn't be able to convince them otherwise. Tell them about the werewolves and it would be Werewolf Mafia. Darn, they don't have any delivery slots open until tomorrow night."

Decker had gotten lost in the logic. Was mafia a type of bread like matzah or miche? Joshua's parents would think that the king's werewolves were bakers? Decker wasn't sure how Joshua's parents would even find out about the king—unless of course Joshua himself confessed somehow—which he could see Joshua doing. And what exactly was the wolf bakers going to deliver? Oh! Joshua meant the supermarket.

"I'm still going to need to go food shopping after I get done with my homework," Joshua said. "But if I can set up a big food delivery for tomorrow night, I'll only have to grab a few things tonight."

8: JOSHUA

Joshua had never been to a supermarket late at night. It seemed like a totally different place—in a weird alternate universe kind of way. On the plus side, there were no screaming babies nor any little old ladies slowly pushing squeaking carts, managing to block an entire aisle for minutes on end. On the downside, the store had a creepy postapocalyptic zombie vibe. Most of the long, gleaming aisles were empty but lurking around every corner were shambling mounds of flesh. The smelly, heavily bundled people were either homeless, addicts, drunks, insane, or some combination of the above. It was difficult to tell. They could even be zombies; Joshua *was* a werewolf food shopping with a vampire in tow. It was ten below zero outside. Whatever the aimlessly shuffling beings were, they were in the warm store to keep from freezing.

Joshua's furry other half didn't like the zombies. It had growled at two of them so far. He could feel his wolf pressing outward on his skin, wanting to transform into something larger and more impressive looking than a five-foot-two high school senior. He wasn't sure why it felt so intimidated by the other shoppers; even if they were zombies, they probably couldn't hurt Joshua. He'd been shot last week half a dozen times by a Wicker. By the next day, he couldn't even find the bullet wounds.

Even if he wasn't a werewolf, he had a brown belt in judo. He could defend himself without supernatural strength and speed and invulnerability.

What made it all especially annoying was that it was all the wolf's fault that they were at the store so late. Joshua was an honor roll student. He'd been in the running for valedictorian of his class. He had good study habits and normally got his work done quickly and efficiently. The wolf blew all that out of the water—taking over every time it got bored—and it had gotten bored often. Instead of finishing his homework in an hour or two, it had taken nearly six.

He'd been afraid that the supermarkets would all be closed but luckily this one recently had become twenty-four hours, apparently attempting to cash in on pre-Christmas sales. All signs of Thanksgiving had vanished. In its place was a huge selection of stocking stuffer candy, displays of candy canes (he had no idea that they came in so many flavors) and rolls of wrapping paper. The sound system played holiday tunes, which only served to remind him that he wasn't going to be seeing his family during the holidays.

While Joshua was distracted by this thought, the wolf beelined for the meat section and tried to wrangle a six-pound leg of lamb into the shopping basket.

"No!" Joshua shouted as he fought with himself. "I was just going to get lunch food. I don't even know if we like lamb. I don't know how to cook it and I'm not eating it raw. Put it back! It won't even fit in the basket!"

"I'll get a cart." Decker went off, leaving Joshua to deal with his inner monster alone.

"No, no, we've got a big pack of ribeye steaks coming tomorrow!" Joshua managed to drop the lamb back into the cooler, but his wolf countered by grabbing a filet mignon multipack that cost nearly two hundred dollars. "If you want meat, we can get one steak and cook it when we get home. We can get two and have steak and eggs tomorrow for breakfast."

The wolf cooperated enough for him to get the filet mignon back into the cooler, but they ended up with three individually wrapped steaks in the basket.

Joshua sighed. "Fine. Fine. Fine."

One of the zombies came up the aisle, muttering darkly. "The sun is setting. The moon is rising. The stars will wheel about in the sky."

When Joshua was younger, his mom and sister would make

dolls from dried apples. They'd carve faces on apples and then let them dry. The apples would shrink and shrivel up. This old person looked like one of those carved apples. It seemed as if they had no teeth, the gums withering inward. The head was topped with spare gray hair, so thin and short that it didn't cover their skull. They were so old that it was hard to tell their sex. Joshua decided that based on the person's small size, they were female. Maybe.

The old woman wore a patch over her left eye. She smelled of age and seawater.

The wolf didn't like the woman. It pulled the basket closer and growled.

"She's not going to take your steak!" Joshua whispered at the wolf. "Be nice."

"Listen to your wolf when it warns you that creatures of power are near at hand," the woman said.

Joshua jerked back. She knew he was a werewolf? She was a creature of power? She didn't look powerful but neither did Decker or Elise. "What are you?"

"Hungry. What else would I be? We're in a supermarket. I'm Enyo Graeae and you're the lost heir. What name did you decide to keep?"

"Joshua. Joshua Tatterskein."

"Oh, what an odd name," Enyo said. "Nice to meet you, Joshua Joshua Tatterskein."

"No, my name..." Joshua started to protest and then realized that he shouldn't argue with creatures of unknown power. He took a step backward. "You're only here for food?"

"Fate and random chance are two different things." Enyo wagged her finger as if pointing at two objects far apart. "You being a werewolf is fate; there's no way you could have escaped your destiny no matter what odd twists your life took. It is random chance that we're meeting now. Nothing I could say or do would influence your fate—although I could make the road a more interesting journey."

He backed up some more. "I'd rather have a nice boring life."

"Who cares what you want? The universe doesn't care. I don't care. The universe might like a good old-fashioned brawl. I have my suspicions. I think if the universe was pacifist by nature, I would have a harder time stirring things up."

"The universe?" Joshua said. "Do you mean, like, God?"

"Pfft." Enyo waved off his question. "You need to study religion, boy. If you studied enough, then you'd realize there's a pattern to them all. There's always a big nothingness that gets bored with being nothing. It makes gods. They make a world to play in and littler gods to push around. The names get changed but the pattern remains."

"You mean like Odin and Thor and Loki?" He knew those from the movies. "They're just stories. Myths. Legends."

"Reality is like a box of tissues," Enyo said. "Layers upon layers. Not everyone can see into the other layers. Not everyone can move from one tissue to the another. Myths are just events that involve multiple layers, outside the ken of the people you consider 'normal.' Where do you think your power comes from? Where do you think your wolf lives when you're not all furry? Just because you only catch glimpses of the forest that is your Source does not mean it doesn't exist."

The "box of tissues" sounded like what Winnie had told him when she tried to explain how she could talk to the dead.

"The green is a real place?" Joshua said.

"The green?" The old woman cackled at the name. "It is as real as the Wolf King. It is the Wolf King. The Wolf King is it. When the universe shattered itself out of sheer boredom, 'the green' became its own little universe that then created its own god, like a clam making a pearl. The Wolf King used his power to make the alphas like your ancestor, the Prince of Boston, who then made their pack members. Gods beget demigods who beget heroes who beget kings who beget knights who beget serfs. It's a diminishing chain. The power degrades even as it's passed on. Copies of copies. We're not talking about digital here. Flaws are inherent in the creation."

What was taking Decker so long? Surely getting a shopping cart in a nearly empty store should only take a minute or two! The wolf picked up the basket and attempted escape by heading down the aisle in the direction Decker had gone.

The old woman followed Joshua. "Where do you think the angels came from?"

Angels? "Do you mean the Grigori?"

"The god of the Jews made little gods and called them angels. Those angels made children with the daughters of men—demigods called Nephilim. Their god is all about law and order, and the

Nephilim were too flawed—copies being copies. Their god wiped almost everything out in the Great Flood, so he could start over again. He only kept the most orderly of his demigods. Dominions. Virtues. Powers."

"Elise is a demigod?" That didn't sound right. Joshua realized he shouldn't believe everything that some random stranger said to him.

Enyo cackled, nodding her head. "Yes, she is. She could have been a Power, but she chose to carefully chain her power with limits and behavioral restraints. The world would be much more exciting if there were hundreds of Powers wandering around loose, using their strength to erase whatever they wanted. I like a good brawl. I've seen some epic ones. Currently it's like a game of Marco Polo where everyone is blindfolded. Soon the blindfolds will come off and the knives will come out and things will get interesting. I'm looking forward to it."

Marco Polo was hide-and-seek played in water. Not that he actually played it—you needed friends who you could trust not to be jerks while your eyes were closed.

"There's more Wickers?" Joshua asked.

"Oh, the Wickers were only idiots who wanted to be gods. They didn't understand that their minor mind-tricks made them just above circus freaks. If they had true power, they wouldn't need a blood sacrifice to power their toys. They couldn't become gods unless they opened themselves up to a source, and they were too cowardly to do that. The Wakefield coven were simple tools. They were given the spell books of Monkshood coven and let loose to wreak their havoc."

"Why?" Joshua said.

"Have you ever played the game *Battleship*? The first attack has no hope of sinking the enemy's ship. The first attack is to find the enemy."

Joshua's wolf wanted to kill Enyo. It was angry and afraid. It took a snarling step toward her before Joshua managed to wrestle control back from it.

"Who gave the Wakefields the books?" he growled.

"If I told you, you wouldn't recognize the name."

"Tell me!"

"It's useless, I tell you," Enyo said. "You don't understand how it works. Power from another layer needs a vessel to take form here. A body to give shape to pure energy. It would take whoever it can reach. It cares not who. It could be anyone."

"What do you mean by 'anyone'?"

"Anyone." Enyo waved her hand to encompass all of Boston and the four million people who lived in and around the city. "Most gods don't care who they take; they just want access to this layer. What do you think the breaches are? It is a source that pours out, looking for a vessel, taking everything in its path. If it can find a vessel that can hold its power, then it's golden. Of course, if the vessel is too weak, then maybe the resulting turmoil will hit someone stronger. Like it did with Decker. That one might have succeeded if the Wolf King hadn't raced across the planet to put out the fires, root out the weeds, and stitch up all the holes." She cackled, rubbing her hands together. "It's just about showtime again. I'm hoping for sheer chaos. It is almost Christmas and I'm due a good present."

Joshua backed away from her. The wolf was growling. Joshua wasn't sure if he could keep it in check. Where was Decker? Joshua was nearly to the front doors. The carts were within sight. There was no sign of Decker. The wolf worked its nose, caught Decker's scent, and they were off—the wolf, Joshua, and the old woman.

Joshua decided he hated this particular supermarket. It was some weird supernatural magnet. This was where he had met Winnie, who talked with ghosts. She and her spirit guide, Fred, had been giving out samples of organic apple sausage. (A job Winnie quit, saying that they'd met by "fate," and she had to focus on helping Joshua.) There were other supermarkets in the area. It was just random chance that he'd decided to come here tonight and be ambushed by this weird old woman. Or was it?

"You-you-you know . . . something," Joshua said.

"I know everything," she said. "That's my secret elf talent. People try to find me, make me tell them things. Sometimes I let them find me. It's fun to watch them crash and burn. Those Wickers that kidnapped you as a baby—they were so full of themselves. They were so sure that they were going to rule the world. You weren't their first target. They had had their sights on another when they found me. It was fun to tell them that the messenger boy had tasted the cake that he was supposed to deliver untouched. That they had another thirteen years before the one that they needed would be born."

"You're the one that the ghost found. What was her name? Wonder Woman something-or-other." Joshua winced as he realized that the ghost hadn't put much weight in "real" names of people either. "She might have used the name Jazmin. She was a scam artist with an eye patch and a parrot. Are you the one-eyed fortune teller that the Wickers had Jazmin find?"

The old woman cackled again, nodding. "Yes, yes, she had a touch of power, that one. A little baby god. She would have been able to defend herself from the Wickers if she was more aware of what she was. She could convince her victims that what she said was true because she had the ability to make almost anything she said to be true. But she was ignorant of the true range of her powers—so she just used it to fleece her victims. Play with the fire; burn by fire. She got swept up in the chaos. The trick is to sidestep just at the last moment, like playing chicken with a freight train. Fate will not change its course any more than a locomotive."

Jazmin had broken free of the Wickers' control after the coven had killed Joshua's birth mother. She took Joshua and ran. She sold him to his adoptive parents. His life would have been vastly different if she'd left him with the coven.

"You told the Wickers about me," Joshua said. "You got my birth mother killed."

"Everyone dies sooner or later. Even gods." The old woman cackled louder.

The wolf snarled with anger.

Decker was suddenly there. Blood sword out. Eyes full dark. "Get away from him, you heartless old hag!"

"Ah, Silas, still bitter?" Enyo said.

"Yes!" Decker's voice rumbled deep and dangerous with his power. He pushed Joshua back behind him, keeping the bloodred sword leveled at the old woman. "You can see the danger coming but you never do anything about it except stand and watch it mow everyone down!"

Enyo shrugged. "It doesn't take an oracle to guess that your precious Virtues would have been killed by a monster sooner or later. Live by the knife, die by the claw."

"You knew and did nothing to save them," Decker said.

"Oh, I made popcorn." She vanished, cackling, just as Decker slashed at her with his blood sword.

"Where did she go? Hey! Whoa!" Joshua caught hold of Decker to keep him from charging off. Decker was as dangerous as the wolf when he got this way. "Calm down."

They stood a moment, clinging to each other as they struggled with their personal demons.

"She can use her source to teleport." Decker still held his impossibly long sword. He pressed his forehead to Joshua's shoulder and took a deep breath. When he spoke again, his voice had lost its deep and dangerous tone. "Step in. Step out. I think she lives in our world but I'm not sure. First time I heard about her was shortly before the Prince of New York went feral and killed a quarter of the people living in the city. That was over three hundred years ago, and I was still human then. Last time I saw her was the night that Elise's mother was killed along with all the wolves in Boston."

"What? Is she that dangerous?"

Decker took another deep breath. He hugged Joshua like he was the only safety in dangerous waters. Decker used both hands; his sword had vanished back to whatever reality he summoned it from. "Enyo is like crows gathering before a battle; she doesn't kill anyone, but she feasts on the dead."

"She's a cannibal?"

Decker laughed and let Joshua go. "No. She's there to see the carnage. It's like a movie to her. The more dead bodies on the battlefield, the happier she is."

The comment about popcorn made sense now. No wonder Decker was freaked. She'd sat and ate popcorn as Decker's lover died.

Grief settled on Decker as if his loss had been recent. Elise's mother had died three years ago but Decker was over three hundred years old. It probably seemed recent to him.

A security guard came stalking up the aisle. He eyed them with suspicion. The wolf growled at the guard. The man rested his right hand on his pistol. With his left hand, he pointed at his eyes and then at Joshua. *I'm watching you.*

Joshua looked away, clenching teeth on a louder growl. Getting shot would only piss off the wolf. His inner monster would slip out of his control. "Come on. Let's get what we came for and get out of here."

✧　　✧　　✧

Joshua would have preferred using a self-checkout lane, but they were all closed. Only one of the lights above the manned cash registers was on. The lanes were near the big automatic sliding glass doors that let in the arctic cold. The cashier was bundled up and seemingly asleep, head down on the unmoving black rubber conveyance belt.

The security guard had followed them through the store. He banged on the counter beside the sleeping cashier. "Hey! Come on! Wake up. I told you: you can't sleep during your shift!"

"I'm just resting my eyes." The cashier's voice sounded familiar. It was only after she looked up, saw Decker, and yipped with fear that Joshua recognized her. It was Winnie. Hat and gloves covered her signature purple hair and fingernails. Her spirit guide, Fred, loomed over her as a faint shadow.

The guard stepped forward, his hand going to his pistol.

"Winnie! It's okay!" Joshua shouted. "Winnie, it's us!"

Winnie blinked at Joshua a moment before recognition kicked in. "Oh! Oh! It's okay, Harrold. I was just startled. They're friends. I just didn't recognize Decker. He's... He's..." She turned to squint at the vampire. "Brighter? A moon has come out on the starry night, but it's still full of things that scratch at the windowpanes and want to be let in."

"Thank you," Decker said. "I think."

"What?" Harrold glanced back and forth between Winnie and Decker. "I don't like them. They're weird."

Winnie threw up her hands. "You should know by now: all my friends are weird!" She made a shooing motion. "Fred says someone is trying to steal booze out of the wine shop. You should go check on it."

"Don't try anything, Fred!" Harrold pointed at Joshua, obviously thinking that Joshua was Fred. "I've got eyes in the back of my head."

Harrold walked backward toward the wine. "Try anything, and I'll see it!"

"I thought you quit." Joshua started to unload the cart as Harrold bumped into the corner of the aisle and turned around.

"The food-sample lady was a different gig," Winnie said. "Whole different company. And yes, I burnt that bridge to ash. Nothing left, not even blackened timbers. Why do we say 'bridge' when it comes from Cortés burning his boats?"

"I don't know." Joshua was glad to see that Winnie looked no worse for wear. He'd last seen her possessed by the ghost of Marie Antoinette, who was keeping her safe from a Wicker's fetch.

Joshua paused as he discovered an insanely expensive family pack of porterhouse steaks in his cart. Where did they come from? Were they already in the cart when Decker got it? No, there was a lot more than just the porterhouses. Six bone-in chicken thighs. A twin pack of pork chops. How did the wolf get so much into the cart in such a short period of time?

How could he claim to be in control when he did things he couldn't remember doing? That "he" didn't do but his furry other was responsible for. And why didn't his brother Seth seem like he had a split personality problem? Was it because he was mentally better integrated with his wolf, or was his inner self simply better behaved? What did this mean in terms of what Enyo claimed? Was it the Source that wanted pork chops?

"I've been thinking about going back to school." Winnie ignored Joshua's existential crisis. She swiped his purchases past the scanner, making her cash register beep. "I could have gone to college. I was an honor student at Blackridge." *Beep.* "I had a full-ride scholarship; I thought your dad would be pissed off if I didn't get good grades. He scared me. I could have gotten into any of the local colleges." *Beep.* "Except Harvard." *Beep.* "Harvard and MIT." *Beep.* "Harvard, MIT and—I don't know! A lot of places!"

"It's a cash register, not a lie detector," Joshua said.

"One can't be sure with machines." Winnie eyed the cash register with suspicion. "Sometimes they have their own magic. Something has leaked in and changed them. My cousin had a possessed car. It liked polka music and German bratwurst."

"It ate meat?" Joshua said. It sounded similar to his wolf.

"No, once a month it would drive him to Jacob Wirth's downtown on Stuart Street. It wouldn't move until he got three orders of their grill-smoked bratwurst. I think it might have liked the smell. Burnt offerings. The dinners came with red cabbage and German potato salad. Oh, so good! Occasionally he had to pour dark lager on all four tires. That car had attitude. I was so sorry that he lost it."

Joshua resisted asking how the cousin "lost" the car.

Decker visibly wrestled with temptation before saying, "Did it die? Someone killed it? Or did he just misplace it?"

"It left him. It's his fault. The endless polka music got to him. He disconnected the radio. It got mad and left him. Who knows where it is now."

Decker must have been curious. He closed his eyes, lifted his hands, and pointed toward the produce section. "Southwest. Very far away. New Jersey or farther."

"Pennsylvania Dutch. That makes sense." Winnie pointed at the large package of porterhouse steaks still in the cart. "Are you buying that?"

Was he? It was insanely expensive and very heavy. They would have to carry everything back to the house several blocks away.

"Yes, we're buying it," Decker said firmly.

"It's over a hundred dollars," Joshua whispered.

"If the meat is at the house, the wolf won't come back to the store for it when you're asleep."

There was that.

Joshua put the steaks on the conveyor belt. They watched them slide down the counter.

"Anyhoo." Winnie grunted as she hefted the package and waved it over the scanner. "I didn't see the point of going to college. People in education don't believe in ghosts. Even at Blackridge, all of the teachers thought Fred was my 'imaginary friend.' They wanted me to see a psychologist. One would think that a school owned by werewolves would have a staff that believed in things that go bump in the night, but I guess it's safer to hire skeptics. There isn't a degree that would help with what I *want* to do for a living. Even something like World Religion seems to take the stance that the supernatural is what uneducated aboriginals believe in."

It made Joshua think of his earlier encounter. "Do you know who Enyo Graeae is?"

"The sea hag?" Winnie looked up at her looming spirit guide. "She was here? Fred! Why didn't you tell me? I wasn't sleeping, I was..." She trailed off as the guard came strolling back.

"I hate night shift," the guard announced loudly as he returned. "The crazies come out of the woodwork."

Winnie ignored the guard, focusing on bagging Joshua's purchases. "I just started here. It's just a temporary job during the holiday season. I could have worked as a Santa's helper at the CambridgeSide mall but that's kind of dangerous."

"Dangerous?"

"It's a mall!" Winnie said as if that explained everything. Seeing his confusion, she elaborated. "I think Marie Antoinette is in love with some guy. She kept using my credit card to buy stuff for a man. A heavenly smelling men's cologne by Yves Saint Laurent. A shaving kit with a leather bag and silver-tipped shaving brush. A cashmere scarf that was five hundred dollars! I returned everything I could find and cut up all my credit cards! I'm out a thousand dollars until everything gets cleared up. I would report the stupid things stolen but I'm afraid I'm the one that would get arrested. It really sucks. I haven't done any of my Christmas shopping yet and I think I've lost my phone. I can't find it anywhere."

"Can't you get Fred to find it?" Joshua whispered.

"He's not a dowser like Decker. He deals with spiritual things. Ghosts. Spirits."

"He found the winning jackpot ticket." Joshua pointed at the machine that sold the tickets.

"That was your fate. Anything tied up with you has giant neon signs in the spirit realm."

"If the ticket was my fate, why is your grandmother keeping it locked up?"

Winnie threw up her hands as she walked to a small freezer case behind the checkout counters. "I don't know. That's why she's the Wise Woman and I'm not."

All thoughts of the lottery ticket vanished when Winnie thumped a huge, misshaped object onto the belt. It was some lumpy brown thing sealed in plastic, seemingly frozen.

"What's that?" Joshua eyed it with fear.

"Your total is over a hundred and fifty dollars," Winnie said as if that answered the question.

"What is that?" Joshua pointed to make it clear that he was asking about the mystery item.

"You get a free ham with your purchase!" Winnie said.

He realized that the unidentified lumpy brown thing was the cured rind of a large whole ham. It was the biggest ham he'd ever seen; Winnie probably thought she was doing him a favor by giving him the largest that the store carried.

It begins.

Joshua whimpered. He glanced at the plastic shopping bags already holding the expensive family packs of meat. It all had to go into his freezer. Worse, he probably would end up going shopping at least once or twice before Christmas. It was going to be the entire Thanksgiving turkey fiasco all over again.

One good thing about being a werewolf: he didn't get cold.

Joshua could tell it was bitterly cold by the fact his nose hairs froze each time he breathed in. His warm breath out turned into billows of mist. He'd worn hat and gloves out of habit, but he didn't need them. It had started to snow again. It crunched under their feet as they walked. The roads were deserted. The houses were dark, their residents asleep. The night pressed in around them with only the streetlamps keeping the dark at bay. Snowflakes swirled in the light, making him feel like he was in a snow globe recently shaken hard by some giant hand.

Being a werewolf might protect him from the cold, but it didn't make him invincible. He hadn't been able to escape the Wickers' snakelike construct. He hadn't been able to break free of the cage the coven had trapped him inside. Everyone—Winnie, Decker, Seth, Jack, Elise, and himself—had nearly been killed. If they had died, all of Boston could have died too.

What did Enyo know that she hadn't told them?

"Who is she?" Joshua asked. "What is she?"

"Enyo?" Decker said in anger. "I have been told that she's one of the original sea hags."

Winnie had used the term.

"What's a sea hag?" Joshua said.

Decker fussed with the collar of his long, dark wool coat. He turned it up against the cold and pulled his long white scarf tighter. His breath didn't mist in the freezing air. Decker wasn't warm-blooded enough to create the effect. "There's a Greek myth about women born to the sea. Their hair is gray at birth like sea foam. They are referred to as the Graeae. They were considered more monsters than goddesses even though their father was a god of the ocean."

Joshua struggled to remember his Greek mythology. "Enyo's father was Neptune?"

"No," Decker said after moment's thought. He spread his gloved hands in apology. "It's been a long time since I studied the Greek legends. When I was young, they were considered the classics that any well-educated man should know. Before Zeus and Poseidon and all those famous gods, there were lesser-known 'primordial' ones. According to the Greeks, the first god was this unformed mass who fathered Gaia."

"I've heard of Gaia," Joshua said. "She's Earth. So out of shapeless chaos comes matter. It kind of sounds like the big bang theory."

Decker looked uncertain. He probably didn't know the scientific theory for the beginning of the universe.

"Never mind, go on," Joshua said.

"Gaia gave birth to Uranus, who is the god of the sky—or, more basically, anything that wasn't Earth. If you think of it, sky covers Earth like a man lying on top of a woman. The two of them then produced the Titans."

This sounded like what Enyo had told Joshua. Nothing creating a lone god who creates lesser gods, who created a pantheon of even lesser gods. "Zeus is a Titan?"

Decker thought for a moment. "I'm not sure. Somewhere in this inbred mess, a couple of evil fathers were killed by their youngest son. I've lost track of who killed whom. I do know it happened more than once. It's some weird pattern with the Greeks where sons murder their father—either knowingly or by mistake. Lather, rinse, repeat a couple of times until you get down to the generation that Zeus ruled from Mount Olympus. The generations prior to Zeus are considered 'primordial.' Poseidon is the Greek god of the seas that you were thinking of; Neptune was the Roman version of him. The Roman gods followed the same bloody and inbred path as the Greeks but there were different bells and whistles along the way.

"Enyo's father is said to be a primordial sea god by the name of Phorcys, which means he's a generation or two before Poseidon. He had a staggering number of monstrous children with his sister. The most famous story involving these offspring was Perseus slaying Medusa. Perseus was given the impossible task by his evil stepfather in an attempt to kill Perseus. The goddess Athena told Perseus to go talk to Phorcys's daughters, the Graeae, who shared one eye and one tooth between them. They alone could tell him where to find the weapons to kill Medusa."

"The one-eyed fortune teller?" Joshua said. "Enyo does have one eye—and maybe one tooth. You think Perseus really talked to Enyo and her sisters?"

"Perhaps. The story was ancient before I was even born. I'm not sure if Enyo is a fortune teller or merely that she knows a great many secrets. One has to wonder how prophetic the Graeae could have been if they didn't know that Perseus meant to kill their sister, Medusa. But then again, considering how the Greek gods killed family members by the score, perhaps the daughters didn't like Medusa."

"Wait! Do you really think the Greek myths are true?"

"The Greek gods were as real as the Wolf King or Elise or Fred or me are. They were creatures who drew power from another layer. Some could change shape. Some were immensely powerful. Some were monsters that would devour men. Those who were dangerous monsters have been hunted down and killed by the Grigori. A few somewhat harmless ones like Enyo remain."

Joshua stood a moment in the falling snow, mind reeling with the implications. "So...what about where the gods lived. Asgard? Valhalla? Olympia? Heaven? Hell? Are those places real?"

"Certainly, literature would have you believe that people used to pop in and out of Hell all the time. The Greeks even had a word that described going to the Underworld: catabasis. They described Hades as located at the periphery of the earth—an invisible other world, accessed by a cave or sailing to the edge of the ocean. Although I doubt that Hell is the tourist destination that Dante made it out to be. The world has greatly changed since those early days. I was born long after those times. As the Wolf King spread his influence, things became much more...secure. Breaches used to swallow whole countrysides. They're unknown by the common man now. I think the layers were closer in ancient times, allowing for frequent passage between them."

"So...is the Source of werewolf magic a god or a realm?"

"I'm not totally sure if myths and legends are completely accurate," Decker said. "Nor am I sure if we have the words to describe it."

Decker took out his smartphone and held it up. "If I suddenly found myself back in New York during the time of King Charles the Second, I'm not sure how I would describe my phone to someone. I could show him it but all he would understand is that it's a piece of polished glass. I could turn it on and take some pictures—maybe. I'm still struggling with that. I could show him the movies that I know that it can play. And if that person decided to tell someone else about my phone, he would probably call it a magical polished river rock or maybe a mirror of the gods. He certainly wouldn't describe my phone for what it truly is. Even if he somehow understood the technology—I don't—he would need to use words not yet invented. Computer. Telephone. Internet. Movie. Netflix."

"So, you don't know if the Source of the werewolves' magic is some kind of god," Joshua said, "or just kind of a multiversal forest."

"No. Not really. I hope that there's no vampire god that will ever reach out and try to use me like the God of the Grigori is wont to do to its people. I've seen the power of their God with my own eyes time and time again and know that He is real."

Joshua wasn't sure what he felt about...everything. In one conversation, he'd found out that his comic book heroes might be real, that all the silly Greek legends might have actually happened, and that his own god might be just one more tissue layer in the Kleenex box of life. Unsettling as it was, he wasn't sure what he could do about it all. Enyo did suggest that something big was about to happen. He'd been almost utterly useless in the fight with the Wickers. What the hell was he supposed to do up against literal gods?

"Do you think I should call Seth?" Joshua asked Decker. "Tell him about Enyo?"

"It's the middle of the night."

"I meant tomorrow—or do you think that he already knows Enyo's here? She would show up on his Peeping Tom superpowers. Right? His spider sense would be tingling or something."

Decker squinted at him, probably confused by "spider sense." He had a weird gap in his knowledge base; he had lived for years without any media input. Decker didn't know the recent memes.

"She's a magical creature," Joshua said. "She should be easy for Seth to spot."

"If she's actually in Boston," Decker said. "She could have teleported to anywhere in the world. It might be why she's here in the middle of the night—she's counting on Seth being asleep. Supermarkets are only open all night in big cities. All the other large cities in the world have a lot more wolves."

"She could be just getting food, like she said? Because she's hungry?"

"Perhaps," Decker said as if he only partially believed it.

They had reached the house. Fresh snow lay on the sidewalk. It crunched underfoot. There were no tracks leading up to the door. As they thumped up the front steps, onto the wide wooden porch, it occurred to Joshua that Decker was going to be totally helpless in a few hours and he would be at school.

"The wards on the house?" Joshua put down the bags on the front porch in order to unlock the door. Decker stood rubbing his arms, looking as if he might freeze solid from the cold. "Will they keep Enyo out?"

"Yes," Decker said with complete conviction. "Even if she knew where I lived—and it's very possible she does, since *knowing* seems to be her gift—she could not enter the house in any method."

One less thing to worry about. Joshua had so many other concerns that he knew he was losing track of them all.

"It turns out that my school is going on a field trip to the aquarium." Joshua stomped on the welcome mat and walked into the warm house. The furnace was running, rumbling softly, trying to adjust for the rush of bitterly cold air. "We're going next week. It even has the type of penguins that I dreamed about."

After Enyo, a penguin cursing in Spanish didn't seem particularly dangerous.

Decker drifted to the heat duct and stood on it, letting the hot air rush over him. "Next week? Well, we'll have to check it out before that—maybe with Thane Cabot and Elise."

Joshua nodded. Seth was coming up Friday night with Cabot to do the whole Christmas tree and condo-hunting thing. Seth would be able to use his super-alpha power to scope out the aquarium and see if there were any dangerous monsters lurking in the fish tanks.

9: ELISE

"We lost Francis."

Elise fumbled with the shower controls. Surely, she had misheard her cousin, Clarice. She turned off the steaming water, and then flicked off the fan on the overhead bathroom heater. In the silence, Elise stood naked and dripping wet, struggling to contain her fear and grief to ask for details.

"Francis is dead?" Elise asked.

"He is?" Clarice cried with surprise and dismay.

"I'm asking you!" Elise said.

Clarice worked as a dispatcher at the Central Office. She was responsible for assigning missions to the Virtues and Powers of the East Coast Grigori. She would be the first person to know if something had gone horribly wrong with anyone in their family.

"No! At least, I don't think so." Clarice didn't sound positive. "There aren't any unexplained craters in New England. I checked. We just...lost...him."

Elise took a deep breath as relief flooded through her. Francis was her baby cousin, the youngest child of her mother's youngest sister. He had been a sweet, gentle little boy. He liked climbing into her lap to be held when he was a toddler. Even then, though, you could sense his potential. He was there, blistering on your awareness, even when he was asleep on your shoulder. He wanted to train with Elise, Clarice, and his older sister, Theodosia, in Greece to be a Virtue. God had other plans.

Last time she'd seen him, he'd been sitting in the smoking ruins of a tiny Greek village that he'd just wiped off the face of the planet, covered with soot and blood, wailing with remorse. As a Power, there were very few things on the planet that could actually harm Francis. He could, however, take out whole square miles of the landscape by accident.

"He's worse than me with equipment," Clarice continued, accompanied by the furious click of a computer keyboard. "I'm not sure how he goes through so many phones. He kills them nearly as fast as I mail him new ones. I swung a special corporate rate to buy cell phones in bulk. Twenty bucks a phone. If it was me, Grandmother would be howling at the cost, but Francis is a Power..."

"Clarice! Focus! How did you lose him?" Elise hit the speaker button, put down her phone, and picked up a towel to dry off. If this conversation continued in this direction, she was leaving her apartment in a matter of minutes.

The world outside Elise's windows was still gray with wintry dawn. The holidays with the werewolves had reset her sleep schedule; she was no longer on vampire hours. The Wolf King, the prince, and all the Thanes had gone back to New York City in one big motorcade. Joshua had started school yesterday. She'd gotten up early despite her plan to sleep in.

"If I knew how Francis disappeared, he wouldn't be lost." Clarice huffed. "He'd be slightly misplaced—or something."

"Clarice!" Elise cried.

"Theodosia had to drive through Vermont. She decided to stop at the monastery where Francis lives. He wasn't there. She called me wanting to know where I'd deployed him to so she could check up on him. I haven't talked to him for days! He should be home!"

Theo worked out of Bangor, Maine. Her district overlapped with the Viscount of Burlington's territory of Maine, New Hampshire, and parts of Vermont. Francis had chosen the monastery to be close to his only sibling. The monastery was literally in the middle of nowhere, ten miles from the Canadian border.

"Maybe he went to the mall or to a movie." Elise wanted it to be something simple and nondramatic. Her family had already lost one person recently, her cousin Cade, killed by the Wickers.

"No! Francis wouldn't drive all the way to Boston to see a

movie. Theo stopped to check on him because she had a weird bad feeling like that time in Greece!"

"Francis is in Boston?" Elise echoed. "I thought you lost him!"

"I found his car," Clarice said. "I made sure that his vehicle came with OnStar, and it was activated before I had it delivered to him. After Greece, it seemed like a good idea. Francis never leaves the monastery unless I call him. Well...almost never. It's not like there's anywhere to go! There's a ski resort but the one time he tried skiing, it ended badly for the mountain. He buys everything on the internet and has it shipped to him. Some of it is seriously odd. He's into adult—"

"Where is his car?" Elise asked to stop the flood of information. She didn't need to know Francis' vices. They were probably minor compared to her dating a werewolf.

"The Alewife station's parking lot," Clarice said. "I hacked into their security camera system. I'm looking at his car right now. It's just sitting there like it's an ordinary car of an ordinary person that can't reduce all of Boston to a smoking ruin. I feel so useless!"

Alewife station in Cambridge was five miles from her condo. More importantly, it was the terminus for the Red Line subway. It gave Francis a direct line into the heart of Boston.

"He's not allowed that close to a city—is he?" Elise asked.

"Sort of!" Clarice wailed. "Dispatchers aren't allowed to send Powers into heavily populated urban areas without approval from their tribal elder. We haven't been able to deploy Powers into major American cities without notifying proper authorities since the San Francisco 1906 incident. That is always an interesting conversation to have with a newly appointed bureaucrat. But that ban only covers deploying a Power on an active mission, not them visiting those metropolitan areas. That's just frowned upon since it's a bad idea. Francis is fine with the informal restrictions—I think. He's never talked about wanting to visit Boston. Besides, Montreal is closer, has no standing orders about Powers, and sorry, it's way cooler. It's like Paris without the jetlag. The thing is, sometimes God steps in and is all hands-on, and then it's anything goes. Francis just ends up places, at the right place at the right time—like in Greece."

One could argue that it was the wrong place at the wrong time considering the destruction that followed.

Either reclusive Francis was blatantly ignoring rules in place for over a century or God sent Francis to Boston. It was terrifying that the second seemed more likely. God had sent Francis to the little Greek village that no longer existed.

Elise wrapped the towel around her head. She was dry enough. She needed to find Francis before something horrible happened. "Theo is still in Vermont?"

"I just texted her. She's heading to Alewife but it's two hundred and thirty miles."

It would take Theo at least three hours to get to Boston. "Okay. I'm on it."

"I know you're going to be mad about this," Clarice said quietly. Carefully. "But you can't tell Decker or the wolves."

Elise swore. "Why the hell not?"

"Well, first off, we don't want Francis accidently nuking the Prince of Boston out of existence. It would be hard on our political ties with our allies, not to mention the ensuing possible destruction that would follow if it turned out that Seth's brother or his cousin isn't strong enough to bear the weight of Boston."

Yes, there was that. Elise pulled on underwear.

"Plus, there's Theo to consider," Clarice said. "She'll be there by noon. Theo. Wolves. Not a good idea."

"Why not Decker?"

"Normally I would say the more the merrier. Decker's dowsing ability would be useful in finding Francis but it's morning. Decker is dead to the world until sunset. Literally. If you try to leave Decker a message, Joshua might intercept it. He might think it's his duty to help a friend find their lost family member. Most people would. It's going to be hard enough to keep the prince out of this. If Joshua gets involved, then Seth will act."

Elise winced as she realized that Clarice was right on all counts. It was one of the reasons that Clarice was the dispatcher: she could see patterns. "Okay. Mum's the word."

"Be careful," Clarice said. "Francis wouldn't do this on a whim. Something is very wrong. Either God sent him to Boston to nuke it to the ground or Francis has finally snapped. He's been a little broken since Greece. Be careful."

"I will." She always was. It was why she was still alive.

Francis owned a big luxury Cadillac Escalade SUV. It wasn't for vanity's sake; not all monsters kept to paved streets. She owned a Jeep Wrangler for the same reason. Francis's car needed to provide a safe, comfortable, and *isolated* retreat; Central couldn't put civilians at risk by having him check into a hotel unless it couldn't be helped.

The SUV had a bright yellow custom paint job, which was a surprise. Virtues drove vehicles that were "low profile" in nature. Black. White. Dark Blue. She supposed the yellow worked like a warning sign. The color said, "Danger, proceed with caution, avoid contact."

Winter had just started in earnest in Boston, but it had already taken a toll on the Cadillac. Its sides were caked with mud and slush. Someone had drawn a smiley face in the dirt. It grinned at her, full of impish delight. *Wash me* had been scribbled under the smile but road dirt had changed the lettering until it seemed to spell out *Watch me.*

Elise eyed the car from the warm safety of her black Jeep. It could be her own paranoia being kicked into overdrive, but the Cadillac felt like a trap.

The SUV sat on the open roof of the parking garage. A foot of snow covered the Cadillac's roof and windshield, serving as proof that the SUV had been there for some time. The cars surrounding it were clean; they were obviously driven by commuters who'd arrived early that morning to catch a train into the city.

Her phone played Clarice's ringtone. Elise took it out and tapped the "answer" icon.

"It's just sitting there," Clarice whispered. "All innocent like."

It wasn't just Elise's paranoia, then.

It was too quiet, she realized. There should be screaming and fire and blood everywhere. The world trembled when Powers went on a rampage.

If any other cousin was missing, she would believe something—a witch, a monster, a breach—had done something to them. She had been ignoring that possibility because Francis was a Power.

"Are you watching me through the security system?" Elise asked.

"Of course! I'm missing one cousin. I don't want it to be two. The Cadillac has an OnStar system. I can disable its alarms and pop its locks when you're ready."

"Pop them now," Elise said.

"Huh?"

"Just in case there's a bomb wired into the locks."

"Oh. Oh! *Oh!*" There was the sound of furious typing. "I hadn't even considered a third party could be involved in Francis disappearing. You just don't think 'kidnapping' when you're talking about a Power. How would you even manage it? It would be like trying to pull the sun out of the sky."

The SUV flashed its lights as Clarice unlocked it remotely.

"Huh," Clarice said. "Well, I guess there's no bomb connected to its locks. There still could be one tied to the ignition—don't try starting it."

"I'm going in." Elise switched to a Bluetooth headset to free up her hands.

It was freezing on the windy rooftop. Elise pulled her scarf up high to protect her face. The blanket of snow cloaked the interior of the SUV from causal view. She would need to clean off its windows to see inside.

There were footprints of someone getting out of the driver's side of the SUV. He or she compacted several inches of snow with what looked like size-twelve boots. The prints were still visible despite the hours of snow that had followed. It would be a mistake to assume it was Francis. Someone else could have driven the car here and abandoned it.

There were tracks on the passenger side, but they seemed too fresh. They most likely had been made by the driver of the car beside the SUV.

She brushed the wet clingy snow from the driver's side windows so she could peer into the Cadillac. It was a lived-in car. There was a paper coffee cup in the center console. A box of donuts sat in the passenger seat. Oddly, a St. Christopher's medal hung from the rearview mirror.

Elise frowned at the medal. To most people's dismay, the angelic weren't Christians. Their religion shared roots with Judaism. The Jewish religious leaders branched off as they decided that acknowledging the existence of angels was in conflict with the idea of one god. To the uneducated outsider, it would seem that the Virtues' rituals were based on the Christian Bible, but they came from the part of the Talmud that formed the Old Testament. Her people saw Christianity as something that didn't include them as they were bound to God by an ancient pact made days prior to the Great Flood. They had taken their name from what the Greeks had called them. "Grigori" was the Greek word for "Watcher," as their angelic forefathers had been commanded to keep watch over humans and protect them from monsters. Salvation for them came from keeping their part of the bargain: to use their abilities to hunt monsters.

Francis might take refuge with the Catholic brothers, but he'd never actually pray to a saint. Why would he have a St. Christopher medal? Was this really his car? The backseat was a nest of blankets, pillows, coloring books, and stuffed animals. It looked more like a family car than something that belonged to a monster hunter.

"What's in the car?" Clarice said. "I can't see inside! You look really freaked out. Is someone frozen in there or something?"

"Clarice, did the monks provide Francis with a driver?"

"Oh God, I thought you knew. Galahad Percival Roustabout has been Francis's driver since he came back from Greece. I didn't think Grandma would allow it—Roustabout being fresh out of jail for manslaughter—but she seemed to think it was fated."

"Manslaughter? What the hell?"

"It's a long, weird story typical of our family." Clarice loudly typed at her keyboard, multitasking as only someone with her talents could. "There were werewolves and hordes of monsters and people torn to pieces—one of them being Roustabout—but Francis raised him from the dead. Anyhoo, Roustabout was dead a good hour or so before Francis revived him, so he had a nice long tour of the afterlife. Francis claimed that he was a changed man. And he seems to be right. Roustabout is in the pipeline to become a Franciscan friar. Apparently, there's a lot more to it than putting on the robes and shaving your head. Wait! Is Roustabout dead in the car?"

"No one is dead in the car." Elise scanned the parking lot. "It's empty. Are you sure that this Roustabout didn't just steal the car and take off?"

"I told you! I don't know anything!" Clarice cried. "I doubt it. Roustabout seems devoted to Francis. Borderline worship. Maybe not borderline—maybe whole hog. Francis is a Power. It would be like meeting Jesus in the flesh."

"What does this Roustabout look like?"

"I have a full dossier on him. I'll send it to you. Here's a picture of them together."

Elise's phone dinged. She took it out of her pocket to look at its screen.

Francis owned a selfie stick. That was surprising. Their family normally avoided cameras. Their angelic blood gave them a supernatural beauty. It went beyond having symmetrical features, stunning eye color, great hair, and good skin. It gifted them with a magical glamour: an aura of attraction that they couldn't turn off. It was a burden, not a blessing, as people didn't see "them" but an idealized version of them. Most strangers reacted strongly to their appearance. People stared at them. Touched them. Tried to have sex with them.

The experience made most of her family abnormally self-conscious; they hated getting their pictures taken. Francis, though, had been in seclusion most of his life. He and Theo had been homeschooled. After he became a Power, it was too dangerous for him to go out in public. Theirs was a jealous and protective God; it punished anyone who was too forward with its Powers. Perhaps Francis hadn't been subjected to the unwanted attention enough to be self-conscious.

Like most of their family, Francis had been a beautiful child. As a young man, he was stunning. He'd let his dark hair grow into a glossy mane of soft curls that made his eyes seem more unreal with their vivid blue color. He smiled widely at the camera. He was still just a teenager in the picture, slender in build. Francis had always been short for their family; his driver made him seem even shorter.

Roustabout was a big brute of a man. He wore a black tank top that showed off a muscle-builder body with every inch of his arms covered with tribal sleeve tattoos. Someone had tried to take out his right eye with a knife, leaving a scar from his heavy eyebrow down to his jutting jawbone. He had multiple piercings—his ears, his eyebrow, and his nose. In the picture, he had on a black knitted cap that covered any indication what his hair color was. Based on his thick eyebrows, she guessed that he had dark hair.

"You've got to be kidding," Elise said. "That's Francis's driver? Grandmother knew about this? She allowed it?"

"Francis doesn't like to drive," Clarice said. "He can do it but he's not very good at it. He's not very good at any of the necessary life skills for living alone."

"He's twenty. No one is good at that stuff at twenty. You only get better with practice."

"Normally I'd agree with you, but he's a Power and he has PTSD. I still don't know how his washing machine could 'startle him,' but he kept reducing it and his laundry room to rubble. I thought I was hard on equipment, but I don't take out the surrounding buildings when I break things. That's why he's at the monastery—it's a nice peaceful place where someone else does the cooking and laundry. Besides, Florida was pissed at him after what happened in Miami. I'm with Francis on that, though: alligators shouldn't be in public parks."

Elise hadn't heard about the alligator or the public park. "I thought he wanted to be closer to Theo."

"That's why he's in New England and not on the West Coast. The brothers at the monastery haven't complained yet but I get the impression he's singed a few of them by mistake. Francis says they're all afraid of him. None of them wanted to be trapped in a car with him, so when Francis asked for Roustabout to move with him, Grandmother allowed it. The man seems devoted to Francis. No matter what is going on, you'll need to be careful of Roustabout. He's a champion heavyweight mixed martial artist. He knows kickboxing, Brazilian Jiu-Jitsu, and Muay Thai. What's more, he'll probably assume that you're as dangerous as Francis. He won't underestimate you."

As if a mentally unstable Power wasn't enough, he came with a brute of a bodyguard and/or kidnapper. Roustabout might be devoted to Francis, but Boston just had an infestation of Wickers that could corrupt the will of any human. The big question was, did Francis need to be saved or stopped or assisted?

Elise searched the interior of the SUV for clues.

The backseat had all the makings of a comfortable retreat. For stuffed animals, Francis had nothing as mundane as a teddy bear. His collection contained a gray elephant, a blueberry-ripple unicorn, a rainbow alpaca, a three-toed sloth, and a golden chicken. Two down pillows and an oddly heavy blanket completed Francis's nest.

Francis liked to color to pass the time. Francis used top quality Prisma pencils in a hundred and thirty-two carefully sorted colors, stored in the original tins. None of them seemed to be missing. His current coloring book was titled *Color Me Calm: 100 Coloring Templates for Meditation and Relaxation (A Zen Coloring*

Book). It contained mandalas, geometric patterns, water scenes, flora, fauna, and natural patterns. Roughly a third had been carefully colored in. It would be quite beautiful except someone had written things like "I'm so fucking lonely" in the white spaces.

There was a wicker picnic basket sitting on the floor on the passenger side. It was packed with thick ham sandwiches on artisan bread, a roasted sweet potato wrapped in tin foil, and two organic apples. If it wasn't sitting frozen in the back of a car, it would seem to indicate that nothing was amiss.

She moved back to the front seat to check the glove compartment. Inside she found a brown paper bag containing a box of yellow pills in blister packs. The brand name was Ativan, which she wasn't familiar with.

Clarice called her. "What did you find? You've been digging around for ten minutes now."

"What is Ativan?" Elise took a picture of the pills and sent it to Clarice. "Is it some kind of medicine for Roustabout or—is Francis sick?"

She'd always been told that Powers didn't get sick, at least, not physically.

"I-I-I'm not sure." Clarice said. "I talked to him, and he was saying things that—at the time—I thought was a joke. They might have been jokes. It's just that afterward, I felt...unsettled. He might not be joking."

"Like what?"

"Well, he talked about going to see a shrink for his PTSD, which isn't that weird. But then he said that the discussion would lead to him confessing to be God in flesh. His entire problem stems from the fact he is God's power given human form. Francis believed that explaining why he has PTSD would lead to his shrink trying to commit him to some kind of mental hospital—which is possible—depending on Vermont's involuntary commitment laws. I really should have looked it up after the second time he talked about it. I thought he was joking. It was funny the way he said it. He made it sound like people tying steaks to their body and going out into the woods to look for bears. You know how sweet and gentle he is. A regular psychologist would have no idea how dangerous he really is. Francis had this entire elaborate scenario mapped out that ended with him accidently killing the psychologist, the hospital staff and any police officers rallied for the committal. Francis said he'd feel so guilty that he'd raise them all from the dead. It would make the psychologist finally believe his claims, but it would be hard on their patient/doctor relationship."

That was a fairly accurate prediction given Francis's PTSD and how most psychologists didn't believe in the supernatural. Elise wasn't sure how the general populace became so ignorant of the truth. Sometime between the witch trials of Salem and the current day, the general populace lost its fear of things that went bump in the night. The chance of being killed by a monster was much higher than being attacked by a shark, one in five thousand to be torn to shreds on land as compared to one in three million bitten in the ocean. It was possible to survive a shark attack. A single nip from a monster—no matter how small a wound—would transform a human.

It was irrational that people were afraid of sharks but didn't believe in monsters. It didn't even make sense that the general population didn't know that the danger was real.

"Ativan is a prescription medicine used to treat anxiety," Clarice said. "I know that Roustabout isn't seeing a doctor; I'm keeping tabs on him. I don't think Francis is actually going to a psychologist. I do have him on the health plan just in case he did manage to accidently hurt himself and for some strange reason God didn't instantly heal him."

"If it's a prescription drug," Elise said, "one of them had to see a doctor."

"Or Roustabout got them—somehow—illegally." Clarice's comment was underscored by her typing on her keyboard. "Huh. That blister pack is what emergency rooms use, not what is handed out to customers by drug stores. I know that neither one of them has been to the ER. Roustabout did spend ten years in prison for manslaughter before becoming Francis's driver. It's possible he bought the pills off the black market or stole them or...or...I don't know...got them off of Craigslist. You can get weird shit off the internet."

Elise eyed the unmarked brown bag she'd found the pills in. Virtues weren't immune to diseases, just highly resistant. The few times she was prescribed antibiotics, the drugstore used white bags with the pharmacy name printed on them. A printout of her prescription and a pamphlet with warnings about the drugs' side effects had been stapled to the outside. This package had none of the standard trappings. "You think Francis would actually self-medicate?"

"Oh, I hope not. The possible side effects of Ativan are scary when you consider Francis is a Power."

"What side effects?"

"Confusion. Hyperactivity. Hostility. Hallucinations. Amnesia."

A Power with amnesia and hostility issues: not a good thing.

Elise felt guilty that she hadn't made the drive up to check on Francis personally. The six-hour round trip had seemed too much effort.

"None of the pills seem missing." Elise offered that up as hope.

The rear storage was totally devoid of normal hunting weapons and paraphernalia. No gun safe, caltrops, traps, or bags of salt. Powers didn't need such things—they were God's ultimate weapon. Neatly packed into the space was a small tent, two sleeping bags, a duffel bag of clean clothes, a plastic baggie of new toothbrushes still in their packaging, a mega pack of wet wipes, a box of shop towels, and a canvas tote of "emergency food." Francis had stocked chocolate candy bars, a box of graham crackers and marshmallows to make smores, and packets of hot cocoa. The rations made it look like he was going camping with Girl Scouts.

While the rest of the car looked like a lived-in mess, the back appeared to have been packed long ago for any unexpected overnight trip into the wilderness.

She'd learned all that she could from the car. She transferred the duffel bag of clothes to her Jeep just in case she found Francis covered in ash or drenched in blood. The question remained, where were Francis and his driver now?

"What have you found out from the security cameras?" she asked Clarice.

"I'm still working on that," Clarice said. "I hacked into the live feed easily enough, but the history was a struggle. I'm in, though, and stepping back through the video to see when the SUV parked in that spot."

Why was the SUV at Alewife station?

People used the subway system because they didn't have personal drivers. Roustabout could have taken Francis to any place that he wanted to go and then waited with the SUV.

Alewife was the terminus of the Boston subway; it sat facing Route 2 with its back to a bird-watching park. It was isolated from anything useful except hot coffee from the Dunkin' Donuts on the lower level. Not far away—but not convenient enough to walk in this subzero weather—was everything from supermarkets to hotels and even some Catholic churches. There was lots of free parking at the places that offered hot food, warm beds, or holy refuge.

Francis wouldn't use the subway system for the same reason that most people wouldn't juggle live grenades in a crowd: it was just too dangerous to innocent bystanders. It didn't make sense for Roustabout to park at Alewife if he intended to pick Francis up someplace else. Did someone steal the car and leave it at the station? There had been no sign of tampering with the ignition.

The garage was too public and too secure for the SUV to remain unnoticed forever. Sooner or later, Clarice would have found it even without tracking devices. Or was that the point? Was the Grigori meant to find it?

Elise found no real clues in the SUV. If the vehicle was parked at the garage to lead her to the train station, then she needed to search the building with caution.

She unsheathed her twin daggers. They flashed in the pale morning sun. She knelt in the snow and rested the tips lightly against the concrete of the parking garage's top deck. Intent strengthened her connection to God, the Almighty. When she was little, she had felt Him, patiently waiting for her to take up daggers and learn the rituals that would make her His tool.

Francis wasn't given a choice. God had put him in harm's path, forcing him to forgo learning the rituals and blades that put limits on the power waiting to flood into them. There were cautionary stories of angelic children who mistakenly believe they were intended to be Powers. Who opened themselves up to God's full glory only to be reduced to ash by what they channeled.

She felt the warmth of His love gather about her. Lightning scented the air with the potential. She whispered the holy words that would shield her from taking harm from God's power even as the ritual used His strength to conceal her.

"Blessed be the Lord, my rock, who trains my hands for war, and my fingers for battle; He is my steadfast love and my fortress, my stronghold, and my deliverer; my shield and He in whom I take refuge. Amen."

Angelic wings—ghostlike in appearance—threw even fainter shadows on the snow. The ritual would cloak her from cameras and the naked eye of normal men. Francis would be able to see her, as would any werewolf, vampire, or other supernatural being. It would only offer limited protection. She would still need to search carefully.

Alewife station was a mix of concrete, steel, and glass dedicated to the function of protecting commuters from the elements while shuffling thousands of people on and off trains. The ticketing machines and fare gates were on the cavernous mezzanine with tall windows to let in sunlight. The floor was an odd mosaic of mismatched beige tiles. Everywhere were accents of red to remind commuters that they were boarding the Red Line. It was lacking anything else. No art. No seats. No clutter. No place to hide.

Noise echoed up from the platforms below. The loud rumble of trains. The occasional sharp squeal of wheels on rails. The announcements over the PA system. The dissonant nature was grating on her nerves. Sensing her without consciously noticing her presence, a flood of people wove around her, rushing off to work in Boston. It reminded her how much she hated crowds.

She thought of the stuffed animals and soft blankets that had been in the back of the SUV. Francis would have found this place nerve-racking.

The gates had tall panels of glass blocking access to the paid area; she needed a ticket to move through them. It seemed unlikely anyone would pay to set up a trap beyond the gates.

"Don't assume anything," she reminded herself as she fed money into the machine. It was the first rule of hunting. Assumptions were a trap; they limited your vision from all possibilities to just those that supported a preconceived notion.

She checked the restrooms that were accessible only to commuters who paid for a ticket. They were surprisingly clean, probably because of how early in the day it was. If there had been any clues to Francis's disappearance, the janitors had wiped them away. Even the trash receptacles were empty.

The platforms were slightly more cluttered than the mezzanine level. There were advertising posters, soda vending machines, benches, and system maps. Tucked into corners, barely noticeable by the general public, were utility closets and storage rooms, all marked AUTHORIZED PERSONAL ONLY. One by one, she broke into them.

Machines. Cleaning supplies. No clues.

She was locking the last utility closet when Clarice called.

"I hate not being able to see you," Clarice said. "I can see slight blurring on the cameras where you're eclipsing objects, so I know that you're fine, but it still freaks me out."

"I'm done sticking my nose into places where I'm not supposed to go." A gleam of white and the flutter of yellow down near the tracks caught Elise's eye. "I think I see something down by the rails. Are there any incoming trains?"

"What? Wait. Let me check. Where did I put that tab?"

As Clarice searched out a train schedule and security cameras of the stations down the track, Elise took out her Bluetooth headset and put it on her left ear.

"Okay," Clarice said after a minute of typing. "I've got eyes on all inbound and outbound trains. You're clear for another ten minutes."

Elise hopped down from the platform into the dark well that contained the steel rails. The gleaming white were feathers from a monster-size bird, six all total, drifting in the air currents trapped within the steep sides of the railbed. Each one was the size of her fist. She stacked them so she could hold all six in one hand. There was something very otherworldly about them. They gleamed, filling her cupped hands with pale white light. Tiny flecks of rusty red spotted the feathers, as if they'd been sprayed with cast-off blood.

The yellow was a scrap of plastic with CRIME SCENE printed on it. It was a fragment of police tape used to mark off crime scenes.

In the Boston Metro area, only forensic teams used this type of tape. Patrol officers were given rolls printed POLICE LINE—DO NOT CROSS. The reasoning was that the printing was more multipurpose, allowing officers to do things like crowd control and marking off dangerous sidewalks and structures, without the ominous implication that the area was part of an active case.

If the police had marked this as a crime scene, something as unusual as the feathers would have been collected—unless a normal human couldn't see them.

She scrambled up onto the safety of the platform.

"A train is leaving Davis," Clarice said. Davis was the next station on the Red Line. "You've got six minutes tops."

"I'm off the tracks." She took out her phone. "Here, I'm going to Facetime you so you can see. Maybe."

"Maybe?"

"Do you see anything?" Elise pointed the camera at her hand once the connection was made.

"I see the floor. I wonder why they decided to go with different shades of beige. I'm not sure if I like it or not."

Elise sighed and canceled her cloaking ritual. "Now what?"

"Still seeing the floor. Should I be seeing something?"

Elise shifted her phone so it pointed at her feet. "What now?"

"I take it I'm looking at your boots. Very nice. Are those Ugg Adirondacks?"

"So you can't see that I'm holding something?" Elise shifted the camera back to the feathers.

"I can't even see your hand."

The feathers were like her wings. They couldn't be seen by most humans or through a camera lens. It meant no one would have seen the monstrous bird that shed the feathers. Whose blood speckled the downy white?

"Do you have access to the recordings from the security cameras?" Elise said.

"I'm stepping through it now while jumping through hoops with . . . Ah-ha! Yes, that's what I wanted. Why did they make that so hard? What's the difference between knowing where your car has been from where is it now? It's your car! If I'd known they were going to make it this hard, I wouldn't have just bought a black-market tracker."

"Clarice!" Elise snapped.

"The car got here last night, around ten," Clarice said. "And cameras say . . ." Some clicking of keys as she backed the security feed up to find the car parking. "Roustabout was driving it. Francis doesn't seem to be with him. Oh, that's not good. Roustabout is running and checking over his shoulder, like he expects to be chased by something. Shit, something wonky is happening with the security cameras. He keeps blinking out."

"Like maybe a giant monster bird is eclipsing him?"

"Perhaps," Clarice said. "What the hell? He was at the end

of the platform all by himself—the camera blinked—and then he's gone."

Someone had sprayed blood all over the feathers.

"Can you check 911 calls for last night?" Elise asked. "Find out why a forensic team was down on the tracks recently?"

A train rumbled into the station, filling up the area that Elise had just vacated. It obscured the crime scene as Clarice searched. Passengers trickled off the newly arrived subway cars. Elise was glad that many had their heads down, studying their phones. Every male who glanced at her came to a full stop. She glared at them, wanting to be left alone. The joy of the Grigori glamour. It was more than just impossible beauty. It was the illusion of sexual perfection that most people couldn't resist.

A hard glare and their own low self-esteem sometimes kept men from harassing her. It was the men who were cocksure of themselves that she needed to hit.

One by one, the new arrivals decided that either they weren't worthy of her or that whatever business they were attending to was more pressing.

Elise sighed out relief when she was once again alone on the platform.

"Oh! Oh! Oh!" Clarice cried over the connection. "One of the subway drivers called in, saying someone fell onto the tracks as he was pulling into the station. He couldn't get the train stopped in time. The John Doe was dead on the scene. An eyewitness said that he saw the man fighting with someone on the platform but couldn't give a description of the attacker. The witness said that the John Doe was pushed."

"Fighting with someone?" Elise repeated. Roustabout was a professional fighter. If his attacker was a normal human that a witness could actually see, maybe it hadn't been Roustabout who ended up on the tracks. "Can you see anyone on the footage?"

"Not from the camera's vantage point. I'm not seeing any possible witnesses until the train gets stopped."

So, the witness was either lying or had a different vantage point than the camera or had enough spiritual power that they could see through whatever glamour was being cast on the area.

"Do you have any description on this John Doe?" Else asked.

Clarice snorted. "Male. White. Adult. It sounds like the body was in fairly bad shape after the train hit it. It's at the county morgue."

Elise closed her hand on the bright feathers. Where was Francis? Why wasn't he in the car? Why would a monster bird be after Roustabout? Was it because it had already killed Francis? She doubted it. Monsters could rarely harm Powers, but it wasn't impossible. If it had, though, she wasn't going to be able to kill the bird by herself.

"Do you have an ETA on Theo?" Elise asked.

"She's still over an hour out now," Clarice said.

Theo had to be breaking the speed limit by thirty or forty miles per hour to be so close.

"I'm going to have to sweet-talk some of my contacts to find out what the police know about the dead man. Tell Theo to meet me at the offices of the chief medical examiner over on Albany Street."

10: JOSHUA

The Goths were gathered by the lone wolf statue at the school's front gate, bundled up against the cold. Joshua had been so concerned about being drafted as the standing army of Unpopular that he hadn't really *looked* at the Goths yesterday. They were all reasonably sized—neither too short nor too tall nor too heavy. They even had abnormally clear skin. Did supernatural powers prevent acne? At lunch the day before they had been wearing their school uniforms and blending in. The uniform policy didn't include the outerwear needed to deal with the brutal Boston winter. In their stylish coats, hats, scarfs, and boots, the Goths really stood out. They looked like models dressed in a line of high-fashion winter clothes. Joshua instantly felt underdressed even though Seth and Jack had bought him a stupidly expensive black trench coat. He felt like he was cosplaying in it. It did not help that he didn't actually need to be wearing it to stay warm.

Ottilie wore a black duffle coat with toggle closures, a luxurious scarf of autumn colors, and leather gloves. She looked suave and sophisticated despite being only fourteen. As Joshua walked up, she gave him a graceful nod and elegantly pulled her hood up. "We should get going before any teachers spot us."

Maisy caught sight of Joshua, grinned and waved. She wore thick knit gloves, fake rabbit fur earmuffs, and a big scarf wrapped around her shoulders until her head was nearly lost in the folds of pale honey-colored wool.

"What's up?" Joshua asked, wondering why the Goths were standing around outside instead of heading into the school. It was hovering around ten degrees out, dipping down into the negatives with the windchill. He wasn't cold but his breath came out in big misty puffs. He knew that if he weren't a werewolf, he would be in a rush to get out of the bitter cold.

Ji Su looked up, surprised and then concerned at the sight of him. She bit her black-lipstick lips. She wore big clunky black boots, black leggings, and a black hooded cape that looked like something out a vampire movie. Her little snake spirit guide, Nam-gi, was wrapped around her neck like a choker, its eyes locked on Joshua. "We need to do an intervention."

"A what?" Joshua asked.

"An intervention," Tal repeated. He had on a very cool steampunk leather trench coat and a slouchy black knit cap that Joshua could never pull off. "It's a medium thing. When someone gets possessed by a ghost without any fail-safe in place, then you need to force the ghost off its mount. We've done it before with Vijay."

The Goths all stared at Joshua with nervous expectation. *We don't want your wolf to come along* hung unsaid in the air around them.

"Oh. Okay." Joshua drifted toward the gate even as they started down the sidewalk. He felt weirdly relieved and yet disappointed. With the exception of Ajax, who had been dragooned into tutoring him, he hadn't talked to anyone else at the school. He'd be back to square one of not knowing anyone. "You found Vijay, then?"

"Sort of," Allie called back. She wore a black parka with a fur-lined hood and lots of pockets. It was very function-over-fashion but still managed to look stylish. "We think he's at the aquarium."

"Wait! Where?" Joshua started to follow them.

"The aquarium." Ji Su started to walk a little faster as if trying to discourage him from following. His sister Bethy used to do it to him all the time when he was little; it stopped working around second grade. "We're going there next week for the school field trip, remember?"

"I think there might be something weird at the aquarium," Joshua said.

"Yeah," Allie said. "A seventeen-year-old boy possessed by a ghost."

"Hopefully a ghost," Ji Su muttered darkly.

"No!" Joshua said. "A penguin!"

The Goths stopped to look at him.

"He's possessed by a penguin?" Allie broke the silence.

"No—at least I don't think so. It's just there's a penguin there..."

"Doh!" Tal said. "It is an aquarium. There are lots of penguins."

"This isn't really a penguin—it just looks like one." Joshua realized how crazy he was sounding. "At least, I don't think it's a penguin. It's definitely not a normal penguin." *No, not much better.* "It might be a were-penguin—if there are such things as were-penguins. This penguin talks. It wants—he wants to hire me."

Oh God, this sounded insane.

"Hire you to do what?" Ji Su said.

"I—I don't know," Joshua said.

"A penguin?" Allie asked.

"A rockhopper penguin from South America with a foul mouth and a short temper," Joshua said. "It speaks Spanish with an Argentinian accent."

"That's weirdly specific," Tal said after a long minute of silence.

"Breach-borne monsters don't talk," Ottilie stated and started to walk again.

Allie remained in place, lifting up one finger to argue a point. "No, they don't—which means it's not a breach-borne monster. So—what kind of monster is it?"

"It doesn't matter what it is." Ji Su started after Ottilie. "If Vijay is possessed, then he's not able to defend himself. We need to find him, especially if he's at the aquarium and there's some kind of weird monster there too."

The others started to walk again.

"I should come with you, though." Joshua trailed after the Goths. "Just in case...you know...if you need muscle."

"That's why I'm along," Ottilie called from the front.

"She's not a Virtue but she's been trained to fight since she was a toddler," Ji Su said. "She's very good at it."

Joshua wanted to say "She's just a freshman" but he worried that Ottilie might knife him if he did. He knew from experience, though, that werewolves were nearly unkillable, but Grigori weren't. Elise was still recovering from lesser wounds taken during the fight with the Wickers.

Maisy touched his arm and shook her head. She let Joshua know in her quiet way that Ottilie's family thought Ottilie was being willfully childish for not going through the motions of attempting to become a Virtue. Ottilie saw herself as a realist, funneling her energy toward something that was guaranteed to succeed instead of chasing certain failure. Her family's criticism, though, had made Ottilie insecure. Since Ottilie had no talent other than fighting, she was clinging to the role of protector. Could Joshua just let Ottilie lead while bringing up the rear?

Joshua nodded his understanding. It wasn't like he wanted to be the standing army of Unpopular. It would be better if the Goths had someone else—someone more stable than him—as their protector. He was just worried that Ottilie wouldn't be enough to protect the Goths from whatever was at the aquarium.

Joshua had researched the aquarium after his dream about the penguin, but he hadn't figured out where it was. He only knew that it was somewhere on a shoreline—but that seemed to describe most of Boston. The Goths seemed to know exactly how to reach the aquarium. They led the way to Porter station, which was little more than a glass wedge aboveground and steep escalators leading down into the underground.

A loudspeaker announced, "This train is full, please wait for the next train," as they rode down the escalators. The train in question pulled out in a loud rumble and shriek of metal wheels on rails.

The wolf didn't like the grungy, dim, loud tunnel far below the street level. It got worse as the next train pulled in as they reached the bottom of the escalator. The cars were all crowded with morning commuters.

"Are you sure it's okay for you to come with us?" Ji Su shouted over the braking train as it rumbled to a stop. What she really meant was "Can you keep control of your wolf through this?"

Joshua wasn't sure. The train was already crowded; if they picked up more people in later stops, they could be packed like sardines before the end of the trip. The thought would have made old, normal human Joshua uncomfortable. The wolf curled back his lips in a silent snarl at the thought.

Oh, come on, work with me! he silently pleaded with his other half. *If we don't stay calm, we won't be able to go with them. We won't be able to protect the Goths.*

The wolf stopped snarling.

The train came to a complete halt and the doors slid open.

As they boarded the train, a tall college guy glanced at Ottilie. His eyes widened—then narrowed. The man pushed his way through the other passengers, stalking toward the girl like a hungry lion.

The wolf snarled—this time out loud.

There was a sudden exodus of everyone except the Goths. The Goths edged away from Joshua until they were on the opposite end of the subway car but didn't look at him.

Ji Su looked like she wanted to ask Joshua again if he was sure about coming with them—but was too scared to.

"Sorry," Joshua said.

The door slid shut and the train started up.

Joshua took out his phone and texted Seth with "What kind of penguin talks?" He wished he had talked more to Decker about the improbable penguin before he went to bed. He hadn't thought that the dream was all that important the day before; he'd had several weird dreams. Running around the school naked. Having a test in a class that he forgot to attend. The two talking statues at the school's front gate. Even the news that they were having a field trip hadn't made the aquarium dream seem that alarming; the penguin had been rude but not violent. It was only the fact that Vijay had been taken by people or spirits unknown that made it worrisome.

"A nun?" Seth texted back.

Joshua squinted at the phone. A nun? Did some nuns turn into penguins? Joshua wasn't a Catholic, but it didn't seem right. It would explain nuns' black-and-white uniforms. He considered what he remembered about the dream. Was there anything religious about the penguin? No, and the bird spoke with a man's voice, so not a nun.

"I think it was male," Joshua texted. "It sounded male. How do you tell the sex of penguins?"

His phone pinged with a text from Winnie. He switched over to the new text box. Her text read, "Mon cher chevalier noir, monsieur le loup, où êtes-vous? J'ai besoin de vous."

Was that French? He'd taken Spanish as his foreign language, so he wasn't sure. He texted back a confused emoji.

"It might be a swan maiden," Allie said loudly. She had taken a seat on the far end of the car. She had her phone out and apparently had done research on the odd creature at the aquarium.

"What's a swan maiden?" Joshua said.

"It's a type of shapeshifter that can transform from swan to human form." Allie read the definition aloud. "It's said that they use a magical garment, normally the actual skin of a swan or a piece of clothing with swan feathers sewed onto it. In most stories, a man sees the creature in naked human female form and steals her magical garments, which renders her helpless. He then forces her to become his wife."

"Sounds more like a rape fetish than a real monster," Ji Su said.

Ottilie gave a negative-sounding grunt. "The part about stealing the skin and forcing them into marriage is the same as the selkie legends. I know selkies are real. They're considered non-monsters by the Grigori. They transform into seals using a magical artifact. They do lose the ability to become a seal if you manage to take their 'skin' while they're in human form. But that's all I know about them—my people have rarely interacted with them. They're fairly peaceful people that rarely live inland, away from the shore."

Joshua felt Seth using his "Peeping Tom" power to check in on him. Seth seemed to do that a lot. Several times a day he could feel his brother watching over him. He was never sure how he felt about that. It was nice to know someone had his back but at the same time, a fellow liked his privacy. Joshua switched to Seth's text box and explained quickly what was going on.

"Well, it seems as if almost every culture has stories about creatures like swan maidens." Allie scrolled down through the Wiki article. "The European folk stories seem to center solely around swans but in some Asian cultures they are cranes and geese and even bats."

His phone pinged again from Winnie. "Monsieur, bonjour, êtes-vous là?"

"So, a male penguin swan maiden..." Tal trailed off as he realized how many steps away from the original folklore their current situation landed them. "It seems like a reach."

"We know that benign shapeshifters other than wolves exist," Ottilie said. "That's the important point. If it is a swan maiden, it is in possession of its skin, else it would be human. If it proves to be hostile, we could try taking its magical artifact. It would allow us to control the creature. In the legends, selkies can never free themselves by killing their husbands or just searching the house to find their hidden skins while their husbands are off working. Usually, it takes one of her kids to find and return the skin to their mother. Basically, the creature is unable to go against the wishes of the man imprisoning it."

"That's messed up," Ji Su said.

Joshua tried to bounce the question off of Seth, but his brother seemed angry about something. The answer came back in all capital letters as if Seth shouted the answer. "Seth says there are no were-penguins."

"Technically, he's correct," Allie said. "Werewolves are created by a wound that connects the creature to the Source of the werewolves' power. It's like the bite punches through the layers of reality to the magic that then pours into the creature and transforms it wholly. They might look human but they're not; they're pure magic. In all the stories of swan maidens, the creatures require a magical device to transform. It means that magic is separate from the creature. It's kind of the difference between a tapeworm and...um...a blood transfusion."

"Allie!" Ji Su gasped, looking to see if the comparison upset Joshua.

"What?" Allie said. "I'm just saying that the one is a separate thing that can be taken away. With the other, it becomes part of you, it's impossible to divide from the receiver once the initial process happens."

Ottilie nodded in agreement. "Werewolves are magic taking human or wolf form. Other shapeshifters are more like witches— they're basically humans that use borrowed magic to change their appearance. It means that they have much less power than werewolves."

His phone dinged with another text in French from Winnie. It dinged again with Seth wanting to know who he was texting with other than him. His wolf growled in irritation.

"This is our stop," Ji Su announced as the train slowed.

11: SETH

"What kind of penguin talks?"

Seth peered at his phone. Texts from his brother were always odd. They were often total random insanity in a minimum number of words. What kind of penguin talks? The question made no sense. Maybe it was like that old riddle about newspapers: *What's black and white and red all over?* In that riddle, the word "red" was actually "read."

What looked like a penguin and talked?

An alternate answer to the newspaper riddle was "a wounded nun." Was this a spin on that solution?

"A nun," Seth typed back. He added a "?" to indicate that he wasn't sure. He didn't recognize the joke. If it was a joke.

"I think it was male," Joshua wrote in reply. "It sounded male. How do you tell the sex of penguins?"

Oh, God, that was a serious question!

Seth reached out to find his brother, cursing inwardly as they were two hundred miles apart. It was nine in the morning—Decker would be unconscious in his basement. If Joshua was in danger from a random magical creature, it would take hours for anyone from Wolf Castle to reach him.

Joshua was on a subway train moving through Boston. It seemed like the Red Line, heading inbound. Despite the morning rush hour, the car only had a handful of other people in with him. One seemed like a Grigori, although registering fainter than Elise normally did. The other people seemed to be human. No, strike that, a tiny spirit guide was wrapped around the ankle of one of the other passengers. That person was some type of medium. Joshua hunched over his smart phone, tapping in text messages. Seth's phone didn't indicate that the message was to him. Who else was Joshua texting? His brother looked up as if startled.

"I'm on the subway with some of the kids from school," Joshua texted, explaining who was with him. "The Goths. We're going to the aquarium to rescue Vijay. He's a Goth. He's missing."

How did Joshua always seem to know that Seth was checking on him? Jack didn't seem to notice—or he did and just never said anything?

"It was a rockhopper," Joshua continued.

A what? Seth frowned at his phone. There didn't seem to be any weird monsters in Joshua's immediate area beyond the spirit guide. What was this evil grasshopper-penguin crossbreed that Joshua was talking about? Seth closed his class notes on his laptop and opened a browser. A quick search of "rockhopper" pulled up the smallest of penguin species. Apparently, DNA testing was the only way to tell the difference between the males and females. The picture showed a penguin with beady red eyes and bright yellow spiky feathers on their head.

It looked evil.

"We think it's a swan maiden—only it's male and a penguin. Do you know anything about those kinds of things or is it some kind of we're—we're—we're—damn autocorrect—were-penguin?"

He typed in "no" because he had no idea what Joshua was talking about. Swan maiden? What the hell was that? The Wikipedia page had a black-and-white drawing of three women bathing naked. The first sentence explained that it was a shapeshifter that shifted between human and swan form. Seth's browser assumed that "were-penguin" was a misspelling of "where do penguins live?" It claimed that the birds were only found in the Southern Hemisphere on islands and rugged isolated continental areas. Boston didn't qualify as any of those conditions. He closed the tab and called up the page on werewolves to see if it mentioned sea birds.

"No w. penguin?" Joshua texted.

The article on swan maidens seemed three times longer than the one that Wikipedia had on werewolves. Why had he not heard of these things before? One thing he knew for sure was that if humans had any inkling about a supernatural being, then it was based on something real and dangerous. There was no smoke without fire. The swan maiden entry was proof that they were real.

Joshua must have decided that his question was confusing as he reworded it. "No, you don't know or no w. penguins?"

"No were penguins," Seth tried to answer but the autocorrect changed it to "No where penguins." He hit send before he realized that the text been changed. He locked down on a growl of anger.

"It's at the aquarium. I think," Joshua replied. "Are you sure there's no w. penguins?"

Seth clenched his phone tight, angry that he was so helpless. "NO WERE PENGUINS!" He typed back in all caps. He felt bad as soon as he hit send.

"Why?" Seth refrained from using lots of "?" and "!"

"The penguin wants to hire me," Joshua wrote back. "Maybe. If my dream is real again."

Seth stared at the screen. His brother lived to hurt his brain.

Seth glanced to the front of the classroom. His teacher hadn't noticed yet that he'd taken out his phone. He didn't really care if he was caught, but it would trigger a cascade of events that he normally avoided.

Joshua said he was with the Goths, and they were going to the aquarium.

Seth scanned the building that his brother was rushing toward. There among the normal penguins was something non-penguin. The tight knot of magic created a small birdlike body. Not a werewolf but certainly not a normal animal either. At the moment it was fighting for its share of fish being handed out by the human staff.

Whatever it was, it barely stood out. If it hadn't been so close to the other penguins, he wouldn't have been able to spot the differences between it and a normal bird. He could have easily missed it. There was no telling how long the creature had been at the aquarium. Judging by the feeding going on, the staff hadn't noticed the ringer.

Oddly, there were two Grigori just a block or two from the aquarium. One felt like Elise—but who was the other? Was it another Virtue? Why were there two Virtues in Boston?

He focused back on Joshua. His brother was still texting but none of the messages were to Seth. "Who are you talking to?"

"Winnie. I think. Either she's butt texting, or she's possessed by a ghost. I think it's French. I think autocorrect hates French. I think autocorrect hates everyone."

When would the hurting stop?

Seth clenched down on a growl of impatience. Contacting the Wise Woman, Sioux Zee, via her granddaughter wasn't a bad idea, if it actually worked. Seth had no idea what the magical creature was, but the Wise Woman might know. The Grigori might also know.

"Mr. Tatterskein?" His teacher had finally noticed that Seth had his phone out during class. "Do I need to take that from you?"

Ah, the battle of wills had started. They never ended well for the teachers. Seth was hoping to avoid any conflict as he actually liked Mr. Hotchkins.

"I'm sorry." Seth stood up. "I need to be excused."

"Sit down, Mr. Tatterskein, and put your phone away."

Seth closed his laptop. "I cannot do that, Mr. Hotchkins. This is a very important matter, and I can't ignore it."

His phone vibrated again. He glanced at it.

Joshua had typed a lone "?" to Seth's lack of response.

"Mr. Tatterskein!" Mr. Hotchkins came toward him, hand outstretched, demanding that Seth surrender his phone.

Seth lost his temper. It flared for a second, fueled by his fear for his brother. In that moment, everyone around him realized— without truly understanding the hows and the whys—that they were in a very small room with a very large predator. There was a sudden exodus for the door.

Mr. Hotchkins backpedaled until he hit the whiteboard.

Seth struggled to get his temper in check. Last thing he needed was to be kicked out of school again because everyone was too afraid to be in the same room with him.

Joshua's safety, though, came first.

"DON'T GO NEAR IT!!!" he texted his brother.

Text sent, he tried for damage control. "I'm sorry, Mr. Hotchkins. You don't have to be scared. I'm not going to hurt you. Shit!" This was because Joshua didn't respond to his text. Mr. Hotchkins whimpered as Seth growled with frustration. Did Joshua not see the text? "I'm not angry with you, Mr. Hotchkins. My brother is being an idiot."

Getting no reply from Joshua, Seth dialed his brother. "Joshua! Don't go there! That thing could be dangerous!"

"Seth? Hi! What? Dangerous? It didn't seem dangerous," Joshua said. "It is a very small penguin."

"That's not what it is," Seth said. "I don't know what it is, and you are not to go near it."

"The Goths are going to the aquarium with or without me," Joshua said.

"You. Will. Not. Go. There." Seth growled the words. "This is a command, not a request."

"I'm sorry," Joshua said and actually sounded like he was. "But I think that I have to. I dreamed about the penguin just like I dreamed about the Wickers. If I had been able to figure out the Frog Pond dream, then those people that the Wickers killed wouldn't have died. Jack wouldn't have nearly died. I don't want anything to happen to the Goths, not if I can do something to protect them. I've got to go. Bye."

The line went dead. Seth struggled not to lose his temper a second time. His teacher was still quivering against the wall.

"I'm sorry, Mr. Hotchkins," Seth said as he gathered his things. "I really am. I'm going home now."

He dialed his cousin as he walked out of the classroom. "Jack! Joshua is doing something super stupid!"

"What now?" Jack asked as if everything Joshua did was somewhat stupid.

Seth explained the best he could about the not-a-penguin at the aquarium. "I told Joshua not to stick his nose into trouble, but he just hung up on me."

"It would take me nearly four hours to drive to Boston," Jack said. "Leung has the king's jet in Vancouver. Even if I tried to catch a plane, I'd have to get to the airport, get through security, and hope this bad weather didn't delay the flight. All that could take up to two hours before I could take off."

Seth glanced out the window. It wasn't snowing hard but weather to the west of New Jersey could have delayed all flights inbound to the airport—thus delaying outbound traffic. "I know, you can't get there fast enough—not with Joshua nearly at the front door of the aquarium already. Can you get hold of Elise? She's just a couple blocks from the aquarium with another Virtue for some reason."

"Another Virtue?" Jack said in surprise. "Okay, I'll call Elise."

12: JOSHUA

By the third station, Joshua was hopelessly lost. He knew that they'd taken the Red Line into the city as he'd been in Cambridge long enough to know that was the color of the subway that went through the area. They got off at Downtown Crossing. From there, things started to blur. They'd gone up a flight of stairs, through a long uphill sloping concourse, and then ran to catch a second subway train. He'd forgotten to pay attention to the color, although it might have been orange. They only rode the second train for one stop. They went up a second set of steps only to go immediately down another staircase to catch a third train. They rode only one stop again, and then took yet another flight of stairs up and emerged out into the gray bleak cold.

Joshua had followed the others blindly down the street a dozen steps before he realized that the land ended just ahead of them. There were large boats tied off at docks. A small hut with a blue whale statue affixed to its roof advertised BOSTON HARBOR CRUISES TICKET CENTER. Beyond the boats was open water.

He'd known that the aquarium was "near the harbor" but he somehow didn't expect the ocean to be right there. His wolf didn't like it; it made unhappy noises as they walked along the boat docks.

Ji Su cocked her head as if listening to something and then turned around to look back at him. Her snake spirit guide was whispering into her ear. She waited as he caught up to her and then fell into step with him. "The school has a pool so everyone can learn to at least doggie paddle. Your family thought it was an important skill, given how surrounded we are by water. Your brothers and cousins liked playing in streams and shallow ponds but none of your family liked the ocean."

He eyed the shifting water just a stone's throw away. "Is it just because the ocean is so big or is there something in the bay that freaks our wolves out?"

"I-I-I don't know," Ji Su admitted. "I never thought to ask."

They caught up to the others at an odd ticket booth—all glass and polished stainless steel at right angles to one another—in the courtyard before the main building. There was a proliferation of signs. Tal and Allie were shaking their heads at the sign.

"It's nearly thirty dollars for adults," Ottilie muttered quietly.

"They don't have a student rate?" Ji Su scanned the prices.

"Kids under *eleven* get a discount," Tal whispered. He glanced at Ottilie as if wondering if she could pass as a ten-year-old.

His classmates might go to a private school, but the Goths were all there on full scholarships. Their families weren't wealthy. They probably got the same kind of allowance he received when he lived with his mom and dad. Back then, he wouldn't have been able to afford a thirty-dollar ticket.

"I can pay," Joshua said.

They looked at him in surprise.

"Seth gave me a lot of money." He was glad that he hadn't thought to leave the cash at home for safekeeping. He took out two of the hundred-dollar bills within his wallet and pushed them through the slot in the window. "Six adults, please."

He collected the change and six tickets. There was a seal exhibit between the ticket booth and front door with five sleek gray harbor seals gliding back and forth. Maisy was leaning against the glass, forehead to forehead with one of the seals, communing.

Red bricks paved up to a row of glass doors. Inside was a massive foyer with one wall all brushed stainless steel. It served as an airlock against the bitter cold of the outdoors. The smell made his nose twitch. It was an assault of sea and fish and wet bird and something else.

It all felt strangely familiar despite the fact that Joshua knew that he'd never been to any aquarium before.

"This place is huge," Joshua whispered. "Where are the penguins?"

"On the first floor," Tal said. "We need to go past them to go up to the upper floors. The place is basically a corkscrew with the center being one giant tank."

"Vijay could be anyplace." Ji Su took off her vampire cape and folded it over her arm. "He could be in the staff-only areas, in the bathrooms, hell, even in one of the tanks."

Nam-gi hovered in midair, there and not there, a dark shadow with bright eyes. He seemed twice the size as he normally appeared.

"Find Vijay," Ji Su whispered to the spirit snake.

The shadow darted away, speeding through the air like a loosed arrow. The Goths surged after it, Ji Su in the lead with Tal and Ottilie right behind her. Allie and Maisy followed in a way that suggested that the two couldn't actually see the ghostly snake.

The front doors had funneled them to the far-left side of the large foyer. On the far-right side was the entrance to the aquarium's gift shop. It was like a toy store had collided with a T-shirt shop. There were racks and racks of shirts and hoodies and hats alongside overflowing shelves of stuffed animals.

Joshua drifted after the Goths, still a little overwhelmed by the déjà vu feeling. Was there a talking penguin just around the corner? Or was the bird in his dream like the frog statues that carried on a full conversation in his nightmare but were just plain regular statues when he saw them in person?

"Monsieur!" someone called from the back of the gift shop. The person waved by raising a hand and rotating it back and forth slightly. It was perhaps the most stiff and formal wave that Joshua had ever seen.

Joshua thought for a moment that the person was a young woman but then realized that he was a boy in a long green princess coat trimmed with black fur. He had on a white cosplay wig that was all upswept curls and ribbons, makeup—elaborate makeup that included a small black heart at the corner of his lipstick-covered lips—and boots topped with black fluffy fake fur.

"Oh, poor Vijay," Ji Su whispered. "He's going to die of embarrassment when we get him back to himself."

Tal nodded while he took pictures of Vijay with his phone.

"Monsieur, je suis tellement content que tu sois venu!" The boy used a soft falsetto to speak in French, making elegant gestures with his hand. *"J'ai utilisé le miroir magique—vous envoyant des notes, vous demandant de venir."*

Joshua's mom had a thing for costume-laden period dramas and movies. It was a weird quirk for a gearhead like her who spent most days in mechanic coveralls with grease up to her elbows. Her favorite way to unwind was a glass of wine in a fancy glass and a movie about beautiful people in beautiful clothes in elaborate palaces. One of her favorites was *Marie Antionette* starring Kirsten Dunst.

When Joshua had met the ghost of the dead queen for the first time, she'd been possessing purple-haired Winnie, speaking French in Winnie's normal voice. There had been nothing about her that reminded him of the movie. Perhaps it was only because the ghost had so little time to save Winnie's life. Marie Antionette obviously had spent days inhabiting Vijay—and it showed. The white upswept wig. The ribbons. The makeup. The clothes that seemed old-fashioned yet stylishly modern at the same time. There was no mistaking the queen.

"She's been texting you?" Tal asked in surprise.

"I guess," Joshua said.

Marie Antoinette must have been using Winnie's missing phone to text Joshua earlier. He'd ignored the French texts because he'd been fighting with Seth at the same time.

Joshua took out his phone and showed it to Tal. "I took Spanish as a language, not French."

Tal laughed at the text. "She calls you Sir Black Knight."

"What does she want?" Joshua asked as Marie was talking again, holding out two stuffed seals.

Tal squinted a moment, listening intently. "She wants to buy a seal for Muffin Man but she's not sure which one to get. They had come to the aquarium on a date—and he loved the seals. Winnie has stolen all the presents that Marie bought and taken all the magic cards, so she's been reduced to selling..."

Tal paused to ask Marie a question, which Marie answered in a flood of French.

"*Le manchot?*" Tal repeated a word that Marie used, sounding as if he wasn't sure what it meant.

Marie gestured toward the door. "*Le manchot.* Manuel."

"What?" Ji Su asked.

"She's raising money by selling information to a penguin by the name of Manuel," Tal said.

They all turned to stare at the second set of doors that led into the main aquarium area. They couldn't actually see the birds, but Joshua could hear the loud squawking noise that they made.

"If she's selling the penguin information," Allie said, "it can't be too dangerous."

"Proves nothing," Ottilie said.

Maisy caught hold of Joshua's sleeve, edging closer to him. He could feel her fear. She thought that they should just do the intervention, free Vijay from Marie Antoinette's influence, and go back to school before they ended up in any trouble.

In his dream, the penguin had said, *It stands to reason that you're the one that she told me about. The new one.*

"She" was Marie Antoinette. God only knew what else the dead queen had already told the penguin. In the dream, he and the penguin spoke English but as far as Joshua knew, Marie Antionette didn't speak English. She also couldn't or wouldn't speak Spanish. Certainly, she hadn't done either to save Winnie's life. Was the penguin some kind of polyglot?

Marie held out the two stuffed seals. One of a huge plump gray speckled seal with a very realistic face. The other was a smaller white—and in Joshua's opinion—cuter seal pup. *"Lequel devrais-je acheter?"*

Maisy petted the head of the white stuffed animal. She thought it was very cute. She would love to get one.

"The white one," Joshua said.

The Goths all nodded.

Tal added, *"Le blanc."*

The queen turned to shove the gray speckled seal back onto the crowded shelf.

"We're here to rescue Vijay," Joshua said quietly as he realized that once the dead queen made her selection, she would buy the toy and leave. "Aren't we? How do we do that?"

The Goth's exchanged looks.

"We're not going to be able to do bell, book, and candle here," Ji Su whispered.

"Do what?" Joshua said.

"As we discussed yesterday, wolves can't use their power against ghosts," Ji Su said as if she was afraid that Joshua might have forgotten. "All wolves do is hurt the mediums."

"I know," Joshua said.

"Okay." Ji Su pushed on. "Mediums can open themselves up

to a ghost, but they can't actually control the ghost without some type of ritual. It normally involves reading a spell from a book, burning a candle, and ringing a bell."

Winnie's grandmother had lit a candle, burned some incense that she said attracted spirits, and rang a bell to end the séance. Joshua had been running on the assumption that he'd never be involved in another spirit summoning, so he hadn't thought to ask more detailed questions. There had been weird books in the room, but none had been used in the ritual. He supposed that summoning a spirit and getting rid of one were two different things. Certainly, Winnie and her grandmother had taken precautions as if driving the spirit out could have been difficult.

"How long does it take?" Joshua asked as they were currently the only shoppers in the store. The two female staff members were by the front entrance, changing out a Thanksgiving display for a Christmas one. They seemed too occupied in their task to pay close attention to the teenagers. "Do we really need the candle?"

"The main difference between wolves, Virtues, and gifted people like Allie and Maisy..." Ottilie started to explain.

Allie threw up her hands. "Now is not the time for Ritual 101!"

Ottilie plowed on, ignoring the interruption. "...Is that while gifted people can observe the flow of magic, most of them don't have any real power of their own. Even when we're young, wolves and angels have a faint connection with their Source. It's not strong enough to save them if they're bitten by a feral, but it protects them..."

"The candle is an easy power source for the spell," Tal said, cutting to the ending. "Crude but it gets the job done. Spirits have a tenuous hold on the world, even strong ones like Her Majesty here."

"We thought we would find Vijay in a less public part of the aquarium." Ji Su put in her two cents.

Joshua glanced around. More visitors were filtering into the aquarium, but none were coming into the gift shop yet. It seemed as if people shopped for souvenirs only after they'd seen the exhibits. Marie/Vijay had discovered a third stuffed seal to consider—this one impossibly fluffy and completely gray.

"We have enough people to block the two doors and distract the staff," Joshua pointed out.

"He's right," Ottilie murmured.

"I'll take the back entrance." Joshua didn't want to do the distraction as his wolf might decide to "help."

"I'll do the distraction." Tal took out a breath mint and popped it in his mouth.

Maisy sighed and pointed at the front entrance. Joshua understood that she didn't think she could actually block the door, but she was going to try.

Ottilie took out a leather-bound book, flipped it open to a pre-marked page. She pulled a wooden match from her pocket and lit it with a flick of her thumbnail. As the match flared brightly, she read aloud a passage from the book: "Be strong and courageous. Do not be afraid or terrified because of them, for the Lord your God goes with you; he will never leave you nor forsake you."

The match snuffed out.

Joshua felt something crawl over him like static electricity. "What did you just do?"

"It's a protection spell." Ottilie pocketed the spent match. "A very low-powered one. It won't stop a bullet or anything like that. It will keep Marie from just jumping to someone else after we force her out of Vijay."

"Right! Let's do this!" Tal headed toward the staff members, radiating charm like a movie star.

Maisy squeaked in surprise and headed toward the front door.

Joshua drifted toward the back door, trying to keep an eye on everyone. He realized that the wolf had stripped off his coat, apparently feeling hot. He hoped that it would behave and not do anything stupid or dangerous.

Ottilie, Allie, and Ji Su closed on Marie Antoinette, who was still debating between the two stuffed animals. They moved with grace that suggested that they'd practiced what each had to do many times.

Ottilie flipped her small leather-bound spell book to a page marked with a red silk ribbon. Ji Su took out a thick bundle of sage and a large feather. Allie produced a tealight candle from one of her many pockets and put it on one of the display shelves.

The three girls glanced at each other, nodding to signal that they were ready.

Ottilie produced a second match. She lit the tealight and then the bundle of sage that Ji Su was holding. Ji Su fanned the smoking end of the bundle with the feather. Allie caught hold of Vijay from behind.

"*Quelle? Non!*" Marie cried out in French, dropping the stuffed seals.

Ottilie quietly read aloud what was written in her book. "The Lord hear thee in the day of trouble. The name of the God of Jacob defend thee. Send thee help from the sanctuary and strengthen thee out of Zion."

Marie/Vijay glanced around frantically until she spotted Joshua by the back door. "*Monsieur le loup chevalier, sauvez-moi!*"

Joshua spread his hands to indicate he could do nothing even if he understood what the dead queen was saying to him. Marie stomped her foot in anger.

Ottilie read on while glaring at Joshua over the top of her book. She seemed sure that Joshua would come to Marie's assistance. He had no idea why she thought that. "Remember all thy offerings, and accept thy burnt sacrifice; Selah. Grant thee according to thine own heart and fulfill all thy counsel. We will rejoice in thy salvation, and in the name of our God we will set up our banners: the Lord fulfill all thy petitions."

"Manuel!" Marie called loudly. "Manuel!"

Ottilie sped up her reading. "Now know I that the Lord saveth his anointed; he will hear him from his holy heaven with the saving strength of his right hand."

Ji Su glanced toward the staff with concern.

Tal was doing an amazing job at keeping the two women distracted. He was juggling four bright yellow toy sea turtles while singing the introduction song of the demigod Maui from the movie *Moana*.

The two staff women looked mesmerized by the show of charm and talent.

Ottilie plowed on. "Some trust in chariots, and some in horses, but we will remember the name of the Lord our God. They are brought down and fallen but we are risen and stand upright. Save, Lord: let the king hear us when we call. Amen."

Ji Su tucked away the feather, took out a small bell and rang it.

The candle went out.

Joshua felt a strong wave of static electricity pass over him. A cold breeze followed. He thought he heard a woman whisper mournfully "*Mais mes cadeaux!*"

"Oh, holy hell," Vijay muttered in a voice half an octave lower as he staggered in Allie's hold. "Not again."

"Yes, again." Ji Su pocketed the bell, pulled out a portable ashtray, and stubbed out the bundle of sage. "We need to go before they notice the smoke."

Allie released Vijay to collect the candle.

Vijay looked in puzzlement at the two stuffed toys on the floor at his feet. As he stooped to pick them up, he noticed then his gem-crusted acrylic fingernails. "Oh, you've got to be kidding me!"

"Crisis later." Ji Su caught his arm and started him toward Joshua. "We've got to go."

"Okay! Okay!" He got five steps before slamming to a stop and pointing at Joshua. "Wolf!"

"Yes, yes, he's with us." Ji Su ruthlessly pulled Vijay onward. "He's the prince's older half brother."

"Older half brother?" Vijay murmured. "Wait, they found Ilya alive?"

"It's a long story," Joshua said uneasily. "But yes."

Allie passed them both. "We should go talk to the penguin before we leave."

"I thought we agreed that it was a bad idea," Ottilie said as Maisy and Tal joined them in the foyer.

"If we don't find out what it wants, then Marie Antoinette could just grab one of us again to finish selling it information," Allie said with her hand on the door into the aquarium proper. "If we talk to it, then she doesn't have a customer."

"She has a point." Tal walked over to join her at the door. Tal took off his coat as if he expected to stay.

Joshua froze as the others slowly drifted after Allie and Tal. It was a good point. Marie Antoinette proved that Joshua's dream had been true: there was a penguin here that talked. Its name was Manuel. What Joshua didn't know was why it wanted to hire him. Seth had ordered him to stay away from the penguin. Chances were good that Cabot or one of the other Thanes or Seth himself was on the way to Boston to make sure that Joshua had nothing to do with it.

Last time he didn't find out what his dream meant, everyone almost died. Winnie. Cabot. Decker. Himself. Innocent people— random strangers that the Wickers used to create their monsters— had died. He really should find out what the penguin wanted.

13: ELISE

"Theo just hit the Albany Street Garage." Clarice named the public parking garage located next to the office of the chief medical examiner. "I thought you should know that I told her about the Thane."

Elise had been pulling favors to get what little info the police had on the murder victim. It took her a full minute to switch gears and process what Clarice meant. "You told her I'm dating Jack Cabot?"

"It kind of slipped out," Clarice said.

"Slipped out?" Elise stopped on the sidewalk outside the sleek modern-looking office building that functioned as the city's morgue. She had permission to see the body and check the dead man's personal effects. She'd better wait; knowing Theo, her cousin would not be stopped by protocols.

"I was complaining about the lack of eligible young men in Philadelphia," Clarice said. "Most normal men are overwhelmed by our angelic glamour. If they aren't, they're *seriously* gay. There are no men in our tribe that are our age ... well, that aren't already married with kids. The Philadelphia pack of werewolves, on the other hand, has a score of men our age. They're immune to our glamour. They're all surprisingly intelligent; most have master's degrees from Ivy League colleges. They're good-looking too, in that backwoods kind of way. Most of them seem single—at least they're living in houses with other guys, not women."

Teaming up with Jack Cabot had been an education on all the things Elise didn't know that she didn't know about werewolves. Her family had only taught her how to kill wolves. She had known nothing about how they lived. Yes, werewolves were surprisingly intelligent. They put a great deal of importance on college degrees from the best universities. They were, though, sheltered and naïve beyond belief.

Her people left home young, trained in a foreign country, and then were expected to live alone once they finished their training at eighteen. Male werewolves never left the home. Never. If an unmarried wolf moved out of their parents' house, it was to move in with the other single young male wolves down the street. The bachelor quarters were like frat houses with fur. Wolves didn't like being alone. They sought out the company of their own kind.

Elise hadn't had a chance to share her observations with Clarice yet. Life kept giving her more important things to discuss with her cousin. How did Clarice know about the bachelor quarters? "You spied on them?"

"I couldn't help it," Clarice murmured. There was the clicking of her keyboard. "I've always kind of taken the wolves for granted. I know they're there, but they run a tight ship, so I never had to get involved in them. But after you started to date the Thane, I was curious. I should know all the wolves in my area. How many there are. How old they are. Where they live. I started out just doing a quick search but then I got a little...obsessive?"

"How obsessive?"

"You don't really want to know. It's kind of creepy. I know *I* would be totally freaked out if someone did it to me."

Knowing Clarice's abilities for gathering information, the mind boggled as to what level her obsession took her.

"Are you tracking them via their phones?" Elise said. "Or did you hack their computers' cameras?"

"Something like that," Clarice admitted in a shamed whisper. "Clarice!"

"I'm lonely! I just got carried away." Clarice proved that she been watching Elise from some nearby security camera by saying, "There's Theo! You should focus on her! Bye!"

Theodosia arrived like an angel of vengeance. She'd always been tall, lean, and angry with the world. Since Elise had last seen her, she'd cut her dark hair butch short. Dressed in hiking boots, worn blue jeans, and a trench coat, she could pass as a man. A cigarette dangled from her lips, completing the "bad boy" image.

"What is it with your family sleeping with monsters?" Theo's voice was husky from smoke and screaming curses. "First Saul and then your mother and now you."

Elise bit back the first dozen snarky things that came to mind. Theo had a thing about appearing strong, so she would never admit how worried she was about Francis. All that worry needed to escape somehow. "Can we just focus on Francis?"

Theo snorted. "His car is in Boston, but do we have any evidence that he is?"

"No. The video shows that just his driver was in the car when it hit the train station. Francis could be anywhere, even still at the monastery."

Theo shook her head as she took a deep drag on her cigarette. "I stopped there first." She snorted out smoke. "Punched a few monks."

"What?"

"I thought Francis would get better there. The monks were supposed to be helping him. He's God's power manifested in flesh. It's their job to help him. They've got him squirreled away from everything and only his driver interacts with him on a daily basis. He's not getting better. He's still totally messed up from Greece."

Clarice had mentioned that Francis had PTSD. Elise hadn't connected the dots.

Francis had been on his way to join them at training like any normal thirteen-year-old Grigori child. In a way that could have been only God pulling strings, Francis ended up on the wrong island. God dropped him deep in the mountains at an odd religious festival where the locals would bring hundreds of harmless snakes to an ancient church in an isolated village. God wanted Francis there when a breach opened within the church, twisting the snakes into monsters. "God wanted" was the only sane explanation for the improbable chain of events. Yes, Francis had leveled the village and killed all its inhabitants, but it saved the rest of the island.

Elise hadn't considered its effect on Francis's mental health. They were Grigori; they were raised from birth to face monsters. To kill or be killed. During training, Theo had been the most unflinching of the Virtues.

"I always thought my parents spoiled Francis rotten," Theo said. "I didn't realize that they were frightened of him. They were afraid to go hard on him. They should have been grinding his nose down into the shit that we would be facing as adults. They didn't prepare him for our life. They let him be all teddy bears and rainbows and sparkles."

Theo flung her cigarette butt down and ground it out with her boot. "They broke him. My parents and God broke him. Then instead of letting him come and train with us, our family tossed him around like a live grenade, not wanting to be the one holding him when he went off. They had him living alone when he was fucking fifteen, saying he was an emancipated minor. They didn't send him to a shrink because 'angels' and 'monsters' and 'God made me' would be signs of insanity for anyone else. A normal shrink would never be able to figure out the crazy from the Power."

"What did the monks say—after you punched them—about where Francis went?"

"No one actually saw Francis yesterday morning. The monks stay as far from Francis as they can get. He's toasted a few in the past—nothing permanent but painful enough to make them leery about surprising him. His normal winter morning ritual was to have breakfast with his driver, Roustabout, and then they would go snowshoeing on the monastery grounds. His driver picked up Francis's breakfast from the kitchen as usual and took it to his private 'office,' which is what the monks call the building that Francis hangs out in during the day. It's on the far edge of the compound. Roustabout brought back dirty dishes and asked the kitchen to pack a lunch. Shortly after that, a handful of the monks heard the car leave but hadn't seen who got into it. They assumed that since the lunch had been for two that Francis left with Roustabout. He only leaves if Central deploys him. It's not uncommon for Francis to be at the monastery for several months at a time. If he wants something that can't be shipped to the monastery, his driver goes out and gets it for him."

Clarice had said something along the same lines. Elise knew, though, that Theo had yanked Francis out on some wild-goose chase at the same time that Elise was heading to Utica to deal with the Wickers.

"You went around Clarice and deployed him," Elise said. "Someone could have activated him without Central knowing."

"I had no choice; Clarice had broken Central's phone again. I had to bully Francis into it. I don't think anyone else could have deployed him. Francis... He... He loves me."

Theo looked ashamed of the admission. The shame shifted into anger at having to admit it aloud.

Elise changed the subject back to Francis's movements. "Roustabout was at Alewife station with the car, but Clarice hasn't managed to confirm that Francis was with him at any point."

Theo gave a dismissive wave of her hand. "When Francis is deployed, he has Roustabout drop him at a safe distance from the infestation site and then leave. Roustabout is wholly human. Francis knows that not even a Virtue would be able to go toe to toe with any monster that a Power was sicced on. It's the whole point of sending in a Power to clean up a mess instead of a Virtue. Powers create too much collateral damage. People remember. Sodom. Gomorrah. Krakatoa. The Great Quake of San Francisco. Markopoulo."

The last was the village on the island of Kefalonia that Francis had wiped off the map when he was thirteen. Only charred rubble, a mile in diameter, marked where it once stood. A world-famous church, a dozen hillside houses, several thousand festivalgoers and an unknown number of breach-borne monsters had been vaporized to ash.

From what Clarice told Elise, Francis had as much control as a thunderstorm as to what his power hit. Anything near him was fair game. If Roustabout was his only friend, Francis probably would want to keep him safe. "You believe that Francis got out somewhere else and sent his driver away?"

Theo hesitated before nodding.

Dealing with any police department as a Grigori woman was like swimming in a pool of sharks while bleeding. Yes, she was "officially" a federal agent working for the Department of Justice with a badge and everything, but none of the American law enforcement agencies played nice together. Add in the Grigori glamour, and every attempt to work with any straight male officer became a battle of wills disguised as a fight over jurisdiction. She restricted her contact to phone messages and emails whenever possible, but the few times that she needed physical contact with evidence, she needed to run the gauntlet of face-to-face meetings.

Worse, it turned out that the homicide detective assigned to this case was Richard Rutledge. "Rick" to his frat boy friends. "Dick" to everyone else. The man thought he was God's gift to women. He was good-looking enough that many women acted like it.

Elise suspected that she could have viewed the unidentified dead body without Rutledge's presence, but he was using it to gain access to her. It was little maneuvers like that that kept her from ever saying yes to the many invitations to drinks and dinner and whatever else that would lead to. Abuse of power started small like that.

She told Rutledge that she wouldn't be alone, but he probably thought that Decker was coming with her. (He didn't know that Decker was a vampire and thus unable to work daylight hours.) Annoyingly, Rutledge was on good behavior around the vampire. She would like to think it was because he was sensitive enough to find Decker's mere presence unnerving—but prying little comments about the nature of her work relationship with "her partner" suggested otherwise. Rick was the type of man who wouldn't take "no" from a woman but respected the prior claims of other men.

Detective Rutledge was waiting in the front lobby of the building, dressed in a dark wool trench coat and a cashmere green tartan scarf. The tips of his ears were red with cold; he refused to wear a hat because it messed up his perfect Ken-doll hair. He had been a chain smoker but quit since she'd met him, switching to an unending supply of Big Red cinnamon gum. His square jaw chomped on the stick of gum as he eyed his reflection in the window. He realized that he was being watched, changed his focus and saw her. The smile would have been charming if it wasn't so predatory.

Rick was so focused on Elise that he didn't notice Theo until she stepped into the elevator with them. Elise had kept her distance from Rick. Theo took up a position beside Elise, looking bored and annoyed. Rick tore his gaze from Elise to glance at Theo—and froze.

The first exposure to a Grigori's personal glamour always hit the hardest, as if the viewer had to build up an immunity to it. It was a rabbit punch to the reptile-brain. It went without saying that homosexuals weren't impacted the same way as they were hardwired differently.

Rick's eyes went wide, and his mouth opened slightly. Then confusion set in, and he took a step back. "Who's this…guy?"

"Theo is backing me up on this case." Elise didn't bother to explain further. She had learned from experience that people didn't react well to federal agents being related to one another. "This is Detective Richard Rutledge of the Boston Police."

"Theodore?" Rick guessed. What he really was asking was "Are you a guy or a girl?" Knowing how Rick thought, he was probably wondering "Fuckable or not?" while being slightly horrified by the thought that he was attracted to a possible male.

"Dick?" Theo replied with the faintest of sneers, giving Rick nothing.

"No!" Rick took another step backward in alarm as if what he really was asked was if he was a lover of men.

Theo's sneer became more pronounced.

"What can you tell us about this John Doe?" Elise said to distract the two.

Rick glanced at her and relaxed slightly, as if relieved that he still found her desirable. "Who?"

"The murder victim?"

"Not much," Rick said. "The train did a number on him. We're guessing he was between the ages of twenty and forty. Dark brown hair—no gray—on the long side. The one eye that remained intact after the impact was brown. He looked like he either really worked out or had some kind of heavy labor job. He didn't have any ID on him."

Theo relaxed at the description. The eye color was wrong for Francis.

"Tattoos?" Elise asked. "Scars?"

"Nah, no identifying marks whatsoever." Rick said.

Not Roustabout then, who had tattoo sleeves on both arms and a scar across one eye. The dead man was still tied to Francis's disappearance as the video camera failed to show him on the platform.

"The security footage is spotty." Richard confirmed that the police noticed the oddities in the video. "They were having some kind of weird problems with the cameras. There were a lot of late-night people on the platform but only a handful saw anything.

Some said that the guy was alone and acting crazy. Other witnesses said that there were two to five men. They believed that there was some kind of running fight that started near the ticket machines. We haven't pulled anything off the security cameras to confirm this."

Elise nodded. It matched up to what Clarice had already discovered.

"What's Interpol's interest in this case?" Rick asked. "Do you know who this guy was?"

Theo surprised Elise by admitting the truth. "One of our agents is missing. His car was parked at Alewife. A John Doe on the tracks? We wanted to know if it was our man."

"Oof!" Rick said in sympathy.

"The accident was close to the same time that our agent's car arrived at the train station. It may or may not be related," Elise said. "Identifying the John Doe might give us a lead—or it might not."

The door chimed as the elevator stopped on their floor. It was a long hallway lined with stainless steel coolers that held the dead. The faint stench of death scented the air. The public address system, though, played "Angels We Have Heard on High."

Theo rolled her eyes slightly at the music. The Grigori weren't Christians. While their holy text shared some of the same books— Genesis, Proverbs, and Psalms—the rest was the ancient events told from the angelic perspective. By all rights, they shouldn't know anything about Christmas, but the overwhelming flood of related media made that impossible. They ignored it—usually— but there was something grating about the Christian version of angels. The white robes. The halos. The heavenly choir. It totally ignored the Christian Bible where some angels were described as flying wheels with many eyes and others were said to have six wings and not much else. It seemed very likely at some point in time the Christians adopted the Greek image of the winged attendants of Zeus for angels. It begged the question, though, of what was written in the Bible. Were the heaven-bound angels different from those set to watch over Earth? Or had the Grigori forefathers been very strange beasts—and their glamour was just vestiges of an ability that made the angels' monstrous appearance seem human? Or was it simply that the ancient prophets were tripping on acid when they "saw" angels?

It was an uneasy question that Christmas stirred up every year as angels festooned every public place that wanted to attract the all-important Christian dollar.

At least the music didn't follow them into the actual storage area. It was tomb silent. Into that silence, her phone gave a deep wolf howl as Jack Cabot called her.

She'd set the call notification sound over Thanksgiving, slightly drunk and feeling ambivalent about the idea of getting calls from the Thane. At the time, it seemed wise to have the little reminder that Cabot was more than a tall, muscular, good-looking man who smelled sexy as hell straight out of the shower.

Her phone gave another wolf howl as he called her a second time.

"You've got to be kidding," Theo said, raising her eyebrow. "You picked that as a ringtone for him?"

"Him?" Rick pounced on the pronoun. "Him who?"

At least Cabot's text notification was a normal ding. She ignored Rick to pull out her phone and look at the screen.

"Hey." Cabot had texted and then "Are you there?"

She could feel a blush burn its way up her ears. She set her phone on vibrate and tucked it into her coat pocket. Most likely he wanted to plan something for the upcoming Christmas school break when he and the prince were going to be staying over at Decker's again. "A lawyer that I'm working with in New York City."

That was vague enough and close to the truth. Cabot was a lawyer and had passed the bar both in New York State and Massachusetts—unbelievable as it might seem.

Elise gave Theo a look, silently telling her to behave around Rick.

Theo snorted but played nice. "Lawyer. Wolf howl. Good choice."

It pacified Rick somewhat. In order to compete with the semi-mythical lawyer, he talked with the staff and finished the paperwork so they could view the body.

The thing on the table only looked human. It was some kind of magical creature. Its appearance wasn't a glamour, which meant it was some type of shapeshifter. Dead and partially dismembered in its human form, it was impossible to tell what its furry form had been. Such things often needed magical daggers or silver bullets to kill but the massive blunt impact of a commuter train would do in a pinch. (Not that Elise ever personally used the method, but her grandmother had once.)

Theo gave her a questioning glance, obviously wanting to discuss the creature but not where they could be overheard.

There were many types of shapeshifters, starting with were-wolves. Theo had dealt with the wolves of Burlington enough to recognize their non-furry bodies. She obviously didn't recognize the person, so it wasn't one of them. Elise had dealt with the three black Boston werewolves, the gray wolves of Albany, and the oddball mix of the Wolf King Thanes. Between those four packs, it accounted for most of the werewolves in Northeast United States.

Elise shook her head. The werewolves were the only ones that the Grigori counted as somewhat friendly. There were other shape-shifters that were considered neutral, such as selkies. It would be unlikely, though, to find a prey animal in the heart of a preda-tor's territory. They favored remote islands for that very reason.

Another predator? The Japanese kitsune and tanuki had not fared well after the Wolf King moved his people into Japan; they retreated into the mountains after losing countless skirmishes. By all accounts, though, their human forms looked Asian. There hadn't been a lion sighting for so long that people were starting to suggest that their source had lost its hold on this world. There had been bear reports in West Virginia—Clarice's little sister was checking into those. Bears tended to be solitary beasts.

The werewolves were an exception to the rule; their numbers and success was thought to be due to the pack nature of their animal form. The Wolf King had been the only predator shape-shifter who successfully spread his people across the planet. At one time the Grigori had waged war against the werewolves, but a thousand years ago they realized that the Wolf King's people guarded against breaches within large cities.

The breach that killed her mother had happened when the Boston pack was at its weakest. The disaster last month in Hun-gary was a result of the Prince of Budapest dying. The world needed its guard dogs.

"Can we see its—his personal effects?" Elise asked.

The clothes were shredded by the impact. The cable sweater had been white, though it was difficult to tell now since it had been soaked with blood. It seemed the only nod to how cold the Boston winter was at night. Over the sweater had been a light-weight loose-knitted poncho. The wind would blow right through the holes—but then shape changers didn't seem to feel the cold the same way as humans. At least the wolves didn't.

"Gaucho," Theo read the clothing tab on the poncho. "Buenos Aires."

A cowboy shapeshifter? It would explain the boots and wide-brimmed hat. The sweater and poncho both seemed too luxurious for actual cattle work. The clothing line might be a fashion brand.

The wallet contained colorful paper currency. Elise wasn't sure if it was a lot of money even though the number "1000" was printed on the bills as it also had "pesos" written under the numbers, which might make them equal to one dollar or a thousand dollars. She wasn't sure which. It also had "Banco Central de la Republica Argentina."

Elise wasn't familiar with the shapeshifters of South America. Theo shook her head to the unasked question; she didn't know either.

"I'll call Central Office," Elise said, meaning Clarice. Their cousin would know who to call to get the information.

They scraped off Rick, dodging invitations to eat lunch with him, and split up to get their cars. They planned to backtrack to Alewife and stop at a small Greek restaurant near the train station. Elise had skipped breakfast and Theo hadn't eaten since early yesterday.

"Order lots," Theo had said when they split up. "Anything we don't eat can stay in my car since it's colder than hell. I can get Greek food when I'm in Bangor but when I'm out in the field, it's mostly burger and fries."

Arriving first, Elise ordered two Greek coffees, a lamb souvlaki plate, a moussaka plate, a side of both grape leaves and spinach pie, a pair of gyros, and two pieces of galaktoboureko to finish everything off.

The diner was a small place with giant murals of Greece painted on the walls that reminded Elise of the island that they trained to be Virtues on. It was a happy time for all of them. Sunshine. Blue seas. Pure white houses. The only living souls around them were other Grigori who were immune to their glamour. You could wear nothing but a smile if you wanted to and be safe and close and loving without fear.

When Theo arrived just as the coffee hit the table, the murals made her lose the bleak tightness around her eyes.

Elise called Clarice and let her know that they found out.

"Argentina?" Clarice said with surprise.

"That's what the money on the dead male says. I can't imagine anyone being in the United States very long and not have at least one American dollar in their wallet."

"Argentina?" Clarice repeated while typing on her keyboard. "That's a long way to go to pick a fight with a Power. Over five thousand miles—like a fifth of the planet. It's like crossing the Pacific to jump into an erupting volcano. Why would anyone do that?"

"I don't know," Elise said. "Let's start with identifying what type of shapeshifter that it might be."

"Okay," Clarice said. "Well, I got a line to the Buenos Aires Central Office and they're saying that it's probably one of the Aptenodytes."

"The . . . what?" Theo said.

"Aptenodytes," Clarice repeated. "I'm getting clarification because I don't recognize the name. According to Buenos Aires, Aptenodytes are . . . Oh, you've got to be kidding. That's a thing?"

"What's a thing?" Elise pulled the souvlaki meat from the skewer to build a sandwich with the pita-bread side.

"Swan maiden penguins!" Clarice cried. "They're like swan maidens but they're penguins. Several different types of penguins. They're strictly Southern Hemisphere so it's not surprising that we haven't heard of them. The name Aptenodytes is a composite of ancient Greek to mean 'without wings diver' because unlike traditional swan maidens, they can't fly. There are full colonies of Aptenodytes scattered all over the Southern Hemisphere. Oh, get this, it's rumored that they have a supreme leader—an emperor penguin."

"Are you serious or are you making a dad joke?" Theo sipped her Greek coffee. "This coffee is heavenly. It's just like the ones we would get during training."

"You're having Greek without me?" Clarice yelped.

"I'm sure there's a decent Greek place near Central," Theo said.

"Well, there's Kanella but it's always so crowded," Clarice complained.

"Penguins?" Elise repeated to make sure that she was understanding Clarice correctly.

"That's what Buenos Aires is telling me," Clarice said as the sound of her typing sped up, which probably meant that she was cross-referencing the text messages from Buenos Aires with her own database on magical creatures. "They're like selkies or swan maidens as they use a device—a feathered cloak in this case—to change shape. Without the cloak, they can't change into a bird. They're not like werewolves, pure magic taking different forms."

Elise really wished that Clarice would stop reminding her—accidently or on purpose, she couldn't tell which—that Jack Cabot was anything but a normal man.

Clarice continued, seemingly unaware of the pain that she was inflicting. "With the cloak—which apparently will be black and white feathers if you find it—the Aptenodytes turn into one type of penguin. Like the werewolves that can be different colors of wolves—the black wolves of Boston for example—each colony of Aptenodytes turn into different breeds of penguins. Buenos Aires is saying that you'll only find Aptenodytes where you would normally find penguins—so basically all along the bottom of the Southern Hemisphere."

There was a pause in the flow of information.

"So . . . is that a yes or no on that's what our dead shifter is?" Elise asked.

Clarice made a frustrated noise and started to type again. "Buenos Aires doesn't know why we would have any in Boston. They say that there's a colony near them—southern rockhoppers. The council of tribal elders has determined that the Aptenodytes are non-monsters—so the South American tribes typically ignore them."

God had given the Grigori the mission to kill all monsters to make up for the crimes of their angelic forefathers. The punishment wasn't for finding loopholes in God's orders to the angels to watch over his creation, the cross-species sex, or the resulting offspring, but for all the insanity that said offspring got into. While the Bible claimed that the sins of mankind triggered the Great Flood, it was because the Grigori children had gotten out of hand like an infestation of cockroaches with superpowers. God created the worldwide extinction event to create a clean slate. He saved all the pure humans that he could find—all six of them—and killed off most of the Grigori. He spared a handful that he thought would make good *obedient* monster hunters.

While humans had gotten a general "thou shall not kill" commandant long after the Flood—the Grigori had immediately been given a very detailed "thou shall not kill" order as if God was worried that they would slaughter all annoying life on the planet—like crocodiles, hippopotamuses, and sharks. The list contained certain threat levels to be met before a creature could be considered a monster.

"Non-monster" was a specific label. It meant that the creature wasn't a natural beast but also wasn't a threat to God's creation plan. It *could* be considered on the "thou shall not kill" list but only if it behaved itself. It was a flexible label that generally meant that the elders would discourage Virtues from actively hunting the creature but left it to the Virtues' discretion if they deemed it necessary to kill any number of them.

Like Clarice and Buenos Aires both said—it wouldn't make sense for such a "harmless" creature to travel a fifth of the planet to ambush a Power.

"Argentina doesn't have any other shapeshifters?" Theo said. "What about werewolves?"

"I'm already asking." Clarice fell silent as she typed the exchange. "Huh. Okay. So, the 'don't know why you would have any in Boston' didn't mean 'it's unlikely that the dead male is one of our Aptenodytes.' It meant 'we don't know how many are in Boston and we don't know why they went there.' The Buenos Aires Marquis was the one that noticed the overnight disappearance of the entire population of the local Aptenodytes. The werewolves paired up with the Grigori to investigate—probably so they wouldn't get blamed for any mass carnage. The entire colony had disappeared. There were some signs of violence but no clue as to what had happened."

An entire flock of shape-changing non-monsters?

"Shit," Elise whispered.

Cabot's flurry of texts suddenly felt ominous.

She swiped on her phone and pulled up his text messages.

Cabot had texted: "Seth has spotted a monster at aquarium. Joshua and classmates are investigating. Joshua said something about a penguin. Joshua won't answer phone. Can you make sure he and the other kids are okay?"

14: JOSHUA

Joshua and the Goths went through the foyer that operated as an airlock to the aquarium. Once into the main building, they passed a fake mangrove biome that contained a shallow pool full of manta rays. Signs explained that visitors could carefully touch the fish. The wolf wanted to stop and play with the manta rays. Joshua sighed and muscled them away from the petting exhibit.

Beyond the manta rays was a big dimly lit space. Right in front of them was the penguin exhibit, looking exactly as he remembered in his dream. The big pool of water, its bottom painted tropical blue. The craggy rocks that formed artfully styled islands so the birds could easily scramble up and down them. Dozens of knee-high black-and-white birds.

According to the website, the aquarium had fifty African penguins of the kind nicknamed Jackass because of their call. They were the source of a loud braying noise that echoed through the dim exhibit area. There was also a flock of rockhoppers, but they were a quieter species of penguins.

On the far side of the exhibit, a massive round aquarium stood, three or four stories tall. A ramp spiraled up the side of the tank. To the left there seemed to be another area that could be explored before heading upward. The skeleton of a killer whale hung from the ceiling, almost as if to menace the poor penguins with their natural predator.

As they walked toward the exhibit, Joshua wrinkled his nose

against the barrage of odors: salt water, fresh fish, and something he couldn't identify but suspected was wet bird.

"Oh, that stinks," he said.

"Yeah, I know." Tal led the way to the penguins. "It's another reason I don't like the aquarium. Oh, it's feeding time. With your nose, you're probably even smelling the sardines or herrings that they use as food."

The floor was cantilevered out over the pool so that the rocks were only a few feet down and out. A handful of penguins were gliding through the water—surprisingly graceful. Most of the African birds, however, were up on the rocks, patiently waiting to be fed. A young woman in a black wetsuit stood in the water. She held a purple plastic basket filled with finger-sized fish. She fed one penguin at a time, fish by fish. From time to time, she would pause to make notes on a clipboard. The penguins seemed incredibly docile, waiting patiently on the rocks for her to feed them. Only one or two would impatiently jockey in close for a fish, crowding out the current bird being fed. A fish or two placated the hungry bird and the woman would return to feeding the original penguin.

There was a low glass barrier that kept the African species separate from the fifteen Argentinian rockhoppers. Somehow one had managed to invade the African enclosure and was impatiently trying to be fed early. For some reason the woman feeding the penguins didn't notice that the bird she was feeding was in the wrong area.

The pushy rockhopper glanced up as they walked in. It saw Vijay and seemed to wave. Then it spotted Joshua. It waddled away from the pack, hopping from rock to rock to get as close to the retaining wall as it could.

"Hey! Kid! Over here!" The penguin repeated the same line it used in his dream.

"Oh God, it actually talks," Allie murmured.

"Why are you so surprised?" Ottilie whispered. "I'm not surprised."

"My life has been much more grounded in the mundane than yours," Allie whispered. "I can't tell if there's anything odd about that penguin—other than it's talking. It *looks* like all the other rockhoppers."

"It's not a werewolf," Ottilie whispered. "It's not connected to a source, so it can't radiate magic. What little is leaking off is from a magical item—probably its feathered cloak."

"Hey! Wolf boy!" The penguin flapped its arms once it got as close to them as possible on the rocks. It shouted just like it had in Joshua's dream. "Hey! Are you blind or deaf or both?"

"Shh! Shh! Shh!" Joshua tried to get the penguin to stop talking so loudly. He didn't want to get the aquarium's staff involved.

The woman feeding the penguins didn't seem surprised that one of her birds had suddenly started talking. Did that mean that the birds all talked? No, she just hadn't noticed that the gravelly voice was coming from the penguin. Maybe it was some kind of glamour that kept humans from noticing how odd the beast was. The woman seemed to be focused on climbing out of the pool, apparently done for the day.

"You're the new puppy? Right?" The penguin again repeated what it had said in Joshua's dream. "There are only three black wolves on the planet and you're too short to be the Thane. It means you're either the prince or his brother. Everyone knows that the prince is still in New York City. It stands to reason that you're the one that she told me about. The new one."

This time Joshua knew that "she" was Marie Antionette. The Goths were wide-eyed and silent, apparently letting him deal with the possibly dangerous monster.

"Yes, I'm the new one," he said. "I'm Joshua. My brother Seth is the Prince of Boston. Who are you?"

"I'm Manuel Alvarez," the penguin raised one wing in greeting. "You can call me Mannie."

"What are you?" Joshua asked.

"I'm a penguin!" Mannie squawked out Spanish curse words. *"No te hagas el pelotudo! Sos un bolundo!"*

"Okay! I got it." In Joshua's dream, he'd been on the school field trip, it had been snowing heavily outside, and he'd been alone. Was this going to be the same conversation or had he changed it by not waiting for the fieldtrip? "I'm a wolf. You're a penguin. What do you want?"

"Good! I want to hire you."

"Hire me?"

"Hire! Employ. Engage. Retain," The penguin listed synonyms—again—in the same order and same inflection followed by the same insult. "Geez, were you dropped on your head as a kid?"

Apparently, the change in day did not affect the outcome. Fate was a terrifying thing.

"Hire me to do what?" Joshua said. "I'm just a normal teenager that became a wolf a month ago. I'm not very good at being a wolf. What do you want me to do?"

"I had something very important stolen from me," Mannie said. "A very powerful, very evil being came to my home. Took everything from me. I followed him here to this place."

"The aquarium?" Joshua asked.

"No!" Mannie shouted. "Boston! *Sos un bolundo!* I'm from Buenos Aires." And then as if the penguin thought that Joshua might not recognize the city added, "Argentina! South America! I have come thousands of kilometers. A quarter of the way around the world! Tracking him here had been simple, but to find him within this city? I decided to lay low, buy some information, find out who I could trust. Her Majesty happened to come by. I knew that she would not betray me, so I asked her if she knew of someone that could help me. She said that you live with..."

The wolf glanced up, growling loudly. All the Goths skittered quickly to the other side of the exhibit.

"What the hell?" Tal asked.

For a moment Joshua wasn't sure what was wrong. The wolf was staring toward the ramp that spiraled up the side of a giant fish tank. From where they stood, they could see the fish swimming through the bright blue waters. But he realized that there was a person standing on the ramp. A little gray-haired woman. She cackled and waved. Enyo!

"Too early for popcorn," Enyo called. "Too cold for soda. I brought Sno-caps."

Enyo liked to eat popcorn while watching someone fight to the death. Joshua had a bad feeling about who was going to be involved in the upcoming battle.

"Something bad is going to happen," Joshua told the Goths. "We need to get out of here."

"Oh shit!" Ji Su whispered, whipping around to look behind them. "Something is coming!"

Tal and Vijay backed up, looking terrified, staring toward the manta ray petting exhibit.

"They found me!" Mannie squawked and dove into the water.

"Is there another way out?" Joshua asked.

"No," Tal whispered.

A sign behind them pointed up the ramp toward MORE EXHIB-ITS. A second arrow pointed the opposite direction, through a set of glass doors. It read FUR SEALS. SEA LIONS.

"I'll distract...whatever it is." Joshua waved in the direction of the side exit. "I'll head out to the seals."

"Quick, up the ramp!" Ottilie ordered.

While the others hurried to the upper floors, Joshua drifted toward the glass doors.

A big, dangerous-looking man walked into the main room. He seemed vaguely familiar. Joshua had seen him before—somewhere. While the aquarium was dimly lit, the man seemed wrapped in darkness that shifted restlessly. He wore a tight white T-shirt that proclaimed BELL BOOK & CANDLE. Through the thin white fabric, Joshua could see that the man had a complicated tattoo on his right shoulder, but a long thin wound ran through it, leaking blood.

Wait. Tattoo? Joshua recognized the man: he'd been at Sioux Zee's tattoo shop. Shortly after Halloween, the man had been in the process of getting a protective rune permanently inked onto his shoulder. Sioux Zee had been copying the rune from the magical book protected by Dorothy. What had been the man's name?

The man made a deep growling sound that vibrated against Joshua like a big tractor engine.

Brutus. His name was Brutus—and it fit him well. What had Winnie said about him?

"Heaven and hell, they're just one quantum state away, two or three tissues up or down, and we merely have to change particle state to move to that existence—to that tissue. Most people around us are only aware of the tissue, but a handful like Brutus and I can see a layer over.... Brutus is open enough to see what most people can't, which makes him valuable as an employee for certain businesses, but it also makes him vulnerable. The runes close him off to anything that could take him over."

Did the bleeding wound mean that the protective runes were no longer active?

At Sioux Zee's tattoo parlor, there had been nothing spooky or odd about the man even though he tried to run Joshua off. Brutus now had a presence about him, vaguely like what Seth could generate when he was trying to be firm. But it was differ-ent: darker, stormier—and perhaps stronger.

Joshua backed up a little faster. He didn't want to wolf out in public. That would be bad.

As the man walked toward the penguin enclosure, dozens of eyes opened on his arms, cheeks, and forehead.

Brutus was not Brutus any longer.

Was he like Vijay and possessed by something less benign than Marie Antoinette? Or was not-Brutus like the monstrous pigs created by the Wickers' breach? Could Brutus be saved, or did he need to be killed before he transformed others?

Joshua didn't know.

If Brutus was the latter, though, he needed to be stopped before he hit the enclosure with seventy trapped penguins.

"Hey!" Joshua yelled to attract the man's attention.

One eye on Brutus's right arm glanced toward Joshua and then all the eyes turned toward him.

That got his attention, Joshua thought. *Great?*

There was a standard operating procedure when dealing with a bully. The first was to attempt to de-escalate. Stand up as tall as possible—on a chair if needed—and maintain fearless eye contact.

Joshua considered the multitude of eyes staring at him and wasn't sure which he should be maintaining contact with.

Step two was to attempt to verbally back the bully down, pointing out things like possible teacher interference, school discipline, and Joshua's known ability to wipe the floor with most people his own age.

"Um, so, you know, someone has probably called the police already." Joshua slid sideways, looking for something to stand on while trying to maintain eye contact. "You might not be aware of this, but I'm a werewolf. It means I'm very strong."

Brutus stalked toward him, all eyes staring at Joshua. The darkness deepened and gathered, forming into thick black tentacles. The man made a weird, deep rumbling noise—bellows, clicks, and snaps in a language that didn't sound like humans should be speaking it. It sounded more like whale song. There was a squishing noise as he walked forward, generating black water with every step.

No, talking isn't going to work.

Step three was running. Joshua backed up to the glass doors that led to the fur seals and sea lions. He went slowly enough that the Brutus monster would definitely follow him and not head after the Goths, but fast enough to stay ahead of the man.

There were two sets of doors, forming an airlock. The reason became obvious as he emerged out of the second set to an icy cold outdoor area, barely enclosed by a transparent overhang and half windows that seemed to be there just to block crosswinds. Just beyond the windows were docks with boats tied off and the shifting water of the Inner Harbor.

Brutus smashed through the doors instead of opening them, showering glass onto the ramp downward.

The docklike walkway sloped downward and turned a corner to another big pool, filled with seals. For a moment it looked like a literal dead end.

A tentacle hit Joshua hard, sending him crashing through a window—out of the aquarium.

Let there be land! I don't want to fight this thing in the water! Joshua hit a wooden deck, inches from the dark waters of the harbor.

The tentacles of darkness reached through the broken window for Joshua. They stretched out thirty feet in front of Brutus as he stalked forward with his squishy walk. Ink-black water pooled on the floor behind the man.

How the hell did you grapple a squid—or whatever this guy was? Did tentacles give the same kind of leverage as arms did? Another one flashed toward Joshua. He caught hold of it with his left hand. It was cold and slimy and boneless.

The first throw in a fight was always the easiest. The bully never expected it. Joshua reached higher up the limb with his right hand, grabbed hold, and then spun as he yanked forward, dropping down to put all that leverage into a throw. At the last moment, he let go, allowing momentum to take the creature.

The monster hadn't expected to be thrown.

It went sailing through the air, black tentacles flailing. It splashed down into the harbor.

Joshua stared at the shifting water. Was that it? Was the fight ended? That seemed too easy.

Black tentacles gripped the edge of the dock.

Nope, wasn't going to be that easy. The advantage of surprise was gone.

What now? *I should...I should...*

Brutus pulled himself onto the dock by the black tentacles. The dozens of eyes scanned the area and locked on Joshua. The man-beast made the weird whale-song noise, but it definitely sounded pissed off.

I should run.

Joshua dodged a second and third slap by the black tentacles and took off running, around the sea lion pool, thinking furiously. He couldn't just run away—not if the monster was breach-borne. If it started to bite people, it would turn them into monsters.

He could hear Brutus squishing and roaring and clicking behind him. He glanced back at Brutus, who was following in odd rushes and pauses. The tentacles trailed behind, waving as if riding an invisible current. Was the man a breach-borne monster? The ruined protective spell seemed to suggest it was some kind of spirit.

Joshua wasn't sure that he could fight the actual monster. The Goths had warned him that spirits knew that wolves couldn't hurt them, just the medium that they were residing in. Brutus might be big and ugly but he was friends with Winnie and Sioux Zee. He'd got the protective rune tattooed onto his shoulder in an attempt to prevent this kind of possession. The real Brutus didn't want to fight a werewolf any more than Joshua wanted to fight the monster.

But if he was wrong about that and Brutus was a breach-borne creature—then accidently running into a group of people with Brutus chasing him was bad.

Joshua went up a short flight of stairs and through another set of glass doors. He was back in the penguin room.

"Damn!" Joshua cried. He'd not planned an escape route. He was running blind. "This is bad. What do I do? Run in circles?"

He couldn't flee the monster. If he lost the creature, it could blunder into the Goths or an incoming bunch of school kids on their field trips or the sales people at the gift shop. None of those people could fight it. He was the standing army for the entire city. He had no choice—he was going to have to make a stand. But where?

Not out by the docks where he could end up in the water.

Here was as good as any place.

Joshua spun and charged toward Brutus. All the tentacles whipped forward, grabbing at him. He dodged right and left, ducking them without thought, focusing tight on the man. Just a man. Bigger than the kids on the football team but not by much.

He collided hard with the man just as Brutus transferred all his weight onto his right foot. With his hand on Brutus's chest, Joshua took him through a *sumi otoshi* throw. He slammed the man hard onto the ground. He didn't dare go for the pin or a sleeper hold as the tentacles flashed toward him.

Joshua leapt clear. The wolf growled fiercely, pushing to be let out. There was a siren wailing in the distance, drawing closer.

"No. Not now!" Joshua snarled at his inner self. "Not with the police coming! I don't want to be shot again!"

The police wouldn't have silver bullets—probably—but it would still hurt a lot to get shot.

One of the tentacles tried to snake around Joshua even as Brutus stumbled to his feet. Joshua dodged to the side, grabbed the black snakelike limb with both hands, and slammed Brutus back to the ground again. Maybe if he could knock Brutus unconscious, the monster would be harmless. Maybe.

Suddenly, he lost control of the wolf. Without warning, he was on four legs.

"Stupid wolf!" Joshua shouted. "What if someone sees us?"

At least he was only the size of a dog—albeit a very large one. Without hands, though, Joshua wasn't sure how he was going to safely fight Brutus.

"No biting," he growled to his wolf. "We can't turn him into a feral."

The wolf figured that "no biting" only applied to Brutus and snapped down on one of the black tentacles.

"Mhat!" Joshua gave a muffled yelp of surprise. The blackness tasted like squid. It filled his mouth with an oddly sweet, fishy flavor. He was never going to be able to eat calamari again. "Mo! Mo! Mot im my mowth!"

The wolf ignored him and shook its head. It tore off the tentacle, much to Joshua's surprise.

Oh, that's a thing! If he just tore all the tentacles off, the man would be much easier to pin.

The siren was getting closer. Joshua needed to deal with Brutus before the police arrived.

The wolf tossed the severed limb aside and bit down on another one. The other tentacles, though, suddenly wrapped around the wolf's body, cocooning it.

As the wolf struggled and snarled, Brutus got to his feet. All of his many, many eyes were narrowed with anger—glaring at Joshua. The wolf doubled in size, making Brutus stagger under the sudden increase of weight.

The siren wailed louder, closing in fast. Joshua needed to get back to being a human before the police arrived. He struggled to break free.

Then suddenly he was standing on the rocks in the penguin enclosure, a hundred feet away from the monster.

"What the hell?" Joshua whispered, surprised and confused. How did he get free?

The black tentacles opened, and the many eyes peered at the empty coils as if confounded by the wolf's sudden disappearance.

Joshua struggled to shift back to human. He couldn't fight as a wolf and the police would be arriving soon. "We need to be human, idiot! Human!"

The monster's many eyes scanned the area. One of the eyes spotted the wolf and the rest turned to look at him.

"Human! Human-human-human!" Joshua backed up.

Elise came through the door, shouting scripture as she pulled her twin daggers. "Blessed be the Lord my strength which teacheth my hands to war, and my fingers to fight. My goodness, and my fortress; my high tower, and my deliverer; my shield, and he in whom I trust; who subdueth my people under me."

She slashed at the black tentacles as they attempted to coil about her. The tips of her daggers left glowing lines in the air, forming a symbol that gleamed brightly. "Bow thy heavens, O Lord, and come down: touch the mountains, and they shall smoke! Cast forth lightning, and scatter them: shoot out thine arrows, and destroy them! Send thine hand from above; rid me, and deliver me out of great waters, from the hand of strange children!"

The symbol flashed. The tentacles vanished. Brutus fell to the ground unconscious.

She raised her right dagger high over Brutus's body.

The wolf realized the danger first. Joshua yelped in surprise as he suddenly collided with Elise to force her back. Only then did Joshua realize that the woman intended to kill Brutus.

15: ELISE

Elise scrambled to her feet, swearing softly at the mess the day had devolved into. Francis was missing. An entire flock of were-penguins *could* be in the city for reasons unknown. Something inhuman was definitely dead at the morgue—killed chasing after Francis's vanished driver. A powerful spirit showed up at the aquarium and picked a fight with a ten-foot-tall werewolf. God knew what else was at the aquarium.

At least there didn't seem to be any humans in the building—probably because of the terrifying aura of the massive wolf.

"Elise!" the elephant-sized black wolf cried in Joshua's voice. "No, no, don't kill him! I know he was a monster a minute ago, but it's not his fault! At least, I don't think it's his fault. He's friends with Winnie, so he's probably not a bad guy. His name is Brutus."

Theo had her pistol out and it was probably loaded with silver.

Elise sheathed her daggers. "Theo, put your gun away. The wolf is safe even though he's scary to look at."

"Me? Scary to look at?" Joshua looked down at his giant paws. "Oh. Yeah. I'm monster-sized again."

Theo blew out her breath but holstered her pistol. "Is this your Thane?"

"No," Elise said. "This is the new puppy."

"That's a puppy?" Theo said. "Shit. And you're sleeping with a Thane?"

173

Elise colored. "We haven't got to the 'sleeping' stage yet. We haven't ironed out my knee-jerk reactions to certain . . . triggers."

Theo laughed.

Elise did not want to be discussing her love life at this time.

Joshua tilted his head as he gazed down at Theo. "Who is this?"

"This is my cousin Theodosia," Elise said. "She's also a Virtue. Her territory is Maine and points north."

Theo lifted a hand in greeting. "Call me Theo."

"Nice to meet you!" Joshua sat and lifted a giant paw. "I'm Joshua."

"Can you do something about your size?" Elise asked Joshua. She didn't want anyone walking in and freaking out over the giant wolf. At normal size Joshua could pass as a large dangerous-looking dog.

"I'm trying." The wolf sat on its haunches and closed its eyes. He made a mediative "Omm" noise.

"Does that help?" Theo asked.

"Maybe." The wolf oscillated between huge and tiny.

"Oh, that's sad," Theo commented on Joshua's inability to stabilize on one size.

"He's a puppy," Elise said.

The wolf managed to stay at puppy-size with only its big paws suggesting that it would grow—rapidly at certain occasions—to something bigger than a beagle. "I'm a little too freaked out to go back to human, I think. The wolf doesn't want to give up control."

"Brutus what?" Elise knelt to examine the unconscious man. "Brutus" might be a nickname as he was a big, ugly man obviously into bodybuilding and looking tough.

"I don't know," Joshua said. "I scared him at Sioux Zee's tattoo place, so he left without introducing himself."

Brutus had a protective rune tattooed onto his shoulder. It looked like Sioux Zee's artwork. Since the Wise Woman wouldn't have worked on someone that she didn't trust completely, it meant that the man might be an innocent victim. There was a long, thin cut through the protective tattoo. The wound wasn't fresh—possibly days old—uncleaned, unbandaged, and slightly infected. It looked deliberate, as if someone meant to ruin the magic of the rune and render the man vulnerable to possession. It could mean that the spirit might have an accomplice.

Elise scanned the area. "Was Brutus alone?"

The penguins broke into donkeylike braying.

The puppy trotted to the edge of the tank to look into it. "I'm not sure. I was talking to the penguin when Enyo showed up with Sno-caps."

Enyo was a known harbinger of trouble; the ancient being liked to watch while people died. She had been in Boston when Elise's mother was killed. Elise wasn't surprised to learn that Enyo was on hand—not with Francis somewhere in the area.

"You were talking to who?" Elise said, sure she misheard the first part of the sentence.

"Talking to what?" Theo said, having heard better.

Joshua moved to another section of the exhibit to scan the birds. "Manuel Alvarez. Mannie for short. He's a southern rock-hopper penguin from Argentina."

Elise glanced at Theo. Another South American shapeshifter.

"Yeah, tell us more about this penguin," Theo said.

Joshua explained that he had had a dream about going on a field trip and one of the penguins talking to him. When he got to school, he discovered that Blackridge indeed had an outing planned. When he found out that the other kids were heading to the aquarium to do an intervention, he had tagged along in case said penguin was dangerous. It turned out the missing student had been taken over by the ghost of Marie Antoinette, who was selling information about Joshua to the shapeshifter to fund Christmas presents for the baker she was in love with.

"There has to be something in the water," Theo muttered. "We don't have these kinds of problems in Bangor."

"I believe it," Joshua said. "Ji Su said that none of my family would go near the ocean. That one tentacle—leg—whatever—that I tore off, it tasted like squid. I used to love calamari. I don't think I could eat it now without having PTSD."

Theo moved to scan the penguins. "None of these are shape-shifters."

"Maybe Mannie ran away," Joshua said. "He said something like 'they found me' and jumped in the water."

They. A flock of Argentina shapeshifters or some other organization?

"The police are here." Theo produced smelling salts from one her coat pockets and tossed it to Elise. "I'll deal with them since you know the area better. Go chase the lead on this Brutus."

Theo strode off, pulling her long coat over her holster as she moved to intercept the incoming police.

It left Elise with the problem of wrangling the big brute of a man and a hyperactive wolf puppy. Grigori were stronger than average humans, but she wasn't going to be able to carry them both. Elise didn't want to leave Joshua with Theo. The puppy wasn't in full control of his wolf and Theo was a loose cannon. It was hard to tell which one was more dangerous. The two together was a bad mix.

Brutus was wearing a T-shirt from Bell Book & Candle, a botanica in Salem. The front of the store was typical New Age bullshit of crystals and essential oils and candles. It also sold a lot of "Witches of Salem" souvenir items to tourists. In the back were the true magical items. Had he been possessed at the shop?

Elise cracked open the smelling salts and waved it under Brutus's nose, hoping to rouse him.

He jerked awake. "What? Oh! Hello, beautiful! Who are you—oh shit, you're a Virtue! Please don't kill me. Whatever I did, I'm sorry! I'll never do it again—whatever it was."

"What's your name?" Elise said.

"Brutus Raymond Clay of the West Virginia Clays. I work at Bell Book and Candle in Salem."

"What day is it?" Elise said.

"Friday," Brutus said with hesitation. "I should be at work. I was at work..."

Once a spirit took the helm, a medium lost all awareness of what their body was doing. Brutus was missing four days or more, depending on which Friday he thought it was.

"Come on." Elise tugged on him to get up.

The puppy pranced back and forth, unsure what to do next. "I should... I should... look around for the others. The Goths were here when the fight started. I don't know if they got away safely."

"The kids that were with you left." Elise scooped up the puppy and then marched Brutus out of the aquarium by the collar. She was glad to see that her Jeep was sitting where she left it illegally parked. Theo's Jeep sat directly behind hers. "I didn't know that there was a Grigori going to school with you. She put in a panic call to Central. She was herding the other kids back to school. They were on the subway when Central hung up on her."

"Oh! That's good!" The puppy squirmed slightly in her hold. "I should look around for Mannie."

"No. You're coming with me." Elise was carrying him because she knew that he wouldn't hurt her. If she put him down, he could go back to monster size just to keep her from manhandling him.

"I don't know if I should leave without talking to Mannie. I had that frog dream and if I'd been able to figure it all out, I could have stopped the Wickers before they tried to kidnap Winnie and killed those people and—"

"You're coming with me," Elise repeated as she opened the front passenger door of her Jeep. Because he was starting to whimper and squirm, she added, "We'll pick up some hamburgers. I know where the best ones in Boston are."

"No fair!" Joshua cried as the puppy leapt eagerly to the passenger seat and wagged its tail.

They put in a pickup order with Boston Burger Company, which was vaguely on the way to Blackridge. (There was an annoying lack of true drive-through restaurants until one hit the far-flung suburbs of Boston.) Joshua—still a puppy—picked out a thing called the Kitchen Sink, which had fried egg, ham, bacon, sauteed peppers, mushrooms, onions, and cheddar, provolone, and American cheese. It sounded like a glorious mess to eat—which probably meant that the wolf had influenced the selection.

"Stupid wolf," he grumbled while inhaling the hamburger. "This is just my second day at school! I've missed half the day already."

It probably would be better not to drag a werewolf puppy to Bell Book & Candle. There was no telling what they might find there. With Theo backing her up, Elise didn't need werewolves. She couldn't go to Decker's, not with Brutus in the car. Nor could she drop a wolf puppy at Blackridge.

So, she did her best at comforting Joshua.

"It will be fine," she crooned while petting the puppy's head like she'd seen Decker do. "Just walk in like you own the place—because you do. No one is going to say 'Boo' to you. They don't want to get fired. The Tatterskeins built the school so their kids would get kid-glove treatment. They fire anyone that gives the kids a hard time. They keep the teachers that understand that. They get rid of any that think that all the kids should be treated the same. Everything will be fine."

"You really think so?" Joshua said.

"I know so. I went to Blackridge, kindergarten to sixth grade. There weren't any younglings in my year, but everyone knew that the teachers weren't allowed to even raise their voices to the Tatterskeins' kids."

She pulled into Blackridge's service entrance by the cafeteria. "Go around this corner and you'll be at the front door. You can do this."

The puppy stared up at her for a long moment.

She really hoped her pep talk worked because she didn't know how else to handle the situation.

"Okay," Joshua finally said. "I can do this. I just need to be human." The puppy squeezed shut its eyes. "Come on. It's lunchtime. Everyone should be in the cafeteria. We can see everyone is okay."

The puppy shook itself and became a boy. "Thanks, Elise. Be careful. Brutus—no hard feelings?"

"No hard feelings," Brutus said, sounding like he was still scared silly of the boy.

Salem was a quaint little civilized New England town—if you ignored its history. The streets were wide and lined with elegant century-old brick buildings. In sections it was as if time had stopped sometime in the late 1800s with a sprinkling of even older houses from the 1700s. In an old, converted church was the Salem Witch Museum dedicated to the 1692 witch trials. The irony of it all was that the witch trials had been orchestrated by the Monkshood Coven to weed out anyone who was resistant to their Persuasion ability.

Bell Book & Candle was a botanica located a few blocks from the museum, run by the descendants of the "witches" who survived the purge. To outsiders, it would seem like the store had a multiple personality disorder. The window decorations all screamed tourist trap, advertising "witch souvenirs." The displays by the front door were postcards, refrigerator magnets, artsy brooms, pointed witch hats, witch-themed T-shirts, soy candles with scents named "Black Cat" and "Autumn Equinox," and even a full range of "Harry Potter wands." The shirts had sayings like DON'T MAKE ME FLIP MY WITCH SWITCH, SALEM LOCAL WITCHES UNION, and SALEM 1692, THEY MISSED ONE. (Elise had never seen a real witch wearing one of these as they knew that there were real angels still hunting down dangerous witches.)

Beyond the front entrance area, the store's personality started to splinter. On the right wall were things made of rock. Little bins of polished pebbles. Shelves of statues and orbs made from semi-precious stones. Display cases of affordable fossils: trilobites, ammonites, cephalopods, megalodon teeth. Locked cases of gemstones, precious stones, museum quality fossils.

To the left were "safe" ritual items. Tarot cards. Crystal Balls. Tibetan singing bowls. Statues of Buddha and Santa Muerte. Prayer candles. Anointing and conjure oils. Bundles of sage for smudging. Herbs like rose buds, tonka beans, lavender flowers, patchouli, and nettle. Incense sticks, cones, and powder. The latter section formed a flood of scents that washed over Elsie the moment she pushed open the front door. A bell hung over it jingled, alerting the salesclerks that they had a new customer.

The store's music system was playing meditation music that sounded like random harmonizing chords and notes played so slowly that they formed no tune. Despite the relaxing atmosphere that the soundtrack was attempting to create, the shop was a place where Elise never had felt comfortable in.

It wasn't surprising that in the middle of a freezing cold, off-tourist-season workday there was only one customer in the front room, mulling over the custom handmade (but still completely non-magical) wands. A young woman, in a long black dress and witch hat, had been organizing the T-shirts.

"He says he's Slytherin," the customer was saying to the salesclerk as she eyed one of the wands closely. "I looked it up. It concerns me that he picked the house that all the villains come from."

"They're not all villains." The salesclerk shifted T-shirts, apparently putting them in size order. She glanced toward the door where Elise entered. "Welcome to Bell Book and..."

She saw Brutus behind Elise and came to a full terrified stop.

"Hi, Samantha." Brutus waved sheepishly at the salesclerk.

Samantha started to back toward the door into the area where the "real" merchandise was stored.

"It's okay," Elise called after her. It didn't stop the salesclerk but drew the attention of the customer looking at wands. The woman might not know who fictional villains were, but she picked up that something was amiss.

While there was no rule against telling normal people that

all the supernatural myths and legends were mostly true, it was never an easy or simple thing to do. Elise moved away from the door, so the customer had an escape path, and then ignored her to stay focused on the slowly retreating salesclerk.

"Is Hank here?" Elise followed after Samantha with Brutus drifting in her wake. Hank Whitebrow was part of the Whitebrow dynasty that ruled over New England occultists after his grandfather married the Wise Woman, Sioux Zee. Hank's dad had bought out the failing tourist trap and made it a hub for all that believed in the supernatural and old religions. Hank had taken over the shop just before Elise went to Greece.

"I'll get him!" Samantha backed through a door labeled STAFF ONLY. There was a ward printed under the sign. It blended into the store's general decoration theme but unlike the many posters on the wall, this one had power behind it. It was geared to the most common monsters like skitter scratches and growlings. It wouldn't have kept out whatever had possessed Brutus. "Hank! Brutus is back! And he's not alone!"

Hank's spirit guide suddenly was in front of Elise, a massive ghost-tree presence that was not happy. It filled the store, its leafy head brushing against the ceiling. Its branches reached for her.

"Oh shit!" Brutus bounced back, away from the guide.

Elise pulled her daggers. "Whoever dwells in the shelter of the Most High will rest in the shadow of the Almighty. I will say of the Lord, 'He is my refuge and my fortress, my God, in whom I trust.' Amen."

The tree spirit howled in a voice of wind blowing through dead branches and twigs scratching against glass.

"Phinehas!" Hank shouted as he appeared in the doorway. "It's fine! She's a Virtue!"

There was the jingle of the bell over the door as the customer escaped.

"Damn," Hank muttered softly. "We really need every sale we can get this month."

Hank was a tall man whose look leaned hard into his Native American bloodline. His black hair was gathered into a long braid, and he wore a suede leather jacket over his charcoal gray Iroquois flag T-shirt. He'd abandoned his typical fringed moccasin boots today for sturdy hiking boots.

"Are you okay?" Hank asked Brutus.

"Battered, bruised, confused—but I'm in one piece and all alone in my skin." Brutus pulled aside his torn collar to show off the ruined ward tattoo. "Your granny is going to have to do my other shoulder now."

"Go wash up and get some sleep—you look like you were dragged through hell." Hank gave Brutus a push toward the front door.

Elise waited until they were alone before saying, "Why didn't you give Central a heads-up when . . . whatever happened went down?"

"I wasn't here." Hank led the way through the staff door to the back area.

His spirit guide, Phinehas, followed grumbling and complaining like a restless wind through winter trees. It had to fold itself nearly in half to shoulder through the door. Elise drifted behind the two, wanting to stay out of reach of the spirit.

There were small rooms for tarot card readings and seances on either side of the short hallway. They stood with doors open, empty and dark. They were dressed for outsiders in lush but threadworn mystical elegance, heavy on red velvet and gold gilding.

"I'd gone on a cruise," Hank explained. "I was in Santo Domingo when Yvette texted me what happened. What with the blizzard, all the flights to Boston were sold out. I just got back late last night. I needed to take inventory before calling Central since it was really too late to be timely."

Elise winced as "inventory" meant that something other than Brutus had gone missing. The store was normally filled to the brim with exotic and dangerous items. "Who is Yvette?"

"My manager," Hank shook his head. "Whiz at the books but doesn't fully believe all 'this mumbo-jumbo' that we deal in. She's the ying to Brutus' yang. She's so nonsensitive that you could hand her the holy grail, and she would think that it's a cheap cup."

"So, she doesn't know about the Grigori to call it in," Elise guessed.

"Exactly," Hank said. "And I really didn't want a Virtue hunting down my security guard. It wouldn't have been the first time Brutus got nabbed by a stray ghost—it's why he's warded—was warded. The thing is—since Yvette is nonsensitive and nonbeliever, she downplayed what had happened. To be fair, she thought that Brutus 'played hooky again' at the worst possible time. She didn't understand that when he disappears it's always against his will. I didn't realize how bad the attack was until I saw the tapes from the security cameras."

The hallway opened into the back room where the more exotic but "fairly" harmless items were displayed in locked glass cases. *Had been displayed.* All the glass had been smashed.

"God Almighty," Elise whispered as she saw that even the steel vault door had been ripped open.

"Yeah, we were pretty much cleaned out." Hank led the way into the vault.

The big walk-in vault was lined with individually locked cabinets. Normally each cabinet held something too dangerous for the general public to even know it existed. It looked like a madman with an axe—or a beast with many giant tentacles—had come through the area. The doors had been ripped from their frames.

Hank waved a hand toward his offices by the back door. "They dropped some of the items on their way out—not much—but enough that I can't just give Central our entire inventory list. So far, the most dangerous things missing are some death-tipped arrows and a soul-eater sword."

"Why is this the first time I'm hearing that you had those in stock?" Elise asked. Both were weapons that could kill just about anything it hit: werewolf, Virtue, and possibly a Power.

"You were in New York fighting Wickers when they came in," Hank said. "Then I left for my sixteen-night repositioning cruise, leaving from Marseille, France, and ending at the Dominican Republic. What can I say? Halloween normally closes our busy season. Tourists don't like Salem's snow and Christmas shoppers aren't usually looking for spooky T-shirts. Our best sellers for December are mistletoe and pine-scented candles. I thought I could take off a couple of weeks."

Hank was explaining too much—like he had something to hide. Elise hoped that the entire list wouldn't contain things that she should have confiscated. Hank's dad had a bad habit of thinking that the Grigori had no right to destroy the dangerous magical items that came his way. When she was little, her mother used Elise to make surprise checks of the store's stock. She would send Elise in ahead to create a distraction and then come in like an avenging angel, swooping straight to the unguarded vault. It only worked because Elise grew so much between each raid that the staff didn't recognize her until too late. Elise hated it; she felt that her mother was a bit of a jerk for staging the raids.

Elise had thought that the change in store ownership made the need for surprise inspections unnecessary. Hank had been extremely cooperative, especially after the Tatterskein massacre made Boston a much more dangerous place. He had called Elise several times in the past three years to turn over things too deadly to sell. Most recently, it had been a soul talisman. In Grigori hands, a Virtue could operate as a Power for a short period of time. In the wrong hands, though, it could be dangerous. She'd stashed it away at her family's depot of magical items in Watertown. It was heavily warded. Nothing but angelic beings could enter the depot—not even Decker. She'd destroyed everything else that Hank had given her: burned it to fine ash and scattered those in multiple points.

"If you weren't here, who was?" Elise asked to steer away from their past conflicts. "Did anyone see what happened?"

"Just Sammy," Hank said. "It was right after we opened. Yvette was late because there had been an accident on her route to work. One of our regular customers came in just as the doors were unlocked. He went straight to Brutus and asked to see something in the back. That's our standard protocol: if there's only one salesclerk on the floor, Brutus handles any request to purchase things from the back rooms. The customer knew that. Sammy didn't hear what the guy wanted to buy but saw Brutus unlock the door as if nothing was weird. As soon as Brutus got the door unlocked, the guy pulls a knife, and Brutus isn't Brutus anymore. Whatever stepped into him started to tear the store apart. Sammy—being a smart girl—ran."

Elsie had to agree that Sammy had been smart. If the girl had tried to tangle with the monster possessing Brutus, she would have died.

"Who is this regular?" Elsie asked.

Hank blew out his breath, shaking his head. "He's always paid in cash. He never told us his real name. We call him 'the Rock Hound.'"

"Rock Hound?"

"We get a lot of geology students from Salem State University as customers. They're why we have such a big rock collection in the showroom. The polished junk—the crystal confetti, heart pendants and bracelets, and most of the small stone statues—those are for people that think that all rocks have some magical powers. The larger and raw pieces—the geodes and fossils—are what geeks the geologists. A couple of years ago, a bunch of them came in to look at the fossils and they were dragging along this guy with them that...well, he was Touched."

"Touched" as in "under the influence of a supernatural being," not crazy in the head, although the two looked the same to the uninitiated. It wasn't the same as possessed, where the person's personality vanished under the weight of the spirit. By strict definition, she was Touched. The difference being that, by DNA, she wasn't human, had been trained from birth to carry the load, and spent her teen years building limits on the power that God could push through her. Pure humans rarely survived the long-term effects of being Touched.

"You knew he was Touched," Elise said with surprise and dismay. "And that didn't alarm you?"

Hank shrugged. "A lot of our regulars are. The old gods aren't dead. Yes, their realms aren't as connected to ours as strongly as they used to be but that doesn't mean that they completely vanished. They've just drifted off, lost contact, gone to sleep. Odin. Isis. Frey. Ishtar. Some of our customers are reaching out, searching for them, and more often than not, connect at some small level. Others? Their god has a hand firmly on them. I imagine they're somewhat like a Grigori Power. You can feel it."

Elise shook her head. "You've never met a Power. I doubt you'd stay in the same building with someone at that level if they walked through your door."

"Perhaps," Hank compromised. "Anyhow, Rock Hound came with the geologists, and they obviously knew each other. There was a really weird power dynamic between them, like maybe he was a grad student or a professor. Rock Hound was really dismissive of all the normal gewgaws—the crystals, the candles, the oils. I wasn't surprised that he was—considering what had a firm hold of him. Then all of a sudden, he picked up on our back room. It was like a hunting dog scenting blood on the wind. He went on point."

"His god sensed something that it wanted?" Elise guessed.

Hank shrugged. "I think it just picked up the fact we had quite of bit of interesting stock in the back room. I didn't want the entire herd of geologists pawing over my good stuff, so I told him to come back later. He came back, would hem and haw over the inventory and then ask if I could chase down specific items. I wouldn't commit to that. Things hidden away are usually hidden for a good reason. After that, Rock Hound would come back and ask for information or old books—safer things to sell. He seemed to be looking for something specific, but I'm not sure what. He'd talk to whoever was on duty. None of us got a complete picture of what he wanted."

"Do you have a picture of this guy? You said something about the security tape."

"The tape is not very good—it's like watching a tornado rip through the store. Sammy handles our social media. Instagram. Facebook. Whatever. I don't keep up with it. She's always snapping pictures of the store and customers—the tourists that come in. Our regulars usually don't want their pictures taken. Tourists act like they're going into the hall of fame. But anyhow, Sammy was taking pictures of a display that she'd just put up and accidently got a picture of the Rock Hound."

Hank pulled out his phone and found the picture. "I had her find it this morning when I came back. I figured we'd have to track him down to get Brutus back—if we could."

It was an odd picture. It was by a practiced eye who understood lighting, balance, and framing. The tall, thin blond man seemed almost blurred while completely in focus. He was standing near the fossils in the front room. There was something disturbingly vague about him. His blond hair was going white at the roots. It had that shapeless look of a short haircut grown out too long and straggly. A once-neat goatee was growing toward an unkempt full beard that was also going white. His eyes were gray, nearly colorless. His skin was pale to the point of looking sickly. His brow, nose, cheeks... they were all... worn, like a statue weathered almost smooth by endless rain.

"You sold things to this... this thing?" Elise said.

"He didn't always look that bad," Hank said. "He's degrading."

The man's parka hung open, showing off a dirty, worn Salem State University T-shirt. The parka itself was bright orange with a patch on its sleeve.

"What does that patch say?" Elise held out her hand for Hank's phone. She zoomed in. While it was difficult to read the actual lettering, she was able to make out the fact that it was a map of Antarctica.

Penguins are from Antarctica.

But what did all this have to do with Francis and his missing driver?

Elise found her name on Hank's contact list and emailed the photo to her phone. She then forwarded it to Clarice. "We're going to need a list of everything taken."

"It will take about another hour to double-check receipts for the last month to make sure what is missing is actually missing and not sold," Hank said. "Yvette got called away on a family emergency and Sammy needs to pick her kid up at preschool. I'm here alone until later this afternoon."

She was sure that this was a bid for time. She was fairly sure his employees would have already made the list. She was afraid that there were things—if they weren't taken—he didn't want the Grigori to know he had. What he wanted was time to make the information less damning.

Being that she didn't have a lead on the Rock Hound or the missing flock of penguins, an hour would make no difference.

"Fine," she said. "Send the list to the Central Office."

Clarice answered her phone with, "According to our teachers, mediums are resistant to our glamour. Not that I really know firsthand because I'm not allowed to do investigations. Anyhoo, they said the resistance is part of the medium's ability to see into the supernatural realm—especially the ones with spirit guides."

All that was true, but Elise wasn't sure why Clarice was bringing it up now. Was this because Hank had a spirit guide?

"Do you think I should check out the Philadelphian spiritualists?" Clarice continued. "They might be safer to date than werewolves."

Elise snorted. She knew that dating Cabot would raise eyebrows with her family, but she didn't think her cousins would get fixated on it. "There's more fake mediums than real ones."

Elise pulled out her keys and unlocked her Jeep. The sky was overcast, threatening to snow again. Early December and she was already sick of snow. She had started to miss Greece's sunny weather early this winter. It felt strange that a Greek island felt more like home than Boston, being that she'd been born in New England.

"It will be fairly easy to tell the real mediums from the fake," Clarice said. "The ones that drool are the ones that are scam artists. So, what does the guy in the parka have to do with everything?"

Elise started up her Jeep to get the heater warmed up. She put her phone into its holder and switched to the car's Bluetooth. She explained what she discovered at Bell Book & Candle. "Between the T-shirt and the fact that he came in with geology students, he probably has some connection with Salem State University. I'm thinking because he looks like he's in his thirties that he might be a professor. Just to be safe, we probably shouldn't focus only on students or professors. Maybe—I don't know, we didn't go to college—he could be a janitor or whatever passes as the lunch lady?"

"On it." Clarice started to type.

Elise drummed her fingers on her steering wheel, considering what they knew about the robbery. "This guy walked off with a shitload of magical items from the store. He probably didn't carry it by hand—so he probably has a car or at least a driver's license. Try the Massachusetts RMV and the New Hampshire DMV."

"Ugh!" Clarice complained. "States and their flip-flopping on names for the same thing. At least they stick to 'motor vehicles' for the same department."

"I think Vermont is like two hours out from Salem—too far out for someone to commute to the university, but I could be wrong. Hank is supposed to email you a list of what is missing. I think since he wouldn't just hand me an inventory dump, he had some stuff that he doesn't want to admit having unless they're actually gone."

"Oh, that's not good," Clarice murmured.

Elise glanced at her Jeep's clock. She had gotten an early start but between the trip to the morgue, the fight at the aquarium, dropping Joshua back at school, driving to Salem, and talking with Hank most of the day had been eaten up. If colleges kept normal "school hours," then she'd missed hunting down staff at the university.

"I'm heading back to meet up with Theo," Elise said.

"Theo called in," Clarice said. "She says that the aquarium staff didn't seem to be aware that they'd had an extra rockhopper in their flock. It suggests that the Aptenodytes have a type of glamour while in bird form. She couldn't find anything in a

three-block radius of the aquarium. I did a search on the name
that Joshua gave you: Manuel Alvarez. I found one arriving at
Logan International Airport on an Aerolineas Argentinas flight
from Buenos Aires on November twenty-fourth. It would have
been a few days after the flock of Aptenodytes vanished."

The Wakefield Coven had ambushed Joshua at the barn on
Halloween. All evidence was that the Wickers had been in the
area for weeks prior to the attack. Sometime in a three-week
window after Halloween, all the Aptenodytes of Argentina had
picked up and moved to Boston. They arrived prior to Joshua
being kidnapped by the fetch on the first of December.

Major supernatural events were rare. To have two overlap-
ping seemed too much of a coincidence. She couldn't think of
any way that the two were related, but she had a vague linger-
ing sense that they were. Of all the places in the world that the
Aptenodytes could head for—why Boston? And why would they
attack Roustabout? What did penguins want with a kickboxer
turned friar?

"You still there?" Clarice asked.

"Yeah, I'm here." Maybe Theo knew something about said
missing driver that Clarice didn't know. "Where is Theo now?"

"She said she's heading back to the Greek place since you two
didn't get a chance to eat much of what you ordered for lunch.
She'll order big and if you show up, you can eat whatever is on
the table. Otherwise, she'll stick it in the ice chest in her car,
along with the leftovers from lunch."

"Okay, I'm heading to the restaurant."

16: JOSHUA

Being the owner of a private school was very different from being a poor and nerdy student at a public school. Joshua stopped at the office, expecting to be scolded for walking in hours after class started. The women staff just smiled kindly and cooed over the fact that he looked like his dad. This freaked him out—thinking his dad was at the school—until he realized that they meant his werewolf father, Gerald Tatterskein. They wrote him out a hall pass without a single criticism.

His lunch period was just starting, so he went straight to the cafeteria. The Goths were at the same table as yesterday, looking a little shell-shocked. They were even in the same seats with the addition of Vijay. The boy had stripped off the girl's clothing and makeup and put on a school uniform. Joshua barely recognized him as the same person. Without Marie's curly wig, his hair was short and dark. Marie's pale white makeup must have been very heavy because Vijay's natural tone was deep tan. It surprised Joshua that the boy didn't look like a girl at all now that all the feminine bits and bobs had been washed away.

The Goths came to life as Joshua sat down beside Maisy.

"Joshua!" Allie and Tal cried in surprise.

"Oh, thank God!" Ottilie breathed.

"Are you okay?" Ji Su asked as Maisy clasped his hand, hoping that he hadn't been hurt protecting them.

"I'm fine," Joshua said. "I was worried about all of you."

"There was nothing we could do against that, so we ran," Tal said.

Ottilie looked unhappy. "I called Central. Dominions can't really fight things like that—not like Virtues. Information is our weapon, not daggers."

"Elise and Theo came to the rescue," Joshua said.

"Theodosia?" Ottilie said with surprise. "What is she doing in Boston?"

Joshua shook his head. "I don't know. They didn't say. I thought she was just visiting. Elise said that they were first cousins."

"Virtues don't team up unless there's something really big that a single Virtue can't take down alone, but not big enough to call in a Power," Ottilie said. "Theodosia's territory is Maine. It's a three-hour drive. She's not in Boston because we went to the aquarium—she couldn't have arrived in that short amount of time. Something must be majorly wrong."

"That would explain how the Virtues got to Joshua so fast." Ji Su turned to Joshua to fill him in. "Nam-gi told me that Elise was at the aquarium when we hit the subway. It's why we didn't go back."

"The Virtues weren't at the aquarium because of Vijay," Ottilie said. "At least Theodosia wasn't. Marie Antoinette is old news—she's been around since the late 1930s."

The date shouldn't be weirdly surprising being that the queen had been dead since 1793. For some reason, though, Joshua had thought Marie had only showed up in Boston more recently.

Ottilie continued to update Joshua. "Central Office didn't explain anything, but she did okay me going to the family's depot in Watertown and getting protection against possession for the kids here at school. I think her theory is you're the epicenter of whatever is going on. I'm going after school to pick up some charms."

Joshua explained that Elise had exorcised the evil—whatever—out of Brutus, found out who he was, and was going to go to his place of work to see how he'd ended up possessed. "Elise dropped me off here. Theo stayed at the aquarium to talk to the police—and probably try and find the penguin."

"It fled," Ji Su said. "Nam-gi said it left the same time we did."

"It couldn't be too hard to find," Tal said. "A penguin wandering around in the streets..."

"It's not a simple skitter-snatch or growling," Ottilie said. "It's a shapeshifter. It speaks at least three languages fluently. Central Office thinks it flew here from Argentina on an airplane—so it probably has money, and a passport stashed someplace."

"Marie Antionette did say it was paying her," Joshua said.

"Oh, yeah! Money!" Vijay started to search through his backpack. "I don't know what Marie thought she was going to use as money to buy that stuffed seal that you guys told me about. She didn't have any American money on her—me—in her purse." He gave a slightly embarrassed laugh. "I'm not sure where she got those clothes—not out of my closet."

"Winnie has returned everything she's found," Joshua said.

"Maybe Marie Antionette has clothes stashed someplace," Ottilie said. "She's been around forever, so she might have found someplace she could safely leave private items decades ago."

"Or she's very good at thrifting," Allie guessed. "My aunt loves mid-century furniture and vintage housedresses. Very June Cleaver. I don't understand it."

"Ah, here we are!" Vijay pulled out a vintage beaded change purse with a kiss lock closure. "I tried not to handle it."

He opened it to reveal colorful bills, odd-looking coins, and bits of metal.

"What the...?" Tal leaned close to eye the contents of the purse but was careful not to touch them.

"I think it's the money that the penguin gave Marie," Vijay said. "I found the coin purse in the pocket of the coat I had on. I think that Marie had just talked with Mannie and gotten paid right before you caught up with me."

Maisy wondered if this meant that penguins had pockets.

Vijay pointed at the colorful bills inside the purse. "This stuff is Argentinian for sure, and the writing on some of the coins look Spanish."

"Now we're talking!" Allie said.

Joshua glanced at Allie in confusion.

"My gift is psychometry," Allie said. "That's why I'm going into Forensic Science. I figure with my ability I'll be able to crack murder cases easy."

"Psychometry?" Joshua vaguely remembered Ji Su explaining something about it on his first day. "That's the touching things tells you stuff?"

Maisy put a hand on his arm and let him know that Allie's special power let her read the history of an object.

Ottilie explained a little more. "She's a 'touch witch.' We Grigori see it as a divine gift as it sees the underlying pattern of God's blueprint on the world."

Allie snorted. "I see it more as the disruption of the pattern as crime scene materials are usually linked to disrupting God's plan."

"Oh, I see," Joshua said.

Allie shook the coin purse so that two of the odd-looking gold coins fell out. She cautiously tapped her forefinger to one, as if she expected it to be dangerously hot. Her eyes went round. "Oh!" She lowered her finger again to press it firmly to the metal. Her eyes went distant, as if she were searching her mind for a long-lost memory. "This was on a wooden sailing ship. Its sails were full of wind: it was running from its enemy. There was a battle—warships firing cannons at each other. So many cannons! They boomed like thunder!" She flinched slightly. "O. M. G. The magazine must have blown! There was a massive explosion—everything flying apart in a huge ball of fire and smoke. Everything falling into the water and drifting downward: bodies, gold, silver, cannons, tattered sails, tangled rigging, broken timbers. The coins sat under the waves for hundreds of years, surrounded by lost souls."

Ottilie took out her prayer book and a match. She blessed the coin quietly.

"So, they're like doubloons or pieces of eight?" Tal asked.

"Pirate money?" Vijay said.

"Spanish main money," Ottilie corrected him. "They're Spanish dollar coins that were irregularly shaped because the milling machines weren't invented yet. Each was worth eight reale coins—hence the name 'pieces of eight.' You could literally snap off a section of the dollar coin and use it as if it was a reale. The Spanish would send a treasure ship once a year from the New World back to Spain. It didn't always make it to Spain."

The Goths looked at Ottilie in surprise.

"Numismatics for five hundred, Alex," Ottilie quipped and then shrugged. "Part of being a Dominion is learning a warehouse full of obscure historical information. Coins are often buried with things that need to be kept dead, or they were lost during a violent battle. They attract dark magic and are sometimes possessed or cursed."

"So, this penguin looted these coins off a sunken ship?" Tal asked.

Allie nodded. "He picked it up with his beak and swam to a tidal pool to drop it off. One by one, he gathered dozens."

Joshua cocked his head, considering the implications of the loot. Mannie did say that he wanted to *hire* Joshua. "So, he's a *rich* shapeshifting penguin?"

"And a thief," Ottilie grumbled.

"Well, if the ship is sunken, is it really looting?" Vijay asked.

Ottilie shook her head. "There are salvage laws that govern shipwrecks. Treasure hunters need to report sunken ships since they have historical importance. If you find something in the ground in countries like England and Ireland—even if you own the land—you have to turn it over to the government. There's usually a bounty for turning it in—basically legal tender near the value of the found treasure. The law was put into place because there were so many cursed items littering the countryside. All newly unearthed treasures need to be checked just in case they can turn people into monsters because of some weird curse."

"It depends on how old this Mannie is," Ji Su pointed out. "Supernatural beings are sometimes immortal. He could have recovered it soon after the ship sunk."

Ottilie thought hard. "Hm, in legends of selkies, it's never suggested that the monster wife doesn't age."

Maisy thought it was important that Allie said that the coin had been in the ocean for centuries, which meant that Mannie had only recently found it. She also thought that a penguin would have an easier time finding things underwater since they could stay submerged for twenty minutes at a time. The penguin could go to the location of a famous shipwreck and search it more thoroughly than any human could.

"Hm," Ji Su said. "The coins explain how he could pay Marie Antionette for information but not why he was hiding out at the aquarium."

"Well, I thought the monster that showed up explained everything," Tal said.

"Yeah, the monster definitely was after Mannie." Allie put the silver coins aside. "Let's see if the rest of the money has any clues."

Joshua thought about asking Marie what the penguin told her—but decided that the dead queen probably wouldn't cooperate. So far, she hadn't. He also doubted that any of the Goths would volunteer to do a séance.

Ottilie studied the change purse. "We can probably assume that most of the odd coins are going to have a stronger psychic imprint of how they were lost than current events. The paper bills are normal money—probably without any supernatural entanglement beyond Mannie."

Allie picked up one of the colorful rumbled bills. It was labeled "Banco Central de la Republica Argentina" and had a large "100" printed in one corner. "Oh, this one is useless. He got it as change from a McDonald's."

"In Boston?"

"Buenos Aires." She made an odd face. "He got a Big Mac and Coke."

"Huh, so as a human, he can eat something other than herrings," Tal said.

"I wonder if the Argentina McDonald's doesn't have fish sandwiches," Vijay said.

"The ones in Oklahoma don't have lobster rolls," Tal said.

"The ones in Hawaii have rice and spam for breakfast and will give you chopsticks if you ask," Vijay said.

"Can we focus here?" Ji Su said.

Allie slipped another colorful crumbled bill out of the purse. "Hm, more change from McDonald's. Same meal. Oh, the girl handing him the change had a good look at him. She thought he was cute. He kind of looks like a rockhopper. He's a little older than us—not as tall as Tal. Dark hair with streaks of blond at his temple. He would pass as Hispanic with dyed bangs. His eyes are an odd color—brown almost to the shade of red. I suppose he's kind of sexy—in that scruffy beach-bum animal way."

"But he's a bird!" Ji Su said with dismay.

"The cashier didn't know." Allie took a third bill out and immediately dropped it with a look of dismay. "Okay, that one is scary." She took a deep breath and lightly pressed her fingertips to it. "It's night. Something is coming. A man—I think it's a man—is running. Fleeing. It's a small coastal town and he knows that he needs to get to the beach. He has something that he needs to keep safe. If he can get to the water, he can protect—" She jerked her fingers back. "Oh! Oh. Oh shit. I don't even know what that was. Some kind of monster. It hit so fast."

She was trembling.

"We can skip that one," Joshua said.

"No!" Allie snapped. "I need to be able to do this. I can't get all wimpy at every murder—Hey! This is my first murder case!"

"Yes, it is," Ji Su said soothingly.

"Okay. I can do this." Allie put her fingertips to the bill again. "Mannie found the body. He's swearing and crying. He searches for what the man had been carrying. 'Oh no, they took it, they took it,' he says over and over again. He takes the dead man's wallet and apologizes as he takes the money within."

Maisy wondered if the missing object was the "very important" thing that Mannie said that the evil being had taken from him.

"Very powerful, very evil being." Ji Su amended Maisy's "comment," proving that all the Goths could "hear" what Maisy was thinking. "Whatever this being is—it's here in Boston now. Mannie is chasing after it to get back whatever his friend was protecting."

Allie picked up the crumbled bill and pressed it to her forehead. "The thing that concerns me is that what little I got about the monster that killed mystery man wasn't what attacked us at the aquarium. I just got a quick impression of it, but it was more like a...a...millipede? Or maybe a crab with more legs than normal?"

She went silent, eyes closed, bill pressed to her forehead.

"What are you—" Joshua started to ask.

"Shhh!" All the Goths hushed him.

"Oh, give me a pencil and paper," Allie whispered.

Vijay pushed a charcoal pencil and sketchbook in front of Allie and flipped to a blank page. Judging by the sketches that he passed, Vijay was a surprisingly good artist with a manga-like flair. For some reason, Joshua hadn't expected a hard science nerd to be an artist.

Allie kept the bill pressed to her forehead with her left hand and drew with her right. She drew three oblong forms. At the bottom she put concentric circles of dots, one connected to each misshapen oval form. At the top she put a smaller dotted circle with long spikes between each dot.

"What the hell is that?" Tal whispered and got hushed.

Two large solid dots and a slash between them made a vague facelike pattern. Maybe.

"The dead man—before he was attacked—had this in his hand. It was this egglike...thing...maybe a rock. Maybe an actual egg. I'm not sure. We're talking penguins here. It had this picture on it." Allie started to line the oblongs with dots.

"Are those penguins?" Tal asked.

Allie shrugged. "I don't know."

"They kind of look like people to me," Ji Su said. "Or angels. Those spikes could be a halo."

"Angels don't have halos," Ottilie growled. "That's just an artistic flair from the first century that got carried forward. Since the early Christians didn't know what Jesus looked like, they decided to copy Apollo for Christ. They're both 'son of the father' figures. The statues of Apollo often had sunrays behind his head to denote he was the god responsible for the sun's passage across the sky. Later artists, not realizing what the earlier ones were copying, just stuck on glowing circles without knowing what they were. Fast-forward a few centuries and people all think we got these little hoops of gold floating over our head."

"To be fair, you do have that glowing aura." Vijay turned to face Ottilie and waved his hands in tight circles. "To us who can see auras, we could spot you in an unlit room just by the glow you put off."

Ottilie frowned as if she was trying to decide if she'd been insulted or not.

Joshua was surprised that he couldn't see this so-called glowing aura.

Maisy thought that the concentric circles might be eggs.

Everyone leaned forward to stare closely at the circles at the bottom of the figures.

"Yeah, she's right." Joshua pulled out his phone and found a picture of a penguin with an egg. "Look at how big the egg is to its little feet."

"So, a picture of three penguins with eggs," Vijay said.

"The man had the mystery egg rock when he died," Ji Su said slowly. "Did Mannie find it on him?"

Allie thought for a full minute. Eyes closed. Bill pressed to her forehead. "No. The thing that killed the man must have taken it. There's no other psychic impression on the bill other than some residual from Marie Antoinette."

Ji Su summed up what Allie had learned. "A monster comes to Mannie's town, kills his friend, and takes this weird rock. Mannie then travels half the world to chase after it. He wants Joshua to do something—and I'm guessing it's probably to kill the monster and get back the rock."

"The real question is, why did the monster come to Boston?" Ottilie said. "And how? Monsters are normally localized to specific areas. They don't cross half the globe unless they're highly sophisticated. Grigori, and werewolves are just about the only nonhumans that cross oceans—even sea monsters generally don't swim to new locations. Charybdis and Scylla never left the Strait of Messina—they literally stayed centuries next to the rocks that they lived under."

"Those are real monsters?" Joshua said with surprise.

Ottilie nodded. "They were. They're dead now. A Power took them out about four hundred years ago."

Allie put down the bill. "I can't get anything else off it. The murder kind of overwrote anything else that might have been on it."

Allie extracted a couple more Argentinian bills from the plastic baggie, muttering, "Trash. Trash. Trash."

"I still don't know how Marie Antoinette thought she was going to buy anything," Vijay said. "This was all she had. I'm fairly sure that the aquarium doesn't take currency from other countries."

Ottilie grunted, looking at her phone. "And according to this morning peso-to-dollar exchange rate, she barely had enough for the smallest of the seals."

"Really?" Vijay said.

Ottilie nodded. "Since 2015, Argentina has gone through rampant inflation. No wonder Mannie was doing treasure hunting. The pieces of eight are worth between two hundred to a thousand US dollars apiece."

"But you said it was stealing," Joshua said.

"Technically yes," Ottilie said. "We Grigori don't care about the morality; we care about monsters. As long as he didn't pick up some kind of cursed item, it's fine."

Allie reached into the purse but suddenly dropped it. "Oh! That's...that's...what is that?"

A coin slid out of the dropped change purse. Joshua could feel something dark and sinister. It was like something with many limbs moving within blackness, unseen. Something waiting to grab and hold and drill in. If coins could have emotions, this one raged with anger.

Everyone at the table shifted back, away from the coin. It was a black metal disk made of tarnished silver or maybe stamped lead. It had something with lots of tentacles stamped onto it.

The wolf peeled back its lips in a snarl. Joshua locked down on a growl.

"Oh, that is scary," Ji Su whispered.

"Seriously," Tal breathed.

"What is it?" Vijay said.

Maisy thought that it was terrifying and that they shouldn't touch it.

"I'm not going to touch it," Allie stated firmly. "I can feel the bad *juju* from here."

"I think it is some kind of Charon's obol," Ottilie cautiously leaned forward to eye it closely without touching it.

"What's that?" Joshua said.

"Charon was the ferryman of Hades that carried the souls of the dead to the Underworld," Ottilie said. "It's hard to tell if Charon was a mythological figure or an actual being. It could have been both—certain realms seemed like they were more easily accessed than they are now. An obol was a type of coin, minted by the Greeks. In a lot of the ancient cultures, the dead are given coins to pay Charon or some similar ferryman for passage to the final resting spot. Sometimes it's two coins laid on their eyes. Sometimes it was only one coin placed in their mouth."

Ottilie pointed at the black disk. "Ancient coins usually featured the face of the emperor or king or such that controlled what value the coin was worth. It was kind of a guarantee of its value but also who you owed taxes to."

"Well...we just can't leave it sitting on the table," Ji Su said as the bell announcing the end of lunch sounded.

"I can't take it." Ottilie took out her phone and took pictures of it. "I can feel the chaos on it. We're diametrically opposed. There's no telling how it would affect me. Either I'm very weak to it or very strong. I'm not sure which—but I'm worried that I'm the worst one of us to handle it."

Vijay suddenly leaned forward, picked up the coin, and dropped it quickly back into the change purse. He dropped the purse as if he was afraid it would bite him. "I figured that Marie Antoinette had put it into the purse—so I should be able to handle it. I really don't want to carry it around, though."

Everyone else in the cafeteria was funneling out of the room, heading toward the next period class.

"What do we do?" Allie said.

Ottilie glanced at Joshua. "I think...Werewolf magic is aligned with life. It's not diametrically opposed to chaos like I am. I think Joshua would be the best person to take them."

The wolf did not want to touch the purse, but Joshua trusted Ottilie to know better than him. He forced himself to pick it up. It felt like the coin squirmed inside the purse. He was going to take it to his locker and put it in his coat. That way he didn't have to carry it around the rest of the day.

17: SETH

Keeping tabs on Joshua as he was jumped by a mysterious monster—hundreds of miles away—had been a mistake. By the time the Virtues had arrived at the aquarium to deal the final blows, the hallways of Seth's high school were completely evacuated. He emptied his locker knowing that he wouldn't be coming back. Both fire and police were outside with more units arriving, triggered by reports of an active shooter, a wild animal on the loose, and a possible fire outbreak. Seth walked away from the chaos, shaking his head.

Having been kicked out of the nearby private schools, his current high school was twenty minutes by train away from the Castle. Normally he didn't mind the commute but with his temper slipping out of his control, it was a recipe for disaster.

Elise had driven off with Joshua—at least Seth assumed it was Elise. It was difficult to tell the two Virtues apart, although Elise seemed to be the stronger. She was headed toward Cambridge with Joshua, so at least Seth could stop worrying about his brother. The other Virtue seemed to be searching the aquarium, probably looking for the mysterious penguin that Seth had picked up on just prior to the fight. The monster that Joshua had been fighting had vanished like a ghost—perhaps it had been a spirit possessing a human body. Seth couldn't pick out mediums from the general populace if they didn't have a spirit guide linked to their soul. Elise had taken a human with her, so she must have exorcised the monster.

Joshua was still a wolf; his phone was … someplace else. They hadn't been able to determine where exactly his belongings went when he changed shape, only that everything came back in the same exact place afterward. Shoes on feet. Wallet in pocket. Joshua's phone might be unharmed, but it was currently without signal in some mysterious void.

Since Seth couldn't call his brother, he called Jack instead.

"I need a ride," Seth said when Jack answered his phone.

"It happened again?" Jack guessed the reason.

"Yeah," Seth said without elaborating.

"You're not graduating this year if you keep getting kicked out of school," Jack said—obviously without thinking because half a second later, he swore. "I'm sorry. I shouldn't have said that. I'll be there as fast as I can."

Seth's phone rang with an incoming call from Kate. It was not quite noon for him, so it must be early morning for her.

He answered with "Hi," trying not to let his emotions also flood into their relationship.

"Have you been keeping an eye on our territory? What the hell is going on with our puppy? What the hell is he fighting? Is he going to be okay with those Virtues? Why are there two in our territory? I thought we just had the one! How does he get that big?"

"I asked the Virtues to intercede." Seth answered the one question he knew the answer to. "There's no way anyone else could get to him in time."

"Why is he even alone up there?"

Seth sighed. "I don't know. The king refuses to let me move back to Boston with Cabot."

"Can't you just go? You're the prince. It's our territory."

"I could just go—but then the king would probably drag Joshua to his castle. I had to beg him to let Joshua stay in Boston. I really, *really* don't want him in New York."

"Why not? He seems like some kind of trouble magnet."

The sidewalk emptied as Seth struggled to contain yet another flare of anger. "The king's son, Isaiah, is a dangerous bully. He hates me. We were both born to be the prince of a city, but he's got none of what I have or had. He hates that my parents obviously loved me before they were ripped to shreds. That they threw me birthday parties. That I had little brothers. That I became prince at thirteen and that I have a wife. He would love to take everything and anything that I have away from me."

"What an asshole!" Kate said.

It felt good that she automatically took his side.

Seth continued to explain. "If I give the king any reason to go back on his decision to leave Joshua in Boston, Isaiah will do his best to beat the snot out of Joshua. I'm not sure that he could— but I don't want to find out that I'm wrong. Joshua doesn't have control of his wolf yet and he could go feral if pushed too hard."

"Oh, yeah, that happened to one of my second or third cousins on my mom's side," Kate whispered. "He was in a bad car accident about a month after he was changed. It was one of those 'over the cliff and start to burn after it finally stopped rolling' kind of crashes. He went feral while pinned inside the burning car. My grandfather had to put him down. I was wondering why the king sent me back home with my folks but if that's how his son is, then he probably thought I was safer here in San Diego."

"Whatever you do, don't come to New York."

Kate gave a bitter laugh. "Oh, Isaiah better not try to mess with me—but I hear you. Stick to Boston."

A quick check on Joshua revealed that his brother still hadn't reverted to human. Elise had stopped to pick up takeout—probably to coax Joshua back to normal. The fight obviously rattled his brother's wolf.

Seth was failing as a prince. He wasn't even sure how to fix the problems that faced his pack.

"I talked to the king about getting you money," Seth said. "He didn't give me an answer."

"He didn't? That's weird."

"No, that's the king for you. I'll ask him again in a few days."

"The thing is: Thane Leung showed up this morning with a brand-new minivan. It kind of says 'soccer mom' but I'm fine with that. Wheels are wheels."

Thane Leung had taken the king's private jet to Vancouver yesterday. He must have flown south to San Diego immediately afterward. The king would have given Leung orders shortly after talking to Seth.

"Oh," Seth said in surprise. "No one told me. I'm glad, though, that you got it."

"He also gave me a wad of cash...so...thanks!"

What did this mean for their bachelor house, then? Did the king act on that request too? When was anyone going to tell him? Had one of Isaiah's lackeys sat on the information just like they delayed Kate's message?

"I would like to send Jack to Boston," Seth said to fill her in on current events. "But Jack is still a little messed up from fighting the Wickers. The king healed Joshua, so he bounced back faster."

"We don't have enough wolves," Kate said sadly.

"No, we don't."

They said their goodbyes with promises to keep in touch. Seth checked on Jack. He was a block away.

Jack had picked one of the BMW sedans from the motor pool. The recent heavy snows hadn't been totally cleared from parking spaces. Seth walked out into the street to meet him. He got in the front, tossing his backpack onto the backseat.

"Joshua got attacked at the aquarium," Seth said. "I'm not sure what it was—maybe a spirit possessing a medium. The Virtues helped deal with it. Elise is taking Joshua to Blackridge."

"Good!" Jack took the next right onto Broadway to loop them back toward the Castle.

It took them past the wooded mall of Columbia University where the king wanted Seth to go to college. Seth stared out the window at it, dreading the future. Four more years trying to manage Boston from New York. It was going to be a disaster—this was just the tip of the iceberg.

"I haven't actually talked to Elise," Jack continued, unaware of Seth's thoughts. "I texted her. She didn't respond. I thought she was ghosting me—but then she texted that Joshua was safe, so I figured she had been too busy getting to him to reply earlier."

A reasonable possibility. Seth wished Jack had actually talked to the Virtue, but it could not be helped.

"Do you want me to go to Boston?" Jack asked.

Seth blew out his breath in frustration. He wanted Joshua protected but not at the cost of Jack. His cousin had come close to dying twice in November. It made him realize how much he leaned on Jack's presence to keep stable. Jack was his big brother, father figure, and only friend in New York rolled into one. Seth would be utterly crushed if Jack were killed.

But if Joshua went feral in Boston, he could take out Blackridge and a good part of Cambridge before anyone could stop him.

As much as it hurt, Seth had to be a good prince for his territory. Too many lives counted on him.

"The king would have to agree to it first," Seth said.

"We already planned to drive up Friday," Jack said instead of stating that it was unlikely the king would give his permission. "It's so close to the Christmas break that you might not get into a new school until January."

In other words, since Seth had been kicked out of school, he could stay in Boston for the rest of the month. Seth doubted it—it would be too much like rewarding him for losing his temper. "The king will probably agree to just you heading up early. He might yet pull his permission for the entire Christmas visit. Kate picked up on Joshua's fight, so the king might be aware of it."

"If he doesn't know, Bishop will tell him the moment your school calls," Jack pointed out. "You haven't lost your temper like that for nearly a year. The king is going to want to know why, and you'll have to tell him."

On paper, Jack was his legal guardian but only because it might look weird for a person unrelated to Seth to act as his guardian when he had an adult cousin. It was a lie for the human government that might sniff around a wealthy orphan. Things like Seth's schooling got funneled through Bishop's law office. All the calls from Seth's school would be fielded by Bishop and then reported to the king.

"I called a real estate agent this morning," Jack said to distract Seth. "She said that construction just got completed on a new apartment building in Cambridge—they got the occupancy permits off the city about an hour ago. It has several four-bedroom units. She sent me an email with all the information on the apartments. They look really nice. I wanted you to see them before I said yes to them."

Jack stopped at a red light, pulled out his phone, and handed it to Seth. "We could nab two or three of the units now, let them stand empty."

"It would be expensive as hell," Seth said as he eyed the price. The four-bedroom unit was nearly five thousand dollars a month. It was, however, a three-story apartment with two separate living rooms and three bathrooms. He checked the location. It was just a few blocks from Blackridge. "This is perfect for us."

"I'll call her and tell her we'll take them," Jack said.

"Did the king give us permission to rent a bachelor house?"

"We need permission to move to Boston, not to rent a place."

That was best-friend Jack speaking.

"We won't be able to use our funds until I'm eighteen," Seth said. "That's nearly two years of rent without the estate paying for it."

"We could bill it to Shelter and Assistance."

Shelter and Assistance was for wolves traveling outside their territory. A pack was required by king's law to provide safe, dry, warm housing, food, and anything else needed to travelers passing through their territory. The expense was taken out of the tithe to the king, who in turn billed the traveler's home pack for the cost. It was handled in that way so that there would be no question of being asked for help, providing it, and then being short-changed by the traveler.

Seth supposed that Bishop might quibble over the questionable billing method—but since Boston didn't have any housing, he and Jack did fall under the definition of "traveler." Once he considered it, Joshua would also qualify but he was safer at Decker's warded house.

"I suppose so," Seth said slowly. He knew that he shouldn't encourage Jack when Jack stepped out of the "father" position. It would make Boston stronger, though, to have a place to stay that didn't belong to Decker.

Their territory could easily afford the rent on three apartments. As one of the oldest packs in North America, they were also the wealthiest. The king had paid for Seth's private schools, so even that hadn't been a drain on their finances.

They reached the entrance to the Castle's underground garage. Jack punched in the keycode to open the door. Samuels had driven a BMW coupe to the barn where a dozen high school students had been killed. Seth had totaled a Porsche in the fight with the Wickers at the nursery. (Isaiah had custom-ordered the sportscar and claimed it as his, but its registration listed it as a company fleet car.) Bishop needed to report both cars as stolen to avoid being connected to the crime scenes. The keycode security system had been put into place afterward to reinforce the lie that several cars had been taken out of the garage by strangers.

"I'll call the agent, let her know we want the apartments."

Jack pulled into the BMW's stall. "She said that there was an application process, so I'll have to see what that entails."

"I'll go tell the king that I got thrown out of school again," Seth said glumly.

"Cook sent his breakfast up to his suite," Jack said. "I don't think the king has come down to the throne room yet."

At least it would limit the size of the possible audience to Seth's humiliation.

Seth hated the elevator in the Wolf King's Castle. It was an ancient thing installed when the Castle was built back at the turn of the last century. It went all the way down to the lowest floor of the underground garage and up to the king's private penthouse suite. It was a rickety gilded cage with a simple lever labeled UP and DOWN instead of buttons to select individual floors.

It always felt like a trap.

That feeling was reinforced when the doors opened, and he found his foster brother Isaiah waiting for him.

"Ah, the mighty hunter." Isaiah lazed against the back of the elevator like he had no place to go. He must have just parked in one of the lower levels where the Bentleys were stored. "I hear you bagged a teacher today."

Seth clenched down on a growl. He needed to keep his temper in check. He really didn't want to fight in the small cage moments before meeting with the king. It wasn't surprising that Isaiah had heard the news. Because the king refused to use a phone, information was passed from person to person until it landed where it needed to go. Everyone knew bits and pieces of everything. Someone must have passed the information to the king and—at the same time—to Isaiah.

"How many times is this?" Isaiah didn't wait for an answer. "The fifth time you've been expelled? You've really got to stop attacking your teachers."

"I didn't attack him." Seth stepped into the elevator. Isaiah probably would get off on the first floor. If Seth waited for the elevator to come back to the garage, there was a good chance that Isaiah would jury-rig the door so the cage wouldn't move.

"That's not what he says," Isaiah said.

"He's still alive, isn't he?"

The quip surprised Isaiah into laughing. "I suppose that is

true. The school said something about an illicit phone call. What did your dorky brother do?"

"Nothing." Seth didn't want to discuss Joshua with the man.

Isaiah was the king's only living son. There were rumors of other children, hundreds of years in the past, born to strengthen various bloodlines. The king needed to breed wolves strong enough to hold powerful territories and he was the strongest wolf ever born. It was possible that the king was even one of Seth's ancient ancestors. When he was younger, Seth never had the desire to dig through the old family records. Now the family records were ashes.

New York wasn't the first territory where Alexander had stood as its prince. He'd held Athens back before Troy fell. Then hundreds of years later, he'd been the Prince of Rome as it rose up to control the world. Paris and London followed as the cities became more than just thatched huts gathered on the banks of a river. He had been the Prince of Moscow during the 1500s and 1600s before coming to newly founded New York. Each time he held the city until he could breed a bloodline strong enough to hold the territory.

Isaiah had been born to be the Prince of New York—someday. For reasons unknown, the king hadn't dropped the mantle on him. Isaiah was twenty-nine—nearly twice Seth's age. He was older by almost a decade than the last Prince of New York, Wolter Eskola. It was true that New York had just been a collection of villages in 1690. But Isaiah was even older than Seth's father when Gerald took on Boston.

Every passing birthday made it more unlikely that Isaiah would ever be made the Prince of New York.

All of that meant that the man was insanely jealous of Seth, who was "given" his territory at thirteen. Since Seth outstripped him as Prince of Boston, Isaiah focused his spite on the weaker Jack. At five foot two and a hundred twenty pounds of pure nerd, Joshua would be a natural target for the man.

"I still can't believe your freaking luck. Wah, wah, wah, my whole family is dead. Oh, except this one older brother who conveniently disappeared long enough for me to inherit the city. Oh, he cooked me Thanksgiving dinner. Oh, he wants to do Christmas. We're going to go out and cut down a tree and trim it just like I used to do with our dad. Eighteen years of having no idea he's adopted and he's still willing to do Norman Rockwell holidays with you like you're actually his beloved baby brother."

Isaiah had yet to lay eyes on Joshua. If Seth had a breath in his body, Isaiah never would.

Seth's temper slipped. His anger filled the area with a low menacing growl. They had gone past the basement and ground floor, but Isaiah made no attempt to stop the elevator. "Are you getting off?"

"No. I'm going to see my father."

Seth was never sure if Isaiah was impossibly brave or just that stupid that he'd let himself be locked in a small cage with a powerful wolf that hated him. Hopefully Isaiah would be smart enough to be silent until they reached the top floor.

Alexander's penthouse suite was on the top floor of the Castle, taking up the entire floor. The elevator opened to a long foyer paneled in mahogany. Seth knew that hidden behind the panels were a half dozen secret passages. He knew there were three large closets, a butler's pantry, the even more questionable freight elevator that went to the ground-floor loading dock, and the fire stairs. He wasn't sure which doors led to which.

Seth controlled the urge to open one of the panels at random and stuff Isaiah into whatever was behind the secret door. He didn't want Isaiah to be part of any conversation involving Joshua. Knowing Isaiah, he'd be championing Joshua being moved to New York City "for his own protection." His brother would be safer in Boston than within Isaiah's range of attack.

Seth had to contain himself or Alexander might just listen to his son. Seth let Isaiah swagger down the hall with the confidence born of the fact that he wasn't the one in trouble. If Isaiah arrived first, Alexander might send him on some errand, giving Seth the privacy that he wanted.

At the end of the hallway were double doors into Alexander's private domain. Isaiah knocked.

"Who is it?" Edward Bishop's muffled call came from within the room.

Seth sighed. As the king's lawyer, Bishop should be at his office at this time of day, overseeing all the legal problems that a worldwide organization could embroil itself in. If Bishop was in audience with the king, it meant that there was something that the king alone could decide. It also meant that the king would have little time and patience to deal with Seth's trivial problems.

Isaiah opened the door as if Bishop had said "Come" instead.

Warm air carried Alexander's ancient scent mixed heavily with wood smoke to Seth. He imagined that everything in the room was saturated with the mixture. It made him think of the four musketeers in Albany, still cleaning out their grandfather's home for the new marquis. Ewan said that the scent made everyone too uneasy to work long at the project. Ewan had also offered to take Joshua into Albany for a few years if the king insisted that he couldn't be left alone in Boston. Joshua would be safe there but if anything happened to Ewan, Joshua would probably inherit the alpha. That would be a disaster for the besieged Albany.

Seth clenched down on another growl. If it weren't for Isaiah, this wouldn't be a problem.

With the exception of the three elder Thanes—Bishop, Mandeville, and Chakrabarti—everything in the room was centuries old. It gave an impression of age that museums would envy. The rumor was the contents of the room had been brought from the king's last residence, nearly a hundred years before the Revolutionary War. The massive stone fireplace, the oriental rugs, a marble statue by Michelangelo, and a painting of Toledo by El Greco. It was as if someone had lifted a medieval castle and plunked it down on the roof of a Manhattan mansion.

Alexander was asleep in his leather wingback chair by the fire. His hair was as white as his wolf, but nothing else about him gave a hint of his age. He looked fifty years old, not two or three thousand. It was odd, though, that he was sleeping at noon in his living room.

The two elder Thanes stood with Bishop, obviously in mid-discussion when Isaiah walked in without warning or permission. All three were in human form, wearing impeccable three-piece business suits and worried looks.

"Your father is asleep," Thane Mandeville told Isaiah. He was the oldest of the Thanes: tall, thin, and grizzle-haired. Despite decades of living in New York, he still had his strong native French accent. "Away with you."

Isaiah made an impatient noise, sounding like an annoyed child. "That's what you said last night when I asked to see him. I want to talk to him. Now."

The Thanes were the oldest and most trusted of Alexander's

wolves—but they weren't strong enough to stand up against Isaiah. They wavered visibly against his dominance.

"Don't be such a child," Mandeville said. "Belgrade exhausted him. Let him sleep."

"Belgrade took much out of me," Alexander had said yesterday. "I grow weary."

Seth had thought that the king had just brushed him off with a lame excuse. He hadn't considered that the king might have actually been tired. Then again, Alexander never lied—he had no reason to. His people had to accept the unreasonable along with the reasonable.

Seth felt a twinge of guilt. He'd been so caught up in his own problems that he hadn't considered that Alexander might be struggling with the aftermath of Belgrade or some other equally large difficulties elsewhere. It was alarming that the king had drifted off to sleep without seeking his bed.

Seth's grandfather had faltered that way before he died. The territory's true heir had been killed by a feral, along with all the other pack children. His grandfather had not been strong enough to hold Boston, but he was all that they had. He was given a strong wife and encouraged to have many children as soon as possible. Boston burned him out young. All of Seth's memories of Grandfather Tatterskein were of him asleep in random places. The living room couch. His office chair. The dining room table. The garden courtyard. Sometimes as a man. More often, a wolf grayed about the muzzle when he was barely in his forties.

"Quiet, *abuelo* needs his sleep," he'd be told by his mother. "It keeps him strong enough to bear the weight of everything."

One day, his grandfather simply did not wake up. He laid asleep for a week before dying.

It was unimaginable, though, that Alexander was faltering in the same way. He'd been alive for thousands of years. He'd seen the rise and fall of the Roman Empire. Yes, he was ancient—but as far as they knew he was as immortal as a god.

But then again, in the Norse myths, even Odin slept to restore his health.

"Father!" Isaiah said loudly. "The Prince of Lagos called. He wants an audience with you. He wouldn't tell me why—the damn prig. He said he'd call back in twenty minutes. What am I to tell him? Father! Oh, stop this charade and open your eyes."

Did Isaiah know his father that little?

"Leave him to sleep," Seth commanded.

Isaiah turned to face him with a growl. "You are not my master."

"You are not yet Prince of New York," Seth said. "You might have the dominance to make the Thanes obey you, but you are not their elder, nor one of your father's official advisors. If they say he needs to sleep, you will let him sleep."

"This is not Boston," Isaiah snarled.

"I am still a prince," Seth said as calmly as he could. He didn't want to fight all the Thanes in the room, just Isaiah. "You can choose to leave under your own power, or I can make you go."

Isaiah glared at him but didn't move closer, which he used to do, trying to use his big build to intimidate Seth. Being that Seth had gained over a foot in height during the last three years, it would not work as well as before.

"Call me when he wakes," Isaiah finally said to the elder Thanes. He turned and stormed out of the room. Angry as he was, he did not slam the door. It was the king's private door and even in his anger, he obviously could not bring himself to abuse it.

Seth sat down on the couch, at the farthest point from the sleeping king as he could get. "I'll stay for a little while to make sure no one disturbs the king."

Isaiah did not return. Seth sat in silence, measured out by the ticking of the clock on the mantel. The fire crackled and snapped. The Wolf King slept, breathing deep and measured. The older Thanes came and went quietly as Seth stood guard.

Seth couldn't stop thinking of Grandfather Tatterskein. All of Seth's strongest memories of the man were of him asleep. It seemed harmless when Seth was very young. As a toddler, more than once he lay down and napped beside his grandfather. Only as he grew too old for naps did he realize that something was wrong. That no one else slept in the afternoon or early evening. That all the adults spoke in worried tones and gave the man concerned looks.

Surely the king wasn't seriously ill.

Seth's grandfather hadn't been born with the strength to be a prince. He was the youngest of many children born to Seth's great-grandfather. The true heir had been identified and was already being groomed to one day become the prince. But it was not to be—a new puppy nipped his youngling sister, changing her into a feral that tore all the other children of the pack apart. Siblings. Cousins. An entire generation gone in one afternoon. The only survivor, his grandfather, didn't have whatever genetics needed to shoulder the alpha successfully. It was decided that he would stay in place to bridge the gap between his dying father and his young son. He took the mantle knowing that it would kill him just so the next prince would be of the Tatterskein bloodline.

One could not compare his sacrificial grandfather to the ancient Wolf King.

Surely the king would be fine after a short rest.

Bishop returned to report that Isaiah had left the Castle, and that Seth could step down from guarding the king. Seth had been so distracted by the king's condition that he'd forgotten why he was there in the first place.

Bishop provided a painful reminder as he walked with Seth to the elevator. "Your school called. They reviewed your records. They apparently hadn't given credence to the reports from your last school that you were 'terrifying.' In light of today's 'incident' they have reconsidered and requested that you not come back."

Seth expected that much. "I cleaned out my locker when I left."

Bishop glanced back toward the closed door to the king's private suite. "I do not know what the king wants in regard to your schooling. I will have my office look for a suitable school—but until the king wakes, I cannot assume what he plans for you going forward."

Seth nodded. That was what he expected: another private school in New York City, probably requiring a train ride of more than twenty minutes. His only disappointment was that he might not be able to bully the new school into overlooking his four-week-long absence. Money bought a lot of forgiveness, but it only went so far.

He got onto the rickety old elevator and rode down a floor to his room. He felt slightly disoriented as if the elevator was shifting him through worlds with vastly different problems. Being thrown out of school was minor compared to the king being sick. He hadn't been in the last school long enough to make friends. The only difference was the length of the commute and if the new school would honor his first term with so many days being absent.

The root of his problem was Joshua. Things had been rocky in New York before, but they had been manageable.

Seth reached out for Joshua. His brother was back to being human and back at Blackridge, standing in the hallway at what seemed to be his locker. There was some kind of small knot of strangeness inside of the narrow space along with what probably was Joshua's coat.

What the hell?

Seth called Joshua.

"What do you have in your locker?" Seth asked.

"The hell if I know," Joshua grumbled as the bell rang to indicate that the next period was starting. "A coin or something. We couldn't leave it sitting on the cafeteria table, so I took it. I need to find Mannie and ask him what it is."

"Who is Mannie?"

Joshua shut his locker with a clang and headed down the hallway, still talking. "He's the penguin at the aquarium that wanted to hire me to do something. The monster showed up before Mannie could explain what he wanted me to do. But I think I know—he's chasing after something that stole a weird egg-shaped rock thing from him. At least Allie says it was probably stolen by a monster."

Allie Thompson was a touch witch who had hung out with their female cousins before the massacre. She was able to pick up the psychic vibrations that strong emotions and acts of violence left on objects.

"Can you tell where Mannie is now?" Joshua asked. "I want to find out what the hell is going on."

"No," Seth snapped. "Leave the penguin alone. The Virtues can handle it."

"I'm not sure if the Virtues know..."

"You can text Elise anything you think she needs to know, but that's it," Seth ordered. "You will not go back to the aquarium. You will not go looking for the penguin. You will stay away from the Virtues. As far as you're concerned, this is a closed case."

"What? No!" Joshua gave a distressed whine. Or more exactly, his wolf did. "Oh, shut up! Why are you suddenly a scaredy cat? We were handling that thing."

"Look," Seth said. "Things aren't good here in New York. I don't know if I'll be able to leave to come help you out of a bind. Decker is asleep. And that new Virtue might happily stab you if you annoy her."

"Theo? Yeah, she seemed like the stabby type."

"Promise me you won't go looking for the penguin." Seth knew that his brother was a true-blue Boy Scout type. If he made a promise, he would keep it.

"I had a dream about it," Joshua said, trying to wiggle out of making a promise. "If I had known what the toads were actually saying, then I might have found the Wickers before they started to kill people."

Seth rubbed at his temple, since talking to his brother was giving him a headache—again. He had no idea what Joshua was talking about. What toads? "Promise me."

"Fine. I won't go looking for the penguin."

18: DECKER

Something was wrong. Decker knew it instantly when he woke. He could hear Joshua upstairs in the kitchen. Over the last month, he'd learned that a happy Joshua was fairly quiet, often even still and silent as he intensely focused on something that brought him joy. Watching a movie. Playing a video game. Reading a book.

Joshua got noisy when he was upset or angry. It was actually kind of cute as he attempted to stomp as loudly as he could with his short, lightweight frame. Joshua was stomping about in the kitchen, banging pots and pans together as he worked on his dinner. Something had gone wrong with his boy.

Once again, it was before sunset proper, surprising Decker. He glanced longingly at the sunlight in the foyer but headed into the kitchen. Joshua needed him.

There was a surprising number of shopping bags sitting on the counters. The food that Joshua had ordered via the internet had arrived minutes ago. While steaks sizzled in a cast-iron skillet, Joshua focused on putting away the groceries while yelling at his wolf and his kitten.

"We're not eating it raw again! You will let it cook to medium rare! A hundred and thirty degrees! I want the insides to be at least warm! No more cold, raw... Trouble! No!"

This was while scooping up the kitten, who was trying to claw open a package of chicken thighs on the counter.

"Here! Take him!" Joshua shoved the kitten into Decker's hands.

Trouble decided that cuddles were just as good as food and started to purr.

"The two of them are driving me nuts!" Joshua meant the kitten and his wolf. He continued talking but it seemed as if he'd changed subjects. Maybe. "It's like the entire universe got twiddled when I became a werewolf. It wasn't just me that got changed or something. I don't know. Either that or I have this invisible sign on my back that says, 'kick me.' I really don't understand how I became this giant walking weird magnet."

Should Decker ask? Maybe it would be better that he didn't ask. No. He should ask. "What happened?"

"I don't know." Joshua picked up a pair of tongs and did an odd sideways creep toward the skillet. "I'm not allowed to figure it out. My brother is a control freak."

Decker raised a finger. How did they get to Seth? Decker didn't want to make Joshua angry (that would be bad in so many ways) but he wanted to know why Seth felt the need to be a control freak. "What exactly aren't you allowed to do?"

"Find the penguin and ask him what he wants me to do. No!" Joshua shouted and flung the tongs aside, nearly hitting Decker. "Just because I flipped it over doesn't mean it's done!"

Decker felt like he lost the thread of logic someplace. "I thought we determined that penguins don't talk."

"This one does!" Joshua picked up a small black device and stabbed a metal spike into the cooking steak. "One hundred and one! That's not even rare! We are going for medium rare!"

One mystery solved. How and why Seth had gotten involved were still unsolved. There were times Decker truly hated his curse. He had obviously slept through something important.

"And Seth doesn't want you to find the penguin?" Decker guessed.

"I'm not *allowed* to investigate. Strictly forbidden! 'Let the Virtues deal with it!' Mannie didn't want the Virtues, he wanted me!"

Mannie? The penguin had a name now?

Joshua continued to rant on. "He's probably going to just hide from Elise and Theo. If he wanted to talk to them, he wouldn't have left the aquarium after they showed up."

"Theo?" Decker felt alarm jolt through him. "Theodosia is in Boston?"

"Yeah. The two of them showed up at the aquarium after Brutus jumped me. I think Seth called Elise and sicced her on Mannie. Which—if Brutus hadn't shown up—would have been totally unneeded."

Which implied that Joshua had needed help with this so-called Brutus.

Two Virtues in one spot? Something was very wrong if Theo was in town. Virtues normally worked alone since there weren't enough of them in the world to overlap territories. Enyo's presence at the supermarket seemed less like coincidence now. And who the hell was Brutus? What was Brutus? He wasn't human if he'd survived Joshua's defensive reflexes. Decker was nearly indestructible to normal damage, and it still hurt when Joshua tossed him across the room by accident.

"Seth doesn't know what Mannie is or what Mannie wants to hire me to do. Seth got all 'I'm the prince' with me. My wolf got all freaked out about the fight with Brutus. It took me forever to get back to human. My wolf is like 'Seth's the prince' and just wants to stay home and eat."

Decker felt like Seth was right in this regard but didn't want to anger Joshua more. It seemed like the boy was barely in control as it was. Decker had overheard Seth's conversation with the king. Seth didn't want Joshua in New York City as he was concerned that—if pushed too hard—Joshua could still go feral.

Joshua stuck the probe back in the meat. "There! One hundred and thirty—"

He didn't get to finish the sentence. The wolf took control, changing to its draft-horse size, and attempted to pick up one of the steaks with its teeth.

"Hold on! Let me!" Decker picked up the tongs and moved the steaks to a waiting platter.

Knife and fork were ignored. The beast all but inhaled the steaks. Where did Joshua put all that food? Did the contents of his stomach go to the same place his clothes went to when he was a wolf? There were certain things about magic that defied logic.

The wolf glanced toward the front of the house. "Someone is coming up the front steps. Who the hell is visiting at this time of night? It better not be those Christians again."

From what Decker had gathered, a group of Christian missionaries had come to the front door a couple of times while

Decker was asleep. Joshua had been too nice to firmly tell them to go away; he had been tied up for an hour each time as they tried to convert him. While Joshua kept them out of the house, they had left pamphlets and promises to "check back" on him.

Decker snickered. "Go ahead. Answer the door that way."

"Decker!"

"I was kidding. It's probably Elise." Decker silently asked his talent to find Elise. It pointed firmly at the figure walking toward the door. "It is."

Elise rang the doorbell, which was odd. Normally she used her key and walked in as if she lived there. She had done so for years. After Joshua unearthed the upstairs hall bathroom and scrubbed it to shining, Elise had even started to bathe in the big clawfoot tub. True, Joshua had only recently repaired the doorbell but that hadn't changed Elise's behavior pattern.

Last time Elise knocked on the door, she had brought her cousin Lisette to meet him.

Decker caught Joshua by the scruff of his neck. "Let me answer it."

"Why?"

Because Theodosia was in town.

Decker pulled Joshua back from the door. "I don't think Elise is alone."

The doorbell rang again.

"Stay back," Decker said.

Virtues were dangerous to surprise. Currently Joshua was a wolf the size of a draft horse. Only when Decker was sure that Joshua was out of dagger range did he open the door. Winter blasted in with bitterly cold air. The furnace rumbled to life, trying to drive back the chill.

Elise wasn't alone. She stood between Decker and a tall Grigori. It took Decker a moment to recognize the Virtue as she had cut her long, beautiful hair into something very short and mannish.

"Theodosia," he said.

"Hello, Decker. Please, call me Theo." Her voice was low and mannish. Was Theodosia unhappy being a woman or was this some kind of attempt to defeat the effects of the Grigori glamour?

The Virtues stomped the snow off their boots. Theodosia lifted an eyebrow at the doormat, which was decorated with paw prints and ordered WIPE YOUR PAWS! She seemed unsurprised at Joshua's size. He must have changed to a very large wolf at the aquarium. It reminded Decker that he still wasn't sure what had happened during the day except it involved inhuman beings called Mannie and Brutus. (For some reason, the two names made Decker think of an old sock-puppet show on television that featured a dragon called Ollie.)

"Hi, Theo," Joshua said.

"Hi, kid." Theodosia nodded to Joshua.

The two Virtues drifted into the foyer.

Elise moved so she was looking Decker straight in the face.

"What's wrong?" Decker closed the door against the cold wind.

"We need you to find something." With a flick of her eyes toward Joshua, Elise added a silent coded message that she needed to keep her mission a secret from the boy. "Can you get dressed quickly?"

Going out would require warm street clothes. Decker was still in his gray cashmere pajamas. "I'll get changed."

Where had he left his clean clothes?

Decker used life's little chores to fill up the empty hours after Joshua had gone to bed. While the world was dark and silent, he washed laundry. He'd found a strange comfort in the warm fabric and meditation of folding clothes. Between loads last night, he'd searched through his books, looking for information on Enyo Graeae. He'd found nothing useful; he'd never replaced the ancient tomes that burned in his Philadelphia home half a century ago. Modern books had her as a footnote to Perseus's legend. All stories about her appearing at Pompeii prior to the eruption, in Rome during Nero's reign, and at the sites of other similar disasters had been lost. He'd given up at dawn and retreated to his casket. He'd forgotten, however, to carry his laundry down to his room. The basket still sat on the floor of the library.

The wolf paced the foyer, unsure it should follow Decker into the library or Theo as she wandered deeper into the house.

"This is the same house that you've always lived in?" Theo called from the living room.

"Yes." Decker sighed as he discovered that Joshua's ginger kitten, Trouble, had lived up to his name and made a bed out of the clean clothes. There was orange hair on the whites and white hair on the darks. How did a kitten shed so much?

"Huh," Theo said. "What I remember was a dump so filled

with crap that it seemed easier to just burn it down than try to clear it out. This doesn't look like the same house. This is nice. A little bare. You could use some art on the walls. It feels like you just moved in. It still smells a little of paint. You've got a cat?"

"What's wrong with that?" The wolf decided that his kitten might need to be rescued from the Virtue.

Decker wasn't totally sure Joshua's kitten was safe from Theo—or that Theo was safe from Trouble. The kitten was odd about who he liked and disliked. The kitten couldn't stand Bethy, which was strange, since she was the only normal person to ever set foot in the house. Trouble had ambushed Bethy over and over on Thanksgiving Day.

Decker hurried to the living room, carrying the basket.

The orange tabby was twining through the massive wolf's feet while Joshua stood guard over it.

"There's nothing wrong with a vampire owning a cat." Theo ignored the horse-size wolf as she continued investigating. "It's just a little ironic. This place used to look like some little old cat lady died here and no one noticed. A refrigerator and a range? So, the whole housemate thing is permanent?"

"It is what it is." Decker refused to be cornered into that conversation.

He placed the basket on one of the island's chairs and picked out a black sweater and pants that wouldn't show blood. He assumed that the Virtues meant to kill whatever they wanted him to find. He didn't know Theodosia well enough to gauge what her reaction to him changing clothes would be. He stepped into the small laundry room off the kitchen to get dressed. He didn't want to go farther away from Joshua. He wasn't totally sure that Elise could protect Joshua from her cousin.

"Did you find the penguin?" Joshua asked as Decker changed clothes.

"I didn't find any signs of shapeshifters at the aquarium," Theo reported. "The sea hag disappeared on me too."

Enyo had been at the aquarium? Was that the fight that she hoped to witness, or was there another—perhaps worse—yet to come?

"Oh! I forgot about Enyo!" Joshua said.

Decker returned to the kitchen to find that Joshua had shifted back to human. The boy started to look for his phone by patting his pockets. (Decker had seen the beginning of the search enough times to recognize the pattern now.)

"I haven't told Seth about Enyo Graeae yet," Joshua said. "I probably should."

"How do you know her?" Elise asked.

"She was at the supermarket last night," Decker answered for the boy. He dropped his pajamas into the laundry basket. "She thinks something big is coming. She's looking forward to the show."

"I should tell Seth something." Joshua's pockets proved to be empty. He started to sort through the clutter on the kitchen island of newly arrived groceries, textbooks, and school notebooks.

Elise caught Decker's gaze and shook her head. She didn't want Seth in Boston. Most likely she didn't want the prince in harm's way or anywhere near Theodosia.

"I'm not sure you need to mention Enyo," Decker said. "She's harmless herself. We don't know why she's in Boston. It would be kind of like mentioning that it's snowing in December. The information is so vague that it's pointless."

Trouble jumped up in the basket to investigate Decker's pajamas.

"No. No! Don't put your hair on my pajamas!" Decker scooped up the kitten and deposited him back on the floor. It was one thing to remove the cat hair from his cotton clothes, it was another to pick it off cashmere.

Theo snickered at Decker as he moved his pajamas into the empty cool dryer.

Joshua had found his phone and was tapping on the screen.

"You're talking to your brother?" Decker guessed. He was also a little surprised how he was able to accept this new odd "magic" of instant messages on the impossible portable phones. He'd remembered how difficult it had been for him to adapt to the first phone installed into his home, back around 1920. It was nearly laughable that, at the time, he thought those primitive devices were horribly complicated.

"No," Joshua shook his head. "I texted Bethy earlier to ask her what she wanted for Christmas and if she had any suggestions what I should get my folks. I'll need to mail their presents soon so that they get them before the holidays."

Joshua paused, his eyes widening a little and he looked at Elise. "Are you going to come for Christmas? Do you do Christmas?"

Elise looked startled and then pleased and then embarrassed, which made Theo snicker again. Elise shot her cousin a hard look. "We don't do Christmas. We're undecided on if Christ was truly the son of God. We were slightly distracted at the time. We were still having running fights with the Wolf King at that point."

"So...do you want to still come? It's not like we're going to do the whole church service thing." Joshua glanced at Decker. "I don't think we can do the whole church thing." He quickly added, "My family never did—at least not after Bethy threw a hissy fit about me being baby Jesus three years running!"

"You?" Elise said with confusion and disbelief. "Baby Jesus?"

Joshua shrugged, frowning at his phone. "The woman that ran the Christmas pageant was a little touched in the head. She apparently went on and on about me being the perfect son of God. Bethy was pissed because she always got cast as a wise man, had to wear a beard, and sing 'We Three Kings.' The song still makes her froth at the mouth."

"Oh, fuck Christmas!" Theo said. "We need to go."

"Yes, I'll be here," Elise said even as she headed toward the door.

Decker got his scarf, gloves and greatcoat from the closet.

"Remember your phone!" Joshua took it from the charger on the foyer table. "That way you can call if you need help or anything."

Decker pocketed his phone. "Don't wait up. You have school tomorrow."

He wanted to tell Joshua to be careful, but if he did, then the boy would probably be even more worried about Decker. Joshua might even want to come with them if he realized how rare it was for Virtues to work together. Theo might be one of Saul's grandchildren, but she was a stranger to Decker. He didn't want to trust her with Joshua's life. He wasn't entirely sure he could trust his own survival with her.

It had started to snow. There were two black Jeeps outside. The one with Maine plates sat in his driveway. Elise's Jeep was parked blocking his drive. A fine dusting of white already covered both vehicles.

"What do you need me to find?" Decker asked as Elise brushed off her windows.

"My brother is missing," Theo said.

"Francis?" Decker stepped back, shocked and dismayed.

"His car is here in Boston—and maybe his driver," Elise said. "We think Francis might be too. Can you get a bead on him?"

Decker closed his eyes and forced himself to ignore the fear that was racing through him. A Power! One of the few things that could vaporize everything that Decker held dear. If the Virtues didn't know where he was, then Francis was operating on God's will alone. It meant that somewhere in the city was a force that required a Power to root it out. This was the fight that Enyo came to see.

Enough. Calm. Focus on the man.

Decker had never met Francis, but he'd heard family gossip about him since his birth. Saul's daughter Petronilla was Theodosia and Francis's mother. Like Clarice, she had been born with a magical power that made her too valuable to be made a Virtue. It was a blow to her ego. She laid her hopes on her children recouping her lost honor. She married to a strong Virtue and hoped to give birth to only Powers.

Lauretta had complained about the fact that Theodosia's mother had treated her daughter as a disappointment when it became clear that the girl would "only" be a Virtue.

Francis was a handful of years younger than Elise, making him not much older than Joshua. One would think he would be a spoiled golden child, having achieved his mother's ambitions. The truth was that Petronilla's ambition was a thirst that could not be slaked. Nothing was good enough. Every fault magnified. Examined. Ground out with grim determination. Francis was, by reports, a sad little boy, desperate to please, always failing to gain the warmth that he wanted.

When Lauretta had died, Elise took over her mother's territory. She rarely saw her cousins and didn't like talking about them to Decker. He was left without a source for family gossip. He had no idea what the sad little boy had grown into.

Where was Francis? He lifted his hand and pointed.

"East?" Elise said. "Oh, he must be close by."

"How can you tell?" Theo said.

Elise pointed east. "The ocean is a little over six miles from here."

"There's boats." Theo would not be persuaded. "And Francis can walk on water."

Of course he could. Powers were all the miracles of Jesus wrapped up with the deadly intent of an atom bomb.

"He's close," Decker said. Unnervingly close to Joshua. "Let's go."

He climbed into the backseat of Elise's Jeep since Theodosia was making no move to clear her vehicle of snow. He left the front passenger seat for Theodosia, who climbed in and belted up.

Elise got in. "Show Decker what I found at the train station."

Theo frowned at Elise. "I said he didn't need to know."

Petronilla had always been jealous of Decker. She wanted to be the center of her father's affection. Saul had fathered children merely to fulfill his duty to his tribe. He thought Petronilla too much like her mother, whom he could barely stand. But even if Decker didn't exist, it was unlikely Saul would have treated his daughter any differently.

Theodosia seemed to have been poisoned by her mother's opinion on Decker. Hopefully Francis didn't drink from the same well. It could make finding him messy. Theodosia was being somewhat polite because it would be rude to kill your cousin's work partner. Francis wouldn't need to follow normal social conventions.

"This is my territory." Elise started her Jeep. "It means I have lead on this case. Decker has always been loyal to our family. He's over three hundred years old. It would be stupid not to tap that knowledge base."

"I know how your family taps his knowledge base," Theo said.

"Do you want to work alone?" Elise snapped.

Theo glanced eastward, toward where Francis might be. She took a deep breath and took gleaming feathers out her pocket. She leaned between the seats so Decker could examine them. She glared at him, warning him with her eyes that he wasn't to touch them.

"Have you ever seen anything like these?" Theo asked.

"Possibly," Decker said. "A breach had opened south of Philadelphia over two hundred years ago. It was during the Panic of 1819. I was working with Melatiah..."

Melatiah had been their great-great-great-great-grandfather born in 1791. At that period of time, Decker would have been under their tribe's protection for nearly a hundred years.

"Were you sleeping with Melatiah too?" Theo asked.

"No." He struggled to leave it at that, but he couldn't help it. He added, "He preferred men of much more bearish nature than me. He struggled with the duty to produce children."

Elise glanced in the rearview mirror, eyes narrowed, willing him to behave.

He didn't add, "Just like your grandfather, he had to be ordered to sleep with a woman."

"Tell us about the feathers," Elise said.

Decker considered the gleaming feathers and their current problem. "It was very long ago. My memories fade over time. I remember that the site was in an odd place for a breach, deep within the wetlands. A vast flock of seabirds had been twisted by the magic. Sea pies. You probably know them as oystercatchers. They're black-and-white birds with long, thick orange beaks. They were once much more common; they might even be extinct now."

"These oystercatchers dropped gleaming feathers?" Theo asked impatiently.

Decker shook his head. "Melatiah wanted to be sure what type of monsters we would be facing. He'd brought feathers like these along for me to use as a touchstone. He said that he'd been taught that there was something odd about crossing birds with magic. They are elusive by nature. They become even more so when magic is applied to them. They become nearly invisible to every ability that normally could be used to locate them."

"So, you're useless?" Theo said.

Decker did not trust Theo enough to be completely truthful. "I can find them, but it is slow and tedious work."

"Every ability?" Elise asked. "What about Seth?"

"I believe that it includes the prince," Decker said. "It is why the Grigori were hunting the breach-borne in the marsh and not the Marquis of Philadelphia."

"Where did Melatiah get the feathers?" Theo said.

"In Greece," Decker said. "Even then the Grigori sent their children across the ocean to be trained. I don't remember now if Melatiah had actually fought the beast while he was in training. He might have been given the feathers as proof of the monster's existence. If I had been able to sense the beast close at hand, though, he planned to call in a Power. The feathers are from a firebird."

"God almighty!" Elise whispered. "We were told that they were most likely mythical."

Two hundred years had apparently erased the creature from the Grigori's collective memory.

"Melatiah believed that the breaches were how the old gods once established toeholds in our realm and why they slipped away, lost, as breaches became less common. The creator of shapeshifters like the firebird rose and fell before the dawn of our civilization—there's no record that it once held sway over our realm. There is no myth to explain most of the bird shapeshifters, they simply are—acknowledged but not explained."

"Can we focus on Francis?" Theo snapped as she tucked away the gleaming feathers.

Decker paused to focus on the missing Power. For a moment, there was nothing, and worry that the boy was dead spiked through him. Then, like the sun coming out from behind a cloud, the way was obvious. "Northeast."

"I thought you said east," Theo said.

"I rarely can go in a straight line to what I want. It is more a matter of triangulation. As I said, it is tedious. The more stressed I am, the slower it goes."

Theo slumped back into her chair to glower at the darkness.

"Did you fight firebirds in the marsh?" Elise asked.

"Luckily, no," Decker said. "Melatiah thought that the breach indicated the return of an old god and that we should be prepared for the worst. The marquis, however, managed to close the breach while we tracked down the birds."

"Did Melatiah tell you anything that is actually useful to us?" Theo grumbled.

"That the firebird was a shapeshifter—hence why it seemed mythical. Yes, it hatched from an egg and grew within a nest, but if it desired, it could take the form of a human."

"Like the werewolves?" Theo asked.

"The werewolves start as men." Decker wanted to remind her to keep Joshua safe. "They are, at their core, as good or evil as any other man. They are non-monsters. That they can live peacefully for centuries beside normal men is proof."

"Loyal?" Theo muttered. "It's been a month, and he's switched sides. So much for three centuries of service."

Service. Yes, that was what it was. To most Grigori, he was nothing more than a pet. A bloodhound.

No. Don't let the anger in. Especially trapped in a small car with two Virtues. Find Francis quickly, for everyone's safety.

He focused on Francis. Nothing. He closed his eyes and pressed hard. Again, the sense of the sun coming out of the clouds, he sensed the boy. "South now."

Forward and back, they went. Their way was made more difficult by a multitude of one-way streets. Elise occasionally ignored the signs and the law and went down them the wrong way. They made their way slowly to the eastern end of Cambridge.

"In there." Decker pointed at the massive, glass-front building. People were streaming in and out of the doors.

"The Cheesecake Factory?" Theo read the sign above the nearest door.

"Give or take a hundred feet," Decker said.

"Oh, God Almighty, the CambridgeSide mall?" Elise cried. "Two weeks before Christmas? Shit!"

Theo jumped out of the Jeep. She didn't even close the door. In three quick strides, she was across the sidewalk and into the mall.

"Fuck!" Elise cried. "Yes, let's talk about what our plan of action is before we run off in separate directions! Damn it, Theo, you're better trained than that!"

But she was talking to an empty seat. Snow drifted in the open door.

"God damn it!" Elise growled. She leaned across, grabbed the passenger door handle, and slammed it shut. "Damn it." Ignoring angry horns and startled shouts, she backed the Jeep up until they were nearly touching bumpers with the car behind them and then pulled into a space labeled CURBSIDE TO-GO PARKING.

"This is illegal as all shit," Elise said. "Stay with the car. I'm not sure if Francis won't nuke you on sight. Clarice and Theo both say he's jumpy as hell. He's blasted some of the monks at the monastery 'by accident.' I don't want to test how flammable you are." She pulled out a police light and put it on the roof of the Jeep. "I'm putting out all my 'I'm a law officer' stuff but that doesn't always fly. There are no guns in the safe, so if someone wants to tow my car . . . try to talk them out of it but don't fight with them." She added in a mutter, "I just want to put out one fire at a time."

And then she was gone.

"I probably should have mentioned that I keep losing track of Francis," Decker said to the empty car. "Something seems to be throwing my ability off."

Too late now. He sighed. Was Francis still in the mall?

The mysterious nothingness.

What about Elise?

Nope. Nothing. Like she had vanished into a deep hole.

What about Joshua?

Joshua was in the mall.

"Oh, no!" Decker fumbled with the door handle and half fell from the car in his hurry. "No, no, no. What is he doing here?"

And then mysteriously nothing—as if Joshua had joined the others in the well.

19: JOSHUA

For some insane reason, the Elf on a Shelf was wildly popular at the CambridgeSide mall. The bloodred doll was everywhere. Watching Joshua with a sadistic grin. Judging him. Finding him naughty.

His wolf didn't like it.

Joshua knew that it was just a marketing ploy sold to parents to guilt trip their kids into being good for the entire month of December. *The Elf on the Shelf is watching. It sees you doing bad things. It will tell Santa Claus.*

His wolf was a four-year-old with sharp teeth.

Joshua stifled yet another growl and shifted so the elf couldn't see him.

He'd texted Bethy before the arrival of the Virtues, asking what she wanted for Christmas. She'd texted back that she wanted gift cards. He'd called Bethy after Decker left to find out what kind of gift cards. She had dumped a load of crazy on him: all hell was breaking loose with his family because he was still "missing" as far as their parents and the police were concerned.

"You said gift card," Joshua said to Bethy when she answered her phone. "What kind? Dunkin' Donuts? Home Depot? From where?"

"Hold on," Bethy said quietly. "Let me close the door to my dorm room."

He listened as she moved closer to some loud female voices, which were apparently girls gossiping in the hallway outside her dorm room. The voices muffled as she shut her door and then silenced as Bethy crossed back to her desk.

"Cash gift cards," Bethy said. "Something like Visa cards. I'll be able to use them at any place that takes a credit card—so gas stations and supermarkets. I'm completely broke at the moment."

"Oh? Oookay," he said. Normally their grandparents handed out pre-Christmas cash to "the exceptional grandkids" on Thanksgiving Day. (Joshua never qualified—something that had mystified him until he found out that he was adopted.) Because of the blizzard, the meal had been postponed until the weekend. He'd assumed that since she left Boston early Saturday morning, she had made it to the postponed meal and gotten her money then. "Didn't Grandma and Grandpa give you your Christmas cash?"

"No," Bethy snapped.

Joshua waited for more information. For a moment there was only silence.

Then Bethy explained in a deep growl worthy of a werewolf. "I had a fight with . . . with everyone. They're all being impossible. I don't know where even to start. I don't know if I should even tell you. It's all petty and stupid and mean. Really, really stupid. I didn't think our parents could be this dense!"

He sat down on the floor, suddenly aware the house was empty and silent, and he was all alone in a strange town. "What happened?"

"I remember that woman—the one that claimed to be your mom—very clearly. I guessed that she stole you almost the moment she started to talk. I kept saying, 'She's lying,' but Mom and Dad never listened to me. I was four at the time. Almost five. But the woman kept going on and on about how she grew up in an orphanage and met the father of her baby there and that he had been killed in a car accident before they could get married, so she didn't have anyone to turn to for help. I don't know why but I kept feeling like I was listening to one of Grandma's soap operas. It just didn't feel real. I don't how many times she said, 'My baby doesn't have any other family than me.' The thing is, soap operas repeat shit like that, so you don't forget the important plot points. After the third or fourth time, I figured it was a story where the main plot twist was going to be that you did have someone other than her. I thought that the only reason she was lying about that was because she stole you from somewhere."

He could remember when they were little, Bethy had told him that he was stolen from someone else. His parents always told him that she was lying. At some point, she stopped teasing him that way.

Had she tried to tell some of the truth to their parents? She couldn't tell them the whole truth. There probably wasn't anyone that would believe the whole truth. Her little adopted brother had been stolen out of his crib and sold to his parents by his kidnapper. He was now a werewolf living in Boston with a vampire, hiding out from witches. (Okay, Joshua didn't think she *knew* about the vampire angle, but the rest was enough to keep her silent.)

Bethy plunged on. "Well... I met up with Mom and Dad at Grandma's house for Thanksgiving. They had gotten that card that you sent them. And oh my God, the crazy stupid theories that everyone came up with. I was going to tell them that I saw you, but I recognize unsolvable stupid when I hear it. I decided not to say anything and just try to put out fires before it could burn down the house, but nothing worked."

"What fires?" Did she mean actual fires?

"Mom and Dad still believe the stupid 'no other family' lie that woman kept saying. I tried to point out that they never got your birth certificate from her, and they had no proof that she was actually your mother. But no, no, let's believe the woman that drove away and never once called to ask how her baby was doing! They'd much rather ignore their prelaw daughter with a four-point-oh average and think you've been kidnapped by bad people who are brainwashing you with lies about being related to you. *It's Stockholm syndrome!*"

The last was in their father's angry bellow.

"They didn't believe anything I wrote in my card?" Joshua said.

"Oh, it's worse than didn't believe!" Bethy cried. "Grandpa decided that the law should be called in. Mom and Dad are going to give him the card and he plans to turn it over to the FBI."

"What?" Joshua leapt to his feet. "Tell me that you're not serious! Why?"

"Because Grandpa is Grandpa!" Bethy grumbled. "He knows best, and he'll cut the purse strings of anyone that says otherwise.

Never mind that his granddaughter, who is zeroing in on summa cum laude, has looked up 'Tatterskein' and found out about the murder/kidnapping case that happened the same day that bitch broke down on the turnpike."

Shit. Bethy knew everything. "You told them about that?"

"No. They were past making sense. I didn't trust Grandpa to keep his mouth shut about it. But the FBI will probably figure it out. How many newborns were kidnapped and never found the week you got adopted? I went back to Mom and Dad's house before they got home and found your adoption paperwork. I have not a clue what Great-Uncle Morton was smoking but they're not legal at all. Half the form isn't filled out! I'm not even sure it got filed with the right state agency! There's no seals or countersigns any-place. New York requires an investigation of the adoptive parents' home—which I know was never done. There has to be proof that the natural parents are voluntarily giving up their rights to their child. None of that legwork was ever done. I have no idea how Mom and Dad got you into school with so little legal paperwork! But put the shifty paperwork together with the murder of your birth mother, and Mom and Dad are in deep shit!"

Great-Uncle Morton was dead, and his law office was closed down. There was probably no one left to vouch that his parents had been led to believe that the paperwork had been properly filled out. The fact that his parents hadn't told the police that he was adopted—even after his holiday card showed up—made it seem like they were hiding the information. Add in the shoddy paperwork, and the police might decide that his parents had killed Anastasia themselves. Only her murderers could have taken him out of his crib and carried him away.

"Since you talked about finding your birth family in your card, the first thing the FBI is going to do is ask for your adop-tion papers!" Bethy said. "They'll want to know who your real parents are. They're going to try and track down that woman who claimed to be your mom."

"Oh, she's dead. She drove into Cayuga Lake near Ithaca a few hours after she left our garage."

"She did? Oh shit. Well, that's a literal dead end. We don't even have the freaking photograph of her and the car anymore. Seth took it and I forgot to get it back from him! The little dipshit!"

What photograph?

"I'm seriously considering just burning the damn adoption papers," Bethy muttered.

"No! Don't do that!" Joshua cried, sure that it would only make things worse. "Why would Mom and Dad even give the card to Grandpa?"

"Because of crazy Great-Aunt Ginny and her quack spiritualist!" Bethy shouted. "She's had a dream about getting an invitation in the mail but when she got to the party, the host said she wasn't invited, and that the invitation was faked. Her spiritualist convinced her that the dream meant that you didn't write the card. Someone killed you and your body is buried somewhere close at hand. For a hefty price, the spiritualist will track your gravesite down!"

"What?" Joshua started to pace the living room. "You've got to be kidding!"

"I told you that I fought with everyone because they'd all gone insane. I swear if I hadn't seen that giant wolf that you become when you're freaked out, I would have driven them all to your doorstep right then and there. As it was, I could barely keep from smacking them all. I don't want to test your wolf's patience—not after seeing Cabot tear that red-haired jerk-face into pieces."

"He did what?" Joshua hadn't heard about that before. She probably meant one of the Wickers in Utica. At least he hoped she meant one of them.

"If I hadn't talked to the Jensens and heard what jerk-face did to them, I might actually have more of a problem with Cabot— but I'm fine. I'm fine."

She didn't sound fine. And how did the Jensens get involved?

"Aunt Ginny talked Mom into believing all the spiritualist bullshit," Bethy continued. "Mom wants to pay the finder's fee, so she needs to get the money off Grandpa and Grandma to pay for it. Grandpa is demanding your card in exchange for the money for the quack. And I wanted to wipe the floor with all three of our cousins! They kept guessing who killed you and where you might be buried! Ian kept saying I killed you. I just wanted to choke-hold him so bad!"

"No, no, Mom shouldn't be paying for that! I'm not dead. Maybe I should call..."

"No! Don't you dare! The FBI will back-trace the phone call

and come for you! You do not have your act together enough to deal with a raid! Even if you don't rip the FBI agents to pieces, it will be a freaking media circus. You have no idea what November was like for Mom and Dad. There were a dozen camera trucks parked at the garage for two weeks after Halloween! I had to leave the first press conferences because I nearly lost it. You will not be able to hold it together."

"What can I do?"

"You can get me some gift cards. Soon. Grandma and Grandpa are pissed off at me and I'm broke now."

His Thanksgiving Day card to his parents had only made things worse. The phone call with Bethy had left him feeling helpless and horribly guilty.

His wolf must have decided that buying the gift cards immediately would make things better. It took him out the door at a full run, coat unbuttoned and flapping in the wind behind him like a cape. He was at the mall minutes later—thankfully still human.

He had been to the CambridgeSide mall only once, shortly after Halloween. It was three stories with a glass roof over the wide central hallway. Since he'd visited it last, it had been decorated with giant red and gold ornaments dangling on red banners. It was crowded with a mysterious horde of little kids all dressed in fancy holiday clothes. Joshua spotted a Santa's workshop with a photographer and "helper elves" who explained that mystery. Parents were bringing their little kids to get their picture taken with Santa.

He found the mall's directory. Where could he get gift cards? T.J. Maxx? CVS? He decided since the drugstores normally had greeting cards that CVS probably would have gift cards. At least CVS wasn't as crowded as the department stores. He found a rack holding a wide range of options. Restaurants. Clothing Stores. Coffee shops. Amazon. Theaters. The Visa ones had a dollar value that ranged up to two hundred and fifty dollars. Bethy had burned through at least a hundred dollars to drive across two states on toll roads to spend Thanksgiving with him. She would need another hundred to get home for Christmas.

Luckily, the wolf had remembered his wallet. It had a stack of hundred-dollar bills in it. Joshua decided to buy two of the two-hundred-fifty-dollar Visa gift cards. He also got a book of twenty stamps, a pack of Scotch tape, three rolls of wrapping paper, and a box of Christmas cards with a simple picture of garland and the words "Peace on Earth." No "Happy Holidays" or "Merry Christmas" for his family but hopefully some peace. He could wish them that without feeling like he was betraying them.

He put the gift cards into his wallet so he wouldn't lose them even if he transformed into a wolf. Coming out of the drugstore, he spotted a display of home-spa gift baskets. To be exact, the wolf noticed the vanilla scent that Elise often wore and took Joshua to it. Elise had been coming over to use the big clawfoot bathtub on the second floor. She said that her condo only had a walk-in shower, and she liked an occasional hot soak during winter. Was it weird to get bath supplies for an older female friend? He would need to get something for her if she was coming for Christmas dinner. He decided to just buy it and hope it wasn't weird.

That made him consider the rest of his gift list. He was already at the mall, and it was a little over two weeks until Christmas. He might as well get as much as he could. He'd planned to send his parents presents. He wasn't sure if it was a good idea. It seemed like just sticking his finger in a leaking dike that held back an ocean's worth of trouble. At the same time, he didn't want to make his parents suffer by not letting them know—from time to time—that he was still alive and "happy." If he didn't send something, then the belief that he was dead and buried might grow.

Should he get something for his parents?

Yes. He should. He was at the mall now. He could express-mail them in the morning with hopes of them arriving in time. The question remained of just what to get his mom and dad.

"Something inexpensive but not cheap." He wasn't sure if his wolf would try to find any other presents, but he should at least give it guidelines. If Marie Antoinette could figure out credit cards, surely his wolf could too. "It should say 'I'm doing fine' without saying where I am. Their presents should be small enough to mail easily. Okay?"

Did the wolf understand? Joshua wasn't sure. It detoured him to a food stand selling something called mochi donuts. There had been a long line that suddenly evaporated. The customers sensed the danger of the hungry wolf waiting impatiently behind them and fled. It was clear that the shoppers didn't know what they were running from; they kept looking over Joshua's head for something more impressive looking.

Joshua bought a twelve-pack assortment of oddly shaped donuts to make his wolf happy. It would be bad for his furry self to pop out in such a crowded place. They were right beside a mockup of Santa's workshop. A sign identified the mock elf village clustered around the foot of a massive Christmas tree as THE NORTH POLE. Green- and red-clad Christmas elves shuffled little kids on and off a massive chair with Santa. It was weirdly similar to the one at his hometown mall, Sangertown Square. The only addition was a scary-looking reindeer that seemed to be guarding Santa or something.

His wolf growled at the reindeer as it looked his direction. Joshua distracted his inner beast by shoving a Fruity Pebbles-covered donut of goodness into his mouth. He should find gifts for his parents and leave.

Donuts in hand, his wolf allowed him to wander the mall, eyeing the various stores for gift ideas. There were a lot of shoe stores, but he didn't know his parents' shoe sizes. Same with clothing. The donuts were gone by the time he looped back to Santa's workshop. There was a Kay Jewelers beside it with brightly lit cases of jewelry. Maybe a necklace for his mom? She didn't wear rings or bracelets since she spent a lot of time working on car engines, but he could get her a pendant and chain. There was a small silver snowflake with black diamond accents that he liked. Oh! No! Not at that price! Actually, none of the pieces were under two hundred dollars.

There was an Elf on the Shelf on the glass display case of necklaces, warning him with a grin to not buy anything for his mom at the store. She would freak out just seeing the name of the store on the box.

"Something inexpensive but not cheap." He chanted the criteria for the presents like a mantra against the Elf on the Shelf. He considered adding "nothing naughty" to the refrain. No. That would only feed the wolf's insecurities. "Something inexpensive..."

"You keep repeating that." Decker appeared suddenly beside him. "Are you worried that you're going to forget?"

Joshua managed to not fling the vampire toward Santa's workshop. The wolf kept hold of Decker. Normally Decker was a sea of calm that the wolf liked to wallow in, but the man seemed unusually tense. "Decker! Where's Elise and her cousin?"

"They're here someplace. Why are you here? Are you shopping for presents? We can shop tomorrow. Please, go home."

"I can't wait for tomorrow." Joshua released the hold he had on Decker. "I called Bethy. I wanted to know what I should get her for Christmas. She dropped this huge load of crazy on me. My parents are still going nuts over me disappearing. They think I've been kidnapped and have been brainwashed or have Stockholm syndrome or something. Apparently when Wonder Woman What's-her-name—the ghost—Jazmin sold me to them, she cooked up some tidy little 'no other family' story to feed them. My parents still believe that whole load of bullshit! They're sure that I'm being deceived by bad people who are just pretending to be related to me."

"To what end?" Decker caught him by the elbow and started to walk them toward the mall exit.

"Exactly!" The wolf turned them around. It didn't want to leave; it wanted to buy presents to solve the problem. It veered into a toy store to pick out a white stuffed seal. "No. Put it down. We're not getting my parents a stuffed animal. Yes, it's very, very cute. My parents don't want it. They don't need it. Oh, God, it's like being chained to a four-year-old! Fine! We'll give it to Maisy! She loved the one at the aquarium." Joshua got in line to pay for the toy. "It gets worse! My grandfather is going to turn my Thanksgiving Day card over to the FBI! I said I was kidnapped as a baby in the card! I didn't think they'd show it to the police! My parents still believe Jazmin was my mother and that whoever took me—in October, not seventeen years ago—made that story up to make me cooperate with my own kidnapping."

"What? Why?"

"Enyo said that Jazmin had some kind of magical power—one that made people believe anything she said. I think that Jazmin put a whammy on my parents so that they would believe her story about being an orphan, having a conveniently dead boyfriend that was the father of her baby, and everything. Bethy never believed Jazmin—I think she must be immune to magic like Jazmin's the same way she's immune to Persuasion. Jazmin must have also put a whammy on my great-uncle Morton. He was the lawyer that handled the paperwork—and it's all messed up, like he was on drugs when he filled it out. Nothing was filed properly. It was all bogus."

Decker had picked up the bags of wrapping paper and fancy bath soaps that the wolf dropped to take possession of the seal. He looked around as if he wasn't actually listening to Joshua. "That stuffed seal is cute, but do we really need to waste time buying it?"

This was because the line barely moved.

"I'm not the one that wants it!" Joshua wanted to fling the stuffed seal across the mall. He couldn't. The wolf had a death grip on the toy. More importantly, with his luck, he would probably nail Santa or one of his elves with the plushie. Doing so would piss off the scary reindeer who was already staring hard at him. He did not want to fight Santa's entire posse in front of a mall full of preschoolers.

"I don't know what to do!" Joshua wailed. "Bethy believes me because she's seen me in every size that my wolf comes in! My parents aren't going to believe witches and warlocks and werewolves without me turning into a wolf—and I don't trust my wolf. I don't think it would hurt them, but what if I'm wrong? What if they freak out and that makes my wolf freak out? What if it's mad that they lied so long to me? I know that I'm upset. You have no idea how many times I asked them if I was adopted, and they straight out lied to my face. Why would they do that to me? If it pisses me off, my wolf is sure to be angry."

"Calm down," Decker said.

Joshua closed his eyes and took a deep breath. Decker was right, it wouldn't do to get upset here. His wolf might pop out. What a mess that would be. Calm refused to come. "I'm worried that even if I tell them my birth mother was murdered, my family still won't believe me. My grandfather plans to go to the FBI. Up to now, the local police didn't know that I was adopted, so they never connected the dots to Anastasia's murder. The case is seventeen years old and in another state. If the FBI finds out I was kidnapped as a baby, they'll check for all the kidnappings in North America. They'll realize I'm Ilya Tatterskein. My 'adoption' would be a smoking gun against my folks."

Joshua opened his eyes to find that the line had vanished. The other shoppers had sensed the wolf lurking just under his skin and fled. Unfortunately, so had the cashier. "Oh, no!"

The wolf decided that chewing on the seal's flipper would be a good thing.

"Really?" Joshua mumbled around the fake fur.

"It might be better if I pay for it." Decker patted his pockets. "Oh. Oh dear, I left the house without my wallet."

Joshua gave Decker enough money to cover the toy, found an identical seal for the cashier to ring out, and then wandered out into the mall trying to pretend he wasn't chewing on a shoplifted stuffed animal. Once the cashier came back, the toy wouldn't be stolen, but until the transaction was complete, technically it was.

This seemed to bother Santa's reindeer. It started to drift toward Joshua, hampered by a crowd of toddlers trying to hug it. (Joshua really didn't understand why the little kids loved such a scary-looking creature when Santa Claus was making all the babies cry.)

The wolf went in the opposite direction to put distance between him and the reindeer. As he reached the far exit, three tall, thin men came through the glass doors.

The center man had flame-red orange hair so striking that it had to be dyed. His eyes had orange irises with dark brown pupils. He wore a cape of gleaming feathers of red, yellow, and orange. The two men flanking him were white-haired with fully black eyes. There was something strange about their faces, too thin and angular, as if someone had grabbed their foreheads and chins and pulled their heads into a long oval. The men didn't seem to notice him. Their attention was on a stone that the man on the right held in his hand. It glittered and pulsed.

The wolf growled at the sight of the men. It didn't like them, and it really hated the way that the weird stone glittered in a way that the light leapt across the crowded mall directly at Joshua. He decided to turn tail and head back to Decker. Things were getting too strange. It was time to flee the mall.

Joshua ran into the reindeer before he found Decker.

At least, he thought it was a reindeer. The furry mascot costume was mostly brown with the exception of a white belly and face and four black "hooves." Instead of deer antlers like most reindeer he'd see, it had horns like a goat. It was only inches taller than Joshua's five foot two but somehow it seemed to loom over him. Its mouth was stitched into a permanent grin that looked terrifyingly sinister.

The wolf growled at the reindeer through teeth locked on the stuffed seal's flipper.

"Just move along, reindeer," Joshua said, or at least, tried to say. His mouth was full of cotton and fake fur. It came out as "Hhst mmmm mmmmm, hmmdmmh."

The reindeer cocked its head, puzzled.

"Chamois." The reindeer's voice was definitely male. He sounded young, like he might be a high schooler or college student with a part-time job.

"Hmm?"

"I'm a chamois, not a reindeer." The person inside the fur suit reached up with their black glove "hooves" to indicate the costume's horns. "See? Reindeer are cervid; they have antlers like their cousins, the white-tail deer. Chamois are bovid, or goats. They have horns."

Joshua pried the stuffed toy out of his mouth as he eyed Santa Claus, the workshop, the massive Christmas tree, and the dozen elves trying to corral tired children onto Santa's lap. "What... what's a goat doing at the North Pole?"

The wolf clamped down on the seal's flipper again.

"Purging evil with holy fire," the chamois said. "Or at least that's what I thought God wanted me to do. It's quite depressing, if you think about it much, so I try not to. Maybe, though, I was just supposed to meet you here. I thought you were in New York, with the Wolf King and your cousin the Thane. What are you doing here with Silas Decker?"

Joshua froze in surprise and alarm, thinking *Oh shit, oh shit, oh shit.*

He found himself suddenly looking down at the chamois. He'd transformed into an impossibly huge wolf, standing six feet taller than the goat. The stuffed seal dangled from the wolf's mouth by one flipper, which was good, as Joshua was afraid he might have swallowed it.

The chamois did an amazing mime of surprise, flinging its arms wide while leaping back. It put its hands to its oversized head and wobbled back and forth. "Oh, no, no, no!" the chamois cried as it shook its head. "Don't startle me like that! That's so dangerous!"

The crowd stopped and stared at the massive wolf suddenly looming over them. They gaped in amazement, like the goat had just done a magic trick: pulled a giant wolf-shaped balloon out of his sleeve. They "ooh'd" and "ahh'd" without fear.

"It's a hologram," one man said confidently.

The toddler on Santa's lap decided that it had had enough. It didn't like the big man in the red suit. It didn't like its matching Santa suit. It didn't like the big black "dog." It clawed the red hat off its head, flung it hard on the ground, and let out a primal scream of fear and distress.

The scream worked like a hard slap on the crowd. For one stunned minute, they stood, completely silent, eyes wide as they realized that the massive wolf was real. The sudden silence was painfully surreal. The chaos that erupted afterward was almost a relief.

"Oh, it begins." The chamois was an image of limp disappointment, sagging forward, arms dangling, head shaking. "The screaming. The fleeing in terror. The fire."

"What fire?" Joshua roared and accidently spat the stuffed seal at the chamois.

The chamois dodged the seal missile without seeming to notice. "There's always fire when I get lost. Sooner or later. God wills it."

The crowd washed away, leaving behind the three strange-looking men with the glittering stone.

The one holding the stone gazed down at it and hissed in anger. "*Cazzo!* I've lost it! It was nearly close enough to reach out and take it—and then it was gone!"

"I don't see that *stronzo* Alvarez." The other white-haired man had turned his back to Joshua as the crowd fled. He stood scanning the fleeing shoppers. Both of them had a thick Italian accent. They didn't sound Argentinian. Were they some other kind of shape-changing bird? Or a different kind of monster?

The red-haired man *stared* at Joshua, hissed a curse that might have been Russian. "The black wolf prince! We can't allow him to stop us."

Joshua backed up. "No! Wait! I'm not—"

No, don't tell them. Protect Seth.

The Italian man on the left flung open his long coat, revealing that he had a sword sheathed at his side. He grabbed the hilt and pulled the blade. It was a weird misty black, as if an evil miasma had partially solidified into a weapon. Darkness crawled over the blade and wafted around the swordsman.

Joshua could feel the power and knew with no uncertainty that he did not want to be hit by the sword. It would do terrible things to him. The silver bullets were harmless in comparison.

"Run!" Joshua scrambled backward.

There was a blinding white-hot flare as a pillar of fire punched through the ceiling of the mall. It hit the floor just feet from Joshua with a deep throaty roar of flame. Heat flashed over Joshua.

Joshua blinked rapidly, trying to clear his vision, too stunned to flee. *What? What?*

There was a hole punched through the ceiling to the black sky. Snow started to fall down through the opening. The column of flame had hit too close to the brightly colored Santa's workshop. The little building caught fire and was burning merrily.

"Jiminy Cricket!" the chamois cursed very softly. The North Pole sign exploded. The chamois slapped its hooves over its suit's muzzle.

"It's a Power!" the Italian man on the right cried, pointing at the chamois. "Kill it quick or we're all dead!"

"A Power?" Joshua echoed in confusion. The chamois was a Grigori like Elise? Was this another one of Elise's cousins?

The swordsman charged toward the chamois, screaming. A second column of white-hot flame flashed downward. Joshua leapt backward even as it hit the swordsman in a blinding strike.

When his vision cleared, there was a pile of white ash at the center of a blackened scorch mark where the swordsman had been. A misshapen lump of blackness was all that remained of his blade.

His wolf was backpedaling from the remaining two men. It didn't want to be anywhere near them. Joshua agreed with it completely, but he was worried about Decker. Wouldn't holy fire be like silver to the vampire? Joshua scanned the fleeing crowd. Had Decker done the smart thing and run?

The man in the feathered cloak hazed into a shimmering blood red light, rippling as it expanded. It solidified into a dinosaur-looking bird even larger than Joshua. It was covered with scales and feathers. Its feet and belly were yellow. Its tail was an iridescent teal. Its head was deep red with a spiky cockscomb like a rooster's while its back was a fiery orange red.

The massive bird turned toward the chamois, who was now miming panic by wind milling his arms. The giant beast gave a deep threatening rumble that Joshua could feel against his skin. Its orange eyes—the size of dinner plates—blazed with anger.

There was another column of white-hot flame, this time

aimed at the bird monster. The fire roared down over the beast. A shimmering shield blocked the searing blaze inches from the brightly colored scales. The beast shook off the fire with an angry hiss. It lunged toward the chamois. The chamois looked like a stuffed toy next to the massive bird.

"Watch out!" Joshua cried.

His massive wolf pounced on the bird. They slammed to the ground at the feet of the chamois. Elsie's probable cousin threw up his arms and scampered to the side crying, "No! No! You're going to bring the whole mall down around our ears! Think of all the innocent bystanders! The children! Santa Claus!"

The bird roared and shook the wolf from his back. As Joshua scrambled to all four feet, he realized he still had no clue how to fight as a wolf. He had no "hands" to grab hold of leverage points. He wasn't sure how to judge the balance of his foe. He backed up, trying to figure out how to pin the monster.

The bird took a deep breath. All Joshua's instincts screamed "Dragon breath!" Could this dinosaurlike bird breathe fire too? Joshua ducked behind Santa's wide red throne just in case. With a deep "woof" the bird breathed out a gout of flame. The chair hadn't been wide enough. Joshua's tail caught fire.

The sprinkler kicked on, raining water down onto them, putting out Joshua's tail and dampening the spirits of the burning chair.

"The Power!" the one man still alive shouted. He gestured toward the chamois. "Kill the Power!"

The bird roared in annoyance and turned toward the chamois.

The wolf took it as an opening. It leapt for the base of the bird's neck. Its teeth hit thick scales.

"No, no, not there!" Joshua cried. The base of the bird's neck was too close to its center of gravity. He couldn't get leverage to shift it.

The dinosaur bird spun. Its heavy tail hit Joshua hard. It sent him tumbling across the floor.

"I'll kill the wolf!" the remaining man shouted as he produced a bow. "Get the Power!"

The bird ignored his companion. It lunged at Joshua with stunning speed. Its massive jaws caught him in the hip. Joshua howled in pain as the teeth snapped together, tearing open a wound.

A black-tipped arrow whined past Joshua's head trailing dark mist.

There was a brilliant flare of light as the chamois reduced the bowman to ash.

The bird roared with anger. It flung Joshua away and whirled toward the chamois. It breathed in deep to ready its flame.

Was the Power fireproof? Joshua doubted it. If the bird was like a chicken, then its weakest point was where its neck met the base of the skull. A hard enough twist would kill it.

Joshua dashed forward to gain momentum. He aimed for the bird's throat. His jaws locked down on the narrow column. He flung himself forward to jerk the monster off its feet. He heard the sickening crack as the spine separated. The bird thrashed wildly; its limbs flailed as all its nerves fired in protest of its death.

The wolf shook its head, making sure that the bird's spine was broken.

Only when it went limp did Joshua remember it had been a human, just like him.

He'd killed a man.

Not for the first time. Somehow the Wickers had been less traumatic; he'd felt no remorse after watching Rowan Wakefield kill his own daughter.

Joshua had been buying Christmas presents. Minding his own business. How did it end up like this?

The wolf gave the bird another hard shake, making him horrifyingly aware he still had the dead shapeshifter in his mouth.

Joshua tried to release it. The wolf growled and shook the bird more.

"It's dead! Put it down!" Not an easy thing to say while your mouth is filled with meat and blood. "Oh! Stop it!" This was because the wolf went into overdrive, shaking the dead body. "Bad wolf! Bad wolf!"

"It's not really dead," Decker said, appearing beside him. "You've only paralyzed it temporarily. It will heal the wound and attack again."

Yay? Joshua hadn't actually killed the man but now he was stuck with an angry fire-breathing chicken monster in his mouth.

"Put it down." Decker's eyes were fully black. His blood sword gleamed wet red in his hand. "I'll dispatch it."

The wolf dropped the bird and backed away.

Decker swung down his sword. The red gleaming blade sank

deep into the bird's neck. Power roared up the sword to Decker's hands. The beast went still, withering as Decker fed on its magic.

"No, Decker!" the chamois cried, waving madly. It covered his eyes and turned away.

That can't be good.

Joshua snatched Decker up in his mouth and leapt to the second-story walk. A moment later, a massive flare went off. The heat of the explosion washed over them. When he could see again, there were bright feathers mixed with white ash where the bird had lain. His tail was singed a little more and Decker's coat was steaming.

"Decker!" Joshua put him down to pat massive paws over Decker's coat. "Are you okay?"

Decker grimaced with pain. "I feel like I stood in the sun too long. It hurts but it will heal quickly. You're hurt."

"I am? Oh, yeah, it bit me." It was Joshua's turn to wince as Decker examined the wound on his hip.

There was the sound of someone clapping slowly. On the other side of the mezzanine, Enyo stood at the railing. "I'm glad I brought popcorn!" She lifted up a red-and-white-striped bucket. "It was a good fight!" She took a handful of fluffy white kernels and made a show of stuffing them into her mouth.

"You bitch!" Decker snarled.

She cackled, spitting out popcorn, and vanished.

20: ELISE

Elise was on the third floor at the other end of the mall when the fight broke out. She had just spotted Theo disappearing into Macy's when there was an odd, abrupt silence behind her. It made her aware that moments earlier the mall had been filled with the loud chatter of hundreds of people. For some reason, the crowd had gone completely silent. She turned as the screaming started. A giant black wolf that loomed over the holiday shoppers was the obvious cause, the crowd parting like the Red Sea around it.

Joshua? What was that overgrown puppy doing here? Had he followed Decker? No, that didn't make sense—not with the path the Grigori had taken to get here. Fate was an odder travel agent than random chance. God needed the boy at the mall—but why?

Both escalators were packed with shoppers standing and gawking down to the first floor, instead of running away like reasonable people. She pushed her way through the people, swearing at the mall's limited access between the various floors. There were only two escalators to the lower levels, one each at either end of the long mall. She could see that the pair from the first floor were even more crowded.

The large Christmas tree and Santa's workshop blocked Elise's view of whatever had triggered the werewolf. She headed for the escalator between the first and second floors, cursing inwardly. Joshua had little control over his beast. They could be up to their necks in ferals if he bit anyone not already connected to a magical source. What was he fighting?

There was a supernova of light from the center of the mall followed by a curse-born explosion.

"Oh, God in heaven!" She breathed. Francis! What did the holy fire hit? The wolf was still standing. Where was Decker? Did he stay in the car like she told him to?

There was an odd shimmer near the wolf that expanded and transformed into a firebird.

"Oh shit," she whispered. "I was hoping those would stay mythical."

Elise pushed through the crowd on the escalator from the second floor down to the first. It was even harder as the shoppers—unable to cram themselves through the mall's exit—were fleeing up both sets of escalators.

"You can't get out that way," they said between curses as she shoved through them.

"I don't want out!" Elise cried.

At the other end of the mall was the roar of flame. The mall's fire suppression system went off. Water rained down from sprinklers high overhead. More flares. Roars. Wolf howls and growls and snarls.

Elise was nearly to the combatants when the massive black wolf snatched Decker up in his jaws and leapt upward to the mall's second-floor walkway. Thus warned, Elsie ducked into a shoe store for cover. Seconds later, white holy fire blasted away the dead firebird, the Christmas tree, and the already burning Santa's workshop.

She carefully stalked forward, daggers out, ready for attack. Francis should be the only thing standing but she couldn't see him. There was only someone in an animal fur suit, gripping their head in an overtly dramatic reaction to the destruction around them.

"Francis?" Elsie shouted, hoping to draw out her cousin. "Francis?"

The person in the costume turned. "Elise? Elise!"

Oh, it is Francis in the fur suit. Elise sheathed her blades as the chamois (at least she thought it was a chamois) bounded toward her, crying, "Elise! Elise!"

She was hugged as if Francis wanted to be picked up and carried. "What are you wearing?"

"I'm a chamois!" he cried.

"Yes, I can see that, but why?" she asked and then realized it probably wasn't the most important information about him currently.

"Fur suits are like a security blanket that you wear." Francis petted himself. "It's like when they swaddle infants. I find it comforting. I've been collecting fur suits. I get them online. I think this one was made in France. I also started traveling with a weighted blanket. It helps me stay calm."

That explained the oddly heavy blanket in his car. Clarice had started to say something about Francis buying animal something-or-other. Elise hadn't let her finish. It was probably "fur suits."

Elsie scanned the ruined mall as the fire suppression system tried to put out the burning Santa's workshop. "What are you doing in Boston?"

"I don't know! I was sitting at home yesterday morning, eating breakfast and watching Drew Barrymore, when God just up and dropped me in the North End of Boston!"

He was wearing the fur suit while eating breakfast? No wonder Theo thinks he's broken.

Francis continued explaining the last day. "I've been wandering around since then, trying to figure out what God wants me to do. I even wandered around in the bay for a little while—totally freaked out some people in boats."

"Why didn't you call Central?" Elise tried to stick to the important details. "Call me? Call Theo?"

"I'm sorry. I know I should have called Clarice, but I didn't have my phone." Francis patted his furry chest. "I don't have my street clothes on under this. I normally keep my phone in my pants pocket. It's probably still in my bedroom with my jeans—maybe. Roustabout might have picked it up to bring to me. I tried to find you, but I just know you're someplace in Cambridge. I don't even know where Decker lives. I thought I might be able to find your Jeep but bleep-bleep there's a lot of black Jeeps in Boston!"

Francis couldn't swear as his words were actual curses that could destroy anything he was facing. It was the one of the many reasons Elise never attempted to become a Power.

Francis continued to explain why he hadn't called anyone. "I borrowed a phone off a man walking an entire pack of dogs to call Roustabout and let him know where I was. I was lucky to be able to make that call—the man only trusted me because all the dogs fawned over me, as usual."

Very young children and animals recognized their creator in Powers. Their behavior toward Powers bordered on worship.

Francis continued to explain. "Even then, the dogwalker kept hold of his phone and had me shout at it—so the conversation was stilted," Francis said. "I really couldn't call Central to tell Clarice that I'd been deployed by God or call you to warn you about impending doom. By then I figured out you lived somewhere near the Red Line, so I told Roustabout to meet me at Alewife. I thought I'd be able to use his phone once we met up. But when I got to Alewife, Roustabout never showed up."

That explained much.

"Elise!" Decker called from far overhead. "I found Francis!"

"Yes, I know!" Elise shouted back.

"The firebird bit Joshua," Decker called. "I would like the royal vet to see him. I'm calling my work here done. We're going to get a cab and go there."

"We have phones, you know!" she shouted back, not liking to air their private business in public. There were already idiots with phones creeping back to film them. At least Francis was in the silly fur suit. Still, she didn't want to show up on video on the nightly news. "Francis, go into area-cloaking mode."

Francis made a gesture. Ghostly wings sprouted out of the back of the fur suit. He drifted off the ground. The area around them got less smoky and the cold wind from the broken ceiling stopped blasting over them.

"I'm sorry about the fire!" Francis called up to Decker. "God smites any dark powers operating near me! He never consults me on what he's going to smite!"

"Yes, I know. I should have remembered that!" Decker called back. "We're going now! Goodbye! Godspeed!"

"He's nice," Francis said to Elise quietly. "But I always assumed he was—given our family's history with him. Theo!"

Francis leapt to his sister, who allowed herself to be hugged tightly.

"We need to get out of here," Elise said.

Francis wasn't done hugging his sister. "I didn't expect to see you here, Theo!"

"You up and disappear, what else was I to do but look for you?" Theo said gruffly. "Let's go."

Elise led the way back to her Jeep. As they walked, she pulled out her phone and called Central Office.

Clarice answered the phone with, "Did you find Francis? If you didn't, try the CambridgeSide mall. It just lit up like a Christmas tree on a bonfire!"

"We're leaving there now with Francis," Elise said.

Francis leaned in to say, "Hi, Clarice!"

"Oh, good! You've got about one minute before the police arrive in force," Clarice said. "Hi, Francis!"

"Can you call Roustabout and let him know that I'm okay?" Francis said.

There was a slight pause and Clarice said, "Sure."

"My place is a bit too small for all three of us," Elise said. She didn't say she really didn't want all her clothes nuked out of existence if something startled Francis in the middle of the night. "Clarice, we're going to the depot. There's a ton of space there."

"Understood!" Clarice said.

They reached her Jeep and climbed in just as screaming police cars and fire trucks came pouring into the area with lights flashing, sirens and horns blaring. Luckily everyone was more focused on the fire and the crowds than on her vehicle. Elise was able to pull out and drive away as if the chaos had nothing to do with them.

21: JOSHUA

The wolf was rattled. The wolf didn't want to change back into human.

After two fights, with several different kinds of monsters in one day, Joshua wasn't sure that his wolf was totally wrong. Somehow, he'd become a weirdness magnet, and strange things kept happening to him. Deadly things.

His wolf did shrink down to puppy size and allowed Decker to carry him and all the shopping bags of Christmas presents and wrapping paper out to the waiting cab. It complained with whines and howls and grumbling noises, mostly with its head hidden under Decker's arm.

Decker kept up a soothing patter of conversation. "We'll go and see the nice vet. She'll look at that bite wound and tell us not to worry and send us home with doggy treats. We'll order pizza and watch a movie. Something without monsters. Maybe a musical. *Singin' in the Rain* was fun to watch. Or a Christmas comedy to get into the spirit of things."

The wolf howled at the word "spirit," remembering the weird ghost tentacles.

"A musical, then," Decker promised. "One without monsters."

Dr. Huff, the royal vet, had a combination home and veterinary office maintained by the Prince of Boston. The lights were off in the office, so Decker carried Joshua around to the house entrance and rang the doorbell.

Dr. Huff answered the door with a quilted bathrobe thrown over a granny nightgown. One of her braids was undone but her Goth makeup was still in place. Having met the Goths at Blackridge, Joshua now wondered where she had gone to high school and if her signature style perhaps had been influenced by the "gifted" students.

"Silas Decker!" Dr. Huff pointed at Joshua with both hands, "Is that . . . ?"

It was the first time she'd seen him at puppy size.

"Stupid wolf won't let me change back," Joshua answered for himself.

"He's been bitten by a firebird." Decker added. "I'm worried."

"I thought those were mythical! Come in!" She stepped aside, shooing back her three dogs, who were excited at seeing Joshua again. The Jack Russell terrier was leaping up and down like he was on springs. The pitbull and the three-legged black lab were trying to nose past Decker's fending hand to lick Joshua's face.

"Not the face! Ugh, doggy spit! Stop wagging your tail, you idiot," Joshua grumbled, the last directed at his wolf, who liked the attention.

"Let's go to the examination room." Dr. Huff led the way through her home toward the door into her clinic.

"I'm not that hurt," Joshua said. "It's just a scratch. It's just that weird, terrible things keep happening to me. I just want to live a normal life. Go to school. Take my math test tomorrow—hopefully not fail it. Graduate. Go to college. Figure out what I want to do with my life. I have to do something! I can't just sit at home all day playing video games. It would be fun—for a while—but I want to matter. I want to make things that help people or help people in trouble or something. I don't know what."

"Well, he's not going feral if he's worried about tomorrow's math test," Dr. Huff said. "Wolves are very much the here and now. The only reason why werewolves can run businesses is because the human stays at the helm."

At the door to her offices, she paused to take out some dog treats. She gave one to Decker to feed to Joshua and then split another one up among her three dogs.

The wolf ate the treat while Joshua grumbled, "I want to change back."

It did not help that he could feel Seth and the Wolf King

doing their "Peeping Tom" thing, watching from afar in what was probably insane worry. If he changed back, he was sure that his phone would start dinging with demands that he stop doing what he was doing. (Like he *wanted* to be doing what he was doing!)

"Let's not be hasty," Dr. Huff said. "Magical bite wounds are nasty things. You might not be able to change until the wound is cleaned with Earthblood. Besides, you heal faster as a wolf."

"Seth and the king—or someone else; who knows, I might have some weird fairy godmother—keeps checking on me. There. Seth is doing it again."

Decker's pocket vibrated with an incoming call. He set Joshua down on the polished steel examination table and took out his phone. "It's the prince."

"See, I told you!" Joshua said.

Decker pushed ANSWER on his phone and speaker (although it wasn't clear if he did it on purpose as he looked surprised when Seth's voice came out of the phone so loud and clear).

"How badly is he hurt?" Seth asked.

Dr. Huff pulled on gloves and examined the raw-looking wound on Joshua's hip. "The bite doesn't appear to contain poison. I'm still going to rinse it with Earthblood to be sure. The wound itself is large, but the bite isn't deep. No bones were broken. He should be fine with a night's rest."

"Did Elise tell you why there's a second Virtue and a Power in the city?" Seth asked.

Joshua glanced toward Decker since he didn't know.

"God deployed Francis without his phone," Decker said slowly, as if cautiously picking his words. "As far as the Grigori were concerned, he just vanished out of Vermont. That's Theodosia's territory and he's her little brother, so she was the first to notice. He had called his driver to come pick him up, and his car is here in Boston, so the Virtues believe that the driver drove down from Vermont. Elise thinks the driver was jumped at Alewife station by shapeshifters. She and Theodosia were focused on quickly finding Francis. His driver—a man by the name of Roustabout—is still missing. From what the Virtues told me, my guess is that Francis will not leave Boston until he finds Roustabout—dead or alive."

"Joshua, how did you end up fighting... fighting... whatever that was?" Seth asked.

"I was Christmas shopping!" Joshua growled. "The stupid thing just showed up and jumped me."

"I believe it was one firebird and two male swan maidens," Decker said. "One of the swans had a witching stone. It works much like my ability—it allows someone to find items of great magical power. While dowsing is considered a divine power by the Grigori, the creation of such a stone is done by blood magic. A witch kills a dowser and ties their soul to a crystal. The Grigori destroy such items when they find them. Between the rarity of the true dowsing ability, lack of witches willing and able to do blood magic, and the Grigori's general policy, witching stones are exceedingly rare. I've only seen one other in my entire lifetime. The swan maidens—males—also had magical weapons that I didn't recognize."

"What were they tracking?" Seth asked. "Joshua?"

"They said something about almost finding something and then it disappeared," Decker said. "Since Joshua was impossible to miss at that point, it wasn't his wolf."

"I doubt it was me as a human either," Joshua said. "They thought I was you. You know, big black wolf—must be the prince. But if they were chasing me—Joshua—then they wouldn't think my wolf was you."

"Yeah, that makes sense," Seth said. There was a moment of silence from the phone, and then his brother asked, "Could it have been that weird thing you had in your locker? It's not there now."

"What weird thing? Oh! That! Um…" Joshua tried to remember what he had done with it. He'd barely beat the grocery delivery truck to Decker's house. He was trying to cook dinner and put away food when Decker woke up. Then the Virtues showed up. He talked to Bethy and then his wolf ran him to the mall. Oh, yes, his unbuttoned coat had flapped like a cape during the entire run to the mall. "I never took it out of my coat. So…it's wherever my coat goes when I transform."

"It might be better if it stays there," Seth said.

"I'm not staying a wolf!" Joshua said.

"Yes, you are," Dr. Huff said. "I need to wash out that wound and then you need to heal. Stay! Don't move."

She headed back into her home.

Decker raised a finger. "What exactly is that 'thing' that we're discussing?"

Joshua explained the strange coin that Vijay found in Marie Antoinette's purse after they returned to school. "It's creepy as all hell. Since I was the one in the least amount of danger from it—whatever it is—I took it and put it in my coat pocket."

"Which is now...elsewhere," Decker said. "A place only you can reach."

Joshua nodded.

"I agree with your brother," Decker said. "The witching stone was destroyed when Francis fire-bombed the swan carrying it. It's unlikely that the swans have a second witching stone. But we're up to our ears in odd fowl monsters. If you transform here, we put Dr. Huff in danger—especially if the monsters arrive after we leave."

Joshua was going to protest but as Decker finished his argument on why he should stay a wolf, he let out a small "Oh" of realization that Decker was completely right. "Okay, I'll stay this way until we get home."

22: DECKER

The problem of having a reason to live was it came with the fear of losing it. It was a terrible, dark feeling. Decker hid it the best he could as they waited in the bitter cold for the cab to arrive.

"Will it actually be safe for me to change back to human at the house?" the puppy in his arms asked.

"Yes, it will," Decker said with more certainty than he felt. "Sioux Zee Whitebrow put wards on my house before I moved in. The prince is the only one that can scry anything within the walls of my home. It is the nature of his Source; it comes from the land itself. No one else can sense what lies within my house nor force their way into it. For anyone using magic to seek me out, it would be as if I had vanished into a void—much like where your coat is now."

"So, you knew Winnie and her grandmother before I met them?" Joshua asked.

"No. I have never actually met Sioux Zee. The prince—your great-grandfather—arranged it."

"Really?"

It was a painfully bleak time in Decker's life. "After my house burned down in Philadelphia, Saul thought it best to move me completely out of the city. I . . . I didn't care. There seemed to be no point." He wanted to be left alone to mourn all that he'd lost. His entire staff of servants, some of whom had been with him for decades. Everything that he'd gathered over the centuries; many of the items were all he had left from Grigori that he'd loved who were now long dead. The sense of safety and normalcy. He was a monster once again—fleeing before the hordes armed with pitchforks and torches. *Burn the monster out.*

"There was no way I could have stayed hidden from the prince," Decker said. "Like Seth, he would be able to spot me from anywhere. Saul met with him to ask permission for me to move into Cambridge. Luck—if you want to call it that—had it that it was shortly after the tragedy of all the pack's children going feral. The prince had to consider a future where there would be few wolves to protect the city. The Grigori had settled in Philadelphia shortly after William Penn was granted what would be Pennsylvania in 1681. They have a peaceful relationship with the wolves who arrived roughly twenty years later. Well, 'peaceful' might be overstating it. They mostly ignore one another except in extreme emergencies—but it meant I was a known quantity to the Philadelphia pack. The marquis gave me a letter of introduction for the Prince of Boston..."

He was rambling, uneasy with all that had happened during the day. He paused, trying to remember why he'd been talking about days past. Oh, yes, the wards on his house.

"The prince had opened Blackridge to all those with gifts, since it would be years until there would be younglings to attend it. It made him aware how many of the people under his protection could easily stumble across my resting place. Since the marquis had reassured him that I was a worthy ally, the prince decided that he would have the Wise Woman place wards upon whatever home I moved into."

Joshua surprised him by asking, "So by 'Wise Woman,' you mean Sioux Zee?"

It was hard to remember, as Joshua shifted in and out of wolf form, that he didn't grow up within a community of wolves who were familiar with the occult side of the world.

How should he explain Sioux Zee? Now that he considered the question, Decker realized that all his knowledge of Wise Women was secondhand. He hadn't actually spoken to one, face-to-face, during his entire three-hundred-plus years of existence. Not before he became a vampire and certainly not afterward.

"They are women from certain families that are blessed with very strong divine gifts. I suppose in some ways, they are like

Enyo—their gift is to know things. They can foresee the future, speak with the dead, commune with the spirits of nature and any other number of things. Over the centuries, they've amassed a great deal of knowledge that they pass down to their children. You could call them scholarly mages. While they have no real organization beyond family ties, every major city has one woman who bears the title Wise Woman."

"Oh wow, so Sioux Zee is a big deal?"

"Her family are the oldest line of Wise Women in North America," Decker said. "Barnabas Tatterskein, the first Prince of Boston, extended his protection to them during the Puritan rule of the area."

The puppy cocked its head. "I suppose Winnie knows a lot about weird things."

"Sioux Zee had married Arnie Whitebrow, who was a powerful medium. The ability to be a Wise Woman, as the name suggests, is typically inherited by females. Sioux Zee had all boys, and Winnie is her only female grandchild. It is quite possible she's training Winnie to be Boston's next Wise Woman."

The cab pulled up to the curb, cutting short their discussion. As they were wont to do, they got out at the corner instead of in front of the house. The snow crunched underfoot as he carried the puppy and his shopping bags home.

Decker stood on the furnace grate, letting hot air blast over him once the door was firmly locked. He closed his eyes and focused on his ability: where were the active wards on his house? One by one he picked them out, flicking his finger from hidden ward to hidden ward. The nearest one was above the door on the inside of the coat closet, covered by a piece of oak paneling. Another was by the back door, hidden behind the wainscoting of the mudroom. Others were inside window wells where the counterweights hung. Every possible entrance was covered. None of the spells seemed damaged or inactive. Sioux Zee had been very thorough.

At the time he gave it no thought, assuming that what the prince wanted, the prince received. Considering the decades since, Sioux Zee must have wanted the extra protection that Decker afforded the city as much as the prince did.

It was an oddly comforting—although belated—realization.

Decker opened his eyes as the puppy squirmed in his hold. Putting its paws on his shoulders, it looked deep into his eyes.

"Are you okay?" Joshua asked with concern in his voice. "Francis did get close with that last nuke."

"I'm just cold," Decker lied slightly. "I was in a little pain at the vets, but I heal quickly, and the pain has passed."

"You sure?" Joshua pressed. "Do you need to feed?"

Healing drained his energy stores. It was lucky that he'd killed the firebird, otherwise he would be ravenous beyond control. He probably could hold out. Considering how the last two days had been, that might be a bad assumption.

"Maybe a little," Decker admitted.

"Let's practice, then," Joshua said.

It was something they'd worked on for the last week since the fight with the Wickers. Their first two times of feeding, Decker had been famished and barely in control of himself. Doing it when he was only slightly hungry meant that it didn't have to become something big and emotionally messy.

He leaned his head down and touched foreheads with the puppy. Concentrating, he slowly fed on a trickle of power. Warmth flooded through him. It reminded him of the play of sunshine he'd seen in the foyer. The light was seeping back to his world.

After a few minutes, he broke the contact. "I'm good now."

"Great!" The puppy jumped down to the floor. "Whoa, you're going to need a new coat. That one is really singed."

"I have some old coats—someplace." Decker pulled off his gloves, loosened his white scarf that was now gray, and unbuttoned his long woolen coat. His fingertips turned black from soot. There were small holes in the wool. Joshua hadn't cleared out all the closets. The coats Decker had set aside over the decades should be in one of them.

The thoughts of lost coats reminded Decker of the discussion at the vets. "Let me see this mystery-coin thing that you got from Marie Antoinette."

The puppy shook itself, growling slightly.

"We're home and safe! Just change already!"

Joshua shook through various sizes of wolf—small to huge to normal and back to small—before becoming human. "Finally!"

The boy took a coin purse out of his coat pocket. Snapping it open, he carefully spilled a black coin onto the foyer table.

Decker could feel the crawl of power even from where he stood. The tarnished silver disk was stamped with a squidlike figure. It emitted a dark chaotic flare against his awareness, not that much different from his own power.

"Ottilie said that they're a Charon...obil? Obal?" Joshua stumbled over the word.

"Obol. I suspect she's right."

Decker knew very little about his source, despite the hundreds of years that it had enslaved and preserved him. The only reason he wasn't an utter monster was his dowsing gift, which was divine in nature. It reinforced his soul enough that he could withstand and control the power that his source connected him to. It was similar to the werewolves who could shift back to human only if they hadn't gone feral. There was a human soul to give pattern to the body.

He wasn't sure what the coin would do to him. Destroy his control on his power and make him a true monster? He didn't want to admit to Joshua how fragile his hold on humanity was. "Charon obols were often magical in nature to keep a soul that might become a ghost from staying with its body. A priest's last rites work along the same line, although the church has attached the idea that the clergy intercedes between a common man and God, making them indispensable for reaching heaven."

"Whatever." Joshua shuddered. "My wolf doesn't like the ghost-be-gone whatchamacallit—and neither do I."

"I do not like it either," Decker admitted.

They stood and stared at the disk for another minute in silence.

"So...what do we do with it?" Joshua asked.

Decker's experience with magical items was limited and all bad. "I have several boxes of various sizes where such things can be stored."

Joshua gave him a puzzled look.

"Over the last few hundred years," Decker hesitantly explained, "I've encountered several things that should be carefully contained until they could be safely destroyed. My condition affords me some protection—and I'm very sturdy—so when we find such things, normally I hold onto them until something can be done with them."

"Great. Well, I've got a test tomorrow that I need to study for," Joshua said.

"Already?"

"Well, it was on the class syllabus from the start of the semester. I was just unlucky about when I spawned in."

Decker shook his head. Sometimes Joshua's sentences went off in odd directions. He went in search for his shielded boxes. Luckily, he kept them in the library as it was the one space that stayed semi-clutter-free—if one didn't count all the books stacked up in towers and overflowing off shelves. Joshua had left the room untouched during his cleaning whirlwind, so they should still be within the library.

It took Decker an hour to find his smallest shielded box. It was on one of the lower shelves by the door, buried behind a collection of Reader's Digest Condensed Books.

The Philadelphia house fire had wiped out Decker's old library. At first, Saul would take him out in the wintertime to quiet antique bookstores scattered throughout Boston and occasionally to a department store. Cambridge was all new to them and exploring it was a peaceful adventure. It was an idyllic time.

It didn't last.

When Saul turned thirty, he was given a wife by the tribal elders and told to father children. While his children were small, Saul made every effort to spend time in Philadelphia to be with them. When in Boston, he and Decker only had time to hunt. All the shopping trips ended. The darkness started to creep in.

While Lauretta trusted Decker enough to take him as a lover, she refused to take him out in public, as if he were a mad dog that needed to be kept on a short chain. Desperate for new material, Decker had subscribed to a collection of abridged novels that arrived four times a year. Most of the material within them was not to his taste but he'd read them all multiple times, waiting for the next selection to arrive.

The Reader's Digest books were a grim reminder of that time.

He stacked the books in the foyer and added a note reading: "I would hate to just throw these away, but I no longer want them."

Joshua was clever at figuring out the modern world. He'd know what to do with them.

Decker stepped back into the library.

The shielded box was only the size of a cigarette case but surprisingly heavy. It was made of rowan wood, lined with lead, and inlaid with spell glyphs. As he lifted it off the shelf, something slid about inside.

What had he forgotten inside? He couldn't even remember the last time he'd seen the box.

He cautiously cracked open the lid. A book of matches lay within, from the local Irish pub that Saul liked to drink at. It was like finding an old friend. Nostalgia washed over Decker. He picked up the matches, running his fingertips along the rough striking surface.

Saul liked to smoke clove cigarettes. The scent clung to everything. The faintest trace of the spice lingered on the matchbook. It conjured up memories of Saul sitting on the bank of the river, night cloaking the city, a bottle of mead in one hand, a cigarette in the other, wreathing him in smoke, laughing his warm laugh. "I won't live long enough for cancer to kill me."

Saul had been right about that.

"God, I miss you so much," Decker whispered.

Decker put the matchbook on the shelf. He had so much junk and yet so little of it linked him back to the people he had loved.

He didn't want to touch the sinister coin that still lurked on the foyer table. He went into the kitchen for tongs. Joshua was sitting at the island. His schoolbooks were scattered around him. He was so focused on doing complicated math problems that he didn't seem to notice Decker slip in and take the tongs with the longest handles.

Decker returned to the foyer and carefully shifted the sinister coin into the box. He felt better when he closed the lid and could no longer feel the menace that it projected.

Where to put the box until they could take it to the Wise Woman to destroy the coin? It felt unsafe to leave it by the door where any visitor might open it out of curiosity. There was the kitten to consider too: Trouble had a love of pushing things off tables and shelves. The library seemed too close to the front door.

Decker wandered around the first floor with the box in hand. It was surprising how few hiding spaces were left now that Joshua had shoveled out the clutter of Decker's life. The dining room was devoid of everything except chairs and table. The number of cat toys under the couch in the living room suggested that that was the domain of Trouble now. The mantel was empty—because of the kitten. The kitchen cabinets were full of dishes and glasses, spices and cereal boxes and packaged cookies.

"What are you looking for?" Joshua asked without glancing up.

"Nothing," Decker lied and wandered out of the kitchen again.

In the end, he put it back on the bookshelf and buried it under books again.

At midnight, Joshua's phone sounded an alarm, warning him of the late hour.

Joshua went yawning to sleep, leaving Decker alone as the winter wind moaned outside like a lost soul. Drawing the curtains against any spies, he checked the wards again.

23: ELISE

When Elise had seen the start of *The Hobbit* movie when Joshua was showing it to Decker, she had thought, *Oh, Bag End is like the depot!* While the depot lacked the round windows of Bag End—or any windows at all—it had the same warm wood paneling, arching plaster ceilings, round doors, tiled floors, old Persian rugs, and heavy wood furniture. It was large enough to fit an entire extended family but small enough to be cozy doing so. The underground warren in Watertown had been built between the late 1600s and 1700s, using a combination of ancient angelic technology and magic. It was warm in the winter, cool in the summer, dry and airy at all times. It had been updated from time to time for more modern conveniences like electric lights, but parts of it were ancient, like the brick oven in the kitchen.

The Grigori had arrived in New England just behind the Pilgrims and the werewolves. Because of the Puritans, the Grigori had operated as secretly as possible. Yes, the Grigori were angelic, but the Puritans were religious zealots at insane levels with full control of the local government—as evidenced by the Salem witch trials and the hanging of Quakers in Boston Commons. Puritans had little tolerance for those operating outside their views of how God should be worshiped. Hence the reason the depot had been built underground. It was a place of secrets, warded against every type of creature except the angelic.

As a kid, she couldn't understand why she and her mother

didn't live there instead of their cramped rented apartment in Cambridge. As an adult, she knew that she couldn't keep it hidden and live in it full time.

At some point the land around the depot had been made into a sprawling parklike graveyard. A chapel had been built atop the main entrance. There had been a hidden underground stable for horses and space for wagons that had been converted into a four-car garage.

Elise had dropped Theo and Francis at Theo's Jeep and had driven on ahead. As Elise pulled into the first stall, Clarice called her.

"You should know that Grandmother gave Ottilie permission to take some things from the depot," Clarice said.

"Who?" Elise walked to the open garage door for a stronger signal. The one drawback of the underground quarters was it had little to no signal reception.

"The wannabe Dominion that was with Joshua at the aquarium," Clarice said as a reminder. "She's a little rebel but she seems to have the chops to be a good Dominion. Her family was against her ditching training in Greece, so she had to do all the groundwork of applying to Blackridge herself while she was twelve. That had to take a lot of guts—getting to Boston, interviewing with the werewolves, nailing down a full scholarship all by herself. I'm a little jealous—Greece is still stuck in the Bronze Age...except for the combat driving class. Like I ever get out to drive! Ow! Stubbed my toe! No, no, don't fall!"

There was a long cascade of things falling with little cries of dismay from Clarice. Her clumsiness was one of the reasons she was a desk-bound Dominion.

"I can't imagine not going to Greece," Elise said. It was the happiest part of her life. Being a Virtue, though, was something that she was ambivalent about. She had grown to hate the loneliness—although part of that was her own fault for keeping Decker and everyone else at arm's length.

"I suppose I wouldn't want to give up Greece either," Clarice said. "Anyhoo, I had serious catch-up to do with computers and such once I came back to Philadelphia."

"What did Ottilie want from the depot?" Elise asked.

"Protection charms for the mediums who are in close contact with the new puppy. He's been chaos central for the last month, so

I asked Grandmother if Ottilie could take some charms from the depot. I had to beg and plead a little, but she okayed it in the end."

Elise decided that she better check that Ottilie hadn't left any doors open or somehow cancelled the protective wards. It was doubtful—they had been in place for hundreds of years—but she knew nothing about this young girl. Closing the garage door, she made a quick circuit of the depot. She turned up the boiler that fueled the in-floor heating system. All the emergency exits were closed and untouched. The wards seemed fine. She would need a closer inspection of the supply room later.

Theo and Francis were climbing out of Theo's Jeep when Elise returned to the converted stables.

"Huh, so that wasn't the Prince of Boston, then?" Francis scratched his goat head as if he wasn't wearing anything bulky and weird. Had he spent all his idle time learning how to mime? "Well, it makes more sense why he was there with Decker. But does that mean that all wolves can get that big if they need to?"

"Pfft, beats me!" Theo took her ice chest filled with lunch's leftovers out of the back of her Jeep. She held it out to Elise. "I'm not the resident expert on werewolves."

Elise took the chest, expecting Theo to add the fact that Elise was dating Thane Cabot. Both siblings looked at Elise with curiosity. Maybe that discussion had happened en route.

"No," Elise answered the question. "They can't. They don't know how Joshua is getting that big—or the other weird things that he can do. It might be that he wasn't raised by wolves, so he didn't have certain limits trained into him."

"Don't open yourself completely to God's power," Francis quoted the advice against attempting to become a Power because most people who tried went up like a lit match.

"Amen." Theo took out a duffel bag of clothes and slammed shut the Jeep's tailgate.

"You two can decide who gets the tub first," Elise said to change the subject. She'd showered that morning while her cousins had both been without sleep and change of clothes for several days.

"You can be first, Theo." Francis sniffed at the fur of his goat suit. "I want to take care of my suit first. I smell like I was pelted with caramel apples. I guess the firebird's breath was composed mostly of its source's magic."

✧   ✧   ✧

Elise unpacked Theo's ice chest in the kitchen. There was some freeze-dried emergency food stored in the pantry but that wouldn't compare to Greek takeout. Despite being in Theo's ice chest in the back of her Jeep, everything was partially frozen.

While the brick oven was original to the kitchen, parts like the sink's plumbing and the range had been updated over time. Elise had replaced the microwave from the early eighties last year. She put the lamb into the microwave to defrost. As it revolved, humming occasionally, she went back out to the garage. She had gotten Francis's go bag out of his SUV that morning, but she hadn't mentioned it earlier. It didn't seem like Theo had told Francis yet about his missing driver. He was going to realize something was wrong when he saw his bag.

She set the bag on the armchair behind Francis. He didn't seem to notice. He'd stripped off the chamois outfit in the living room. He wasn't completely naked under the suit; he had on a balaclava, ankle socks, and blue, fitted Under Armour. There were more pieces to the chamois fur suit than Elise had guessed. The hooflike gloves were straightforward. Inside the suit were several pieces of padding, giving bulk and shape to the goat body. All the various pieces made a small mountain that he carefully separated into piles of what needed immediate attention and what could forgo care.

"It stinks so bad from the firebird that I'm worried that if I don't wash it that it will be ruined," Francis said.

"My mom put in laundry machines in the wash room," Elise said. "She'd leave me here whenever she went out hunting with Decker, so this place was like a second home."

Or third, considering how much time they'd spent at Decker's.

"This place is nicer than what I have in Bangor." Theo came down the hall, hair still damp, smelling of soap. She wore a clean change of clothes. They were a variation of the same theme of what she wore before: worn blue jeans, flannel shirt buttoned over a solid color T-shirt. "Mine is much more a *Phantom of the Opera* grotto kind of thing."

"I don't know." Francis sniffed at the inner padding. "The interior padding doesn't smell too bad. It's a new suit and I was out in the cold most of the time, so I didn't sweat that much. It's nothing compared to the suits that I was wearing in summer in Florida before I realized that I needed Under Armour to wick away the sweat."

He wrinkled his nose as the sniffed the outer fur. "The outer skin needs to be washed, then hung up to dry and brushed out. I wish I could just wait to clean it at the monastery. Roustabout does the actual laundry since the monks don't want me near the machines. He's really good at washing these."

Theo shot Elise a worried look. Elise frowned at her. They had to tell Francis sometime. Now, in this quiet time, would be better than later—perhaps as they stumbled across the driver's mangled body. It was Theo's call, though, since Francis was her brother. "I'll throw them in the washing machine. Since there's no television or radio here, I used to do all our laundry and make cookies while waiting on my mom."

The microwave beeped as the defrost of the lamb finished up.

Theo sighed. "Yeah, why don't you get dinner ready, Elise, while I catch Francis up to speed on this mission?"

Elise heated up the Greek leftover dishes one at a time while listening to Francis's heartbreaking "Why? Why would God allow him to be taken from me? Why?"

Once all the dishes were heated, they sat at the long trestle table in the kitchen to eat together as a family. Francis was silent as Elise placed down the hot dishes. His eyes were filled with sadness. It hurt to see him so openly grieving for his missing driver.

"I don't understand," Francis murmured. "Only God knew I was in Boston. If Clarice didn't know where I was, then Roustabout hadn't told her that he was going to Alewife. How could a firebird have jumped him at the train station? Why? What would attacking him gain a shapeshifter? How could they even know how important he was to me? The monks don't gossip about me to outsiders. While they're frightened of me, they are quite protective."

Theo made a noise that indicated she didn't believe that. She said nothing, dividing up the lamb souvlaki and moussaka into equal shares.

"There are spirits involved." Elise split the grape leaves and spinach pie. She had ordered more than two people could eat at one sitting but divided three ways, it was a little bare. "There was one at the aquarium that was possessing a medium who worked at a botanica in Salem that had been ransacked on Friday. It seemed to be after a penguin shapeshifter who is somehow mixed up in this. Spirits know things that no normal human or shapeshifter would know."

"Enyo was at the mall and at the aquarium," Theo added. "She would have told the shapeshifters any secret they asked if it made her day more exciting."

The air in the kitchen went up ten degrees and took on the smell of lightning.

"Stay calm," Theo reached out to touch Francis's shoulder. "We will find him. And if he's dead...you can just raise him. You've done it before. You don't even need all his parts, just some of them."

Elise glared at Theo, who shrugged, probably because while it was painful, it was still the truth.

Francis got up and went to his go bag to take out a coloring book and an eight pack of colored pencils. He returned, opening the book to a page filled with butterflies fluttering around the balloon letters that spelled out: *For every minute you are angry, you lose sixty seconds of happiness.*

The "how" was probably answered but the "why" still remained.

"This Roustabout," Elise cautiously started. "Does he have any ability—divine or otherwise?"

Francis shook his head as he started to color intently. "He's a good man—that's it. He grew up in an orphanage and didn't do well in school, so he trained to be a professional fighter. It was that or the military and he felt like if he joined the military, he'd have to kill people. He learned Brazilian Jiu-Jitsu and Muay Thai. He got really good at them. Once he actually started fighting—even though he was winning—he didn't like it. He didn't like hurting people. One day he accidentally broke the leg of his opponent. As the man was lying there, crying in pain, Roustabout felt so guilty and ashamed. He quit after that fight and got a job working security at one of the biggest nightclubs in Miami."

Theo made a face but didn't say anything.

"Roustabout liked working at the nightclub. He likes people and they like him. The club was like a constant party. People were there to dance and be happy and have fun. The dancers had all sorts of cute names for him like Teddy Bear and Sweetness and Honey. They called him that because most of the time he could talk troublemakers into quieting down and being good. He said you just needed to listen to them. That they were acting up because they were in pain. He believed that if you acknowledged their pain, they saw you as their friend and would do what you asked them to do."

Dancers? The place sounded like a strip club. No wonder Theo made a face. It was probably not a place that Grigori—male or female—could have gone safely.

"How did he end up your driver?" Elise asked.

"It was fated," Francis stated firmly.

"Clarice fucked up," Theo growled.

Francis colored in the letters of "happiness" in bloodred as he ate the moussaka without relish. "When I was just about to turn sixteen, God suddenly yanked me out of Greece and deployed me to Florida. Much like two days ago, I had no money, no car, no spare clothes, and no place to sleep. I didn't even know what country I was in. I thought I was in Cuba for a while: parts of Miami are very Cuban. I did have my phone, so I called Clarice. She figured out where I was, but she didn't know why I was there any more than I did. She conferred with the elders, and they decided that I should stay in Florida—at least until God moved me Himself. Clarice set me up in what was supposed to be a fully furnished house with a car. Only I didn't have a driver's license. I was just fifteen, after all."

Elise hadn't heard how Francis ended up in Florida.

"It left me sitting in an empty house with a car I couldn't drive, with no food or clothes or even sheets for the bed. Then Roustabout showed up."

"Just out of the blue?" Elise said.

"Clarice had cut some deal with the Prince of Miami to get a driver that could be trusted," Theo explained with great annoyance—probably at the elders who hadn't coughed up a caretaker who was Grigori.

Francis picked up his narrative. "It was kind of impromptu. The prince called Clarice, wanting to know why there was a Power suddenly in his city. Somewhere in the discussion, Clarice mentioned that I needed a driver. They had to be someone who could be trusted around an underaged Grigori—glamour and all. I think she was trying to get the prince to volunteer one of his wolves—but he wasn't willing to do that."

"The prince found a random normal human to do the job?" Elise guessed.

"Basically," Theo said.

"Roustabout wasn't random," Francis said. "It was fate. The prince owned the nightclub where Roustabout had worked. The prince knew he was a good man that could be trusted."

"Only he'd killed a customer, gone to jail for manslaughter, gotten out, and couldn't go back to working security as an ex-con," Theo added.

The temperature in the room rose again.

"It wasn't Roustabout's fault," Francis said. "The bleeping idiot had gotten banned because he was stalking one of the dancers who had a restraining order on him."

On "bleeping" the empty serving dish nearest Francis trembled violently as if it was about to fly to pieces. Theo moved it out of blast range of Francis's mild curses.

"He wasn't allowed anywhere near her," Francis continued as if he didn't notice the dish. "When Roustabout told him that he couldn't get into the club, he pulled a gun on Roustabout! There were people all around them, so Roustabout tried to point the gun upward as he disarmed him. The gun went off and the bullet ricocheted off the marquee overhead, killing the man. There were a dozen witnesses. Roustabout shouldn't have even been arrested but the police department had a beef with the Prince of Miami. It wasn't fair. Roustabout was only trying to protect the dancer and the people around him."

Perhaps normal people would be shocked by Roustabout killing someone to protect others, but that was all the Grigori did.

"It's okay," Elise said to calm Francis. "The prince needed someone he trusted, and Roustabout needed a job, so the prince sent him to you."

Francis nodded. "He'd gotten out of jail the day that God yanked me to Florida and plopped me down in the Prince of Miami's territory. He was in front of the prince, asking for a job other than bouncer, when Clarice told the prince about me needing a driver. Roustabout had meant to go earlier in the day but the bus he was taking broke down and he need to walk halfway across the city. Yes, if it wasn't the day that he met me, the bus thing would be just bad luck. But Powers are ruled by fate—and everything that comes within our sphere of influence is intertwined with our fate."

It seemed like the only thing that made Roustabout special

was the fact that he was Francis's driver. While he might be entangled with Francis's fate, he obviously didn't receive God's protection. Maybe the shapeshifters hoped to use Roustabout as a hostage. Elise suspected Francis would be willing to move mountains to get him back.

She felt like she was missing something obvious. If a firebird had taken Roustabout as a hostage, why hadn't the three shapeshifters at the mall brought him as a deterrent? Or was this some kind of weird war among the various factions of the bird shapeshifters? Had the male killed at the train station been an ally of the penguin at the aquarium?

Theo yawned again. "I've been going since Sunday morning. I need to crash."

"I'll be better able to control my temper if I take a bath and sleep," Francis admitted.

"Besides," Theo added, "I think the shapeshifters are just disposable tools. Cannon fodder."

"With me being the cannon," Francis said.

"Hank Whitebrow said that his store was attacked by a Touched of an unknown god." Elise shared the photo of the man with Theo. "The only lead we have on his identity is that Hank believes he might be connected to Salem State University's geology department somehow. Maybe. The guy came in with some geology students, but he might not have anything to do with the university."

"That is thin," Theo admitted. "Salem is like, what, an hour away?"

"More or less, depending on traffic," Elise said.

"I want to go to Alewife," Francis said. "There might be something Elise missed in my car. Something out of place. Something that should be there and isn't. I don't know."

Theo looked unhappy. Elise knew that she wasn't happy with the idea of Francis staying in the area, nuking holes in random landmarks. If God wanted him in Boston, though, it was best that he stayed until they found out why.

"We should move your SUV if nothing else," Theo said. "Bring it back here. Elise, do you have a backup phone that Francis can use?"

"Yeah, I'll get it."

Elise cut one of the two gyros in half and took it with her as she headed to the vault. The depot was where her family stored over three hundred years' worth of things that might come in handy in their fight with evil. She'd been in it just days ago to replace the Earthblood that she had used to save Cabot's life. That had been a pain—filling blessed glass bottles from the magical spring while the wind chill was near negative ten. She didn't want to be caught without it. If it weren't so cold out, she'd put one of the bottles in the back of the Jeep. But she didn't want to risk the liquid freezing and breaking the bottle.

Most of her contribution to the vault had been in practical items. Bullets. Guns. Cast-iron spikes. Bags of salt. Everything needed to be neatly organized so that any visitor, like Theo or Francis, could find what they wanted in the hundreds of items collected. The catalog sat by the door so things could be found and signed out.

The catalog wasn't turned to her last entry, the Earthblood. She scanned the page, momentarily confused. Why was it turned to this set of entries? Then she saw the unfamiliar signature. Ottilie had taken the soul talisman as well as the protection charms that she'd asked for.

"Shit," Elise whispered.

The talisman was dangerous for a Virtue like herself or Theo to use. For a Dominion, it was certain death.

She took out her phone. She had no signal. More importantly, it was nearing midnight. The kids who lived at the dorms of Blackridge had a strict "lights out" bedtime of ten o'clock. Clarice would also be asleep, so long as one of the other East Coast Virtues weren't needing her help.

"One fire at a time," Elise said, putting away her phone. She'd come to the vault to fetch one of the smartphones that she kept as backup. She'd deal with their little rebellious Dominion in the morning.

24: SETH

Seth woke up before dawn as usual. He started through his typical weekday morning route half asleep. Go to the bathroom. Brush his teeth. Pick out clean clothes. He was packing his schoolbooks into his backpack when he remembered that he'd been kicked out of school again.

When he was a child at his parents' house, he would have crawled back into bed, glad for the unexpected luxury. The four previous times he'd gotten kicked out, he had gone out exploring the city—trying to distract his wolf with a sense of adventure and accomplishment before diving into a new unfamiliar school. Today he could only stare out the big window of his suite at the still dark city, feeling lost.

A few months ago, he thought he had life handled. He'd worked hard for three years so he could graduate from high school early. He thought at that point, he would be deemed adult enough to return to Boston. He'd be a freshman at Harvard, after all. Freshman lived "away from home." At Harvard it was a requirement for freshmen to live in the dorms, although exceptions could be made (and usually were for his family).

Everything seemed to fall apart when the king announced that Seth had to go to Columbia University in New York City instead. What a naïve view of the world Seth had had. Then the Wickers nearly killed Jack—twice—and enslaved Joshua. It had been one harrowing but educational nightmare. It shifted all his priorities.

Just two days earlier, Plan B seemed simple and clear. He would buckle down and go to Columbia. A few years more in New York City would kill no one. What was important was getting the bachelor house set up and then figure out how to recruit young ambitious wolves to Boston. He should network with his neighbors—if for no other reason than their puppies might be willing to shift to a territory still close to home. It seemed all so doable.

Now, he wasn't so sure. Something was very wrong with the king. All of Alexander's mysterious refusals might have been because the king knew that he was failing.

Surely not dying.

Yet the possibility was there.

The old Marquis of Albany had said that the king had a use for Isaiah.

If Alexander was perfectly healthy, he could father another son, hopefully stronger than Isaiah. Alexander had already anchored the city for three hundred years. What would twenty or thirty or even forty years matter?

A bride would need to be found with the proper bloodlines. Alexander had spent the last three hundred years breeding up Raisa Artemyeva, Isaiah's mother, to produce a son strong enough to take New York. She'd been the eldest child and only daughter of the Prince of Saint Petersburg and the only granddaughter of the Prince of Istanbul. It meant there had been no bride in that bloodline for Alexander to quickly replace Raisa. If Seth remembered correctly, Raisa's father boasted of the fact that his sons had given him all grandsons.

When Raisa killed herself, Alexander must have started over, but he'd been set back at least two generations. He would have needed to line up brides for Raisa's younger brothers and then again for her nephews. How old would Raisa's great-niece be now? Isaiah was twenty-nine. If Alexander had started on the day of Raisa's death, his possible bride would be...eight? Six? Two? Not yet born?

Alexander had waited until Raisa was eighteen before sending Jack's father, Anton, to fetch her from Russia. It meant that even if the king's new bride was as old as eight, he'd probably wait until she was an adult to bring her to the United States. Her children would not be changed from youngling to wolf until they were thirteen. Assuming her first child was male, it would be nearly thirty years before her offspring could safely take over New York. While unbending, the king was not cruel. He wouldn't have allowed Isaiah to go fifty or sixty years thinking he would be prince. Alexander would have dashed that dream long ago if Isaiah had no real chance.

But if the king was failing, he would keep Isaiah close as a stopgap measure. Yes, the power of New York would burn out Isaiah quickly, but by the time he died, some other fix could be found. In other words, Isaiah was insurance that if the end came faster than the king expected, there would be someone—no matter how flawed—to take the massive burden of New York City.

It was a horrifyingly logical reason for the king to delay infinitely. The moment Isaiah became the prince, the clock would start to tick before the power killed him. Alexander was delaying it until the last possible moment. Meanwhile, Alexander suffered with the weight of being the king as well as the Prince of New York.

When Alexander woke up, would he shift New York to Isaiah? It would take that strain off the king for some period of time. Seth's grandfather had carried Boston for twenty years. Surely Isaiah could hold New York for that long.

When Isaiah became the Prince of New York, though, there wasn't anyone on the planet other than Alexander who could stand against him.

The king had slept through most of Joshua's trouble yesterday. Jack was the only other person at the Castle who knew that Joshua had spent the entire day fighting monsters. If the king found out, there was no way he would leave Joshua in Boston.

Moving Joshua to the Castle was a recipe for disaster while Isaiah was merely being the strongest of the Thanes. It would be an utter catastrophe if Isaiah were the Prince of New York.

Seth headed into his shower, vowing that he had to keep whatever was happening in Boston a secret. He just wished that there were someone other than Jack or Kate that he could talk to—someone with experience whom he could trust not to tell the king or the elder Thanes.

He was halfway through his shower when Joshua suddenly appeared beside him.

"Joshua!" Seth yelled as Joshua's first reaction—to bolt—slammed the boy into the marble-tiled wall of the walk-in shower. "Don't run! It's just me!"

Joshua rebounded and did a double take. "Seth! Where did

you come...? Where the hell am I? Why are you naked? Why is it raining in here?"

"You're in my shower! Why are you in New York?"

"I'm not! I'm just trying to call you!" Joshua held out his phone as evidence. It had CALLING SETH on the screen. Over the falling water, Seth could make out the faint buzz of his phone on his nightstand. "Why aren't you answering your phone?"

"I'm in the shower! And so are you!"

"No, I'm making my breakfast!" Joshua cried. "Oh geez, my eggs!"

And he was gone.

Seth stared at the empty space as the water washed away the scent of his brother. *What...the...hell?*

He rinsed off the soap quickly, skipped washing his hair, and got out of the shower. His phone was buzzing again. He was halfway to the nightstand when Joshua appeared with a smoking skillet. His school uniform was soaked and dripped water onto the wood floor of Seth's bedroom.

"Oh geez!" Joshua cried. "Will you answer your phone?"

"I'm trying to!" Seth snatched up his phone as evidence that he was doing exactly that.

"Thank you!" Joshua cried. "Something is seriously wrong with me." He glanced past Seth at the clock on the nightstand. "Oh damn, I'm going to be late for school!"

And he vanished.

Seth swore and punched ANSWER on his phone. "Do *not* go to school today!" He picked up the land phone and hit his cousin's extension. "Come up here now! No! Not you!" This was to Joshua, who had reappeared, this time minus his school uniform. "Where are your clothes?"

"I took them off!" Joshua shouted into his phone, seemingly unaware he'd changed locations again, frantically running in tight circles. "They were soaked. This isn't my bedroom!"

And he was gone again. Seth focused on Decker's house. The vampire was still awake; apparently Joshua ate breakfast with him in the mornings. Decker sat at the kitchen counter, but his focus was clearly on the upstairs as the boy bounced off the wall of his bedroom.

The door to his suite unlocked and his cousin burst into the room. He must have run the entire two flights between their suites.

"What's wrong?" Cabot asked.

"It's Joshua!" Seth held out his phone and hit SPEAKER to add his cousin to the loop.

Unfortunately, Cabot asked, "What did the tiny terror do this time?"

Joshua appeared wearing a dry white shirt of his school uniform. He held his phone in one hand and a stuffed seal in the other. He stood on his toes, inches from Cabot but a foot too short to be impressive, and raged, "I am not tiny!"

"I told you not to go to school," Seth said.

"The Goths might be in danger!" Joshua said. "We don't know what these monsters want but they tracked me to the mall. They might figure out that I go to Blackridge. Most people—special people like Winnie and her grandmother—know that the wolves run the school. We were wearing our school uniforms at the aquarium. The bad guys might figure out that we go to Blackridge."

"If they think every black wolf in Boston is me, then they're not very smart." Actually, it wasn't very comforting, but it was all that Seth had to offer.

Joshua powered on. "Besides, I have a test in fourth period, and I need to give Maisy her seal before my wolf drives me nuts with it!" Joshua shook the stuffed seal at Seth.

"Grab him." Seth told Cabot as he realized what was coming next.

Cabot caught hold of Joshua even as he asked, "What's he doing here...?"

And then both of them were gone.

Back in Decker's kitchen, the vampire didn't react as Joshua and Cabot appeared in front of him and then Cabot went flying, landing in Seth's bedroom in New York.

Cabot lay sprawled out on the floor. Stunned. "How did he do that?"

"I have no idea." Seth stayed focused on Joshua, who seemed mystified as to where Cabot had disappeared to, since he was looking under tables and behind doors. "He doesn't seem to know either."

Decker was still at his kitchen counter as werewolves came and went like mad yo-yos. Seth glanced at his cell phone and saw that—not surprisingly—he'd lost the signal from Joshua's phone. He went to his contacts, found Decker's number, and called him instead.

Decker answered his phone with: "Is Cabot with you?"

"Yes, he is. Tell Joshua that he can take a makeup test. They will allow it; that's the point of owning the damn school."

And then Joshua was there, in person, stuffed seal and phone still in hand. "Makeup tests are always harder and I'm way behind because this is a freaking private school with high standards instead of a redneck public school."

"You're guaranteed to get into Harvard," Seth said. "Your grades don't matter. All you need to do is make up the needed number of days—by August—and you'll get a diploma. In five months from now, nothing from high school will matter except the fact that you graduated."

"This is Harvard!" Joshua cried.

"With two different buildings built by the Tatterskeins," Seth said. "You will get in."

"I don't want to screw this chance up!" Joshua's voice trembled and rose in pitch, nearing the high keen of a distressed puppy. "I never thought I could go to Harvard! Hell, if I didn't get a scholarship, I wasn't going to any college, except our local community college. Which would have really, really sucked, because I'd be going with all the idiots from high school that I wanted to get away from!"

Seth wished Decker were there. He realized now that he and Joshua were nearly the same level of dominance, which meant that Joshua wouldn't look to him for comfort. It left him with just normal methods to calm his brother down, and he had little experience at that. "You're an honor student, you scored really high on your SATs, and you're an athlete that competed at the state level. You're the type of person that colleges drool over. You could get into Harvard without us pulling strings. The only decider really was the money, and that's in the bag. Okay? Calm down. Calm. Calm. I think you broke Cabot."

They stood over Cabot, gazing down at him. Their cousin still hadn't moved from where he'd landed.

"Are you okay?" Seth asked Cabot.

Joshua edged away from Seth and whimpered slightly. "I'm sorry. I didn't realize he'd come with me and then it scared me when he just showed up in the kitchen like that."

"That was really, really creepy," Cabot spoke but stayed on the floor. "How did you do that? How did he do that?"

"I don't know," Seth and Joshua said.

25: JOSHUA

Joshua was nearly late for school.

Seth argued and argued with him but in the end, Seth was in New York City and could do little to stop him. Joshua locked the front door of Decker's house two minutes before homeroom bell. He was momentarily distracted as he checked the time while tucking away his keys and when he looked up, he was standing in front of his locker at Blackridge.

He really hoped that he'd gotten there by his wolf teleporting and not that he'd simply forgotten about walking to school like in the movie *Memento*. Joshua tucked the stuffed seal for Maisy and his coat away in his locker. He ducked into his homeroom just as the bell rang.

It turned out that Vijay was part of his homeroom, which made sense since they were both seniors. The boy was putting on an odd-looking necklace as Joshua sat down in the row in front of him.

"Ottilie passed out protection charms," Vijay said as he tied his school necktie. "We'll have to give them back eventually but for now, Marie Antonette and anything else won't be messing with us."

"That's good," Joshua said.

"Did you see the videos going viral this morning?" Tal asked when he and Allie sat down on either side of Joshua. Tal's school necktie was undone. He tucked away an identical protection charm necklace and redid his school tie.

Joshua shook his head. *Oh, please, don't be the mall fight.*

But there he was, a black wolf the size of a Macy's Thanksgiving Day Parade balloon, dwarfing the three-story Christmas tree. Several people—apparently with no sense of self-preservation—had filmed the entire mess, so there were multiple camera angles. (One cameraperson had come close to being turned to ash as they tried for a closeup on the witching stone.) The chamois had been overlooked by all the idiots who stayed behind to document the fight—apparently, they thought he was one of Santa's reindeer and a hapless bystander. Joshua had to admit that nothing in the videos suggested that the chamois had anything to do with the columns of fire smashing through the roof of the mall, reducing things to ash.

None of the videos, however, showed the firebird. Even when his wolf had it by the neck, it seemed as if he was alone. The action looked like a rough green-screen scene in a movie that hadn't had the CGI effects added yet.

"You're obviously fighting something that breathes fire," Tal said. "Was it a dragon?"

"A firebird." Joshua told them about the swans and the firebird showing up in human form with a witching stone. "Did anyone catch me on film? Non-wolf me?"

"It doesn't seem like it," Vijay said. "What was a firebird doing at the mall?"

"We think it was tracking that creepy coin," Joshua said. "It was in my coat pocket a few minutes before the fight broke out."

"Where is it now?" Allie said.

"Someplace safe." Joshua was glad that the bell rang as he didn't want to talk about where "safe" was. Decker had some weird storage box that he'd stashed the coin away in until both of them could go see Sioux Zee. It made Joshua nervous to leave Decker alone with the coin since the vampire slept through the day. He didn't want to bring it to school, though, and have monsters show up there.

"What do you have next?" Tal picked up his backpack, preparing to leave.

"I have no idea." Joshua took out his phone and checked his schedule with the school's app. His stomach dropped. "Shit. Gym."

In theory, he should like gym class. He'd gotten into martial arts at an early age. The weekly lessons—with Bethy as an at-home taskmaster—meant he'd worked hard at strengthening his body and improving his coordination. He had always been better at sports than most kids his age. Gym class, however, usually was some kind of team sport. Football. Basketball. Soccer. Field hockey. Volleyball. And the very worst: Dodgeball. Joshua would have to suffer through being picked next to last, just one ahead of Reggie Werring, who ran like he had his shoes on the wrong feet and was legally blind. When they played Dodgeball, everyone always seemed to target Joshua, even his own teammates. After class, he had to run the gauntlet of taking a shower and getting dressed while the gym teacher sat in his office and did paperwork.

After the insanity of yesterday, he didn't want to go.

"I don't even know where it is," Joshua added on top of his reluctance. Maybe he could pretend to be lost for an hour.

"You can come with me," Vijay said. "You're in my class. We're going to start tennis today."

Joshua took a deep breath. So much for that excuse. Maybe it wouldn't be so bad: no one at the school knew anything about him beyond the Goths. There was no reason to bully him—although it was his experience that bullies didn't need a motive.

"Thanks." Joshua stood up and then remembered he would need gym clothes. Had he remembered his gym clothes? Yes, he brought them Monday, just in case the unexpected happened. So far, a lot of unexpected had happened, but none of it resulted with him running around the school naked. At least that dream hadn't come true. Yet. He hoped that it stayed that way. "I need to hit my locker first."

"It's on the way," Tal said. "The gym teacher is Mr. Payne. He's been here forever, so he's taught all your brothers and cousins, along with both of your parents. He knows how to deal with Tatterskeins."

"He knows about us being werewolves?" Joshua whispered.

The Goths glanced at each other and shook their heads.

"I don't think so," Tal said. "It's just, after all these years, he knows what to expect."

Mr. Payne had a fringe of gray hair on his mostly bald head but had the body of a twenty-year-old. He wore a crisp white T-shirt, dark knee-length shorts, flawless tube socks, and a gleaming whistle. He seemed like the epitome of gym teachers. He might have taught Seth, Cabot, and Joshua's biological parents in past years—but no one had warned him about Joshua. With much grumbling, he dropped the planned introduction to tennis and switched abruptly to archery.

"Less of a temptation to fetch," Mr. Payne said mysteriously.

Joshua agreed that having his wolf wildly swinging a tennis racket and lobbing balls, God knew where, would be a bad idea. He wasn't sure if sharpened missiles were an improvement.

They moved from the gymnasium to an archery range in the basement. It was a big room with a dozen targets set in front of a Kevlar backstop. The rest of the class seemed surprised but not angry at the change in sport. For some reason, Vijay was bouncing with excitement.

Mr. Payne unlocked the storage closet and handed out quivers of arrows, saying, "I wish this didn't need to be said but experience has taught me that I must. These might look like nothing more than long pencils but they're weapons. You're to treat them like weapons. You will not play with them, twirl them, spin them on the ground, fence with them, poke each other with them, or put them up your nose."

The boys laughed.

"Yes, laugh all you want," Mr. Payne said, taking down lightweight bows and handing them out. "But if anyone uses these bows and arrows in an inappropriate way, they'll be suspended.

"Joshua." Mr. Payne reached deep into the closet to take out a bow that was thicker than the others. "This is the Tatterskein bow. Please be careful not to break it. *Gently* pull the string back."

Mr. Payne showed them how to stand with the left foot forward, nock the arrow, draw back the string, and release it. After having them repeat the protocol for ceasing fire and retrieving arrows, he let them shoot.

The first arrow Joshua shot missed the target by five feet and hit the backdrop so hard that it shattered. The second arrow missed by a foot—and shattered.

Joshua stole a look at the other targets. Most were equally devoid of arrows. Only Vijay's bull's-eye had two arrows in it. A dozen arrows lay on the ground. While most of the other boys weren't doing any better than him at hitting the target, their arrows survived.

It must be a werewolf thing.

If the bow was like a hunting rifle, then he should be able to imagine crosshairs that needed to be raised or lowered in order to hit the mark. Both shots had been too high, so he needed to tip the arrow point down slightly.

He aimed carefully. The third arrow hit the target, burying itself halfway to the feathers. Somehow it didn't seem right.

Mr. Payne paused behind Joshua and grunted at his buried arrow. "That's a Tatterskein for you."

So, it *was* a werewolf thing.

Just like his old school, everyone had to take showers before their next class. It made sense back home as it often seemed that many of his classmates only showered when forced. They were a grungy pack, smelling of old sweat. The Blackridge boys, though, smelled mostly of soap, deodorant, aftershave, and hair products.

The class bullies always picked on Joshua during gym class showers at his old school. They equated naked with defenseless. Annoyingly, they were right. Joshua couldn't run if he didn't have any clothes on. Even with a brown belt in judo, he couldn't dodge insults. He had to be vigilant to guard his street clothes, never leaving them in an unlocked locker. He'd even had to pack a towel, just in case the bullies soaked all the ones that they didn't use so he'd have nothing to dry off with.

Since he wasn't in complete control of his wolf, any brush with bullies in the locker room could end up with someone dead. He used a trick he'd learned at his old school: he undressed so slowly that the others would be done, dressed, and gone before he even stepped into the showers.

All his care seemed to be unnecessary. Vijay and the other boys in his class had talked to him in a friendly manner. They focused on being neat and tidy before leaving the locker room— apparently the wealthy put a lot of importance into looking good. When he got to the stack of dry towels that Mr. Payne had put out, there were still several left for him to use beside the tall wire hamper to hold the damp used ones. The shower room was a big, echoing room with ornate tile and marble and recently updated fixtures. It might be a school gym locker room, but it felt like something out of a palace. Knowing that he was alone, he was able to relax enough to shower thoroughly.

"*Che*, you're a hard man to find," a deep rough voice said as he rinsed his armpits.

Joshua yelped and leapt sideways.

A rockhopper penguin stood at the entrance of the shower room.

"Where the hell did you come from?" Joshua twisted off the water.

"Buenos Aires." The penguin sounded like Mannie but maybe all penguins sounded the same. "Although my mother is originally from Islas Malvinas."

The shower room's doorway was wide. Joshua tried to edge around the penguin. His wolf growled angrily at the bird.

"What?" the penguin squawked and backed away, allowing Joshua to escape out of the shower room.

"You nearly got me killed at the aquarium." Joshua snagged a towel from the pile of dry ones. He quickly dried off as he hurried to his locker.

"*Che*, do you think I was hiding out at the aquarium for free fish?" Mannie waddled after him, getting uncomfortably close. The penguin seemed to have almost no clue what personal space or social distancing were.

"I don't know," Joshua grumbled as he tried to open his combination lock only to snap the hasp. The wolf growled again. Louder. "Why were you there?"

"Where else would a penguin blend in?" Mannie squawked. "It's not like I can check in to the Four Seasons and hang out at the pool."

"The Four Seasons doesn't serve free fish." Joshua opened his locker and pulled out his clothes.

"*Che*, you want to fight? I will fight you!" The penguin head-butted him in the knee. "*La re-puta que te pario.*"

"Ow!" The wolf punt-kicked the penguin in response. The bird went flying and landed headfirst in the wire towel hamper.

Joshua dressed quickly while the penguin squawked upside down, trapped in the wire bin. The bird seemed to be cursing in Spanish although in an accent so thick that Joshua couldn't follow it.

The hamper tipped over and dumped out the angry bird and a small mountain of damp towels.

"What are you doing here?" Joshua said.

"*No te hagas el pelotudo.*" The penguin complained but kept his distance this time. "I told you, I want to hire you. Well... not you, but Silas Decker!"

"Decker?" Joshua echoed. Somehow the addition of Decker had been missing from both his dream and their conversation at the aquarium. "Marie Antoinette told you about Decker?"

"Yes!" Mannie squawked. "I told her I needed a witching stone to find something stolen from me. She said that there was only one witching stone in the area, but it was locked in a strong vault, closely guarded. She thought she might be able to get it, as there was a guard open enough for her to possess him, but then she discovered that he'd gotten a protective rune tattooed onto him. She said that instead I should hire the dowser Silas Decker, who lived with the new black wolf puppy in Cambridge. She told me that I would have to talk to you first—for some reason—but she could get you to come to the aquarium."

That sort of made sense—as much as the dead queen of France talking with an Argentinian were-penguin at an American aquarium made sense. (Since Marie Antoinette refused to speak both Spanish and English, did this mean that Mannie knew French?) It didn't explain, however, the weirdness at the mall.

Joshua decided not to bother with his tie and pulled on his school blazer. Clothes made him feel more confident about handling the situation. "How did you know where to find me?"

"*Che*, you were wearing school uniforms!" Mannie waddled over to point his stubby wing at the Blackridge crest on the breast of Joshua's blazer. "I've been to the States before. I know what's what. It meant you kids all went to a private school. There's only a handful in the area that require uniforms and only one has a mascot of a black wolf with a crown."

Joshua had been worried that their uniforms would be a sure giveaway. Why in the world had the school founders picked a wolf mascot if they wanted to be all hush-hush about being werewolves? Did that mean that the spirit at the aquarium could figure it out too?

That reminded him that Seth had forbidden him to talk to the penguin.

Joshua put on his socks and shoes. All the puddles on the floor and benches—left by his showered classmates—made it tricky to do without getting either his feet or pants damp. "The prince said I'm not to talk to you—and I think this time he might be right. Bad things keep happening and I've been lucky so far that people I care about weren't hurt."

The penguin squawked with anger. "*Sos un boludo!* You know nothing about the world! Take me to Decker!"

"No!" Joshua shoved his gym clothes into his gym bag. "I'm not letting you anywhere near him."

The penguin launched himself at Joshua. "The queen told me that his house is warded! The only way I can find him is by you taking me home with you!"

Joshua expected the move and blocked it with a foot on its forehead. "I'm not taking you home!"

The penguin squawked and flailed its stubby wings.

"No! No! Not doing it!" Joshua shouted, keeping it at bay with his foot.

Someone cleared their throat. "Mr. Tatterskein?"

Mr. Payne stood in the door to the hallway. He paused a moment, eyeing Joshua and the penguin. "The bell rang, Mr. Tatterskein. You're late for your next class."

There was something seriously wrong when everyone in a classroom ignored the penguin standing by your desk, glaring at you. Joshua was in the back row by the window, but there were at least six people with a clear view of the bird.

Joshua took out his phone and texted Seth. "Help! It's here!"

"Mr. Tatterskein?" Ms. Silvers, his teacher, said from the front of the room. "What are you doing?"

Joshua looked at his teacher. Looked at the penguin. Looked at his teacher.

"I'm texting my brother because I have a talking penguin stalking me."

Ms. Silvers nodded her head and kept nodding, as if she was looping through the sentence, trying to parse it. After a full minute of nodding, Ms. Silvers said, "Okay. Miss Rodriquez, can you answer question six?"

"*Che,* I am not stalking you," the penguin muttered. "I'm asking you for help and you're ignoring me. There's a difference."

"What's there?" Seth texted back.

"Penguin!" Joshua texted.

He felt Seth use his Peeping Tom ability to check up on him from a distance.

"Do not wolf out at school!" Seth texted. "It's important that you don't bite anyone! Not even the penguin!"

This was followed by lots of exclamation marks as if Seth had gotten his finger stuck on the "!" key.

"What should I do?" Joshua texted back as he knew his wolf was not happy with the penguin staring at him.

"Stay calm!" Seth sent a minute later. "Jack is on his way. This is why I told you not to go to school!"

"You said nothing about penguins at school!" Joshua felt the need to text back.

Seth apparently didn't have an answer to that—Joshua's phone stayed silent.

He stared at his phone, torn between feeling victorious over his brother and lost without any helpful advice.

"Are you going to help me?" Mannie asked loudly.

"Why aren't other people seeing you?" Joshua whispered to Mannie.

"Because I don't want them to," Mannie said without bothering to whisper. "Most magical beings can cast some kind of glamour. Some are stronger than others. Do they not teach you anything in this fancy school of yours?"

"It's not that kind of school." Joshua had been glad that Blackridge wasn't supposed to be like Hogwarts. He didn't want to deal with random deadly school events, endless dark arts teachers turning out—surprise—to be dark, and unexpected monsters showing up. Mannie must not have gotten the memo on "no monsters."

Joshua couldn't sit there and seemingly talk to himself—especially with his wolf twitching under his skin. He needed to get out of class and someplace private. "Excuse me, Ms. Silvers, I'm...I'm not feeling well. I need to go to the nurse's office."

"Let me write you a pass," Ms. Silvers said after a moment of thought.

Joshua wondered what in the world the staff had been told. *Let him do whatever he wants!* He gathered his things, snatched the pass from Ms. Silvers's hand, and fled the room.

"You didn't answer me!" Mannie waddled after him, muttering what sounded like Spanish curse words.

Joshua didn't know the school well enough to know where to go. He couldn't go home. He didn't want Mannie and some unknown number of monsters knowing where Decker was—asleep and helpless. All the other places he knew were stores. Target.

Home Depot. The hardware store. The supermarket where Winnie worked...

He could go to the grocery store; the place was supernatural central. They probably bulldozed a graveyard or something like that to build it. Mannie would fit right in. But Winnie might not be on duty. She'd been there late at night on Monday. The way he was feeling, his wolf would eat the shelves bare if he stayed there until Winnie showed up or dusk fell.

At his old school, there had been an oversized closet that the robotics club used to store all their equipment. It was where all the geeky kids hung out before school, after school, and during study halls. He couldn't remember during the morning announcements if there had been any mention of a robotics club or any other geeky after-school activity. There had been things like lacrosse and rowing and mock trial. He *could* go to the nurse's office. Maybe he should call Dr. Huff. But would it be okay to get the royal vet involved? It seemed as if she was just a normal person with a doctorate in animal medicine.

"What is that doing here?" Ottilie whispered as she came down the hall toward Joshua. She was pointing at Mannie. She was the first person to acknowledge the penguin's existence.

"You can see him?" Joshua said.

"Yes, of course she can!" Mannie squawked. "She's a little baby Grigori—although I don't know why she's here and not in Greece. Maybe she failed out... *Squawk!*"

This was because Ottilie had roundhouse-kicked the penguin. It went tumbling backward.

"Can we not fight in the halls?" Joshua said, struggling to keep his wolf in control. It had kicked the penguin once so far. It was all for doing it again. "I need someplace private."

"This way." Ottilie motioned for Joshua to follow her.

The library was a cathedral of books with a great vaulted ceiling, stained glass rosette windows, two stories of cherrywood bookcases, sliding ladders on brass rails, and a hushed reverent atmosphere.

"Wow!" Joshua winced as surprise had made his exclamation louder than he intended.

"Shh!" Ottilie whispered, "The first Prince of Boston was a first cousin of the Prince of London and had studied at Oxford. He had his architects copy the style of the Bodleian Libraries."

"*Che*, what delusions of grandeur," Mannie grumbled.

"Do you want to be kicked again?" Ottilie led the way through a maze of bookcases to a small, secluded alcove.

Mannie muttered something in Spanish that Joshua didn't understand. It made his wolf growl in annoyance.

"I'm just saying that all you really need in the world is food in your belly and a safe place to nest," Mannie said.

"Which is why you're looting sunken ships illegally?" Ottilie asked.

"Bleah, stupid humans tanked their economy in Argentina and we're the ones that are made to suffer. If we want to keep our nesting lands free and clear of human control, we need to own it and pay taxes—which is nearly impossible when inflation keeps making our capital worthless."

In the back corner of the alcove, Ottilie reached into one of the bookcases and triggered a secret door that opened soundlessly. "This is an area that is only known to the Tatterskeins and the Goths over the age of thirteen. None of the faculty or normal students knows it exists. It houses the Tatterskeins' collection of reference materials. I spend a lot of time in here."

She waved them through the secret door and then closed it behind them.

The space was lined with floor to ceiling bookcases matching the ones in the larger public area. On the shelves were hundreds of hardcover books that smelled of age. On one side of the room were four wingback chairs in a conversation circle defined by a silk oriental rug. On the other side were a desk, a chair, and a surprisingly modern lamp. There was a book open on the desk with a laptop; Ottilie's backpack hung off the back of the chair.

"Why are these books in here and not out with the rest of them?" Joshua asked.

"Because all these books have to do with the occult," Ottilie said, closing the book and shutting down her laptop. "They have real spells, wards, information on monsters, the works. It's all low-powered artillery but not anything you want curious teenagers mucking around with."

Joshua didn't point out that Ottilie was a teenager mucking around with the books. She guessed, though, the direction of his thoughts.

"I arranged to have access to this part of the library when

Thane Cabot accepted me to Blackridge. Allie and Tal told me about your fight yesterday at the mall. I have a study hall right now, so I signed into the library and came down here to look up information on firebirds. There isn't a lot known about them. I was thinking of calling Central and conferring with them."

"*Che*, I could tell you about firebirds," Mannie said.

Ottilie glared at the penguin. After a long moment of silence, she growled out, "Then tell me about them."

"In the beginning there was nothing," Mannie said. "The universe lay still—it was a shapeless kind of matter surrounded by darkness and silence. Then out of the stillness came the god Chaos. It was a being without shape or gender. By its existence, the universe was stirred. Everywhere that it touched divided into light and dark, sound and silence. But there was no land, only water swirling in disorder. Chaos brushed over the ocean and out of this swirl, the waters divided into sweet, fresh water, the begetter, and the saltwater sea, she who bore them all. They mingled their waters together and brought forth many gods."

Ottilie frowned but started to write notes as Mannie talked. "Do these two have names?"

"Who knows if they had a concept of names. We called them..." Mannie finished by squawking twice. "Which of course, you don't understand. Their names translate roughly to Rio and Mar. It matters little as they are dead and only have a little to do with what is happening now."

"So why are you telling us about them, then?" Joshua said.

"Because it is the egg from which this all hatched." Mannie waved him to be quiet. "Rio and Mar gave birth to many gods, great and powerful. But as the two were formed by Chaos, most of their children were wild and untamed in nature. The greatest among them was..."

Mannie squawked again. "Which roughly translated means the Dark One—although at first, he was not dark; that came later. He was the greatest of their children, gleaming like the full moon. But then he slew his father. He tore Rio's body apart and used its power to create a palace for himself, surrounded by a great city and lush land. Enraged, Mar rose up against him and his siblings that had gathered to him. She created powerful weapons for the children still loyal to her and many horrible sea monsters. Their war shook the very foundations of the world. The land that was created from Rio's body was splintered into many pieces and set adrift."

Ottilie shook her head, making notes. "This was a layer close enough to overlap with our world? Travel between the two layers was possible—like Midgard once was—but is no longer?"

Mannie flapped his short wings. "What we know are the tales that we're told as chicks. Our history is all oral. We have no use for written books. Far as I know, no one has ever seen the places of our legends. It is said that when the land was split asunder during the war, the Dark One's palace drifted south, while his city went north. Is this true? Who knows? Not us in Argentina.

"After he killed his sire," Mannie continued, "he told his siblings to lure their mother out, saying that they had captured their father's killer and was holding him prisoner. Once they had her alone, they surrounded her and slew her with magical weapons. With her dying breath, Mar cursed her traitorous son. The Dark One lost his gleaming aspect—he became like the new moon, dark and hidden, unable to bear the light of the sun. Wounded, he fell into a deep slumber within his ruined palace, lost under ice as the land it sits on drifted to the very bottom of the world. No one knows what happened to his city.

"As the pieces of the land that once had been Rio's body drifted hither and yon, some of Mar's blood and bones washed up against its shore. They mixed with a rivulet of fresh water welling up from underground. Three children were born from this mixing. These sisters were the first of my people, those that you call the swan maidens. They are neither of land nor sea nor air but are still part of all of them. Their primal gods dead, the swan maidens fled to all corners of the world. They turned to whatever faith their new homes kept, be it Christian or Buddhism or Shinto."

"Those were your people that attacked me last night at the mall?" Joshua said.

Mannie shook his head. "No! Not really. The sisters each had seven children, each one different, but yet the same. We adapted to our environment—as by nature our form is fluid as water. Some became swans. Some cranes. Others firebirds. We can all take human form, but we all prefer to spend our lives as birds. As we're very different birds, we have very little to do with each other. Before the start of written history, while men were all still living in caves and using sharpened sticks as weapons, we went our separate ways. We penguins answer to our emperor. What I know of the swans and firebirds, I learned from my grand-mère Manon."

Ottilie snorted in disbelief. "It's total coincidence that you're hiding out at the aquarium and the firebird shows up at the CambridgeSide mall?"

"I would not say that." Mannie gave a squawking laugh. "You see, the Dark One stirs."

"By 'stirs' you mean he's waking up?" Joshua said.

"We've been told in stories that our people have repeated since the beginning of our kind. A warning that the Dark One is not dead: he is asleep. Waiting. Just because we turned our backs on him does not mean that he forgot us. He has enslaved all of my people! Those that attacked you—they did not want to fight you."

"They didn't?" So far everyone that Joshua had come up against seemed more willing to fight to the death rather than talk things out.

"On the shore that the sisters were born, there was a bone. A piece of their mother, Mar, worn smooth into the shape of an egg. It's more than a sacred relic to my people. Whoever holds this relic can hold my people in thrall."

Joshua remembered the picture Allie had drawn at lunch yesterday. The weird egg-shaped thing that Allie thought was a stone with the three figures painted on it. He took out his phone and found the picture of her drawing. "You meant this?"

"Yes, that's it!" Mannie squawked. "You have it?"

"No," Ottilie said. "One of our people is a touch witch. She drew that picture after handling the things that you gave Marie Antoinette."

"That is the Mothers' Stone." Mannie waved his wingtip toward the drawing. "I need to get it back to free my people. All of them!"

The "stone" sounded like the leash that the Wickers had fashioned out of Thane Samuels's skin. A part of the body of the creature that had made Joshua a magical beast. Mar's bone must act in the same fashion.

"The damned Touched has the Mothers' Stone hidden somewhere, along with the bulk of my people. He took them all. Our eggs. Our fledging children. Our elders. Everyone!"

"Who are the Touched?" Joshua asked Mannie.

Mannie flapped his stubby wings. "Time and time again, the Dark Lord has managed to reach out and contact a human open enough to hear his voice but unschooled in the ways to protect themselves. The first had been Juan de Cartagena, the bastard son of a Spanish cardinal who had been marooned on one of our nesting islands after he mutinied against Magellan. My people had never seen Europeans before and missed the signs that Cartagena was Touched. It must have been then when the Dark One realized that the Mothers' Stone was in our possession. Cartagena escaped off our islands and made his way back to Spain. He went empty-handed and luckily tripped over a wiser flock of swan maidens who recognized what he was. Cartagena was put down but there have been others over the centuries. I do not know the name of the one who is currently listening to the Dark One's voice."

"What about you?" Ottilie said. "Why aren't you in thrall?"

"I say 'my people' but I am not fully a swan maiden," Mannie admitted. "My mother was, as were all those before her, but my father was not."

"What was he?" Joshua asked since he wasn't sure it would be automatically "human."

"He was the seventh son of a seventh son, born to a Wise Woman, on the island of Saint Barthélemy," Mannie said proudly.

"Saint Barthélemy," Ottilie murmured, squinting in thought. "Your grandmother is a Blanchard?"

"Yes!" Mannie said. "Madame Manon Blanchard! As my grandmother's gift passes through the female line, she cared not that her sons followed their hearts. My father travels the world on his catamaran, looking for adventure and treasure. He met my mother at Carnival in Buenos Aires, and they fell instantly in love. Ah, but it was not meant to be. Penguins do not mate for life and my father's eye roams despite his love for my mother. They remained fond of each other as they passed me back and forth."

Ottilie cocked her head. "Most of the stories imply that children fathered by humans on bird people are human and unable to transform. Obviously, that's wrong..."

Mannie flapped his stubby wings as if angered and frustrated by the assumption. "When a man drags a swan maiden to his home, locks her away, hides her feathered cloak, and forbids her to teach her people's way to their children, then no, those half-breeds can't transform. My father is not a brute. He went with my mother to her people and lived among them for some time. He thought her people were most elegant when they were swimming, so he would dive with them often. I would spend my summers with my mother, learning her ways. In winter, I lived with my father. He and my grand-mère Manon taught me all that I know about humans. When I was ten, the flock gathered together enough feathers to weave a cloak for me so that I could transform."

"If you can be a human, why don't you just be a human?" Joshua said.

"If you can be a wolf, why don't you just be a wolf?" Mannie said.

"Those two things are not the same." Joshua struggled not to kick the penguin as he recognized it as the wolf's response. "Why are you running around Boston as a bird only found in the Southern Hemisphere?"

"*Che*, I only have magical powers when I'm a penguin," Mannie said. "As a human, I am not much different from *la oveja* students at this school. Yes, I'm stronger and faster than a normal man but I can freeze to death in the cold, and I can't erase my presence from other people. I'm alone in a city full of enemies. I can't afford to be human."

"What exactly do you hope to do?" Ottilie said.

"We need to find the Mothers' Stone! If I can get it back, I can free my people from the Touched!"

"We? As in you and me?" Joshua said.

"No!" Mannie cried. "I've told you over and over again, I want to hire the dowser, Silas Decker! I don't know where he is, but you live with him."

"You live with Silas Decker?" Ottilie said in surprise.

"It's supposed to be a secret," Joshua growled. "Please don't tell anyone."

"Tell me where he lives and I'll leave you alone," Mannie said.

"No!" Joshua cried. "It's a secret! Besides, he's not awake right now."

Mannie swore in Spanish. "I'll wake him up!"

Ottilie raised a finger and asked, "You do know that Silas Decker is a vampire?"

"Anyway . . . What?" Mannie said.

"Vampire," Ottilie repeated and then detailed further. "Creature of the night—as in dead to the world during the day."

"Ottilie!" Joshua warned as his wolf was peeling back its lips in a silent snarl.

"So I've heard." Ottilie cringed back from Joshua. "He's been protected by our tribe for three hundred years. It's common knowledge among the Grigori. There was a breach along the King's Highway during the time that the Monkshood Coven tried to leash the Prince of New York."

Mannie cursed and spat on the ground. "You mean when the Touched tried to open a pathway for the Dark One to reenter our world! They knew that the Wolf King and the Grigori would join forces against their cursed god. The leash on the Prince of New York was just to give his Touched a guard dog against the powers that be in this world. The leash failed because the heir was too weak to hold New York. While the Wolf King and the Grigori were distracted, his damn Touched had fumbled an attempt to bring him into our world. His darkness spilled out and corrupted all that it came in contact with."

Ottilie shook her head, making notes. "My family has dealt with Touched before—mostly in Europe—but we didn't know that one was involved in the death of the Prince of New York. It would make sense, though, as much of what the Monkshood Coven had done seemed atypical of Wickers. The fire in London. The witch trials in Salem. The magical items that they created in their attempt to leash the Prince of New York's heir."

Decker had been living as a human in New York City shortly after the Dutch sold it to the English. He'd been run out of town by people who thought his divine gift was the work of the devil. On his way to Philadelphia, he'd been attacked by a pack of monsters. If he'd known the true origin of the creatures that had changed into him a vampire, then Ottilie probably would have known about it too.

Mannie swore in Spanish. "We had thought that the Grigori had hunted down his creatures and destroyed them all."

"Normally we would have," Ottilie said, "but Decker was a special case. He was considered a non-monster and allowed to live."

Mannie squawked. "The monsters that his corruption makes share the Dark One's curse—like him they suffer the sleep of the living dead. I can't trust something so aligned with him."

"Decker isn't 'aligned' with anyone except me and Elise," Joshua said.

"Virtue Elise," Ottilie clarified.

Mannie squawked, flapping his wings. "I don't know how Decker's not overwhelmed by the evil that is the Dark One's influence, but it makes Decker weak to his power. I cannot go raiding their nest for the Mothers' Stone with him in tow."

"Raiding their nest" sounded like opening a beehive and stirring around with a short stick. It was bound to be dangerous no matter who was involved.

"Where is this nest?" Joshua asked.

"If I knew that, I wouldn't need Decker!" Mannie squawked.

"Why did this Dark One even come to Boston?" Joshua asked. "What does he want? And why hasn't Seth noticed all the weird magical birds in the area?"

"I was wondering that too," Ottilie said. "I'm guessing that there's something here in New England that the Dark One wants."

"He wants his lost city!" Mannie muttered a few curses in Spanish. "Since Mar cursed him, he has been locked away in his palace, unable to act directly with the dominant world except through his Touched. That his messenger came to the aquarium means that his Touched has found a way to the lost city. That is where his Touched most likely has the Mothers' Stone and the bulk of my people."

"Well, there are dozens of sites scattered across the prince's territory that have mystical connections." Ottilie pointed to a map cabinet across the room. "Up to three years ago, they were heavily guarded by the Tatterskeins. It should be fairly easy to find your flock if they're using one of those locations to hide from the prince. We would only need to check the areas with mystical connections instead of having to search the entire tristate."

Do we really want to find an entire flock of mind-controlled were-penguins?

"There's a map to these areas?" Mannie said.

"Of course there is." Ottilie went to the cabinet to pull a large map out of the top drawer. She spread it out on the table. "There are at least five within range of the subway system."

"Really?" Mannie jumped up into one of the chairs to scan the map. "Ah, yes, this is what I should have asked Her Majesty. My mistake. Growing up on islands, you don't think of land like this."

Joshua paced back and forth as Ottilie and Mannie discussed the map. If what Mannie said was true, what happened to Decker could happen again. A wave of monsters could flood over the land. Decker had been at an isolated inn, away from any large city. If it happened within Boston, everyone in the city was in danger. Last night, though, he would have lost the fight if Francis and Decker weren't there.

"I'm going to call Central," Ottilie said. "I should update them as to what is going on here."

"What do you think I should do?" Joshua said. Ottilie might be three years younger than him, but she'd grown up with all this weirdness.

"I think you should call your brother," Ottilie said.

26: SETH

The king was still asleep.

Seth took the ancient elevator up to the king's private quarters, hoping to find him awake.

Bishop answered the door, looking equal parts distressed and relieved to see Seth. He stepped back, inviting Seth into the sitting room. The fire had been freshly lit, snapping and cracking as it rushed through kindling wood and crumbled newspaper. The chair by the fireplace, however, was empty. The king was in his bed in the room beyond.

"I'm hoping that we will not need you." Bishop was immaculately dressed as usual in an Italian business suit, but paced the room like a caged beast. It was the first time that Seth had ever seen the man unsettled. "You're too young to shoulder all this. But the king is not awake yet and Isaiah is sure to be here sometime this morning. He's like his mother, Raisa. Once she got something into her head, there was no dealing with her. Anton Cabot was the only one that could sweet-talk her into reasonable behavior. We were hoping that it was simply she was young and anxious from being surrounded by strangers in a foreign country. Once the king sent Anton to Boston to marry your aunt, Raisa grew more and more unmanageable. We thought that once she knew us better and had children of her own to care for, she would mature. Knowing Isaiah, though, I now don't think time would have solved her willfulness."

Isaiah's mother proved to be so unstable that she had killed herself just a month after Isaiah was born. Her insanity was now casting a shadow on what Isaiah's possible actions would be in the face of the king's illness. The elder Thanes might be older and wiser, but they couldn't stop Isaiah.

"Do any of you know: has the king ever slept like this before?" Seth said after he closed the door behind him. He considered locking it—would Isaiah go as far as breaking it down? He decided to leave it unlocked.

"We believe so," Bishop said. "The oldest princes have all called the Castle. London. Los Vegas. Tokyo. Lagos. Isaiah has fielded their calls, so the conversations have been unfortunately stunted. They haven't explained to him why they're calling, just pressed for an audience with the king. We think that they may have noticed a shift in their alphas and recognized the source of the discomfort."

"They've been through this before," Seth murmured as he understood the implication.

Bishop waved his hand. "It's speculation. We didn't see the implications at first. We take calls all day from various packs ranging from territorial issues to financial difficulties. We noticed a pattern only this morning that it was the oldest of princes who only asked for an audience for unspecified reasons—something that they would never do if they expected the king to respond."

"Have you called any of them? Asked them to confirm?"

"Thane Mandeville is calling them now," Bishop took a seat on the couch. "Cook has been with the king the longest, fifty years. He does not remember any episodes like this. Thane Chakrabarti is checking the records of the king's vet prior to that."

Seth had so many questions, but he doubted that Bishop had answers for most of them. While the elder Thanes were close to the king, the last three years had been an education on how Alexander never explained himself. "What exactly happened in Belgrade that weighed so heavily on the king?"

"The breach had grown to a massive size by the time we reached the city. It took a great deal of power to close it. Your brother was not the only one wounded that week. Normally the prince would have healed his own people, but he was deep in alpha amnesia. There was much to do, and the king knew that you were dealing with Wickers. He did not rest so that we could rush back. We were all staggering by the time we reached Boston. I should have known that any normal being would collapse under all that, but I thought—as did the others—that the king was beyond such things as exhaustion. We thought him godlike."

Seth took a seat in one of the winged chairs, needing to feel grounded in the face of the other man's nervousness. What was safe to tell Bishop? "I need to send Thane Cabot to Boston. Something is happening there—but I'm not sure what. There's too many Grigori in the area when there should only be Virtue Elise."

Should he mention the Power? No. That would be too alarming. His vague description was true, just misleading.

"I told Jack to get ready to go," Seth said. "And that I would see how things stood with the king..."

He trailed off, not sure what was safe to add. Seth could do anything he wanted while the king was asleep—no one could stop him. The elder Thanes would report everything that they knew, when the king eventually woke up. Repercussions were sure to follow. If Isaiah was about to become the Prince of New York, Seth had to be sure that Joshua was not dragged to the Castle.

Bishop nodded after a moment of thought. "Yes, it would be wise for him to go but you need to caution him. Nothing can be said to the Grigori about the king's condition."

"Why not?" Seth had been so focused on Joshua it hadn't occurred to him that Jack might say something inappropriate to Elise. It was entirely possible that Jack wouldn't even talk with her; Elise had partnered up with Jack a few weeks ago because she was vastly outnumbered by the Wickers. If there was a Power working with her, it might not even be safe for Jack to approach the Virtues.

Bishop sat down in one of the armchairs to face Seth. He clasped his hands together and carefully picked his words. "Boston has long enjoyed a peaceful relationship with the East Coast Tribe of the Grigori. I don't know how it came to be—I suspect it's related to the Great Fire of London or perhaps to the Prince of New York going feral. It happened long before I came a Thane, and you know how the king is not wont to speak of times gone past. I can only guess. I know, though, that we do not exist peacefully with the other tribes elsewhere. There are two hundred tribes scattered across the world, each descended from one of their forefathers who took humans as wives. According to biblical text, they had a single a leader—Shemihazah—but far as we can tell, the Grigori tribes operate much more like the United Nations. It took hundreds of years to establish the treaty with all the tribes. It could, however, be broken in a single day. If the Grigori thought that the Wolf King would fall, any one tribe—or all of them—might break the peace treaty between us."

"Why?"

"Because without the king..." Bishop paused as he clasped and reclasped his hand in a slow-motion wringing of hands. "The Grigori know what happens when an heir goes feral under the weight of the alpha. The entire pack is lost—like a collapsing bridge when its main support gives out. New York City was nearly wiped out when the Prince of New York died, and his heir could not stand against the alpha. Hundreds of humans died that day. Torn apart or worse—bitten and made into a feral wolf that spread the madness. While the Grigori see us as useful guard dogs, if they thought we all might run mad, they would start a wholesale cleansing of our kind."

That made entirely too much sense.

The idea of Alexander dying was terrifying. Seth doubted that he could hold Boston utterly alone. The fact that he accidently broadcast his anger at school was proof enough that without the king's support, Boston would sink Seth into being feral. Would Albany hold? Ewan was just days into being marquis—would he be able to withstand a flood of additional power? What about the civilization as a whole if vast numbers of humans in every city either were killed or went feral?

No wonder the older princes were calling the Castle, wanting to know what was going on.

"I'll tell Jack not to say anything to the Grigori," Seth said.

The next few hours were a revolving door of the Thanes who trotted at Isaiah's heels. They had flimsy excuses—dropping off the king's newspaper, clean laundry, and random phone messages from other packs. They collected dirty clothes and bedlinens and the tray of Seth's breakfast dishes. When they ran out of true errands, they just knocked timidly at the door. Seth was surprised to realize that some of them had never been to the king's private quarters before. They used the intrusions to gawk.

Seth had known that Isaiah had collected the weakest of the

Thanes—all hoping that one day they would form his inner circle when he was made Prince of New York. He hadn't considered what that meant for the city. If Isaiah wasn't strong enough to hold the city, then the stronger the wolves that made up his pack, the better. It was one of the reasons Jack's father was shifted to the Boston pack. Normally Seth's aunt would have married into another pack, but Boston needed her to stay. Since his grandfather was collapsing under the weight, his wife, children, and their spouses needed to be strong to help carry the load.

But Isaiah wasn't gathering together the strong wolves. He deliberately courted those he could bully with a glance. Anyone who could stand their ground and point out his failings, he rebuffed. That didn't bode well.

The interruptions—and the implications of Isaiah's alliances—distracted Seth from his brother. Joshua had gone to school despite being told not to. He was down in the archery range, seemingly safe for the time being. Jack had just crossed into Boston's territory, just south of Hartford, Connecticut. He was driving the motor pool Bentley like a low-flying black rocket—cruising at over a hundred miles per hour. He was still over an hour from Cambridge—unless he got stopped for speeding.

The Power was at the Grigori supply depot in Watertown. It seemed to be still asleep, as was one of the Virtues. The other—he assumed to be Elise—was driving north for reasons unknown.

It was the first time Seth had had a Power within his territory. The king had always warned him that the Grigori Powers were worthy of their name. They were impossibly strong. It felt like a bright burning star had bedded down in the middle of Watertown. Even the Wolf King didn't feel as strong as the unknown Power.

How had Seth not noticed the Power before it suddenly appeared at the mall last night? Was it out at sea where he couldn't reach? Why was Joshua at the mall? One minute he was safe at Decker's house and then holy fire was being rained down around him at the mall. And now there was Joshua's mysterious teleporting power—if it *was* Joshua's power and not someone messing with him.

Damn Isaiah. If it wasn't for Isaiah, Seth could have brought Joshua to New York weeks ago.

When they were fighting the Wickers, Elise hadn't called in a Power. What in the world was she squaring off against now?

What did it have to do with the mysterious "penguin" that Joshua had encountered at the aquarium?

Having Jack talk to Elise was probably a good idea. An exchange of information—some but not all—would let Jack know what was going on in Boston. Until the king woke up and could order some of the older Thanes to reinforce Seth's pack, it was just Jack and Joshua. (Decker proved himself willing to fight but he was unconscious during daylight hours.) Seth didn't like the odds.

Isaiah knocked on the door even as he swung it open, not bothering to wait for anyone to answer it. Considering that his lackeys probably gave him detailed reports, he probably knew that Bishop had left.

"What are you doing here?" Isaiah said. "Shouldn't you be out trying to get into a new school?"

"The king needs to pick one. Until he does, no, I'm not enrolling anywhere." Seth's phone vibrated. He glanced at the screen. A text from Joshua read, "Help! It's here!"

Seth frowned and then smoothed away the expression as he didn't want Isaiah to know there was something wrong with Joshua. Seth couldn't keep Isaiah from heading to Boston with a car full of his lackeys. Last time it happened, it turned into a mess.

"What's there?" Seth texted quickly back to Joshua and tucked away his phone so he could glare at Isaiah.

The older man was drifting toward his father's bedroom. "Sucks to be you. So much for graduating early."

"It is what it is," Seth said, refusing to be baited. "Leave your father be, Isaiah."

"What is this charade that my father is ill? We don't get ill. He took no wounds at Belgrade."

Seth stared at Isaiah in surprise. "Have you learned nothing about holding an alpha? How can you whine so much about becoming prince without making the effort to learn the basics?"

"When was I supposed to learn? Was I supposed to learn from Cook, who spends every waking moment thinking only about food? The elder Thanes like Bishop and Mandeville were much too busy to teach me. Perhaps in Russia where I didn't speak the language, and no one spoke English? When I got back, I didn't get to tour the world with my father, meeting other princes, getting wined and dined. I'm not even sent out to check on barons and counts. I'm stuck here in New York, taking care of the cars in the motor pool and playing messenger to local businesses."

It was ironic that he was jealous of Seth being dragged around the world when the king would have left him in New York if he knew that Isaiah wouldn't attack Seth.

"The elder Thanes would have made the time if you'd asked them," Seth said. "You could have been nicer to Jack. Hell, if you had been civil, I could have told you."

"Oh, that is rich: bending a knee to you," Isaiah said.

"Asking a simple question is not groveling." Seth's phone vibrated with an answer from Joshua. He pulled it out to glance at the screen. The reply to "What's there?" was simply "Penguin!"

The penguin is at Blackridge?

Seth reached out to check on Joshua. He was in one of the first-floor classrooms, surrounded by other students. Inches from him was the strange creature that had been at the aquarium. Joshua was nearly vibrating in place.

"Do not wolf out at school!" Seth texted. "It's important that you don't bite anyone! Not even the penguin!"

Isaiah took advantage of his distraction to cross to the king's bedroom door.

"Isaiah!" Seth snapped, tapping the "!" icon to drive home his point. "There's a limit to how much power a person can handle day to day and not be burned out by it. It's like a car engine—it's fine if you drive around town at fifty miles per hour but if you try to drive down to Florida at a hundred and fifty miles per hour, you're going to tear the engine apart. My grandfather wasn't meant to be the prince—the true heir had been killed young. Boston burned him out before he was fifty."

"But this is my father," Isaiah said. "He's the Wolf King."

"King or not, he's done too much," Seth said. "Sealed the breach at Belgrade. Healed the wounded. Put out too many other fires in too short a time. He's run too fast for too long. He needs to rest."

His phone vibrated with another text.

"What should I do?" Joshua had texted.

Seth locked down on a growl of frustration. He typed in, "Stay calm! Jack is on his way. This is why I told you not to go to school!"

"If you're going to block me," Isaiah said, "don't ignore me!"

Isaiah slapped the phone out of Seth's hands.

Seth had been distracted by Joshua and hadn't realized that Isaiah had moved in front of him. He shouted in surprise and dismay as his phone flew out of his hands. He heard it vibrate with another text from Joshua before it smashed against the fireplace bricks. It fell to the ground, dark and silent, the cracks in the screen visible from where he stood.

"Just tell me plain!" Isaiah shouted. "When is my father going to wake up?"

Seth snapped. It had been a bad morning from the moment he'd realized that his plans for the future had utterly crashed and burned. All his fears for Joshua and his territory and the king being deep in Odin sleep—it just rose up and overwhelmed him. He roared and leapt at Isaiah, shredding clothes as he transformed. His wolf went for Isaiah's throat, fully intending to tear it open.

Isaiah threw up his arms to protect his neck. He stumbled backward, tripped over the leather ottoman, and fell to the floor.

"Damn it!" Isaiah yelled as Seth savaged his left arm. "I just bought this suit! Get off me! Get off!"

There was a small, quiet inner voice telling Seth that he couldn't kill Isaiah, that the king needed him. His wolf, though, drowned out that rational thought, filled with dark rage. Isaiah was a big, spoiled toddler determined to destroy everything that Seth loved out of spite.

They tumbled across the floor as Isaiah tried to free himself. They slammed into the hundred-year-old chairs around the dining table, smashing them into pieces. Isaiah tore himself free, leaving Italian silk and blood in Seth's mouth. Isaiah rolled under the table a man and emerged out the other side as a wolf. Seth leapt over the table and dove on top of him. They crashed through the sitting room, growling and snarling, seeking an opening.

As wolves, Seth had the advantage of size. Isaiah, though, had over a decade more experience at fighting. Isaiah met every attack with his fangs. Their lip and muzzles grew bloody with deep cuts. Seth caught Isaiah by the left ear, shredding it as Isaiah twisted out of his hold. They circled, attacking each other.

Isaiah started for Seth's throat and then dipped down, catching him by the leg. Seth roared in pain as the bone snapped. He lunged forward and caught Isaiah by the throat.

"Seth! Seth! Get a hold of yourself!" Bishop shouted as he, Mandeville, and Chakrabarti attempted to pull him off Isaiah.

If I kill him now, can we find a replacement someplace in the world? Anyone would be better. Anyone might last just as long holding New York.

"Shame on you, boy!" Chakrabarti shouted. "Fighting in a place like this! Look at what you've done to the king's sitting room!"

Seth let himself be dragged back, letting go of his hold on Isaiah's throat.

They'd broken one of the winged chairs, the couch, and the dining table and taken the front doors off their hinges. At least they hadn't destroyed the statue or the painting.

Isaiah bled from half a dozen wounds.

Seth staggered back and shifted to human. He could taste blood in his mouth and knew it wasn't his. He had a storm of emotions flooding through him: rage, shame, and remorse. Isaiah was an asshole, but the king had ignored his son once he knew that Isaiah wasn't a strong enough wolf to survive New York's alpha. Once Seth arrived, Isaiah must have seen how he should have been treated as a future prince. It had to grate.

Would it have been kinder to tell him simply that he would only become prince in case of an emergency because it would kill him?

Seth wasn't sure. Jack might have been fine with it but not Isaiah. The man had too much ego. It might be that Isaiah became egotistical because it was the only way he could survive being so neglected.

Why had the king ignored Isaiah so much? Isaiah was still his son.

"Come, I'll take you down to the infirmary." Mandeville got Isaiah to his feet. "I'll have the vet come look at you."

It left Seth alone with his guilt and the elder Thanes. "He broke my phone..."

"No reason to try and kill him—especially with the king... as he is..." Chakrabarti said.

Seth struggled to keep his temper in check. "I know. I'm... I'm having a bad day with getting kicked out of school and... and what's happening in Boston. I was texting with my brother when Isaiah broke my phone. I need to answer my brother before he does something stupid."

"Call him on the Castle's landline," Bishop said. "Well, the one in your room. You two broke the one in here. I'll send out one of the Thanes to get you a new smartphone. You'll have it in an hour or two."

Seth nodded and added a polite "Thank you" and escaped to the elevator. He hadn't memorized Joshua's phone number. Jack had given him a slip of paper with the number on it to program into his phone—it might still be on his desk. If not, he could call Jack. He had Jack's number memorized.

He checked on Joshua. His brother had left the school and was pacing the inbound platform of the subway station a block from Blackridge. The penguin waddled beside him. Where were they going? Decker was only a few blocks from the school—Joshua wasn't going home if he was going into the station.

The paper with Joshua's phone number wasn't on Seth's desk. Both of his trash cans were empty. Seth flipped through his school notebook to see if maybe he'd written it in there. No. He checked to see where Jack was. He was on the last stretch of Route 90, nearing the Natick service station.

He called Jack and said, "Hey, can you pull over to the Natick service station?"

"Yeah," Jack said. "I needed to stop at it anyhow; I'm almost out of gas. What's up?"

"I have to update you, and I need Joshua's phone number."

"Okay, I'm pulling into the service station now. Ah, good, no one is at the pumps. I should be able to get in and out fast."

Seth updated Jack as he filled up the Bentley. "I'm not sure where Joshua is going with the penguin. It might not be dangerous, but Joshua is fairly rattled. I think he might be close to losing..."

"Why aren't you answering your phone?" Joshua said, suddenly beside him.

Seth yelped and swore.

"He did the blinky thing again, didn't he?" Jack said.

"Yes," Seth said.

Joshua waved his phone frantically in the air. "Mannie wanted to hire Decker to find the monsters that stole his flock. Well, not the monsters but the bone that they're using to control his people. It acts like the leash that the Wickers put on me. It sounds like a good idea to get it off the bad guys, but I don't know how to do this! It's the chicken and the fox!"

"Chicken and the fox?" Seth echoed in confusion.

"There's a penguin and a chicken and a fox now?" Jack said.

"What fox?" Seth asked as the predator sounded more dangerous than a chicken—assuming it stayed a chicken and didn't become something else.

"Does Blackridge not teach riddles?" Joshua said. "The chicken eats the grain! The fox eats the chicken! We need Decker to find the Mothers' Stone but he's weak to the Dark One—or at least that's what Mannie says. How do you track down the lair of an evil god without having your vampire taken over? How do you work with the penguin without letting him know where the vampire lives? If Mannie can't find the Mothers' Stone, he *will* show up on our doorstep regardless of the danger if he knew where we lived. He's like a neighbor trying to sell Amway."

Seth rubbed his forehead as another headache loomed in his future.

"So . . . what happened to the penguin?" Jack asked over the phone. "Is it there with you?"

"No. Joshua didn't bring it with him," Seth said. "It's still at the subway station."

Seth reached out to double-check. Yes, the small, weird, nearly-impossible-to-sense knot of magic that was the penguin was waddling back and forth on the platform—probably confused about where Joshua suddenly vanished to.

"Mannie is going to check a mystical site that Ottilie said was near Alewife station. It was the closest one to the school. There's four more that you can get to by subway."

"You're not going anywhere with that penguin," Seth said, just in case Joshua disappeared back to Cambridge again.

"I'm not planning to!" Joshua cried. "My wolf had enough of the spooky scary stuff—I barely managed to walk Mannie to the subway station! I didn't want him at Blackridge. I don't want to be there either—I've become some kind of weirdness magnet. If Mannie could find me, maybe the bad guys would show up too. That's why I was calling you. I don't know what to do."

"What exactly did Mannie tell you about this leash?" Seth asked Joshua.

Joshua picked up a pen on Seth's desk. He drew an odd picture in the open notebook while explaining the penguin creation myth. "From what Mannie told me, this bone operates on the same principle as the Wickers' leash. The body of the parent allows you to create a magic item that can control its progeny. I suppose it's not exactly the same—Samuels wasn't my father, but he did make me a werewolf. The three figures on it are the first three mothers of the swan maidens sitting on the eggs that were their first children. The penguins had the bone at a village in Argentina, but it was raided while Mannie was away. He came home to find his people gone."

The Grigori had crossed Joshua's path too many times in the last two days for the penguin to be unrelated to their mission. Neither Jack nor Joshua could take on whatever summoned a Power to Boston. Until they knew what was going on, it would be stupid to blindly follow any clues that might lead to whatever evil the Grigori were hunting.

"Here, give me your phone." Seth held out his hand for Joshua's phone. "Isaiah broke mine. I'll be getting a new one but until then, we'll have to use yours."

Seth took a picture of the drawing and emailed it to Jack. He checked Cambridge and the surrounding towns carefully, looking for monsters. There was nothing he could spot other than the penguin and the two sleeping Grigori in Watertown, which meant that Blackridge was currently safe.

"Elise is near Salem State University," Seth told Jack over the landline. "Why don't you meet up with her and trade information. See if you can find out why the Power is still in our territory. Just remember, whatever you do, don't mention what's happening here at the Castle."

"Sure thing," Jack said. "I'm done pumping gas. I'll head there now."

Seth said goodbye and hung up. That should keep Jack safe. He pulled up Joshua's contact list and wrote down the handful of phone numbers that he didn't have memorized, including Joshua's, just in case his brother teleported again. As he did, Joshua rambled on about a weird magical coin that the penguin had given Marie Antonette.

"Decker is right: talking to Sioux Zee is the wisest course of action," Seth said as he handed Joshua's phone back to him. "Wise Women are trained from birth in wisdom of the ages. If anyone knows what that coin is, she will. Go home and when Decker wakes up, go to Sioux Zee with the coin."

"I don't know," Joshua said. "All of Mannie's people need to be rescued..."

"All evidence says that they're alive and kicking," Seth said. Kicking Joshua to be exact. "They'll probably stay that way—at least for the next few days. Until we know what we're up against, it would be reckless to charge in. Think of it like a boss fight. We need to prepare better than last time."

That obviously hit Joshua hard. He looked at anything but Seth, nodding his head. "I suppose the last fight would have gone better if I'd gotten help in saving Winnie. I didn't know that she was in trouble. I didn't know what that thing was wrapped around her or what it could do. I didn't know—"

"You did the best you could," Seth said as all the "could haves" reminded him of his own mistakes. He'd nearly lost Jack and Joshua that day. "We'll work at being better next time."

"I sincerely hope there is no next time," Joshua muttered. He started to drift around the room, idly examining what was on Seth's desk and bookshelves.

Seth had been angry when he'd been sent to live at the Wolf King's Castle for an unknown period of time. He'd brought an embarrassment of items—most of them toys he'd already outgrown. The few mementos that actually had sentimental value were enshrined on his bookcase.

"It's just that weird stuff keeps happening to me," Joshua said as he eyed each treasure closely. "I can't believe that I went seventeen years without even a whisper of ghosts or vampires or talking penguins or angels in goat suits throwing fireballs..."

Angels in goat suits?

"It's because we're magical beings," Seth said instead of asking. "The laws of the universe are different for us than for human beings."

"That's what Winnie..." Joshua trailed off. "Is this... was this...?"

He'd picked up the framed photograph from Jack's farewell party.

Three years and it still made Seth's eyes burn just thinking about his dead family.

"Yeah," Seth managed to say after swallowing hard. "That's our dad and my mom and our little brothers. The king didn't want Jack taking the alpha if something happened to my father: he would have died young—like my grandfather. That picture was taken when Jack left Boston to be a Thane. It's Jack's goodbye party. I was eleven in that picture. That's Aiden. He was nine. That's Luis. He was seven. And Juan. He was five. Fenway—because he was born at the ballpark—was three. Jack took a lot of photos. They're the only ones I have—everything else was lost in the fire. There wasn't time to take personal effects out of the house after . . . after they were killed."

"I . . . I . . . I can't even imagine," Joshua said. "I thought Bethy hated me—and we're not really related—but it was still hard to think I might not be able to ever see her again. At least I knew that she was okay and that things might work out . . . like they did."

Seth nodded. Growing up, he'd thought often about his stolen brother, wondering what had happened to him. He knew it could have just as easily been himself who had been taken or one of his little brothers. He'd hoped for a fairy-tale ending but as he grew older, he grew sure that Ilya had died as a helpless infant, cut up into pieces by the Wickers to fuel some monstrous wooden creation. Seth had nightmares where he encountered the construct and recognized it as his older brother.

"Do you have any other pictures?" Joshua said. "The kids at school keep talking about our cousins and I have no idea who they're talking about."

Seth hadn't looked at the pictures since Jack had given them to him. He'd gotten numb to the pain triggered by the photo of his parents and brothers. Looking at all the smiling faces of his extended family had been too much. Joshua, however, deserved to know their family.

Seth powered on his laptop to find the photos. "We're the result of three hundred years of breeding. The first Tatterskein pack arrived in Boston in the 1640s. Grandpa was the only kid of his generation to survive but the king gave him a bride while he was still young to protect the Tatterskein bloodline. They had ten kids—four boys and six girls—before he got too weak to do much more than sleep . . ."

That made Seth think of the king. If Alexander was weakened, could he father another child to take New York? Surely the king had some kind of plan. He'd known for years that Isaiah wouldn't be strong enough to be prince.

Seth found the folder with the pictures that Jack had given him. Concerns of the future were flooded out by the pain of the past. To Joshua the photographs contained nameless strangers. It was up to Seth to explain what they lost.

27: ELISE

Black ice was one of the things Elise hated about living in Boston. The roads looked dry and clear of snow. An invisible layer of ice, however, coated the highway, turning it into a giant ice rink. Add in Boston's aggressive drivers, and getting anywhere during morning commute hours was pure frustration. She made the mistake of trying to avoid the heavy traffic on Route 1 and took the Salem Turnpike. Deep in the Rumney Marsh Reservation, she got stopped by a five-car pileup that blocked the northbound lanes. A Jersey barrier between the lanes kept traffic from moving around the accident.

Unable to move, she called Clarice.

"Central," Clarice answered and yawned sleepily. "Ow! Darn, the same toe as last time! Hi, Elise! Are Theo and Francis with you?"

"They were still asleep when I left," Elise said. "They're going to pick up Francis's SUV at Alewife once they get moving. I'm heading to Salem State University, but I'm currently stuck in traffic."

"Oh, okay." Clarice typed on her keyboard. "I was up half the night trying to suppress news on the fight at the mall. I hate people that film disasters instead of running for their lives. What are they thinking? 'Oh, with this I'll win the Darwin Award!' I gave up. The videos just spread like wildfire. Why can't werewolves be invisible?"

"So only Joshua showed up on the film?"

"Mostly. One giant wolf fighting something invisible breathing fire," Clarice said. "Luckily no one caught him before he transformed, so no 'missing teenager from New York is now a werewolf' video. Francis in his new goat suit was caught on camera but only on the sidelines as an innocent bystander. No sign of you or Theo."

"We were late to the party," Elise said.

"That explains it. Oh! Today is the last day of classes at Salem State! That's not good. There's a 'reading period' where it seems like students are on campus but not attending classes, and there's finals—which I think are tests. After that, everyone including the janitorial staff has a long break for the holidays. What I'm seeing suggests that they lock all the doors and basically shut down once finals are over."

"How long is this reading period?"

"It looks to be about a week long. Maybe."

In other words, today was the last day that professors and students would be around. The students would hole up wherever to study and then, after the test, scatter to the winds, heading home for the holidays.

Thinking of students reminded Elise of Ottalie.

"We might have a problem at Blackridge. Our Dominion-in-training signed out a soul talisman from the Watertown vault."

"Oh, no she didn't!" Clarice whispered. "Well, yes, she did—if you say so—but I thought she was smarter than that!"

"She might not realize how deadly it is. I wouldn't use it unless, like, the entire Eastern Seaboard was at risk."

"I'll call her and make sure she knows what she's dealing with," Clarice said.

Elise found a parking space close to Meier Hall where Clarice said the Geological Sciences offices were located. It was a modern four-story yellow brick building with lots of windows and one corner stairwell made entirely of glass. She'd been stuck behind the accident on Salem Turnpike and again at the bridge over the Saugus River. It was nearly noon before she arrived, yet the day remained biting cold. Her breath misted as she walked toward the building.

The geology department was on the third floor and seemed

to be in chaos. It was difficult to tell if this was their operating standard or if they merely were overwhelmed because of the wooden shipping crates taking up much of the hallway.

A slender older woman with long blond hair was attempting to pry open one of the crates with a crowbar while scolding a young man. "Seriously, Beau, do you not think before speaking? You really need to learn to school the words coming out of your month. Antarctica is in the Southern Hemisphere, which means it is in its summer while we're in our winter. It had taken me six years to set up my sabbatical, so I was at my dig at the La Meseta formation on Seymour Island until the last possible moment. I took the last plane out in March. After that, there are no flights or ships in or out of the continent. It's too dangerous. My finds weren't able to fit on the last load, so they sat waiting for October to ship."

"Aw, come own now, Ah'm just pickin' wid ya." Beau had a thick Southern accent that went with his name. "Don't pitch a fit about that, Dr. Boggs."

"And you need to work on that accent of yours." Dr. Boggs waved the crowbar at the man. "It makes you sound like a dumb hayseed. I used to have a West Virginia accent nearly as bad, but I got rid of it."

"What accent?" Beau said. "Aye don't have an accent."

Dr. Boggs paused in prying the large wooden crate to glare at the boy.

"Fiddlesticks," Beau whispered. "Ah swear you could start an argument in an empty house."

"Isn't there somewhere else you need to be?" Dr. Boggs growled.

Beau glanced at his watch. "Ah suppose so."

Dr. Boggs noticed Elise. "Can I help you or are you just going to stand and gawk?"

"I'm looking into a missing person case." She took out her ID case and flashed her badge. She made it fast since most people were clueless as to how the American branch of Interpol worked. She used pulling out her phone as an excuse for why she didn't allow Dr. Boggs time to study her identification closely. "I've been told that this man might be known to the geologists from this department. I'm hoping someone can identify him."

Dr. Boggs frowned at the picture, concerned but puzzled. "That is Trey. He's a professor here. His name is Caleb Danforth the Third, but he goes by Trey. He's missing? I thought I saw him yesterday. Wait—if he's been reported missing, wouldn't you know his name?"

"He's a suspect not a victim." Elise texted Danforth's name to Clarice. "Do you have a home address for him?"

"Trey? Kidnapping? He's got a screw loose but he's not the dangerous type. I wouldn't go out on the ice with him if he was."

"The ice?"

"We've done explorations together in Antarctica. I'm the professor of Paleontology and Geobiology. His area of study is geophysics, studying the area where the Scotia Plate is subducting under the Antarctic Peninsula. An expedition isolates you on the ice with wind chills down to the negative thirties even in the middle of summer. It takes years to coordinate a study, to get the money and needed personnel in place, competing against the entire world's scientific community who all want the limited space and resources that the outposts afford. The people that you work with need to be trustworthy."

"People change," Elise said. "Just because he was sane when he went out on the ice with you doesn't mean that he's not dangerous now. 'A screw loose' isn't how you describe someone that you'd trust with your life's work."

Elise didn't say "with your life" because she'd found that people would socialize with extremely unhinged friends, willing to overlook dangerous habits in the name of friendship. People were more protective of their hard work, especially those who had to struggle against prejudices to succeed. If Dr. Boggs had ground out her backwoods accent, then she had faced enough bigotry to feel the need to hide her real self.

Dr. Boggs bobbed her head. Elise couldn't tell if she was agreeing or disagreeing with her. It seemed as if the professor was arguing with herself. "Winter in Antarctica is not easy for people to endure. The extreme cold causes Polar T3 syndrome. T3 is a thyroid hormone that is a neurotransmitter that is also used to regulate body temperature. When the body uses it to keep warm, the brain is left with a less than adequate supply of the hormone. It's quite common for people that winter over to be forgetful, moody, and cognitively impaired."

"So, he wintered over in Antarctica?" Elise asked to be sure she understood the situation.

"Yes, and it did not end well for him. Trey almost froze to death when he wandered out onto the ice alone. He said someone was calling him—needing help. He's been...odd since he returned but not dangerous. It's entirely possible he had taken some brain damage that has been slow to heal."

Maybe...or maybe something had gotten its hooks into the man and hadn't let go. Hank Whitebrow would recognize Touched when he saw it but normal people wouldn't.

Dr. Boggs continued to explain away her colleague's behavior. "I really haven't seen Trey much since his...his accident. We professors usually don't see each other a lot during the day as we have different classes, office hours, and areas of expertise. He's not my type—he's got a motor mouth and an ego the size of Mount Everest—so I kind of avoid him if I can. The geology department, however, takes joint field expeditions out to seriously rough wilderness areas, so we make it a habit to socialize as a group during the week. Trey has been skipping all our gatherings for the last year or so. The chair is pissed off at him but it's not part of our contracts."

Elsie's phone vibrated to alert her to an incoming text from Clarice. She'd found Danforth's driver's license that listed his residence. Clarice added that she was accessing his credit history so she could use his credit cards, vehicle, and smartphone to track him. "Do you know if Danforth still lives in Danvers, Massachusetts, at..." And she rattled off the address Clarice had provided.

Dr. Boggs snorted. "I guess he's still living at the insane asylum."

"He lives at an insane asylum?"

"Sort of. The Danvers State Insane Asylum. It's a historic landmark about ten miles north of here. It was built sometime in the 1870s or 1880s. After it closed in the 1980s, it stood empty for years. You ask me it was a creepy place to pick to live. The place is supposed to be haunted."

"Haunted?" Elise echoed.

"You hear all sorts of horror stories about the place," Dr. Boggs continued. "People misdiagnosed, locked in with truly crazy, violent patients. Straitjackets. Electroshock therapy. Lobotomies. Rape and assault. Accidental deaths, suicides, possible murder, for over a hundred years. It's a cocktail of everything that could go wrong when you lock two thousand mentally unstable people in a place designed to hold five hundred patients. I heard that toward the end, they had people being held in the unfinished basement areas. I don't believe in ghosts, but I acknowledge that there is much we don't know about human consciousness. If there was ever a place that could be haunted, it was Danvers."

"He's living in an abandoned asylum in the middle of winter, and you don't think he's dangerous?" Elise said.

"Oh, it used to be abandoned. Some bright lightbulb decided to turn it into offices and apartments. They ham-fisted it all. The historic buildings were mostly torn down, caught fire, burnt down, and then rebuilt, so it's not all that creepy. The only thing left is the brick façade and the graveyard and maybe part of the service tunnels that ran under it."

The place didn't sound appealing to Elise.

"Danforth rented an apartment there?" she asked.

Dr. Boggs nodded. "He moved in right after he came back from wintering in Antarctica. We all thought he was . . . well . . . a little crazy. His grandfather died at the asylum back in the seventies. To move into the place where a relative died under mysterious circumstances? Trey signed the papers while the place was still under construction, sight unseen, and slept under his desk here at the office until his apartment was finished. It all felt a little unhinged."

"He wintered over this year?" Elise guessed. "So, he got back to Boston a month ago?"

"Oh, no, this was a few years back. Three—no, four years ago. I wasn't sure if he was still at the asylum. The rent was ridiculously high. The units are geared more for corporate temporary housing than a normal apartment building. He insisted on the biggest and most expensive apartment that they had. Anyone else would have found someplace cheaper."

Elsie thought of Francis trying to find her. He had only known that she lived in Cambridge, not the exact address. It was odd that Dr. Boggs recognized Danforth's address. How close were they? "You've been to his apartment enough times to have the address memorized?"

"No, no, it's just I'm a trivia buff. Kirkbride was the psychiatrist that came up with the idea of building massive bat-winged insane asylums like Danvers. The United States had hundreds of Kirkbride asylums scattered coast to coast. You see them in all the horror movies. Anyhow, they named the road that the

Danvers Asylum was on after Kirkbride. If you're showing him at Kirkbride Drive, then he's at the asylum."

"Is Danforth here today?" Elise asked, doubting it but figuring she might get lucky.

"I don't know the schedule of the other professors. You can ask Linda, our administrative assistant. I thought I saw him coming out of the library yesterday. I was heading to a class, so I just kept moving. I heard that he's been spending lots of time over there in the map room. It was probably him. He's been wearing that same coat since he got back from wintering over."

Map room? That seemed to indicate he was looking for something, but what? "Has he told anyone why he's looking at maps?"

"Soraya—Soraya Ahmad, she's one of our assistant professors— says that Trey's become fixated on the North American Craton."

"The what?"

"It's the oldest, thickest part of the continent. Like most of the landmasses on Earth, it's drifted about and changed shapes. At one point it was part of the supercontinent called Rodinia. After Rodinia fragmented, the craton drifted to almost the South Pole, so it sort of fits into Trey's study of Scotia Plate—but I'm not sure how. After that, the fragments formed the supercontinent Pangaea and from then on, North America was nowhere near the South Pole."

Elise remembered learning about Pangaea and continental drift at Blackridge. At the time, she thought it was a scientist trying to explain the effect of gods on the planet while denying that they existed.

"Who exactly is missing?" Dr. Boggs asked. "One of our students? Are you sure they're actually missing? College students are just large children, many without any common sense. Drive down to Florida for the weekend without telling anyone? Sure, why the hell not?"

"A store employee," Elise said as vaguely as possible. "The security guard was taken during an armed robbery."

"Armed robbery? Trey's family wasn't the Vanderbilts, but he's got a trust fund that would make you cry about the unfairness of life."

"Another employee identified him." Elise held out her phone again to show off the picture of Danforth. "She had taken this photo of him during an earlier visit."

Dr. Boggs eyes went wide with surprise as she recognized the store in the picture. "Trey robbed Bell Book and Candle? What the hell was he after? There's no way that he's short on cash. Those fossils are nice knickknacks but they're not something you would steal at gunpoint."

"I can't discuss those details." Elise dodged the question. "It's an ongoing investigation."

"Fine. There's not much more I can tell you about Trey. He used to be a fun colleague to hang out with and do trivia night at the Howling Wolf Taqueria or the Flying Saucer Pizza Company. The last few years, though, I have only seen him in passing. I should get back to my *Palaeeudyptes klekowskii*."

"Your what?"

"My mega penguin." She waved her crowbar toward the packing crates. "It's a penguin species from the late Eocene epoch, shortly after a severe mass-extinction event killed off most of the monster-sized sea predators. It was six and half feet tall and weighed around two hundred and fifty pounds. I found a nearly complete fossil during my expedition. To facilitate diving through water, penguin's bones are amazingly dense compared to most bird species. It means that the fossil records for them are plentiful but this is the most intact fossil that anyone has found."

Again with the penguins, Elise thought.

Elise went in search of the administrative assistant, Linda, to find out Danforth's most recent movements.

"Professor Danforth?" Linda echoed. "He's not in his office."

"Where would I find him if he's on campus?" Elise said.

Linda leaned over her desk to peer out the window beside her. "You're out of luck. His car isn't in his parking space. I'm sorry but the man hasn't been in his office for days. Weeks even."

Judging by the tone of her voice, she hated the guy and was happy to complain about him. "The only reason he still has a job here is tenure. That and his family's endowment fund. He has his grad students teaching all his classes. He's been haunting the library but other than that, he hasn't been on campus for weeks. He even spent part of November in South America. Talk about entitlement— to not even be in the same hemisphere of the planet as the class he's supposed to be teaching and still picking up a paycheck."

Elise felt a prickle run down her spine as something powerful came up behind her. She whirled, hands to her daggers—and then released the hilts and relaxed.

"Hey," Jack Cabot smiled and waved sheepishly.

"Woof!" Linda whispered, openly staring at Cabot.

It was one thing to know that Cabot was one-quarter angelic—one grandfather being a Grigori. It was another to witness Cabot getting the typical human reaction to a Grigori. Yes, he was a tall muscular man with shoulder-length, honey-colored hair, dark thick eyebrows, and golden eyes. He wore an expensive suit as if he'd just rushed away from a Wall Street office. A hint of stubble on his chin roughed up the polished businessman image. She knew from experience that under that Italian silk was chiseled muscle that would be the envy of a professional body builder.

Linda's dilated eyes and open-mouth pant-of-desire reaction was purely from the Grigori's magical glamour.

To be honest, Elise was tempted to say "Woof" herself. The three-quarters wolf gave Cabot an animal magnetism that male Grigori lacked.

"What are you doing here?" Elise dropped her hands away from her daggers. "I thought you were in New York."

Cabot glanced at Linda. "There's been . . . developments. We need to talk."

So, he wasn't here because of Danforth. "How did you even find me?"

He leaned in so close that she could feel the heat from his body. He whispered, "Seth pointed me to the right neighborhood. I spotted your Jeep and followed your scent to here."

She blushed as the word "scent" made her hyperaware of his. It was a natural fragrance that had tones of oak moss, sandalwood and amber, and musk. She knew that it wasn't a product of soap or cologne. If the wolves could bottle it, they would be the richest creatures on the planet.

Was there anything else that she needed here? It seemed as if Danforth had abandoned his life at the university. Clarice hadn't reported back, so it wouldn't hurt to find out what the wolves needed.

"Okay, let's go find someplace to talk." Elise's stomach growled, reminding her that she hadn't eaten yet. She'd skipped breakfast as there were only freeze-dried meals left at the depot. She'd planned on getting something quick, but the traffic accidents had eaten away her morning. "Someplace with food."

28: JOSHUA

The photographs of Seth's relatives just went on and on. There were twenty aunts and uncles alone, not counting their many children. No wonder Seth looked so sad whenever he talked about his family. Beyond the picture of Seth with his—their—immediate family, none of the photos were organized into family groups. Married couples weren't posed with their partners. Kids weren't with their parents. Only half of the adults were related to him by blood. Joshua quickly lost track of who belonged to whom.

Joshua's entire adopted family could fit around one big table on the holidays. His mom had lost her only brother when she was young. Her parents had died when he was too little to remember them. His dad had two divorced brothers and three nephews. Great-Aunt Ginny—Great-Uncle Morton's widow—saw both of her children die young, leaving her without any other family. Every Thanksgiving and Boxing Day, they would gather at his grandparents' and eat at their massive cherrywood table.

The food was good because his grandmother usually catered the side dishes from a fancy local French restaurant. The meal, however, was never particularly joyous as everyone felt the need to yell at him for using the wrong fork or putting his elbows on the table. Pre-wolf days were not very wolf-free...

The thought of his family and holidays, though, reminded him of his last conversation with Bethy.

"Some asshole con artist is scamming my parents," Joshua

told Seth. "He's pretending to be a psychic. He says that I'm dead and my parents need to pay him money to find my grave."

Seth blew out his breath. "That's Albany's territory. I don't know how they handle the gifted in their area. That didn't come up during the time I stayed at their bachelor house."

Joshua had looked up the Court of Albany on Google Street View after Seth told him about it. He'd been on Wolf Road countless times over the years. He couldn't believe there had been an entire pack of werewolves there the whole time. But there it was, tucked behind the urban sprawl: a small knot of large Victorian houses.

"I could ask Ewan to look into the guy." Seth held out his hand for Joshua's phone. "Maybe scare him off."

Joshua started to hand over his phone and suddenly they were standing on the snowy sidewalk outside the Court of Albany's bachelor house. It looked just like how he'd seen it on Street View, except this time cloaked in snow. It was painted muted blue with cream gingerbread trim. It had a big wraparound porch, a tower to the right of the double front door and lots of stained glass windows. In certain ways, it was a lot like Decker's house except it had been meticulously upkept whereas Decker's looked as if it was about to fall down from neglect.

"Stop doing that!" Seth shouted.

"I don't know what I'm even doing!" Joshua shouted back. "Do you think I would be here of all places if I knew how to control it?"

The front door of the bachelor house opened, and a man came out, head cocked in confusion. "Boston? What are you doing here?"

Seth rubbed his left hand over his face. "Well, since we're here, we might as well talk to Albany."

They thumped up the front steps to the big wooden porch.

"Hi, Ewan. This is my brother, Joshua," Seth said in greeting. "Joshua, this is Ewan Keir, the new Marquis of Albany."

Ewan looked like a college student. He was wearing worn blue jeans and a red flannel shirt unbuttoned to mid-chest, its sleeves rolled up. His dark brown hair was long and shaggy since werewolf's hair grew to shoulder length when they transformed back and forth often. His eyebrows were thick and dark and expressive. He gave them a look that was a mix of worry and confusion.

"I'm glad to meet you, Joshua." Ewan put out a hand to be

shaken. "I ordered way too much pizza. Since I became the marquis, all I seem to do is eat. Why don't you come in and have some?"

Joshua's wolf decided the offer of food made them best friends and turned the handshake into a full hug.

"He's still just a puppy," Seth said behind Joshua.

"It's okay. We're neighbors." Ewan patted Joshua on the back as if they were long-lost relatives. "It's best to be on good terms."

There was a big evergreen wreath on the door, a tall Christmas tree in the living room, and swags of green wrapping the banister of the stairs. The rooms were grand in scale but furnished in battered mismatched pieces. Despite the fact that it looked very much like a man-cave, there was something very homey about it.

Ewan wrinkled his nose. "Sorry about the smell. Jenna drove over and threw a tree decorating party on Saturday. She's into smelly things, so she's like 'you got to have a Christmas tree and pine candles for the whole scent experience thing.' I think there's something wrong with her nose."

Joshua's mom was very much like that. She would get a big Balsam & Cedar two-wick Yankee Candle and burn it all December. At times the scent of bruised pine was overwhelming. No wonder the place felt homey to him.

Ewan realized that Joshua probably didn't know who he was talking about. "Cameron is my older brother. His girlfriend Jenna is from the Syracuse pack. Sire warned them that if they got married, and Cameron inherited the alpha, that the king wouldn't let them stay married. Syracuse is just a barony and Jenna isn't even the baron's daughter; their kids would probably be too weak to hold Albany. Jenna and Cameron are over the moon that I'm the new marquis, but they still need to wait until the king moves Jenna from the Syracuse alpha to the Albany one."

Joshua's wolf had discovered the pizzas sitting on a large dining room table, freshly delivered. Ewan had gotten five large jalapeño, meatball, peperoni, and sausage with extra cheese from a place called Paesan's Pizza. Joshua's wolf approved. It helped itself to a slice while Joshua was distracted by the conversation.

"Oh, I hadn't thought of that," Seth said with dismay. "I thought alphas could shift new members into their pack. They change younglings into puppies all the time. That's shifting someone into their pack."

It was more a question than a statement.

Ewan spread his hands. "I didn't want to make her feral by screwing it up, but I did try to give her a little nudge. I could do the dominance stuff—but that just scared her. Nothing else. It was like she was out of my reach. I don't know if I'm doing it wrong or if I just can't do it at all. Sire never talked about taking in a wolf from another pack. I tried calling the Wolf King's Castle but the only thing they'd say is that the king is too busy to discuss it."

Seth looked strangely guilty about something. "Things have been . . . weird since Belgrade." And then abruptly, he changed the subject. "We're setting up a new bachelor house in Boston."

"Oh yeah!" Joshua said remembering Seth's text about getting a Christmas tree before condo hunting. "You're coming up Friday for that. I need to go out and get some ornaments!"

Seth stared at him, obviously confused for a full minute, before enlightenment washed over his face. "Sorry." Seth rubbed his face again. "There's too much going on for me to keep track of everything. Half of the reason we lost everyone in the massacre was simply that we didn't have enough wolves. We would have easily had over two hundred adults if Grandpa's generation hadn't all been killed off. I don't know why Grandpa didn't recruit from other packs but his way of trying to repopulate Boston by himself didn't work. Kate doesn't want to be a baby machine, and I don't want her to be like Grandma, having a baby every year and a half for two decades. Grandma was nearly as worn out as Grandpa. We need as many adult wolves as possible—now. To do that, we need to recruit from other packs."

Seth turned to pitch to Ewan. "Boston has some of the best colleges in the country. MIT. Harvard. As one of the first packs of North America, we own a wide range of companies, from banking to importing. And the job opportunities are huge even if they don't want to work for one of our businesses."

"Oh," Ewan said. "One or two of my younger cousins might want to take you up on that. Harsain is graduating from high school in a few months and really wants to study music, of all things. There's Juilliard in New York City but after the bullshit that Isaiah pulled last month, Harsain doesn't want to go anywhere near Wolf Castle. Apparently, two of the best colleges for music are in Boston. My cousin Grannd wants to meet girls who aren't part of our pack. He says that our girls feel too much like sisters to think of them as girlfriends."

"The only girl we have is my wife and I'm not giving her up," Seth said.

Ewan thought for a moment and added, "Syracuse hasn't suffered any major disaster like Boston and Albany, but they did take a hard blow to their local economy when a lot of their big corporations moved out of the area. It's left the pack struggling to provide for all their members. I can ask Jenna if she knows of anyone who wants to shift packs. I've gotten the impression from Jenna that they've got more females than males—which is kind of the reason that she was dating my brother in the first place."

"That would be a big help," Seth said. "Thanks!"

Recruiting more wolves to Boston was all well and good but it wasn't Joshua's immediate problem. His parents going into debt to his grandparents because of some asshole was.

Joshua managed to swallow the pizza he'd been chewing and said, "Con artist."

Seth looked confused for a moment and then remembered what triggered their conversation about Albany. "Oh, yes, the real reason we're here! We need a favor."

Joshua explained everything he knew about the con artist who was taking advantage of his parents.

"You're right that he has to be a con artist," Ewan said when Joshua exhausted his knowledge. "If he had real powers, he would know you were alive and well. He wouldn't dare offer up fake information like that—not without checking with me. Everyone under our protection knows that there was a war between Wickers and werewolves in Utica."

"I knew it!" Joshua shouted and then shook his head. "I sent a card to my parents, but they didn't believe a word that I wrote. No one is listening to my sister—although she hasn't spilled the beans that she actually knows exactly where I'm living. Push comes to shove, she might. I really don't want that to happen."

"Let me make a few calls," Ewan said. "Even if he's a fake, our Wise Woman and others will know who he is, where he is. One way or another, we'll get him to shut up."

"Oh geez, don't kill him!" Joshua said. "Just...just scare him a bit."

"Oh, trust me," Ewan said. "When a pack of wolves show up and *talk* to you, people listen."

29: ELISE

They ended up at the Howling Wolf Taqueria just as the lunch crowd thinned away to almost nothing. Cabot picked the place. Their server was a squeaky-clean college student named Todd who seemed to recognize Cabot. Todd ignored Elise and subtly flirted with Cabot, a sure indication that—despite no outward signs—Todd was very much gay. The werewolf was completely oblivious of the sexual innuendos. Elise would have felt sorry for Todd if she wasn't currently sitting there, an obvious girlfriend.

"Is this one of the Tatterskein businesses?" Elise asked after she shooed Todd off for their drinks. (Mexican beer for Cabot. She would have liked one but not on an empty stomach. She opted for coffee.)

Cabot shook his head, studying the menu that Todd had left with them. "Restaurants are too risky. Sixty percent of them fail within their first year. We own the bank on the corner, so I eat here when I'm in town. With a name like Howling Wolf, how could I not? I like their Howling Wolf Burrito and their Good Wolf Burrito. Not sure which to get."

"I've seen you eat; get both." Elise decided on the Tres Amigos: grilled chicken with verde lime sauce, carne asada with grilled scallions, and grilled shrimp with mango chili sauce.

Todd returned promptly with their drinks. He crouched down as he took their orders so he could stare into Cabot's eyes.

Elise struggled not to kick the man. She was surprised at

how possessive felt. She and Cabot hadn't done anything more than snuggle and kiss. How bad was she going to be once they actually got intimate?

Todd left to put their order in without knowing how close he'd gotten to being booted when he winked at Cabot and said, "Call me if you want *anything*."

Cabot put his left hand out in an invitation. (He'd learned not to just take her hand. It turned out to be one of her hidden knee-jerk reactions. She didn't remember being trained not to let someone restrain her hands but there was no denying the response.)

She laid her hand on his. As usual, Cabot felt like a furnace, radiating heat. He gazed at her with his golden eyes, smiling with happiness at being with her. It made her heart flutter in a way that she hadn't thought actually happened outside romance novels.

She wished the moment could last for hours, but they didn't have time for that. "Why are you here?"

"Seth wanted me to make sure Joshua was safe after getting some panicked texts from him," Cabot said. "The penguin from the aquarium showed up at Blackridge and it rattled Joshua. The situation...changed before I could get to Boston. The penguin left Blackridge, and Joshua is...safe, so Seth told me to track you down."

It was a little disappointing to hear that he searched her out under orders but between the prince and the king, Cabot's life wasn't exactly his to live as he wanted. She knew that going in. She held that knowledge as a shield to hurt feelings that wanted to take root in her.

"None of what's going on makes any sense to us," Cabot admitted as he stroked his thumb across her fingers. "We thought that if we pooled information—you and I—we might be able to figure things out."

"That's probably a good idea," Elise said. While Joshua seemed to be at the epicenter of whatever Danforth was attempting, she only had a photograph and a handful of feathers to link the seemingly innocuous professor to the missing Roustabout.

He smiled warmly. "And I get to have lunch with you, so it's win-win for me."

She blushed as she realized that this was the closest they'd gotten to a normal "date." Despite the circumstances that brought them together, it was really nice. Alone in the peace and quiet of the nearly empty restaurant, holding hands, no monsters to kill, just the two of them...

Until Todd showed up with the appetizer of curly fries and queso. Elise shooed him away again, not wanting the man to overhear their conversation. The food sucked in Cabot's focus for several minutes. Elise had to admit that the fries were amazingly delicious, hot, crispy, crunchy, and smothered in savory Mexican cheeses. Eating the hot fries gave her a few minutes to decide what to tell Cabot—and what to edit out.

"Just after Halloween—probably during all that insanity in Utica—someone raided a colony of shapeshifters in Argentina known as Aptenodytes." She felt like that somehow everything that happened in November connected to the recent events, but she wasn't sure how. "Aptenodytes are classified as a type of swan maidens, but their animal shape are penguins. According to Decker, magical birds are extremely hard to detect, even for Seth. Last Friday, one of the Salem University professors—a man called Caleb Danforth the Third—cleaned out the vault at Bell Book and Candle. He took a shitload of magical items and a security guard by the name of Brutus Clay. Hank Whitebrow claims that Danforth is Touched but he doesn't know by what God. Incidentally, Danforth recently was in Argentina. Tuesday, Brutus showed up at the aquarium, possessed by some kind of weird squid spirit, looking for Joshua's penguin. We don't have any evidence to confirm this, but it appears that Danforth went to South America, captured a bunch of swan maidens—somehow— and dragged them back to Massachusetts and then raided Bell Book and Candle to arm them with magical weapons."

"Ducks with guns," Cabot muttered as he ate the last of the fries.

Elsie snorted in surprise. "Not quite. Swans with bows and magical arrows. Francis reduced some of the weapons to ash. I'll send you the complete list of items stolen. I always thought my mother was being a jerk when she raided Bell Book and Candle but judging by what got stolen, I shouldn't have gotten soft on Hank. The witching stone alone is an abomination that should have been destroyed instantly."

Cabot licked clean his fingers, dried them on a napkin, and then patted down his suit pockets to find his phone. He growled softly as he considered the list. Was it weird that she didn't find it as dangerous sounding as she used to? "I'm going to have a long hard talk with Hank. We did give him permission to stock magical items effective against breach-borne, but he danced around my questions about how dangerous they were to wolves. I put too much trust in him because of his grandmother."

Elise felt sorry for Hank, but it was a mess of his own making. He'd stockpiled the weapons and then didn't report a Touch showing interest in his inventory. If both Francis and Joshua had not been at the mall last night, the fight could have ended poorly to the one there alone. God must have guided them both to CambridgeSide as neither should have been there.

"At least the weapons should be fairly easy for Seth to spot them—if they're still in our territory." Cabot typed in a text. "I'll have Bishop call Burlington and let them know."

The Viscount of Burlington's territory lay another hour to the north. Since it was Theo's district, Elise really didn't know much about the wolf pack beyond the key individuals. One thing she knew for certain: the Grigori wouldn't get as much cooperation from Burlington. Theo burned bridges instead of building them.

Cabot swiped on his phone after sending out the text to Bishop. "The penguin told Joshua that someone—obviously this Danforth—is controlling his people with a magical bone about the size of your fist and oval like an egg. This drawing is etched on it."

Cabot showed her a photograph of a rough pencil sketch and then emailed her a copy of it, which she forwarded to Clarice and Theo. "The penguin claimed that whoever has this bone can control any bird shapeshifters that descended from the first mothers of their species. It operates like the leash that the Wickers put on Joshua. The penguins were guarding it but something big and nasty took the bone after killing its guardian."

Their food arrived. Once again Todd needed to be driven off. Luckily, the place was filling up with the Happy Hour crowd, requiring the server to focus on other customers. There were several minutes of silence as they ate despite the curly fries having taken the edge off their hunger. The grilled shrimp with the mango chili sauce was tender, sweet, and spicy. The steak carne asada was amazing as was the chicken with verde lime sauce. It all made her warm and happy. Cabot was in the process of inhaling his two large burritos.

As Elise ate, she considered the new information. It was odd that Danforth managed to piece together how to gather a small army of magical creatures with dangerous weapons. Everything she'd been taught said that Touched operated on the same rules of angelic beings without the protection given to the Grigori by their blood. If that was true, then the Touched would "hear" very little from their god that was clear and understandable. The Oracles of Delphi were an example. The temple of Apollo gathered priestesses who were open to the power of Apollo. Their god burned through the collection one by one for hundreds of years, handing out oddly worded prophecies like clues to a scavenger hunt.

"When we find this Danforth," Cabot asked between bites of his burrito, "how hard is he going to be to kill?"

"I'm not sure," Elise said. "The good news is that when a human is Touched by an old god, there's a limit to how much power that the god can channel through the person without burning him out. It's akin to a breach or someone going feral after a werewolf bites them, connecting them to the Source of the werewolves' magic. The power overwhelms them. The bad news is that Danforth seems to have a wide knowledge base that I can't account for. Clay had a protective rune tattooed onto his right shoulder. To a normal person, it would look like some random tribal art. Danforth destroyed the rune and his god's servant instantly stepped into Clay. For that to happen, he would have had to use a blade prepared in a very specific and little-known ritual. How did he know that the rune meant that Clay was susceptible to possession and how to get around it? How did he know how to put a leash on the Aptenodytes, let alone even know that they existed? I didn't and I spent six years in intensive study of all things occult. Geology isn't a field that leads someone into the occult. Archaeology? World Religion? History? Yes. Geology? Rocks and fossil do not explain gods—unless you view extinction events as acts of pissed-off gods."

"Were they?"

"Who knows? Possibly. The Great Flood was my God getting annoyed at my ancestors. It's unclear what the dinosaurs could have done to piss off anyone to that extent unless it was that they were atheists."

"Maybe Danforth is from a gifted family," Cabot said. "Something divine, which would explain why he's open to a god."

"Divine is purely a Grigori label," Elise said. "We see God—our God—as a force putting order on the universe. The Book of Genesis basically tells how God gave form and structure directly to what had been void. Because of that, we consider the gifts that are based on ordered magic as divine. Decker's original gift of dowsing allowed him to tap into ambient power within the land and understand the basic pattern that it conveys to him. It's the alignment with order that makes dowsing divine. It's the underlying strength of order that allows Decker to resist the pure chaos of his magic."

"You're saying that Danforth might be gifted but possibly his ability isn't what the Grigori classify as divine?"

"Yes," Elise said more firmly than she felt. After a moment of thought, she added, "Based on the squid thing that possessed Clay, I think the god that has its hand on Danforth is chaotic in nature. If Danforth's gift was divine, I don't think the god could use him as effectively as he obviously is."

"Did you call in the Power because Danforth has a full flock of swan maidens? Or should we be expecting something even more dangerous?"

Elise spread her hands to indicate that she wasn't sure. "Monday, my cousin Francis—the Northeast Power—was yanked to Boston without a clue why God suddenly wanted him in the city. Francis managed to contact his driver and arranged to meet him at Alewife station. Before Francis arrived, however, his driver was ambushed by shapeshifters. One of the ambushers was hit by a train and killed. I found firebird feathers on the tracks. The personal effects of the dead shapeshifter seem to suggest it's from Argentina. Whether it was a penguin or a firebird or a swan maiden, though, we're not sure."

"We've never heard of these types of shapeshifters before," Cabot said. "Seth had to look up swan maidens. He sent me the link to the Wiki article. It was quite long so I didn't get around to any mention of penguins or firebirds."

"Until last night, I would have said that firebirds were mythical or at least extinct. Certainly, they've been laying low for several centuries. One of the attackers from last night at the mall was a firebird. We think the other two were swan maidens. Francis reduced them to ash so there's no way to confirm that. Central Office says that the magical items that they had were all on the list of things taken from Bell Book and Candle. We know that

Danforth took the weapons and Brutus Clay from the store. We know that Clay showed up at the aquarium looking for the penguin that was talking with Joshua. We don't know why Joshua and Francis were attacked at the mall. The assailants didn't seem to expect either one—so they might have just been looking for Joshua's penguin and the boys were collateral damage."

Cabot nodded. "Joshua said that they thought he was Seth."

"Everything seems to point that God wants Francis in Boston to deal with whatever Danforth is trying to put in motion." Elise took out her phone and found the picture of Roustabout. "This is Francis's driver. Galahad Percival Roustabout. He's purely human, no bells or whistles. I'm not sure if he's alive or dead. The lack of a body would seem to indicate he was taken alive. But why take him at all?"

"Could it be that he was taken to fuel some kind of Wicker magical construct?"

"Oh, God, I hope not," Elise said. Francis would be upset if they couldn't find his friend, but he could still "save" Roustabout if the man had been merely killed and buried or dumped someplace. There would be no raising Roustabout from the dead if his soul had been used to power a Wicker construct.

"Do you think Danforth is a Wicker?" Cabot said.

Elise considered the possibility. "I don't see a Wicker seeking out a professorial position in Geology and spending a winter in Antarctica. Yes, they could easily use their Persuasion to fake their way into a university, but generally their ego wouldn't allow them to be an underling. They tend to seek out a higher position. The dean of the college. The chairmen. Whatever. The other professor that I talked to indicated that Danforth knows his stuff—or at least he did until his god got a hold of him. A Wicker wouldn't have bothered to learn anything beyond blood magic. Also, Wickers habitually put anyone that has access to vital information about them on a script. I didn't sense any control on Linda, the administrative assistant. A warlock wouldn't have kept his hands off her."

Cabot nodded along with the points. "Good! I could go forever before having to deal with Wickers again."

Considering that the witches of Wakefield Coven nearly killed Cabot twice, she didn't blame him.

"Until we find out what happened to Roustabout, Francis isn't going to leave Boston," Elise said. "Even if I could talk Francis into going home, God might just yank him back. We don't know what Danforth plans—we don't even know if Danforth is the reason Francis is here. I hope there's not a second possible monster outbreak that we don't know about yet."

"If Roustabout is a normal human, Seth isn't going to be able to spot him," Cabot said. "Some of the gifted in Boston, though, might be able to get a bead on him. The Goths found their missing friend through a spirit guide."

"What else did Joshua find out from the penguin?" Elise asked.

Cabot explained the penguins' creation myth, with the son who murdered his parents being cursed into dark slumber. "Joshua had a write-up that one of his classmates did on it. Here, I'll send you a copy."

She scanned over the document that Cabot emailed her. Clearly Ottilie had written it up; it was classical Dominion style. Clarice might even have a copy by now. "Oh!" Elise whispered when she reached the end. "Okay, things are starting to make sense."

"They are?" Cabot looked mystified.

"This last bit is about a palace lost under ice. The people who work with Danforth say that he went insane while wintering over at the South Pole. He wandered out onto the ice because he could hear someone calling him. If the palace ended up in Antarctica, then maybe the Dark One woke up enough to latch onto Danforth. Gods tend to fixate on power structures that they understand, so the Aptenodytes were an automatic go-to when gathering resources."

"This Dark One is in Boston?" Cabot said doubtfully. "I would think Seth would notice that."

"It's probably still trapped in an isolated layer," Elise said. "It can only act through its Touched. I'm just not sure what Danforth is capable of."

"Have you ever faced a Touched before?" Cabot asked.

"No. But it's part of our training. All the old gods—Zeus and Jupiter and Odin—are real gods that once held sway over our world. Over time, though, their realms drifted away from ours. My teachers cautioned that those gods were still very much alive."

In ancient days, gods and men could freely go from one layer to another, hence all the legends of humans visiting heaven or hell. Her teachers thought it had changed with the spread of werewolves. Over the centuries, the wolves had gone from a tight knot in the Middle East to covering the world, usually just one step behind the European explorers. Magical outbreaks like breaches and such had been greatly reduced anywhere they settled. The tribe elders had decided to make a treaty with the Wolf King once it became obvious that the werewolves acted as guard dogs on areas that they occupied.

There was a chance, however, that the occurrences were more like the drift of continents, some natural slow process that pulled the layers apart. Maybe someday in the future the layers would collide back together, and they would be neck deep in gods again.

Considering the legends of how gods treated humans—turning people into monsters, trees, animals and bugs—Elise hoped not.

Cabot had finished his two burritos and the accompanying rice while she was thinking. "Danforth will fight like a normal human? He doesn't have anything like Persuasion?"

Werewolves were immune to Persuasion, but the Grigori were only resistant. One of the Wakefields had caught Elise off guard and taken her captive.

Elise shook her head. "I don't know. It's possible he has some kind of witch power. We certainly won't find him unguarded. With this leash on the swan maidens, he has control of monsters like the firebird. Then there's the thing that possessed the security guard from Bell Book and Candle. I think it was some kind of servant to Danforth's god. Such things were common in all mythos—a lesser being that acts as a messenger or attendant or mount. In the *Theogony*, it was said that Zeus' messengers 'will not live apart from Zeus nor go except where the god goes before them, but they sit forever beside heavy-booming Zeus.' Odin had his crows. Thor had his goats. The Mesopotamian gods had the *sukkal*—lesser gods or spirits that acted as servants, attendants and envoys. Such creatures weren't true gods—they were spirits. They could take physical form but only through the intervention of their master. Thor's goats could be killed, eaten, and brought back to life from the gnawed bones."

Elise couldn't fathom how any creature would be okay with that kind of treatment, but it spoke volumes about the level of their servitude to their master.

"We find this Danforth, kill him, and take back the leash that controls the penguins," Cabot said.

We. He meant to work with Elise in hunting down Danforth. Considering what Danforth might have guarding him, she could use the backup. She couldn't call Theo in without getting Francis. All things considered, Cabot was more durable than Theo.

"Yes," Elise said.

Her phone vibrated with several incoming texts. Clarice had pulled Danforth's credit history. He had chartered a plane to fly from Argentina to Logan Airport the day that the penguin flock disappeared. He seemed to be existing on food from DoorDash, mostly from a place called Dumpling Garden. His luxury SUV had an anti-theft tracking system that pinpointed the vehicle on Kirkbride Drive. The last ping from his smart phone was off a cell tower near the converted insane asylum. Clarice thought that Danforth was at his apartment. She was going to see if the housing complex had security cameras that she could hack into.

"It looks like Danforth is at his apartment," Elise said.

Cabot pulled out his wallet and threw bills down onto the table that more than covered all their food and a hefty tip. "Let's go."

30: DECKER

Decker woke to a silent house.

He whispered a curse as he pushed open the lid of his coffin. It was too quiet. Unless Joshua was taking a nap after a tiring day at school, something had happened to him. The boy should have been home at...

Decker's digital clock claimed that it was a full hour before sunset.

How was that possible?

He went upstairs, wondering why he had awoken so early. How he could be awake?

Sunlight was pouring through the lead glass of the front door. It filled the foyer with the glorious gold of late afternoon. Even the table with his phone was drenched in light. Joshua's kitten was asleep in a sunspot on the floor. With Trouble sleeping, the house was still and quiet.

Where was Joshua? While it was early for Decker to be awake, it was still an hour after Joshua should have been home from school. Had he returned to the house and gone out again?

The Reader's Digest books were no longer stacked by the door. Joshua's school bag was on the kitchen counter. His coat hung off the back of the island chair. He'd taken both that morning, so he'd been home at some point. Was he asleep in his bedroom? The door stood open at the top of the stairs. Trouble would normally be orbiting Joshua like a small rogue moon, not sleeping on a different floor.

Decker closed his eyes and focused with his gift. Where was Joshua?

Very far to the west. Too distant to be still within the city limits. Maybe even too distant to still be within the state.

Was Joshua back with his brother in New York City? Wolf Castle should be southwest. Straight west would be the Berkshire Mountains. Where was the prince? Yes, the two seemed to be together. That was reassuring.

He could call Joshua on the phone and ask him why he was way out west with his brother. Ask him if he was okay. Ask him when he was coming home...

No. That would be too needy. There was also the fact that if Joshua needed help, Decker couldn't walk out of the house and survive. He couldn't even reach the phone as the table stood bathed in sunlight. There was another hour of sun.

Joshua is with the prince. He should be safe.

The kitten stretched awake and came over complaining that its food dish was empty. (Which it was not—there was half a can of its smelly wet mush in the ceramic bowl. Joshua must have fed Trouble while he was home.)

Decker's laundry basket was still on the floor of the laundry room. Decker changed out of his pajamas. His ruined coat hung by the back door, reminding him that he needed to find a different one. The most logical place to check was the closet in the foyer. He opened the door and objects poured out onto the floor. A regular Fibber McGee hall closet. This is why he didn't open the closets in his house.

He shuffled aside everything that had escaped the closet with his feet. (Didn't that bowling ball have a case? It made an ominous noise as it rolled across the floor—which weirdly reminded him what he had hidden in the library.) Normally he'd just stuff the junk back in after he found what he wanted. It would be best in the long run, though, to just throw away the useless clutter—like the bowling ball—after he found a coat to wear.

Oh, the memories. The first coat he had was a cleric cape that Saul had bought secondhand the day after Decker's Philadelphia home burned. It had a decidedly vampiric look to it, which Saul apologized for and quickly found a replacement. Decker dropped the cape onto the floor with the other junk. He wasn't even sure why he kept it; he would never wear it again.

The *Casablanca*-style trench coat from his Humphrey Bogart phase was far too thin to deal with Boston winters. Toss. The leather jacket from his James Dean phase hadn't protected his legs from the cold. Toss. He pulled out a dark blue peacoat with a massive tear in the side and bloodstains from where he'd gotten bit during a hunt. Toss. A black leather overcoat that had suffered the same fate. Toss. A jeans jacket that was too thin for winter. Toss. A psychedelic jacket featuring pop art cartoons. What had he been thinking? Toss. A suede, fringed cowboy jacket. Toss. Three more dark blue peacoats—he gotten into a rut with them—all damaged beyond saving. Why did he even keep these? He had a small mountain in the foyer. A bright red wool coat—was this even his? No, it was too small; it must have been Lauretta's. He put it back into the closet, reluctant to throw away anything of hers. Oh, his camel-haired double-breasted top coat! Why had he stopped wearing this?

Oh yes, it smelled of Saul's clove cigarettes that had annoyed Lauretta.

Would the spice annoy Joshua's werewolf nose? Decker doubted it. Lauretta disliked it because she felt it was her father's mark on Decker. For now, the coat would do. On the top shelf were old hats, gloves, and scarfs. He'd given up on hats—maybe not a wise choice in Boston. He sorted through gloves, looking for a matched pair. Why did he have twenty left-hand gloves and no right-hand ones? At least the scarfs were plentiful. He picked out a wide white-and-beige tartan-pattern cashmere scarf that went well with his tan camel-haired coat.

He searched out Joshua's large stash of trash bags and found it under the kitchen sink. He bagged everything lying on the floor—except the bowling ball. It rolled into the library with a deeply ominous rumble. It came to rest against the bookcase with the shielded box.

The universe didn't want him to forget what he had stored there.

Something or someone had a game plan for magical creatures, one that beings like Decker couldn't escape. He wasn't sure who or what exactly created the strands of fate. The god of the Grigori? The three Moirai sisters of fate from the Greek myths? The three Norn sisters of the Norse myths? A proto god that was formed prior to any other god? Over three hundred-plus years, Decker had seen the signs too often to miss but still didn't know the origin of his inescapable fate.

Enyo could sense the converging strands. She came for the amusement that such a grand scale collision provided. The universe was giving Decker a hint that the sinister coin would be integral to the upcoming conflict. It could not be hidden in a safe spot to be dealt with at a later date. The signs were there; the universe was pulling his attention back to Charon's obol. Even if he took the coin to the ocean and tossed it in, someone would find it in short order.

There was a change in the house. A sense of it no longer being empty washed over Decker seconds before the smell of fried chicken reached him. There was an odd, muffled noise from the kitchen.

The back door hadn't opened and closed, he was sure of that since the locks and hinges were rusty from disuse. Was it Joshua teleporting in like he'd teleported out that morning?

Decker walked down the hall and into the kitchen.

Joshua had returned from wherever he had been. There was no sign of Seth. The only indication of where Joshua had been were several boxes of fried chicken sitting on the kitchen counter labeled CHICKEN BB.Q, BITE A BIT, THEN YOU WILL KNOW. PLAY WITH BBQ. Joshua had a drumstick in his mouth and one in both hands.

Decker had walked too softly into the kitchen.

Joshua had been muttering "mush mone mat a mime" around the drumstick in his mouth when Decker appeared beside him. His eyes went wide in surprise and suddenly he was a massive wolf.

"You're awake?" the wolf cried in Joshua's voice. Decker was still unsure how Joshua spoke with the same pitch and timbre no matter what his size was. The puppy and the wolf the size of a draft horse both sounded the same as the boy.

"I woke up early again," Decker said. "Even earlier this time. I'm not sure why. You visited with Seth?"

"Yeah—and then accidentally took him to Albany." The wolf lifted its feet and turned in circles. "I met Ewan—the new marquis. He's cool. He likes to read. We talked books for a while. He's more into mainstream than I am so I gave him the books in the foyer. Where the hell did my chicken go? Did you swallow those?"

He meant his wolf.

Now that Decker knew what the wolf was looking for, he scanned the floor. There was no sign of the three drumsticks.

"Oh geez, I bet they're with my clothes!" Joshua cried as the wolf turned in circles again, eyeing the floor. "Oh, gross—I don't know what's all in that place. It smells funny. You are not eating those when we get them back! Ewan got us two whole chickens! There's no reason to eat them!"

The wolf turned back to a boy with one drumstick in his mouth and one in each hand.

Joshua spat the drumstick onto the floor. "Oh gross!"

Trouble darted out of the shadows, a streak of ginger. He grabbed the drumstick that was nearly as big as him. He attempted to run off toward the couch, but the stolen chicken slowed him down to a waddle.

"No, not under the couch!" Joshua cried and realized he was holding drumsticks in both hands. "Grab him, Decker!"

Decker picked up the kitten and the drumstick. He had no choice as Trouble wrapped all four legs about his prize and growled in defiance. "You can keep it, just not under the couch."

"Neither one will listen," Joshua said as he eyed the drumsticks in his hands. "If I throw these in the trash, I'm not sure if he won't just dig them out later."

"There is that," Decker said.

Joshua juggled through getting out a plate and putting the chicken on it to leave by the sink. "I'll figure it out later when he's not as hungry. Although I don't know when that is because all he does is eat. We had pizza with Ewan before he ordered the chicken. Ewan at least has the excuse that he just became the new marquis. Apparently it's common for a new alpha to binge."

Joshua picked up a fresh box of chicken and settled on the couch. "Today was not a good day. This has not been a good week. This has not been a good month—or two. I really want my life to go back to something vaguely like normal. I just want to stay home and watch television and not think."

"I'm sorry, but we need to take the Charon obol to Sioux Zee Whitebrow."

Joshua looked at him with sad puppy eyes. The effect was ruined by the fact that he was gnawing on a chicken bone. "Do we?"

Decker thought of the bowling ball augury. "Yes. If I could, I would leave you here, but I have never met the Wise Woman face-to-face. I believe she holds me in respect. Until we actually are formally introduced, however, I would be just a very scary monster that showed up at her doorstep."

"You're only scary when you're pissed," Joshua mumbled around a mouthful of fried chicken.

"Thank you," Decker said.

31: ELISE

On the way to Danforth's apartment, Clarice had spilled out everything she'd discovered about him in the last hour. She had dug up everything from the make and color of his car (an insanely expensive sea blue Mercedes-Benz G-Wagen) to his family history.

"Danforth's great-great-grandfather had kicked around the United States in the 1880s," Clarice said. "He did everything from prospecting for gold to painting landscape pictures—"

"Great-great-grandfather?" Elise echoed, surprised and confused that Clarice started that far back. "Is this really need-to-know?"

"Yes, it relates. I'll get to it. Also, digging into someone's background is ridiculously easy when you're dealing with famous people. His great-great-grandfather—through weird twists of fate—ended up an oil tycoon in the late 1880s. His net worth—in today's money—was nearly a hundred billion dollars. Some of that went to charities—building libraries and hospitals—but the bulk was put into trust for his three children. His great-great-grandchildren are still living off the interest; based on their estimated net worth, none of them have touched the principle."

Dr. Boggs had said something about a trust fund. It explained the expensive SUV and the extremely high rent—and probably why Danforth felt like he could blow off work.

Clarice plowed on with the family history. "The tycoon's daughter married one of those larger-than-life 'most interesting man' types: Clifford Danforth. The reason the money was locked into a trust was probably cause of Clifford. Reading over his obituary, I'm guessing he was schizophrenic and/or gifted. He was certainly mentally unstable with a whole shopping list of mental disorders disguised as 'derring do.' Heavy drinker. Suicidal tendencies passed off as 'mad stunts.' He traveled the world to seek out shamans, witch doctors, voodoo priestesses, and famous mediums—most of whom were scam artists."

When children were raised in families that had lost their knowledge of their inherited gifts, they often tried to seek out anyone who could explain their powers. The very people that could help them, though, were unlikely to speak to outsiders. The only individuals willing to talk were scam artists pretending to have powers.

"I'm sending you pictures of Clifford Danforth's collection of occult items. With Clifford's destructive tendencies and his wife's money, he seems to have collected everything offered. I think that the majority of them are fake. Scam artists create 'artifacts' right and left. Just from the pictures, I can tell that the 'unicorn horn' is the tip of a narwhal tusk. I know the real location of some of his 'relics.' There's too many for me to discount them all. Anyhoo, his son, Caleb Danforth—the First—inherited both his father's insanity and his occult collection. Caleb had an erratic course through college, changing his major five times, but ended up with a master's in science from Caltech. He was one of the founders of planetary science and part of the team that set up the Amundsen-Scott South Pole Station in 1956. After that, he grew more and more erratic until he was diagnosed as having schizophrenia. His mother committed him to Danvers Lunatic Asylum in 1959. The psychiatric hospital was over eighty years old and was on the verge of financial collapse. Mrs. Danforth funneled a ton of money into the institution, allowing for much needed modernization. It seems that part of the deal was to give Caleb the First free run of the place. He was found dead in the basement ten years later. Coroner ruled accidental death due to falling down the steps, but there were rumors that an orderly killed him. His mother never pushed for an investigation, so it was quietly covered up. After the First's death, his mother pulled all her financial support, and the asylum slowly went belly up."

"What about the Caleb I'm dealing with?"

"Caleb the Second had been born in 1955 before his father

went to Antarctica. He was abandoned by his mother and raised by his grandmother. Despite all that, he didn't inherit the family's schizophrenia and thus was boringly stable. He was a professor at Berkley. He married late, probably because of his father's insanity. He's famous only because he spent his trust money on building a huge rock collection and a museum in California to house it. Your Caleb—the Third—is a throwback. Insanely smart. Unsure of what he wanted to do during his first five years of college, he changed his major three times. The same crazy pranks as an undergraduate. I found an entire page of drunk and disorderly charges that were quietly dismissed. Another page of arrests for dangerous stunts that could have been him flirting with death—again, quietly dismissed and then covered up."

"It could be just privileged frat boy behavior," Elise said.

"That's what everyone else seemed to pass it off as. 'Boys will be boys' especially when they have a billion-dollar trust fund. The episode in Antarctica, though, wasn't a schoolboy lark. He went out alone and nearly froze to death. He lost the tips of half his toes to frostbite. Afterward, they had to lock him up because he was out of his head and kept trying to go back outside. Apparently once the sun goes down for the winter, there's a no-fly rule that they only break in life-threatening emergencies. They seriously considered calling for a plane."

"So, like his grandfather, Caleb the Third is a bigger-than-life wild man who went off to Antarctica and came back damaged."

"As far as I've been able to dig up, yes." Clarice said.

"Did you talk to Ottilie about the soul talisman?"

"Yeah," Clarice said, drawing the word out as if the conversation didn't go well. "I warned her that it was dangerous, that it is meant only for a strong Virtue to use, yadayadayada. She thanked me for the information—but she didn't promise me anything. She apparently felt like she'd betrayed the Grigori covenant when she fled the fight at the aquarium with the other noncombatants instead of staying to help. Not that she could have done anything to a monster of that level—but I understand. 'Thou shalt kill monsters' haunts Dominions. I feel so useless when people call in just before they wade into a bloodbath and the only thing I can do for them is pray. Anyhoo, Ottilie is trying to figure out why Boston of all the places. I think she's right: that's a key point. The Danforth family was originally based in

California and then there's this sudden shift to Salem for what seems—on the surface—no good reason. There were dozens of better asylums to pick from which were closer to the West Coast. The Napa State Hospital is still going strong and it's practically in their backyard."

"It could have been because of the massacre of the younglings," Elise said. "It was shortly before Danforth the First was committed to Danvers. It left Boston relatively unguarded."

"I considered that," Clarice said. "It feels, though, like I'm overlooking something obvious."

The converted asylum came into view. Its gothic façade was straight out of a horror movie. The developer had kept every arch and tower and steeple of the place—and there were a lot of them. It stretched for several hundred feet. The trees, bare of leaves, did little to soften the hard, stark lines of the building.

There were flanking buildings that had had their gothic façades mostly erased by the need to include modern features like patios. It made them less creepy looking. Danforth's address, however, put him in the main building.

"I'm at the asylum," Elise told Clarice. "Any change on his phone or car?"

"Not on his car. I lost the signal on his phone. It last pinged off the nearest cell tower, like, twenty minutes ago. I sent a fake spam text via a burner, but it wasn't delivered. He either turned his phone off or its battery died. I'd hacked into the security cameras before I lost contact with his phone—I haven't seen anyone looking like Danforth leave his building, so I'm guessing that he's there. Somewhere. I've looked up the complex's website. The place is huge. There are rooms for spinning, games, and yoga. I'm not sure why anyone would want to do yoga outside their own personal space. Half the buildings have their own theater room where twenty people can sit and watch a movie on a giant TV screen. Who has twenty friends that can come over for a movie? Do normal humans live that way? I miss Greece. I miss being with you and the others."

"I do too." Elise spotted Danforth's sea blue SUV in the residents only parking area near the main building's entrance. She parked in the small visitor section at the far edge of the lot—the last thing she needed was having her car towed. "Okay, I'm going to go. Call me if anything changes."

The cold was bracing as she stepped out of her Jeep. Was it even colder up here on the hilltop? The afternoon sun was cloaked by clouds. A light crust of fresh snow covered the pavement, crunching underfoot. The wind whistled in an odd way as it made little snow whirlwinds between the buildings. It was weirdly musical, like a song that drifted in and out of hearing.

Cabot pulled in beside her.

"His apartment is in this main building," Elise told Cabot as he climbed out his big luxury sedan. He'd taken off his suit jacket, dress shirt, and tie. It made her cold just looking at him standing in the freezing wind in a white undershirt. She knew that he undressed so he could transform without destroying his expensive clothes. The thin white fabric molded to his muscled chest and six-pack abs.

Woof, woof.

The foyer was surprisingly busy with people: there was a package room near the front door that residents were using to mail out and take delivery of Christmas presents. The area was decorated with a real tree covered in twinkling lights, filling the space with the scent of pine. Elise shook her head, knowing that the first fir trees decorated at the end of the year had been dedicated to the Roman god Saturn. The early Christians had stolen the popular holiday—complete with the decorations—and renamed it and now stoutly defended it.

A sign near the tree explained that the community was doing something called "Secret Santa." What in the world was that? Secretly become a bishop during the time of the Roman Empire? Quietly raise from the dead three children prickled in brine and about to be sold as pork during a famine? (Francis could do it, so Elise didn't dismiss this legend completely.) Oh, how poor quiet Saint Nikolaos of Myra had suffered over the centuries, down to his bones being raided out of his coffin by random merchants and sailors. His name and image were mutated beyond recognition.

At least there was no Christmas music playing in the lobby, claiming to know the truth about the unknowable. A heavenly choir that only seeks out a random band of shepherds? *As if.*

The right-most elevator announced its arrival with a ding. A moment later, the doors slid open. There was no one onboard—someone must have been unloading something big and bulky to keep it on the second floor so long.

"Danforth's apartment is on the third floor." Elise stepped inside. She condensed what Clarice had found out about the Danforth family as they took the elevator up. She ended with: "Clarice is trying to find out why California-based billionaires fixated on the Boston area. His coworker thought it was creepy that Danforth bought an apartment in a building his grandfather died in."

Cabot looked confused. "Most of my Tatterskein ancestors died at Court. It's a peaceful death, surrounded by those you love the most."

Did Cabot know what an insane asylum was like? She had to admit her knowledge was based on horror movies, but they didn't seem like "peaceful" places to die.

The elevator dinged as it came to a stop on the third floor. They turned left off the elevators to head down a long hallway with eight doors spread far apart, indicating that the apartments on this level were very large.

Cabot pressed his ear to the door to Danforth's apartment and listened. After a minute, he shook his head. "I don't hear anyone moving around inside. He could be sleeping."

"If he's in there," Elise took out her lock pick kit. "Clarice could have missed him leaving with someone. He has a small army of swan maidens at his beck and call. He could also be doing something as mundane as working out at the gym or doing yoga or something."

"The mind boggles," Cabot whispered.

"Give me room to pick the locks."

The door had both a dead bolt and a normal lock but didn't seem to have a security system. She guessed it was because there would be a constant turnover of occupants as a rental complex as opposed to condos with homeowners. Cabot probably could have (and would have) just broken in the door, but she didn't want to have to deal with the police if she didn't have to. Her alone interacting with cops was annoying, especially if the responding officer was male, but with Cabot along, it could get messy fast.

Cabot patiently kept watch while she worked her picks through the deadbolt's pins. None of Danforth's neighbors walked out of their apartment. She shifted to the normal lock. Minutes later, she set the last pin. She opened the door and stepped into the apartment.

The place was huge. The living room took up one of the gothic towers, which afforded it a thirty-foot-high vaulted ceiling. Deep casements framed the façade's original windows, suggesting that the walls were over a foot thick. With the exception of the windows, all the gothic elements had been stripped away. In its place was a stark, minimalist open-plan box with stainless steel appliances in the kitchen area. The flooring was modern-looking bleached wood planks. The walls were a subtle light gray. The granite countertop and millwork were gleaming white except for the railing of the stairs heading up to a second floor. She thought the sleek modern style made the place look sterile and cold. It didn't, however, seem like a monster's lair.

"This makes my loft look tiny," Elise said. "I bet he even has a proper bathtub."

"Your place doesn't?"

"No, just a shower. I've been going over to Decker's since Joshua cleaned out the upstairs bathroom with the clawfoot tub."

Cabot made a suggestive "interested" sound but said nothing. It made her blush.

Her place was small but at least it was homey and comfortable. She had hung photos and posters of Greece with its whitewashed houses against the stunning blue of the sea. Her living room had a basic tan slipcovered sofa, but it was accented with a rustic walnut coffee table, a fluffy white flokati rug, a soft blue chenille throw, and a scattering of beautiful throw pillows. It was a warm nest that comforted her lonely soul after a night of killing monsters.

Nothing about Danforth's apartment suggested that anyone—let alone a billionaire—lived there.

The apartment felt insanely cold for indoors. She found the thermostat and verified that the heat was on and set to seventy degrees. She could hear the furnace running in the utility closet. Hot air was blowing out the vent, but the space was still registering at thirty degrees. Odd.

Cabot sniffed the air and then said quietly, "Someone was here recently. Their scent is still warm in the air. I still don't hear anyone moving about, though, so they're not here now."

Elsie gave an experimental sniff. Despite the cold, there was an unpleasant musty smell. They had a limited amount of time to search the place before Danforth returned.

The only furniture in the living room was a molded plastic

folding table and a patio chair. The table served as a messy workstation with books and papers. The floor around the chair held the overflow, some in neat stacks and others looking like they had fallen from the tabletop. On the wall was a conspiracy theorist's collection of photos and notes and maps.

As Cabot searched the rest of the apartment, Elise took pictures of what was pinned on the walls with her phone's camera. Danforth seemed to be searching for something. The maps were from different eras with sticky notes stuck onto them. One was labeled *North American Craton Plate*, showing where various tectonic plates lay west of the coastline. Another had mysterious labels of *Archon*, *Proton*, and *Tecton*. A third showed where the first European colonists had settled. A fourth had areas marked out for Native American territories prior to the waves of Europeans. Scattered among them were satellite photos with red marker circling points of interest. Mixed in were aged notes on faded paper, newspaper clippings from the sixties, pages torn from books that were yellowed with age.

She couldn't even guess what it was that Danforth was searching for despite all the copious notes. In some places it was like Danforth didn't seem to know himself. Many of the pinned sheets were yellow with age and written in a faded elegant cursive but had annotations in the margins done in a fresh sloppy print. The notes read "Where?" and "How far?"

Elise systematically photographed everything and sent it to Clarice. It was Clarice's gift to see patterns in things; she might be able to reason out the mystery.

Cabot searched through the kitchen and downstairs bedroom, growling softly to himself. "God, this man stinks. It's like he waded through swamp water and then took a roll in rotting fish. His sheets are gray as if he's not washed them in years!"

Elise would not have thought that a werewolf would care. She supposed she expected them to have a dog's perspective on staying clean—which was to say that rolling in mud was a perfectly fine activity. The three wolves had showered daily during the Thanksgiving vacation, so perhaps not.

Cabot went to the bathroom and sniffed loudly in there. "There was a second male in here for a time. He stinks nearly as bad but different. He's covered with incense and crushed herbs and bleeding from an open wound."

"That sounds like Brutus Clay," Elise said. "I've returned him to Bell Book and Candle. Hank Whitebrow was there: he should be able to keep Brutus safe."

When Elise was done with the maps, she went through the books strewn across the table. It was a weird assortment of material. There were two old leather-bound journals written in Spanish, the paper brittle with age. A third book was a published history of London with a cover embossed in gold. The binding creaked and flaked as she handled it. There was no date printed on the title page, which meant that it was most likely two hundred years old or older.

Elise eyed the papers on the floor. They seemed to be photocopies of a handwritten book. The wide edges of the print were black, indicating that the original book had been much smaller than an eight-inch-by-eleven piece of paper. The copies had lain somewhere damp and were moldering.

She used her toe to spread the paper so she could see what the book had contained. The corner of a hex slipped into view. She knelt down and flipped through the papers. Someone had photocopied a witch's grimoire! Not just any spell book—these were Wicker spells. She shuffled through the pages quickly and found the coven mark. Monkshead! Was this the same grimoire she and Cabot had found in Utica? It seemed like it.

She'd thought the grimoire was safely destroyed with all the spells of how to trap and enslave werewolves!

"Oh, good Lord," she whispered. These copies needed to be burned. Maybe everything on and around the table needed to be burned. What was in the journal? She knew Greek and Latin but not Spanish. She flipped through the brittle pages. The handwriting was neat and careful but tight, as if the writer expected to run out of paper before coming to his journey's end. A picture made her stop. It was a sketch of a rockhopper penguin.

Goddamn penguins!

She pulled out her phone again and juggled through loading the penguin page into the translation app.

"Seventeenth of August in the year of our lord 1520," the page started out, and continued:

> Almost six months have passed since God first spoke to me, urging me to return to Spain by any means. It is the sixth day since Ferdinand Magellan abandoned us on this island, having found us guilty of mutiny. I am

completely alone with God and the priest Pedro Sánchez de la Reina. However pious he may be, the good priest has not yet heard God's whispers as He speaks to me. I blame him not as I have to strain to hear myself. Pedro believes and that's all that matters. The Lord God urges me not to let the natives know that He is in communication with me. I doubt this is a concern since the unholy beasts know nothing of Spanish or Latin or any other language of civilized man. Their language is the harsh cries of birds. When they are beasts, they are ungainly waterfowl. As humans, they are pale, with red eyes, black hair, and yellow brows. To our dismay, they walk around naked without any sense of shame. The good priest tries to convert them to Jesus, but the lack of a common language makes the effort difficult. The Lord God wants me to leave this island and return to a place of maps and knowledge of the world. I don't know how I'm going to be successful at this. I suppose we could make a raft to take us to the Patagonian coast, but we can't return to San Julián where they know about my mutiny against Magellan. My lord God says that I must find . . .

Find what? Elise swore as she realized that the next page was torn out.

The God of the Grigori spoke to no one. Not His Dominions. Not His Virtues. Not even His Powers. He might lend his power to Francis and shuffle the boy around like a pawn piece, but He gave Francis no verbal instructions.

If Danforth was being whispered to, the voice did not belong to Elise's God. Nor did it seem that Danforth was the only mortal that his god reached out to. Danforth's god had been trying to push its way back into this layer for hundreds of years. Its Touched had centuries to collect together items and manipulate groups of people.

Had it pushed the Monkshood Coven to burn London, start the Salem witch trials, and then attempt to leash the Prince of New York with disastrous results? Had a Touched given the Monkshood grimoire to the Wakefield Coven? Pushed the witches into kidnapping Joshua as a baby? Elsie didn't think that a coven of Wickers would need encouragement to run rampant. But repeated attempts to enslave a wolf prince? That smacked of outside interference.

"This all needs to be burned!" she called to Cabot. "Are there trash bags in the..."

She paused as she realized that Cabot was no longer in the kitchen. She'd been too focused on the photocopies; she'd lost track of the Thane. Had he gone upstairs?

"Jack?" she called softly, aware that they were trespassing. There was no reply. She raised her voice slightly. "Cabot?"

Elise held still, listening intently. There was a faint odd musical noise, like several people were playing random notes on flutes. It was the same whistling wind sound that she had noticed outside. She hadn't given it much notice then as a blizzard had howled over Boston during the entire Thanksgiving weekend. The sound shouldn't be as loud inside the apartment—not with the deep windowsills that indicated thick insulated walls. The noise wasn't coming from the wind.

"Oh, I'm so stupid!" Elise whispered.

She should have realized why Danforth had rented the apartment when Dr. Boggs had said that the asylum was haunted. Contrary to popular belief, most haunted areas weren't caused by ghosts clinging to where they experienced a horrible death. A building or graveyard or forest normally became "haunted" only when two layers of reality drifted close enough together to create a Dissonance: a pocket of space that belonged to neither world. Much of the spooky things that happened in such areas—the mysterious cold, the odd sounds, and shifting shadows—was related to the fact the space was linked to a place that was neither there nor not there.

Elise had never found a Dissonance before. It was something they told her about in Greece, using flutes and whistles to approximate the sound. She had been told to avoid Dissonances. They were easy to stumble into and difficult to leave.

She eyed the stairs leading up. The sound seemed to be coming from the upper level. Elise really didn't want to go upstairs. It felt like a trap—one that had possibly snared Cabot already. But if it had, Cabot might not be able to escape on his own.

She went up the stairs cautiously. The apartment grew even colder as she ascended the steps, her breath coming out as mist. The sound of the Dissonance got louder. At the top of the stairs was a landing that overlooked the living room and an open doorway into a large bedroom with an ensuite bathroom.

"Cabot?" she called again.

"Elise!" Cabot's voice came from far away. "Don't follow me! I don't know where I am—or how to get back!"

Elise whispered a curse. Did the Wolf King teach his Thanes nothing? If Cabot didn't recognize a Dissonance for what it was, it was unlikely he could puzzle his way out.

She took out her phone and texted Clarice and Theo to let her know that she was going into a Dissonance.

"You're going in? Alone? Are you mad?" Theo asked.

"Are you two not together?" Clarice asked.

"I drove Francis to Alewife to get his SUV," Theo replied. "We are heading to Salem."

"I teamed up with Thane Cabot," Elise texted.

"And that is better than being alone?" Theo snarked. "I will bring Francis to burn anything dangerous down."

"There isn't time," she texted. "Cabot stumbled into the Dissonance already."

"He's a Thane!" Theo texted. "He doesn't need to be babysat!"

Elise shook her head. Why did she text the others? "I need to get him out before the Dissonance collapses!"

"No, you don't," Theo responded. "You can wait."

It would be over an hour for Theo to drive from Alewife to Danvers. Elsie didn't feel like she could wait. Besides, she really didn't want to get Francis involved. The apartment complex could end up like the mall: on fire with giant holes in the roof. Cabot had said that only Danforth and Clay had been in the apartment recently so she should only have to deal with a Touched.

"I'm good," Elise texted.

"You're screwed," Theo texted.

"She wishes," Clarice added a winking emoji.

Elise shoved her phone back into her pocket while she blushed so hard she felt like she was going to set her coat collar on fire.

She moved forward, step by step, struggling to keep her fear in check. Her teachers said that she wouldn't be able to see the nexus into the Dissonance. It would be an imperceptibly small fracture in reality. Brushing against it, though, would guarantee that she'd pass into the Dissonance.

Her teachers were right.

One moment she was stepping toward Danforth's unused master bedroom in his luxury apartment, the next she was standing in a long-abandoned building.

32: JOSHUA

Night cloaked the city when the cab dropped them in front of Sioux Zee's Quill Pig tattoo parlor. The storefront window, with the porcupine drawn in tribal style, was dark but the neon OPEN sign was still lit up. It stained the snow piled on the curb a bloodred. Heavy metal music thundered inside the shop, promising that employees were still inside.

"I do not know if I can enter," Decker murmured as Joshua tried the door.

It was unlocked.

Joshua pushed the door open, calling, "Hello?"

Over the sound system, he heard "Don't Fear the Reaper."

"Grannie?" Joshua shouted, as that was what Winnie called the woman.

"An evil stirs," Sioux Zee said from deep in the shadows. "We will need all those we can call to our side to win. Even you, Silas Decker. Come in."

Decker hesitated at the door. "I thought that your place would be warded against me."

Sioux Zee emerged out of the darkness. Nothing about her said "old woman" except the pure white of her hair that poured long and thick down to her knees. Tall and leggy in skinny blue jeans, she looked like she might be only slightly older than Joshua's mom. He knew, however, that she had to be as old as his grandmother since Winnie was her granddaughter.

"The wards on my shop are not as simple as the ones I put on your home," she said. "I knew that those would need to be set once and left to stand. Here, I can alter what can come and go. A ghost. An angel. A werewolf. A vampire. You can enter, if you wish."

Decker stepped forward, over the doorsill, into the shop proper.

"You're not as dark as I expected." Sioux Zee switched off the stereo system and then the OPEN sign. She vanished back into the darkness. "I suppose three hundred years of living with angels would do that. Come upstairs to my work room."

The wood floors were stained black, soaking up what little illumination came from the streetlights outside. Even with his wolf's night vision, Joshua could barely make out the details of the tattoo parlor. Without the customers and the artists, the place felt bigger than Joshua remembered it being. Their footsteps echoed loudly off the exposed red brick walls.

Decker looked around with great curiosity. "I've never seen a place where they've done tattoos before. The natives around New Amsterdam often marked their skin—so of course most white men disdained such practice as barbaric. I was surprised when it came into favor."

"Oh, don't get me started," Sioux Zee said as she climbed the metal spiral staircase that led up to the second floor.

Joshua's wolf grumbled at the sign reading QUILL PIGS ONLY, OTHERS WILL BE NEUTERED. It didn't like the upstairs area that was Sioux Zee's private sanctuary. Weird and spooky things happened up there.

"Oh, hush," Joshua whispered to his wolf.

The second floor continued the stained black oak flooring and exposed brick walls. While the downstairs had been devoid of the occult, the upper sanctuary was littered with it. On the walls were skulls of breach-borne monsters and a collection of antique guns engraved with spells. Sioux Zee went to her big old-fashioned safe and spun the dial through the combination.

"I'm going to give to you the lottery ticket that you brought with you the last time you visited," Sioux Zee said. "Now that you have the resources of the king to call upon, I'm sure you can safely claim the winnings."

Inside the safe were a dozen thick, leather-bound books and a collection of crocks wired shut and covered with odd runes.

Joshua wanted to ask about the jars—something about them was highly unsettling—but he didn't want to derail their mission even further.

"Winnie thought we were going to split it," Joshua said as Sioux Zee handed him the lottery ticket. The prize was ten million dollars; it was more than he needed, especially with Seth giving him thousands of dollars in cash.

"What my grandchild thinks is rarely in line with reality," Sioux Zee said. "Besides, if she gets the money, that French queen would steal it away as fast as she can."

"Yes, probably she would." Joshua took out his wallet and tucked the ticket away. "Marie Antoinette possessed one of the kids at our school and was selling information to buy Christmas presents for a guy who runs a bakery in Cambridge."

Joshua explained about Mannie hiding out at the aquarium, the fight with the possessed Brutus, and Vijay finding the scary magical coin in Marie Antionette's purse. Decker added in information that he'd learned from the Virtues about Francis, his missing driver Roustabout, the fight at the mall, and how the shapeshifters seemed to be tracking the strange coin.

Decker had had Joshua carry the box from the house to the shop, saying that the coin felt too dangerous to him. It was creepy, but Joshua didn't think that it was any worse than the rune-covered jars in Sioux Zee's safe. He had put a rubber band on the box to keep it closed and stuffed it into his coat pocket. He pulled it out now, took off the rubber band, and set the box on the card table.

"We're not sure what this is or what we should do with it," Joshua opened the lid.

He had forgotten how it felt, like the crawl of a weak electrical charge across the skin. His wolf closed the box.

"She needs to look at it, idiot!" Joshua opened the box again.

His wolf closed the box.

He growled in annoyance.

Decker caught him by the shoulders and moved him to the other side of the table. "She can open the box herself."

Joshua leaned against Decker, as his presence often calmed his wolf when he was on the verge of losing it. Wolfing out in front of Sioux Zee might be a bad thing, given all the magical guns on the wall.

Sioux Zee took a seat in front of the box. She cracked open the lid and gave a slight "oh" of surprise. "Yes, this is immensely powerful. No mortal made this. A god crafted this. What a god makes, man can only hide away. Marie Antionette had this?"

"Well, it was in her purse," Joshua said. "Everything else in her coin purse was from Mannie, so I assume she got it from him."

"It would be nice to have an answer from him," Sioux Zee said. "But one can never be sure if you're hearing the truth from a living being. Even ghosts of mortals will lie."

"The question is, what to do with it?" Decker said.

"This Mannie came to Boston to face a god," Sioux Zee said. "If he had this, it could be a weapon against the god or it might be a bargaining chip."

"Can you tell which?" Joshua asked.

"I can ask a higher source." Sioux Zee stood and moved about the room, gathering items. She set candles on the card table, lit them with an odd-looking match that smelled strange in the closed-in room.

Joshua struggled to keep his wolf from growling as Sioux Zee turned off the overhead light and settled across the table with the small gilded box. He wasn't sure what she planned but both he and his wolf were sure it was going to be uncanny and spooky.

"It's fine. You're fine," Decker murmured, patting Joshua on the shoulder.

"I'm going to ask for the help of a spirit," Sioux Zee opened the box. "It will not be able to hear your questions, so if you have any, address them to me—but only if you think it's extremely important. I need to stay focused on the spirit to make sure it can do no harm."

The wolf was not happy.

"This will not be a ghost," Sioux Zee said. "It will be more like a spirit guide. It has the ability to act on its surroundings without a host body. I'm going to be setting up wards, but if I lose my focus, those wards might not be strong enough to hold it."

"Are you sure this is wise?" Decker asked what Joshua was thinking.

"Yes, I do," Sioux Zee said. "Information will be key in the upcoming battle. The universe acts differently for magical creatures. There is no random chance. Things happen because of fate. It is unfortunate but one's fate cannot be avoided. It is only through knowledge that destiny can be...not changed, but softened."

"People keep saying that to me," Joshua complained. "Enyo said that there was nothing she could say or do that would influence my fate."

"Enyo would lie if it made things more interesting," Decker growled darkly.

"Fate is like a game of Monopoly," Sioux Zee said. "Dice are rolled for pieces to be moved. The number on the die might change but the pattern of play remains the same. Each turn, you have choices to make that will determine how well you succeed, but you will always be limited by the board as to what move you can take. Fate will drive you to an end position—how well off you are when you arrive can be changed at every decision point."

Joshua wondered if there was some weird magic on the card table that turned people's minds to games. Last time he was here, he'd kept thinking about the card game he'd played with his cousins. "So, my fate has always been 'become a werewolf and fight Wickers' but I could have died at any point? Basically, be first to go bankrupt in the game?"

"Yes," Sioux Zee said. "Whatever we learn now will allow you to play the game wisely, increasing your chances of survival."

She took what looked like a pack of oversized cards from her gilded box. She shuffled them quickly and then started to lay out the cards, whispering words as she laid them down. He could see the shimmer of power coming off them, like heat wavering over hot cement on a summer day. The energy roiled around Sioux Zee's fingers as she shifted the cards.

Some of the geekier kids in his old school would play with tarot cards. (At least he thought it was "play" as none of them seemed to have mystical powers back then. He could see magic now but could he back then? Certainly, the one "reading" he got from his old classmate had nothing to do with witches trying to kill him, becoming a werewolf or living with a vampire.) The layout that Sioux Zee was putting down looked similar, with the first card being crossed by the second. The next six cards formed a circle about the inner two. There were complicated designs on the cards instead of pictures.

"Are those tarot cards?" Joshua whispered to Decker.

Decker shook his head. "They are wards. She's setting up a complicated barrier around us."

She is? Joshua eyed the dim room. *Oh, she is.* He could see faint wavers in the air around them. Were there similar airborne disturbances in their home that he hadn't noticed? Or because the wards on the house were more permanent in nature, they were more... solid? Maybe it was better he couldn't see them—he'd had his fill of weirdness already.

Sioux Zee placed her hand upon the center crossed cards. "I call upon those that hold the three mothers dear. Their feathered children are in peril. I would speak to those who know of this accursed coin. I implore one of their blood to step forward and give council."

There was a sudden blinding brilliance in the air above the table.

The brilliance coalesced into a shimmering figure. White motes of light drifted about it like molted down.

"Wha'?" the figure shouted out in a voice like a bicycle horn being honked. "Wha' you want?"

Joshua squinted at the brilliance. One moment the shimmering figure looked like a woman with wings instead of arms. In the next moment, it was a massive gleaming swan with an overabundance of impossibly white feathers.

"Thank you for appearing before me," Sioux Zee said calmly. "I seek council on the god known as the Dark One."

The shining being ignored Sioux Zee's greeting. It hissed at Decker. "This one is tainted by the Dark One! He only has to call, and this one will answer. Kill it quick!"

"Whoa! Hold on!" Joshua stepped in front of Decker, arms wide, shielding him. "Are you sure it can't hurt us?"

By "us," Joshua meant Decker.

The figure reared back, flapping its wings and hissing angrily. "Wha'! Stupid wolf! Why is the Beast of the Living Woods protecting his corruption?"

"He is my friend!" Joshua growled.

"It can't hear you," Decker reminded Joshua. "Just trust the Wise Woman. Her wards won't let it hurt me. She knows what she's doing, else she couldn't bear the title."

Joshua wondered who got to decide Sioux Zee's worthiness. Was there some kind of spiritual inspection team?

"Tell me about the Dark One," Sioux Zee said.

"Vile! Evil! Parricide!" the swan spirit honked. "He rose up and slew the Bringers of All Life. He was cursed by the All-Mother as she died! Everything he touches will be corrupted! But the All-Mother did not have the strength to kill him for his betrayal. The Three Mothers have decreed it, that he should be weeded out whenever he takes root and begins to grow. If he is allowed to flourish, he will suck the life from the world. Again and again, we have nipped his plans in the bud, killing his Touched, isolating him once again in his frozen palace. When he realized that we would always block his way, he sought out our one weakness: the Mothers' Stone. He took the sea people first, they who were the guardians of the stone in their desolate home. He had, however, lured the others ahead of time with rumors of his awakening. The firebirds are the rarest of our people and our fiercest attackers. Of course, they followed the rumors to Boston to destroy his Touched. It was all for nought. He had set his trap, and they are all firmly held within it."

"Poor things," Decker whispered.

"Why Boston?" Sioux Zee said.

"If he can place a proper vessel in the heart of his city, his Touched can call him forth. Long has he slumbered, buried in ice. While he slept, his city split from his palace and drifted away. He knows not where his city now lies. It could be anywhere in the world. On top of a mountain. Under the sea. Deep in a forest. Again and again, he has sent out his Touched, seeking it. If he has called his minions to Boston, then he has, at long last, found his city. Enslaved as they are, there is nothing my people can do to stop him."

"Nothing?" Sioux Zee echoed.

The swan dipped its head so that its beak tapped the table before the coin. "This is our only weapon against him—not that it does much good. None of my people can lift a wing against him, entrapped as they are."

"It's a weapon?" Joshua said and Sioux Zee repeated his question. The disk of silver that looked like it would bend if someone pressed down on it too hard.

The swan fanned its wings. "Yes! Yes! It would drive him out of his vessel and send him back to his palace to sleep once more."

That made sense. Decker had said that the point of the obol was to make sure ghosts didn't cling to the dead body, instead going to the afterlife. But how did one "use" a coin?

Joshua's phone rang, surprising him. He hadn't had anyone,

other than Seth, call him since he got it. Seth usually texted him and Joshua had just dropped him at his Castle bedroom. Joshua took his phone out of his pocket. The screen read M. CARTER. He frowned at the name. *Who is that?*

Then he remembered that Maisy's last name was Carter. The Goths had all given him their contact information back on his first day of school. He had understood that Maisy had put in only "M" because her real name was Mary, but no one used it. She had felt that listing herself as Maisy, though, would be somewhat misleading.

He hit the button to accept the call. "Hello?"

There was only hoarse breathing on the other side.

"Maisy?" he said.

There was a slight whimper and then a whispered, "Help."

Fear jolted through him. "Maisy! What's wrong? Where are you?"

"B-B-B-B-Bog Hol-Hol-Hollow," Maisy stuttered through a whisper.

"Bog Hollow?" Joshua repeated. It sounded familiar but for the last month he'd been bombarded with new place names.

"Isn't that the place that Seth was talking about?" Decker said.

Seth was? Joshua frowned at Decker, trying to remember where in all the last few days of weirdness Seth had mentioned the name. They were in Albany last, talking about the bachelor house and Seth's wife.

"The Christmas place." Decker made a triangle shape with his forefingers and thumbs for some strange reason.

Then it clicked.

"Oh! The spooky sounding tree farm!" Joshua wanted to ask Maisy why she was there since cut-your-own places tended to be out in the middle of nowhere with acres and acres of empty space to grow trees. He didn't think she'd be able to answer him; this call for help was the first words she'd spoken to him since he met her.

"Back when this area was just being colonized, any place that was mystical in nature, the wolves bought," Sioux Zee said quietly. "There's a dozen or more places scattered across Massachusetts that the Tatterskeins protect. Bog Hollow is one of those spaces. It's a cranberry bog—or at least it was, hence the name. It's been leased to a family with divine gifts to manage. Christmas trees and wreaths are a seasonal thing, something to bring in money while the cranberry bogs are dormant."

Ottilie had said something about researching mystical places in New England to try and figure out what the Touched was looking for. She might have needed someone to drive her out to the locations in question, but she wouldn't have sent Maisy alone.

"Are the others with you?" Joshua asked Maisy.

"Y-y-yes," Maisy said. "I-I-I mean—no. I-I-I don't know where they are. Th-th-there was a monster—and we ran. I-I-I got lost..."

"Shit!" Joshua cried as fear and frustration roared through him. This was going to end up like his old school's Halloween haunted house: everyone dead at a barn out in the middle of nowhere. But this was going to be worse—he liked all the Goths!

Decker wrapped his arms around Joshua. "Stay calm. Now is not the time to lose it."

Maisy gave a squeak of dismay and pain that tore through any sense of calm that he could gather.

Joshua was suddenly standing in knee-deep snow under a night sky. A lone streetlight threw a pool of light down onto a wooden sign that read:

BOG HOLLOW FARM.

CUT YOUR OWN CHRISTMAS TREE!

HOURS: 11 AM TO 5 PM.

MR. AND MRS. SANTA CLAUS: SATURDAYS AND SUNDAYS.

Maisy knelt beside the sign, whimpering in fear, as she dug her phone out of a snowdrift.

"Maisy! Are you alright?" Joshua cried, helping her up.

She hugged him tightly. She was so happy to see him—although she was confused as to how he'd gotten there so quickly.

They were standing beside a narrow country road. The asphalt gleamed with black ice in the light thrown by the streetlight. The farm's driveway was wide but hadn't been well-plowed since the last snowfall. A brightly colored Ford Transit panel van had slid as it turned into the driveway. It sat buried up to its axles in snow. Its balloonlike lettering proclaimed BOUNCE CIRCUS! CASTLE AND WATER SLIDE!

"Bounce castle?" Joshua read the lettering with surprise.

Maisy nodded. She silently explained that Tal's father rented the inflatable structures out to children's parties on the weekends in the summer. It was his side gig that let him afford his child support payments. Tal had borrowed the van to drive the Goths to the farm, but he'd never driven in snow before. He'd taken the turn too fast and slid into the snowbank. The Goths had tried to push the van out of the ditch but couldn't.

Joshua wasn't surprised that they failed. Vans like the Transit were notoriously bad in the snow if they weren't all-wheel drive. His dad's tow truck business was kept busy all winter long pulling delivery vans out of snowbanks on back roads.

Seth had warned him that he was moving through the Source of the werewolf power when he teleported. Joshua could jump Seth and Cabot back and forth to places without fear, but if he tried it with a normal human, they might turn into a feral werewolf. At least that was Seth's theory on how Joshua's teleporting worked.

Joshua didn't want his wolf to try dragging Maisy and the others through the Source. It would be best if they all drove away in the van instead. Hopefully with his wolf's insane strength, he'd be able to free the Transit. If not, rescuing the Goths might get dangerously messy. Joshua waded into the snowbank, sinking up to his knees. He opened the door to find that Tal had left the keys in the ignition.

Wait. Where are the other Goths? Joshua had forgotten to ask.

He put the van into neutral, made sure the wheels were angled to take the vehicle onto the road, and waded to the rear. As he put his shoulder to the van's back door, he scanned the area.

The rest of the Goths weren't in sight. There were footprints in the snow showing that half a dozen people had walked up the driveway, away from the main road.

"Come on, let's save Maisy and the others," he whispered to his wolf.

For once, his wolf cooperated. A good hard shove pushed the van out of the snowbank and up to the center of the driveway. For good measure, the wolf picked up the frame and swiveled the entire vehicle around, so it now faced back to the main road. He shifted the van back into park and left the keys in the ignition.

One problem solved. Joshua needed to find the others, get them back to the van, and have Tal drive them back to Cambridge.

Maisy caught Joshua's sleeve, stopping him. She wanted to know who was lying beside her in the snow.

"What?" Joshua turned and looked down. Decker laid sunk deep in the snow drift. "Decker!"

Decker's eyes gleamed a deep green, and he stank of moldering forest. "Aaaaah soooo that's the wooolves' Sooource?" He slurred his words like he was drunk. He languidly waved his small warded box above him. Joshua had vaguely been aware of Sioux Zee packing up the obol, but he hadn't realized that she'd handed it to Decker. "Sooo green! Sooo peaceful!"

Joshua could tell Maisy had heard stories about Silas Decker. The vampire wasn't as scary as she expected—nor as old. He looked like a college student. A drunk one.

Decker had been trying to calm Joshua's wolf down by hugging him. The vampire must have been dragged through the werewolves' Source when Joshua teleported to Maisy. Decker had always said that he wouldn't become a werewolf even if Joshua bit him. But he was still clearly overloaded by the power of the werewolf's Source.

"I was only twenty when I was attacked." Decker stood up and nearly fell over. He gestured wildly. "Aye, but to die, and go we know not where."

Joshua wasn't sure what that meant. It sounded like a quote from something. Decker's condition was proof that Joshua couldn't teleport the Goths back to Cambridge without his Source infecting them.

He scanned the area again. Maisy had said something on the phone about running from a monster. "Where are the others?"

Maisy pointed down the lane toward a small lake. She conveyed that she was fairly sure it was a cranberry bog flooded for the winter to protect the perennial plants. The snow had been shoveled off the lake, leaving the ice bare and gleaming in the moonlight. From where they stood, he couldn't see anyone on the surface.

"They didn't fall through the ice, did they?" he asked fearfully.

Maisy shook her head. Cranberry bogs were only hip deep—or, at least they were in the commercials. Ji Su's spirit guide Nam-gi had indicated that there was something odd about the lake. And Mannie had said that they needed to find the Mothers' Stone to free his people.

"Mannie is with you?" Joshua wasn't sure if this was a good thing. The penguin seemed no better at fighting than the Goths and stubborn as all hell. He obviously talked the kids into doing something far too dangerous.

Maisy nodded. They had gone into the city to search for the Mothers' Stone, but it was filled with monsters.

Into the city? "Boston? Or some other little town like Framingham?"

Maisy pointed again toward the frozen lake.

Judging by how much the snow was trampled, hordes of people had walked from the "cut-your-own" parking lot to the cranberry bog. How many of the beings were human was impossible to tell by the footprints left behind. At a distance, the lake looked no different from any other one often used for ice skating. On the shore, an area had been set up with a stone firepit. Bench seats provided a place to put on and take off ice skates. A lean-to shelter behind the seating had one low shelf for boots and a higher one with a camping teakettle, mugs, and a tin of instant hot chocolate. The snow had been shoveled off the ice, exposing several acres that gleamed milky white in the brilliance of a big stadium-style floodlight focused on the lake. Joshua was sure it was a lovely way for a family to spend time together when monsters weren't trying to eat their faces.

As Joshua gazed at the lake, not understanding what Maisy meant by "city," he noticed the air over the ice seemed to shimmer like a heat mirage. Faintly through the haze, he made out a ghostlike city landscape that stretched out into the darkness beyond the far shore. Despite the air being still, there was an odd whistling noise, like the wind blowing hard.

"What the hell?" Joshua breathed.

"Ohhh, I know that sound." Decker seemed a little more stable. Maybe he was sobering up. "It's a Dissonance. It's where realms have drifted close enough that you can cross from one to another. Like rocks skipped across a pond ... ripples that collide with each other ... becoming stepping stones."

He waved an unsteady hand toward the lake. "It's the moonlight city! It's a recurring Dissonance moored to this place by the foundations of a lost city. I'd forgotten about it, so long ago was the tale of its discovery told to me. The natives had told the Grigori of it back ... back ... back in the days. So long ago. Very long ago. Long, long ago."

No, Decker was still drunk.

Joshua hauled Decker to the van. "You two stay here. If you see bad people, drive away."

Maisy let him know she didn't know how to drive. She lived in the dorms with no access to a car. With the subway a block away, there was no real need for her to learn.

"Decker, you do know how to drive, right?" Joshua asked as he started to put Decker into the driver's seat.

"Turn the key to battery and then spin the crank as fast as you can," Decker said.

Maisy might not "know" how to drive but she probably would do better than Decker. Joshua walked Decker over to the passenger seat.

Maisy took out her phone and cued up a video on how to drive.

Joshua hated leaving her and Decker alone. He wasn't sure how he was going to find the Goths, but he was afraid if he did nothing, they'd be lost.

Joshua started toward the lake, snow crunching underfoot, his breath coming out as mist. The closer he drew, more structures appeared on the ice. It was a fantastical city landscape of stone stairs leading up to an oddly shaped arched gateway with weirdly shaped towers looming behind it.

33: ELISE

Elise stood in an impossibly long dim hallway that looked like a tunnel with a window at the far end. Doors stood open at regular intervals, letting sunlight spill into the hallway. The floor was layered thickly with chunks of ceiling plaster and paint that had flaked off the walls. The air was bitterly cold, oddly dry, and smelled faintly of the sea despite them being five miles from the ocean. There was another strange otherness to the scent that she couldn't identify. She zipped up her coat and snugged her scarf tight. A muted restless sound like the surf crashing on a rocky shoreline underscored the odd piping noise of the Dissonance.

Elise looked behind her. There was no sign of Danforth's master bedroom. The hallway stretched out behind her, mirroring what had been in front of her. She glanced into the rooms to either side. They were obvious hospital rooms, with old-style metal beds looking as if the patients and staff had walked away long ago, leaving beds, mattresses, linen, and personal effects behind. The rooms had been designed to hold just one bed but two had been crammed into the space. Dr. Boggs had said that the insane asylum had been dangerously overcrowded when it was finally shut down.

A bright fog pressed against the tall windows, allowing in sunlight but cloaking any landscape beyond in gray. Despite the brightness seeping through the window, ice rime glittered on the casings. According to her teachers, a Dissonance created access to another layer. There should have been a whole world beyond the glass. The building, however, stood isolated in a void. This wasn't a true Dissonance. This was some kind of Splinter, fractured off and left floating. It would take the power of a true god to create such a thing. Judging by the age, it had been created when Caleb Danforth the First had lived and died at the insane asylum.

Dissonances were considered dangerous as they were less solid than normal reality. It was easy to fall into neighboring layers—drifting farther and farther from home. Splinters were far more stable but deadlier. They were created to hold something— usually a monster.

"Cabot?" she shouted. "Cabot!"

"Elise?" Cabot stepped out of one of the rooms behind her. He wrapped her in a warm hug. "I'm sorry. You keep needing to rescue me from my own stupidity."

"It's okay." She hugged him tightly, his presence calming her like a drug. He felt like a furnace in the freezing cold. "I didn't recognize the noise until it was too late. I was too focused on the papers I found."

"Can normal people hear that weird sound?" Cabot winced as if the noise hurt him. "I started hearing it in the parking lot. I thought it was odd that it got louder in the apartment."

"No, not really." Elise mentally kicked herself for not real- izing what the sound signaled until Cabot was trapped. "Some people probably would sense that something is wrong about the building. Most ghost sightings aren't ghosts; they're shadows of things moving within a Dissonance."

"How do you... how do you get rid of them?" Cabot fumbled for the correct words. "Close them off. Make them drift away. Whatever."

Elise blew her breath out as his questions were laying bare how little she knew about it. "I don't think we can easily wrap our brains around the metaphysics of layers. They're like dark matter or something. I get the impression layers are like icebergs in the ocean, they drift here and there. Dissonances come and go all over the world. Sometimes they linger for years and other times they vanish in hours. They used to be common. They're rare now. The biggest danger is when they collapse, leaving you stranded in the wrong layer. This is a Splinter—it runs on different rules because it was intentionally made. It's probably why Danforth wanted that apartment—it gave him access to this Splinter."

Cabot let go of her and stepped back to pull off his white undershirt. His muscled chest and six-pack abs were covered in glossy black hair. It worried Elise how strong the sense of want went through her at the sight of his bare chest.

Down, girl! Down! This is not the time for that!

"What are you doing?" She turned away, blushing.

"We're taught how to fight as wolves since we're stronger and faster when we're in our beast form," Cabot said.

"Are . . . are you going to shift?" Her blush went deeper red as she listened to him undo his belt and unzip his pants. The sound of his zipper was insanely loud in the empty ruin.

Oh, Lord, have mercy!

"Yes, and I still haven't figured out Joshua's trick of storing his clothes." Cabot made a neat bundle of his clothes with his slacks and belt. "I don't want to ruin them. It's a pain to get back to your car unnoticed when you're buck naked."

Elise never had that problem . . .

She checked her phone to distract her from what Cabot was doing. No signal. That wasn't surprising. It would explain why Clarice lost track of Danforth's phone. "Danforth might be in here with us."

"Oh, he's here; his scent is still warm. He's come and gone through this area multiple times."

If the cell phone was blocked, what of their magical powers? Was Cabot going to be able to transform? Would she be able to call on God's holy might?

She took out her daggers, placed their tips to the ground, and tried to clear her mind. She needed to focus on calm piety, not desire-induced embarrassment. She took a deep breath and prayed. "Blessed be the Lord, my rock, who trains my hands for war, and my fingers for battle; He is my steadfast love and my fortress, my stronghold and my deliverer, my shield and He in whom I take refuge. Amen."

God's power poured into her, calming her, filling her with warmth. The light spilling through the tall windows cast pale shadows of the ghostly wings that formed on her back.

"Oh, thank God," Elise whispered. She had been afraid that the Splinter would put her beyond God's power, but it still reached her.

She stole a glance toward Cabot. A black wolf stood in his

place, carrying the bundle of clothes via his leather belt looped around it like a carry sling. A few months ago, Elise had thought he was a massive wolf, but Joshua had changed her sense of scale. After dealing with a wolf the size of an elephant, one the size of a black bear looked small.

The good news was that they were both connected to their sources. The bad news was that Danforth was too—along with any creature he had helping him.

She should explain a little to Cabot about magical spaces in case they got separated again. "There are two types of layers. The first is a Dissonance caused by layers drifting close together. There will be a nexus much like the one that we entered with—a simple invisible threshold that could be anyplace—that we merely have to cross."

"So far, not that," Cabot said, meaning that they hadn't tripped over the threshold.

"A Dissonance, however, often has more than one nexus as it connects two or more layers together, which makes it dangerous to move about. The other type of space is a Splinter. It means that a god has taken control over this space and kept it separate from all layers. When a god does that, they typically change the nexus into something more concrete—probably so their followers don't accidentally move to the primary layer or fall into an alternate layer that is farther out. We'll have to find this nexus and interact with it. It may be a door or a window or a mirror or pool of water."

"Oh joy."

The good news was, if Danforth has been coming and going, his trail should be easy for Cabot to follow it back to the nexus.

"Let's see where Danforth has been going to when he comes here," Elise said.

They moved forward, passing through the light spilling out of the side rooms and through the darkness between them. Plaster that had fallen from the ceiling crunched under Elise's boots. Cabot padded silently behind her, a dark ghost in beast form. He checked the patient rooms as they passed as she focused mainly on what was ahead.

Fifty feet down, Cabot murmured, "There's someone dead in this room."

They detoured to investigate. The man lay beneath a bloody impact crater on the wall. The dry bitter cold of the Splinter had freeze-dried the corpse, completely desiccating it to a frozen mummy. There was no way to tell how long ago the man had died. Polaroid photographs lay scattered on the floor like fallen leaves. Most of them seemed to have been taken within the asylum—the patients seemed to wear street clothes during the day. The clothing and hairstyles in the pictures suggested that they were taken in the late 1960s.

The rumble of the rough surf was softer, as if they had moved away from the source. It wasn't coming from beyond the windows, still obscured by the bright fog.

"He looks like a patient," Cabot pawed the bloody clothing. "These are flannel pajamas. House slippers instead of shoes. He's wearing an ID bracelet. Darrel Smith."

The pajamas suggested that the man had been asleep when the Splinter was formed. He was killed before he had a chance to change into regular clothes.

"Some of the patients might have fallen through to the Splinter when it formed. Maybe the reason that the hospital shut down wasn't because it was bankrupt. It could have been that they lost more patients than they could cover up. The staff might have closed up shop and fled."

Elise eyed the impact crater on the wall. It looked like the man had hit with enough force to break the lathe and plaster. Judging by the bloodstain, he'd burst apart like a water balloon on impact. "There's probably a monster here. Something small enough to fit through the door but strong enough to throw a man around like a rag doll."

"I'm surprised it didn't eat its kill." Cabot turned away from the corpse to study the doorway. "Breach-borne would. No way it's still alive all these years with nothing to eat."

"It might not be alive in a way that we understand. 'Gods can create monsters that defy our understanding of life'," Elise quoted her teachers.

Cabot cocked his head in confusion. "Don't the Grigori believe there's just one god?"

"One true god for our reality. Doesn't mean there aren't gods from other layers attempting to trespass on His creation. We should find Danforth before the monster finds us."

A splash of red in one of the photographs caught Elise's eye. She picked it off the floor. It showed a patient sitting in a sunny solarium with a familiar-looking redheaded woman draped in furs and diamonds.

"Oh shit," Elise whispered. "This woman looks like a Wakefield Wicker."

Cabot eyed the photograph. "Yes, I've seen that red-fox jacket before. What was her name? Dahlia? She was a brunette, though, and witches have normal life spans."

"The woman in this picture would be in her seventies now—if she's still alive. I'm guessing she's Dahlia's mother or grandmother."

"All this is related to last month's insanity?"

Elise thought of the copy of the Monkshood grimoire. "I'm thinking yes."

They found another body, this one out in the hallway and oddly misshapen. The man wore flannel pajamas and house slippers like the first one. He had, however, four eyes and three arms. The third arm was giant size with fingers larger than thigh bones.

Cabot wrinkled his nose at the body. "It doesn't smell right for a breach-borne. Do you think he's what killed the other patient?"

Elise looked around, trying to guess from what direction the creature had come from. "I don't think so. He left a trail." She pointed at scratch marks in the floor. "He was dragging that weird third arm. He came from that direction."

Cabot prodded the corpse with one paw. "He was shot in the back. Someone with a gun took him out. Silver bullets."

Werewolves were fairly indestructible, but they had a fatal weakness to silver.

"If we run into any humans, stay behind me," Elise said. Her protection spell made her bulletproof.

They moved on through the ruined insane asylum. The light through the gray fog dimmed slowly. Night seemed to be drawing near. She took out her phone and checked the time. The sun would be setting in Boston proper. Decker would wake up soon.

"I think that time is moving at the same speed as in our world," Elise said.

"That's not a given?" Cabot asked.

"No. Layers sometimes use different rules than what we have on Earth. They might run fast or run slow. It's the basis of stories like Rip Van Winkle, where a man spends an evening drinking and playing ninepins and wakes up twenty years later."

"The dead men have been lying here, forgotten, for fifty years?"

"Most likely," Elise said. "I think Caleb the First managed to manifest his god—somehow—and it created this Splinter. This is a copy or reflection of the asylum as it was in the 1960s. These poor men, already insane, stumbled into this madness just like you did."

At the end of the hallway, they found Caleb the First's large and private room. Unlike the other patients' rooms, which were crammed full of metal cots, his contained a solid mahogany four-poster bed that looked fit for a king.

Every inch of his walls was covered with writing and drawings. The largest drawing was a fantastical cityscape with towering columns, massive statues, and long walls covered in reliefs. It reminded her of Persepolis. Instead of being surrounded by desert, it was an island in the middle of an ocean.

The handwriting matched the flowing cursive of the paper pinned to the walls of Danforth's apartment.

> In his lost palace, under the cold ice, there he sleeps, dreaming of Nimrus. He laments for his city, built upon the body of his father. His mother is long dead, but her curse remains. Until he bathes in his father's blood, he must sleep, dead to the world.

Elise took out her phone to take pictures of the walls. There was too much to take in. They couldn't stand and read it all.

"Huh. This bit mentions His Majesty." Cabot read something written low on the wall:

> It's not working. The vessels keep being corrupted by his power and needing to be put down. He needs a vessel strong enough to hold him. The Monkshood grimoire says that the Wolf King carefully breeds his children so that they can hold his Source. What I have here is not strong enough. I must find something else. Something stronger.

"Vessels?" Elise glanced back toward the door—and the creature in the hallway. "I wonder: did Caleb the First kidnap the other patients, thinking he could use them to hold his god's power?"

"That's a thing?" Cabot said.

"Basically, that's what a Power is. A Grigori opens themselves fully to God and invites Him to take up residence, so to speak. The Grigori that does it successfully becomes 'God's power manifesting in human flesh.' They're not God in person. It's more like God has planted a small seed within them that remains separate from the person. It's a bit like Joshua's wolf—it's a second personality within the Power's body, acting of its own accord. While it's more civilized than Joshua's wolf, Francis has little control over how his magic protects him. He can't be ambushed because it's always aware of his surroundings, even when he's asleep. It takes its cue from his own emotional state, however, so anything that startles him, like the monks at his monastery or random alligators at a park, gets nuked."

Cabot's eyes widened at the mention of alligators, but he didn't question that. Instead, he asked, "Does that mean that Powers can go feral?"

"In a manner of speaking, yes. Any Grigori can do the ritual to try and become a Power, opening themselves up to God's might. Most would go up like a struck match, leaving behind only ash. Only a handful of us are strong enough to survive and we're born to an angelic bloodline. Caleb the First didn't realize that grabbing a random person off the street..."

Roustabout wasn't quite a random person. He was a companion to a Power.

There were werewolves and hordes of monsters and people torn to pieces, Elise remembered Clarice saying, *one of them being Roustabout.*

And Theo had said, *If he's dead, you can just raise him. You've done it before. You don't even need all his parts, just some of them.*

"Oh," Elise whispered. "Something like that would change a man."

"What would?" Cabot asked.

"I think Danforth took Roustabout to be the vessel for his god," Elise said.

"Didn't you say he was completely normal? No bells or whistles?"

"Francis had raised him from the dead when they were living in Florida. It wouldn't have been something as simple as just restarting his heart. He'd been torn to shreds by something and dead for over an hour. God's magic would have entered every cell in his body. Bones knitted back together. Flesh made whole. Any brain damage from being dead erased. God's breath pushed into still lungs. It would have reforged him into something new— something stronger. Danforth might have Roustabout here, in this Splinter, to use him to hold his god."

Cabot shook his head. "Danforth is the only one that's been in this space. I'm not picking up any other scents. He didn't stop in this room; he kept going toward the stairs."

"We need to follow him to find the nexus out," Elise said.

There had been a massive iron grate blocking access to the staircase down to the next floor. It would have kept the patients from escaping their assigned area. Someone or something had smashed it from its anchor points. The grate lay on the floor, strewn with broken plaster and peeling paint.

The stairs led downward. Based on what Cabot's nose told him about the whereabouts of Danforth, they skipped the second floor, descending directly to the first floor. The sound of the surf grew louder. It was as if an ocean raged against the very foundation of the building. If the penguin had been right, then Danforth's god had been born, cursed, and locked away all in water. His mother had turned the seas against him. Caleb the First wrote on his wall that his god needed to return to his city and bathe in the blood of his father to break the curse. Bathing in the blood of the holy was a universal cure for all illnesses of the soul, perverse as it seemed. The Christians weren't the first to discover the secret, but they were the first to water the experience down to ordinary wine and wafers.

The Spanish journal had mentioned that the god wanted his Touched to move to a place of maps. Caleb the Third had been spending time at the map section of the university's library and had maps pinned to his wall. The Touched had been looking for the lost city.

But to bathe, his god would need a body on the same plane of existence as the city. That was probably where Roustabout came in. The question was, had Danforth found the city? Was that where he was holding Francis's driver?

The iron grate at the bottom of the stairwell had suffered the same fate as the one on the third floor. The area immediately beyond the broken barrier held administrative offices instead of patients' rooms. They looked like a tornado had gone through the rooms, tossing desks, chairs, filing cabinets, and reams of papers into a chaotic mess.

Elise glanced over the papers scattered across the floor. They were patient charts filled with handwritten notes on mimeographed forms. Here and there were black-and-white photos of men and women, eyes forlorn at their fate. Had Danforth's god duplicated the asylum down to these papers or were these the patients' true— and possibly only—records? If they were the original paperwork, it would explain why the hospital staff didn't realize that patients were missing. What the forms didn't explain was how Danforth's god manifested enough to create the Splinter with only a Touched to serve him. Touched were limited as to what power they could handle without fear of becoming corrupted by their god's power. If the god pushed power into Danforth, he would lose his Touched. So how did he make the Splinter, caged as he was?

Just past the offices, they found the answer.

Cabot nudged her in the hip and swung his head toward a double set of doors toward the center of the long hallway. A placard above it read ELECTROCONVULSIVE THERAPY. A cardboard sign on the left-hand door stated, UNDER CONSTRUCTION. The right side was cracked open, letting out a slice of light.

"Danforth went into that room," Cabot whispered. "But there's something big farther down the hall. I can hear it breathing. It's not moving otherwise."

"I was hoping all the monsters were dead," Elise whispered. Caleb the First obviously had killed the humans who had been corrupted by his god's power. There was nothing stopping the Third from making new ones. "Danforth could have made a new monster trying to recreate his grandfather's work."

"We should move quickly, get a door between us and the creature," Cabot whispered. "Deal with Danforth first."

"Right." Elise stalked forward with Cabot moving silently beside her.

The electroconvulsive therapy room was impossibly large, as if Danforth's god had expanded its original footprint. It vaulted upward and back, shifting from lathe and plaster to ancient mossy stones and limestone cave. Moonlight gleamed through breaks in. the cave ceiling. The bitterly cold air smelled of seawater and the roar of the surf thundered loudly. Snow layered the floor.

There was something out of a nightmare in the middle of the room, made of crude electric wiring and spell glyphs drawn on the walls, ceiling, and floor. Connected into the mass of machinery and wire were artifacts that had been in photographs of Clifford Danforth's collection of occult items. The strange apparatus hovered over a hospital gurney like a giant evil spider.

"Oh, dear God," Elise whispered. She could recognize some of the spell glyphs from the Monkshood grimoire. The Wakefield Coven had used them to open the breach under Boston Commons. Did this machine somehow open a breach just enough for a man strapped to the gurney to be taken over by its power? The Book of Enoch said that the fallen angels had taught mankind secrets of the universe, everything from mathematics to alchemy. What had Danforth's god whispered to his Touched over the hundreds of years? Caleb the First had been an intelligent man of science. With immense wealth and his father's collection, he had done what should have been unthinkable.

Caleb Danforth the Third stood on the other side of an observation window on the far wall, right before the lathe and plaster became mossy stone. He was a man whose edges had been smudged by the thumbprint of his god. His lackluster mousy blond hair looked like a wild tuft of dried grass. His bare hands were skeletally thin, the tips of his fingers reddened by cold. While his face was pale and gaunt, there was an odd smearing to his features, like a wax skull had melted in the heat.

"That door is warded, isn't it?" Cabot murmured quietly.

"Yes, it is," she whispered. There were very thin shimmering lines like spiderwebs etched on the window and door of the observation room. It would make sense that if Caleb the First made monsters in this place, there would be a shield for the Touched. Dispelling an unknown ward was a matter of an educated guess followed by trial and error. It might take more time than they had.

Was Danforth trapped within the observation room? No, in the shadows behind him, Elise could make out a door. It could go anyplace within the Splinter or even be the nexus to his apartment. Considering that the asylum housed monsters and trapped patients, it made sense that the back door might be the nexus.

Danforth glanced up. His ice pale eyes gleamed in the dimness of the shadowed room. He hit a button and leaned toward a big old-fashioned microphone. "I'm guessing a Grigori. It's hard for me to be sure: there's no Occult Field Work 101 class. I've been winging it. I've heard that the Grigori are considered the most beautiful creatures to walk the Earth. I'm not impressed: I know it's mostly smoke and mirrors. And a black wolf! Are you the new puppy that the Wakefield Coven let slip through their fingers again and again or the Thane? I doubt you're the prince."

Danforth's voice scratched and crackled as it projected through an unseen speaker. He had the rich timbre of someone well used to speaking to a room full of bored college students.

Elise flicked her fingers, hoping Cabot would understand that she wanted him to distract Danforth. She would need several minutes of peaceful prayer before having the power for more than one attempt at dispelling the protection ward. She drifted backward, forcing herself to be calm.

"I'm the Thane," Cabot rumbled in a voice that was full of menace. He started to pace back and forth in front of the window. "Where is the man named Roustabout?"

Danforth ignored the question, focusing back on the control panel before him. "That man is insanely loyal. The Stanford psychologists were all proud of their marshmallow experiment, but they were about two thousand years behind your god. Heaven is the ultimate delayed gratification."

Dr. Boggs had said that Danforth was a motormouth. She must have meant that the man talked incessantly. Elise took advantage of Cabot's distraction to close the double doors to the electroconvulsive therapy room and lock them against the monster down the hall.

Danforth didn't seem to notice. He continued to rattle on while he fiddled with the equipment in front of him. "Hm, two daggers. It means that she's a Virtue—right? It seems as if there should be a more biblical weapon to be had. A sword. A staff. A sling. Daggers? What was he thinking? A shame she's not a Power—I have questions. Once I manage to bring about the rebirth of my god, he will make me his Power. Handsome beyond compare. Faster. Stronger. Even stronger than the Power that burned down that mall. I'm so looking forward to being able to do that. Money is nice but it doesn't keep you from getting bullied by random idiots who think wedgies are the height of humor. Money doesn't get you girls—at least not girls that you can trust not to steal your credit card and sleep with your best friend."

He was actually whining about how unfair his life was? A billionaire born with a silver spoon? Elise struggled not to roll her eyes as she silently prayed.. *I will sing of thy power; yea, I will sing aloud of thy mercy in the morning.* She didn't have time for a full vestment, but it was comforting to feel the quiet strength of the Lord settle upon her. He was with her, giving her strength to fight her enemies.

"Don't be stupid," Cabot snarled. "Powers are like wolves; if they don't have breeding to hold their Source's strength, they're consumed by it. If you had that ability, you wouldn't be just a piddling Touched."

Danforth impatiently waved away Cabot's statement without looking up. "That is a limit that the Grigori's god baked into them. Different gods follow different rules. That's why werewolves are pure magic whereas the Grigori just funnel their god's power through them, never transforming. I didn't see any gleaming winged people at the mall but obviously the Power was slugging away at max strength."

Unto thee, O my strength, will I sing: for God is my defense, and the God of my mercy.

Danforth was correct that most Grigori didn't transform like werewolves. Their "wings" were not bone, flesh, and feathers but of radiant ethereal power. He was completely wrong, though, about Francis using his full strength at the mall. Francis had been worried about hurting innocent bystanders—many of whom had been children—so he hadn't unleashed anything willingly. His automatic defense system, however, had been blasting any immediate threats. She wasn't going to correct Danforth; it was best that he continued to underestimate the Grigori.

It begged the question, though, had Danforth been at the mall during the fight, or had he just seen the videos? How independent were the swan maidens? Weak Wickers could only command puppets that were nearby. Stronger witches could implant and maintain a script on a handful of victims for a limited distance. Their orders, however, vanished when the Wicker was killed. How strong was a god-level magical device? Was Danforth mentally summoning a flock right now? Would his command over the swan maidens continue after they killed him? Finding the stone was paramount. Did Danforth have it on him now or was it stashed someplace else? His apartment seemed empty of personal effects, but they hadn't searched all the closets or kitchen cabinets. It could be sitting in his fridge, along with DoorDash leftovers.

Danforth rambled on as he pulled something out of a control panel in front of him. "For a god that is supposedly omnipotent, his counter moves are pathetic. A Power in a fur suit? A single Virtue and a black wolf? One little penguin hiding in the aquarium? An entire world to pull an army from and that's what he goes with?"

I will sing of thy power, yea, I will sing aloud of thy mercy in the morning. Danforth had miscounted the number of Virtues, but he was right that it was a paltry number compared to a small army of shapeshifters.

"Your god has been stuck in an ice hole since the beginning of time," Cabot said. "He'll say anything to get out of it. You really think that a being who murdered its mother and father has any concept of gratitude?"

For thou hast been my defense and refuge in the day of my trouble.

Danforth held up the item he'd disconnected. "My god has given me treasures and minions and, most importantly, knowledge."

Elise couldn't tell what the item was, but she could feel the power leaking off it from where she stood.

Cabot snarled in annoyance, which probably meant he could feel it too. "It's given you what you need to free him and his empty promises."

"And the promise of heaven isn't a crapshoot?" Danforth pocketed the magical item, shaking his head. "I like my payout before I drop dead, not after I'm completely at the mercy of a god's whims."

He was going to find out that, living or dead, mortals were always at the mercy of gods' whims.

Danforth continued to prattle. "I thought that the swan maidens would make a proper vessel for my god as they shapeshift like the werewolves, but it turns out that I was completely wrong about that. They have these weird, feathered cloaks that follow no scientific logic. They're a bird when they have the cloaks on but humans when they take the cloaks off—which *should* mean that they're humans pretending to be birds but it's really the other way around. You would think that they have human skins that they put on and wear like that furry outfit that your Power had on. Anyway, firebirds were a failure at being vessels, but they do make good guard dogs."

O Lord, my strength. The Lord is my rock and my fortress and my deliverer, my God, my rock, in whom I take refuge, my shield, and the horn of my salvation, my stronghold.

Elise felt a surge of dark chaotic magic in the room, centered on Danforth.

The man grimaced in pain. "Yes, yes, I know 'less talk, more do!' my lord."

Danforth might boast about having more trinkets than her, but his god was hitting him with a mystical cattle prod to do his bidding.

"Rafael!" Danforth shouted. "Cease your sulking and come deal with this, you stupid bird!"

There was a rumbling noise in the distance.

Cabot growled his annoyance. It was a dark and dangerous sound. "He's called in reinforcements; the monster is coming!"

Elise pulled out her daggers. They blazed with power that she had gathered. "Therefore, thus saith the Lord God." Elise pressed the tip of her left dagger into the center of the door to the observation room. "I will even rend it with a stormy wind in my fury..."

Something big banged against the door to the room. It roared in anger.

"Well, it's been real," Danforth said. "Have fun with my pet."

He ducked through the door behind him.

Elise ignored the fleeing man and the incoming monster and continued her spell. Hopefully her first attempt would work. "And there shall be an overflowing shower in mine anger, and great hailstones in my fury to consume it."

The door burst off its hinges and cartwheeled through the room. It slammed into the observation window.

The beast beyond the door was the size of the firebird from the night before. That and its spiky rooster cockscomb were the only similarities. There was nothing elegant or natural about the creature. It had been denuded of colorful feathers and scales. In their place were a rough hide and stiff spikes like boar bristles. It had too many limbs. One right wing. One humanoid left arm with four long fingers. Three legs that it couldn't quite control. It lumbered, ungainly, rumbling in anger.

Cabot flung himself at the beast and the two went tumbling back into the hallway.

Elise drew the glyphs of power with her right dagger as she finished the spell. "So will I break down the wall that ye have daubed with untempered mortar, and bring it down to the ground, so that the foundation thereof shall be discovered, and it shall fall, and ye shall be consumed!"

The glittering lines flared as the power of her spell attempted to overwhelm them.

There was a sudden roar of flame as the firebird breathed out fire. The hallway went bright and washed into the room.

"Cabot!" Elise shouted.

"I'm fine!" Cabot called from somewhere in the hall.

The beast breathed again.

"Ow! Fine! Just fine!" Cabot called again. "Did you get him?"

The wards were undamaged by her first attempt.

"Working on it!" Elise shouted. She started a second dispel. "Bow thy heavens, O Lord, and come down: touch the mountains, and they shall smoke. Cast forth lightning, and scatter them: shoot out thine arrows, and destroy them. Send thine hand from above; rid me, and deliver me out of great waters, from the hand of strange children."

She drew the glyph with the right dagger. There was a flare that whited out her vision like a camera flash.

In that moment of blindness, Cabot yelped in pain and then cried out, "Elise! Help!"

She blinked, clearing her vision. The protective ward was gone. The way after Danforth was open.

She turned and gasped. The deformed firebird had Cabot in its mutant arm and was about to bite off his head.

"God in Heaven!" She flung her right dagger at the beast's eye. "Hallowed be thy name!"

She felt the faint energy trail as the knife flew from her hand as it was a combination of both her soul and God's will. Her blade struck the reddish pupil and pierced it to the hilt. The firebird jerked back, roaring in pain.

Cabot tore himself out of its grip in a desperate scramble, his claws skittering loud on the hallway's tile.

"Thy will be done!" Elise gripped tight to the energy trail and willed the dagger to return. It ripped itself from the monster's eye and flew back to her.

That drew the beast's attention to her.

"Careful, Elise!" Cabot shouted even as he stumbled through a narrow doorway across the wide hall.

The thing was massive, its head barely fitting through the double doors. It rumbled in anger and took a deep breath.

"Shit," Elise whispered. Her protection spell would shield her from a normal fire but not the magical breath of a firebird. The room suddenly seemed tiny; it afforded no protection beyond the antique hospital gurney. Elise sheathed her left dagger and jerked the bed up like a tall shield.

With a deep continuous roar like a jet fighter taking off, the firebird exhaled. The flames licked around the edges of the gurney, trying to reach her. Heat washed over her. It was like being dipped into the sun. The metal reddened and the railing started to melt. Last night, Francis had reeked of the firebird's breath—stinking of something that smelled like apples and caramel. The monster before her stank of rotten fruit and burnt sugar. The very core of its magic twisted into something corrupt.

The moment that it stopped breathing out, she dropped the gurney, intending to blind its other eye. It glared at her with two blazing orange pupils. Its wounded eye had healed. Its big ungainly body blocked the door.

The inhuman arm came whipping toward her. She ducked its four long fingers.

She could chase after Danforth but that would leave Cabot alone with the beast. She had no doubt that Cabot would fight to the death.

Cabot leapt on the firebird's back. He looked like a puppy attempting to take down a pterodactyl. He couldn't seriously wound it at his size. Joshua had only managed to take a firebird down when he was the size of a bus. Even then his victory had been temporary. If Cabot could kill the firebird, it would heal back from the dead.

"It's going to breathe again!" Cabot shouted.

She needed to get out from in front of it. She vaulted over its head to land on its back beside Cabot. Fire washed over where she'd been standing, reducing the gurney to a melted lump of metal. The firebird roared in anger and thrashed its one wing while fumbling for them with its misshapen arm.

Elise slashed at the hand as it grabbed at her, slicing off its fingers; they instantly started to regrow, only twice in number. If she somehow beheaded the firebird, would two heads grow back, both able to breath fire? Was it like the hydra of Greek myths? If so, this fight was hopeless.

"Follow me, Cabot!" She dropped down into the hallway and took off running. She hoped Cabot wouldn't be heroically stupid and stay behind. Relief bloomed through her as he appeared at her side, keeping pace with her.

"Do we have a plan or are we running blind?" Cabot asked.

"A little of both," Elise said. The firebird might still be some-what sentient, so she couldn't tell Cabot her plan. "I want to get to the second floor."

She wanted to lure the beast away from the nexus. Danforth hadn't given the creature explicit instructions, so it should give chase. If she was right about the layout of the asylum, the ends were mirrored, meaning they could run in one big loop back to the electroconvulsive therapy room.

The firebird roared its anger and frustration as it struggled to turn its warped body. And then, with a sound of furious stomp-ing, it came after them.

"We can't stay in front of it," Elise warned. "Its breath can reach hundreds of feet."

"I can run faster. I could loop back and lure it..."

"No," Elise snapped. "We stay together. There may be more than one nexus out of this place."

"Ah, yes, that's probably wise! It's going to breathe again! Take cover!"

Elise dodged sideways into the nearest room with Cabot on her heels. A moment later, the hallway filled with fire. Heat and the stench of rotten fruit flooded into the room. Random parts of the hallway caught fire. Wooden doorframes. Abandoned chairs. Bits and pieces of ancient broken plaster embedded with horsehair lying on the ground. The exposed lathe in the ceiling above. It created a hellscape as she dodged back out of the room to flee the oncoming monster.

As she had thought, the hall led to a staircase. Like the other stairwell, it was institutional-sized with tall narrow windows. She wasn't sure if the firebird would try to follow them up the steps, but it didn't seem to be slowing down. She and Cabot raced upward. Their footsteps echoed loudly. With every breath, she could smell and taste the musty damp air, heavily laden with crumbled plaster, and the strange otherness of the Splinter.

The second floor was a mirror image of the third. The long dark hallway stretched out in front of them. Random doors stood open creating bars of light in the darkness. The desiccated bodies of dead patients littered the wood flooring, each distorted in a different monstrous way by the Caleb the First's attempts to make a vessel for his god. There were hundreds sprawled out in their path. Elise paused on the stairs' landing, dismayed at the number of dead strewn before them. Had no one noticed this many people vanishing into thin air? How many patients had the asylum "lost" before they realized something was wrong? Had Caleb the First been killed because someone discovered that he was responsible for all the disappearances?

Flame roared up behind them, distracting her from the past.

"It's still coming!" Cabot said.

"That's good," Elise said. "That's what we want."

They raced forward. There was no way to avoid the dead. Bones cracked under their feet. The beast came stomping after them, shaking the floor under foot, not even pausing to breathe.

Elise swore as she saw the end of the hallway. Unlike the other staircases, the iron grating to keep patients from changing floors was still intact. Worse, even as they charged toward it, she could see the thin silvery lines of a ward.

"I'll need to dispel the ward on that before we can breach it!" she warned Cabot.

"Keep going!" Cabot turned around to face the oncoming monster.

Her stomach roiled at the idea of him trying to slow the beast down so she would have time to dispel the ward. At least she knew which spell to use.

She started to pray silently. *I will say of the Lord, He is my refuge and my fortress. My God, in Him will I trust. Surely, He shall deliver thee from the snare of the fowler, and from the noisome pestilence.*

She drew her daggers as she closed on the grate. It was the same ward as before, but the door was locked as well as warded. She wouldn't be able to break the lock until she dispelled the ward.

"One problem at a time!" she whispered as she pressed the tip of her left dagger against the heart of the spell. "Bow thy heavens, O Lord, and come down!"

Behind her was a roar of the beast and Cabot's snarl of anger.

She wanted to turn and look but she knew that she'd lose focus if Cabot was in immediate danger. Her spells required her attention as well as the power generated by her prayers.

"Touch the mountains, and they shall smoke. Cast forth lightning, and scatter them: shoot out thine arrows, and destroy them."

There was a heavy impact that shook the floor and rained dust down her. Cabot yelped in pain.

Stay focused! Elise drew the glyph with the right dagger.

The firebird breathed in a roar like jet engines. The flames didn't reach her, but the heat washed over her, stifling hot. Instantly there was the crackle and snap of everything combustible catching fire. She knew without looking that the hallway was alight.

"Send thine hand from above!" she shouted. "Rid me, and deliver me out of great waters, from the hand of strange children!"

The ward flared brilliant. The steel door was still locked. She sliced down with her right dagger, and it sheered through the bolt.

She heard the monster rushing toward her. She turned to face it. Cabot lay on the floor, fifty feet back, unmoving.

"Cabot!" She ducked a savage bite at her head, sliced through the tendon of the right-most leg, and dodged under the flailing wing. She ran toward Cabot. His eyes were closed but he was still breathing. She turned to face the beast again, crossing her daggers.

"God shall shoot at them with an arrow!" She drew back her right dagger as if it were a bowstring and a gleaming arrow took form. "Suddenly shall they be wounded!"

The arrow leapt from her crossed daggers, brilliant as a bolt of lightning. It punched a massive hole through the firebird's head. It crumbled onto the floor with a heavy thud.

"Cabot! Get up! I can't carry you when you're this form!"

The wolf's eyes fluttered open. "Elise?" He tried to move and growled out a curse. "I can't get up! Not yet. I can heal but it takes time. Go without me!"

"I'm not leaving you here!"

With a deep rumbling growl, the firebird stirred. It opened its flame-orange eyes.

"Oh, no, you don't." She crossed her daggers again. If she kept wounding the beast, she could buy the time that Cabot needed to get on his feet. "God shall shoot at them with an arrow!" She drew back her right dagger. "Suddenly shall they be wounded!"

The beast jerked its head to the right. The arrow cut a groove through its shoulder. Blood sprayed from the wound, but it healed shut even as she readied another arrow.

It took a deep breath.

She could get clear, but Cabot couldn't.

She dropped down, pressing dagger tips to the floor. "Blessed be the Lord, my rock, who trains my hands for war, and my fingers for battle..."

She wasn't going to get the spell off in time!

The firebird swung its head back, dropped open its massive jaws.

Brilliance filled her vision like a thousand magnesium flares going off at once even as she realized that a strange peaceful calm surrounded her.

Francis was in the house.

And he was filled with righteous anger.

The brilliance continued whiting out her vision until Theo shouted in the distance, "Whoa, whoa, whoa! It's dead already! Dial it down before you blow this Splinter apart!"

The brilliance died away, leaving only a purple stain on her retinas.

"What just happened?" Cabot murmured at her feet.

"I told my cousins I was coming here." Elise sheathed her daggers. She wasn't sure how they had gotten there so fast. Maybe God had teleported Francis again.

As her vision cleared, she realized that there was a massive hole in the floor and ceiling. The rubble of broken plaster was drifting upward to a foglike void. Francis had weakened the Splinter with his fury—it was breaking down.

Francis came drifting down the hall, glowing with holy splendor, massive ethereal wings on his back. He crossed over the hole in the floor without seeming to notice that there was nothing under his feet. There was no sign of the firebird or the grate. Theo stood at the stairs, unable to follow her little brother.

"Are you okay?" Francis's voice sounded like he was whispering into a microphone. Soft and gentle but filled with power.

"I'm fine," Elise said. "Cabot is hurt."

"Ah, I'm not very good at healing," Francis whispered sadly. "Not in my toolbox."

The speed of the debris drifting upward seemed to pick up.

"I can carry him." Francis gestured and Cabot floated upward. "We should go."

34: JOSHUA

The wind whistled through the alien cityscape as Joshua searched for the Goths. An aurora writhed in the night sky—something that Joshua thought Boston was too far south to actually see. The buildings looked like they were made from giant dead coral or some kind of huge bones: they gleamed bright white in the moonlight. Everywhere were tidal pools filled with dark water smelling of the sea. The streets twisted and turned in a nightmarish maze filled with dead ends. There were towers and minarets and bridges that connected buildings at odd levels. Huge statues of nightmarish beasts loomed over every open plaza. Here and there were carved murals showing people carrying offerings to raised altars. Everything about the city made his skin crawl. The proportions were wrong. The steps were weirdly short and shallow. The people in the carvings looked strangely wrong. There was something very squidlike about them: the bulbous shape of their heads, their mouths nearly beaks, and fingers like tentacles. Flowing cloaks covered the lower part of their bodies, but Joshua doubted that they had anything as normal as feet and toes. The Dark One had made something only remotely close to humans to worship him.

Joshua ran through the alien cityscape trying not to think of the kids who had died at the barn the day he became a werewolf. "Try" was the operative word as memories of their torn-apart bodies kept flashing through his mind. The smell of blood. The screams of pain. Even if he'd missed all the details that night, the police had photographs of his classmates' gory end. Bethy had told him how the entire town was in mourning for the dead kids. And it was all his fault.

Not directly. The Wickers would have set a trap regardless of where he was—and they needed puppets to make it work. Ten kids had died just so Samuels would be forced to make Joshua a werewolf. They'd died because of Joshua's fate. One way or another, the universe would force him to be a werewolf. But it didn't make him feel better about what had happened.

With the exception of DJ and Chris, none of his dead classmates had ever been "friends" of his. Joshua, however, had known them most of his life. They had been together since first grade. He sat behind or in front or beside them in class day after day, year after year. He knew if they carried their lunches or bought the cafeteria food or got it for free because their families were poor. He knew if they were smart or dumb or just lazy. He knew the brothers and sisters of the ones that rode his bus. He'd met their mothers during holiday classroom parties.

The kids at the barn had been like distant cousins—known, not especially liked but emotionally attached. He always thought he'd be glad if he never saw them again. Now he knew that he wanted them to be happy and healthy and *alive*. Not torn to pieces. Not dead and buried. He hadn't known then—as they lifted dead bodies off him—that he'd been the only survivor. Later, though, when he thought of the kids he'd grown up with, he'd been faced with the fact that there was only black nothingness where a living person had been.

He liked the Goths. They had welcomed him completely, furry alter ego and all. He really, really, *really* didn't want to find them torn to shreds.

Joshua rounded a corner and came face-to-face with a giant snake. The coils of its body were two feet thick, and it head swayed six feet above his. He yelped in surprise and fear, jumping back. The snake bobbed its head up and down. Joshua got the strongest impression that it was laughing at him. Also, it seemed familiar. It looked like Ji Su's spirit guide, only bigger. A lot bigger.

"Nam-gi?" Joshua said.

It flickered out its tongue and bobbed its head.

"Oh geez, you scared me!" Joshua muttered. "Where is Ji Su?"

The snake turned and slithered away. Joshua followed it, assuming that it was leading him to Ji Su.

Nam-gi didn't take him to Ji Su. It took him to where Tal lay on the ground, bleeding out from a massive wound to his torso.

Joshua had gone hunting with his father enough times to recognize a mortal injury. The limp body. The massive bleeding wound. The frightened look in the animal's eyes as they realized that they were dying.

"No, no, no," Joshua whispered. This was the Halloween barn all over again. He knelt beside Tal, his hands flailing over the dying boy, wanting to do something but having no idea of what. He glanced around frantically. There was no one else in sight. Even if they were within hearing range, would any of them be able to help? Decker couldn't heal others. Maisy could only let people know how scared she was. Allie's ability was knowing the past. Ottilie? She said that she had no magical power, that she needed things like flames to fuel the spells that she cast. Shouting for the others would bring no real help. The others could do nothing to save Tal either.

Deep breaths. Calm down. Think. What can you do?

At the barn, the witch Daphne ordered the football team to mortally wound Joshua. They had sliced Joshua's arm down to the bone. He would have bled to death in minutes—just like Tal was in danger of doing. Joshua would have died there in the cornfield except Samuels turned him into a werewolf to save his life.

Everyone had told Joshua over and over again that if he bit someone, they would turn into a werewolf. If he bit Tal, the boy would survive. Maybe. Everyone also said Joshua biting someone would be bad. The person would be "feral." Whatever that meant. Only someone like Seth or Ewan could successfully make a pack wolf. Seth and Ewan had acted as if even trying to move Ewan's sister-in-law into the Albany pack would be dangerous.

Samuels had managed to save Joshua. He was a Thane but so was Cabot and Cabot wasn't much different from Joshua at the wolf stuff. Taking the risk was better than just letting Tal die. He had to try!

Joshua focused on being a wolf. *Come on, we need to save Tal!*

He shifted form as his wolf took over. It was as scared as he was—it compensated by being huge.

"Careful, don't swallow him whole!" Joshua said as his wolf

tentatively opened his mouth wide. Joshua remembered what Dr. Huff had said about his own bite wound on his first visit: *This is a classic bite that wolves use to change their younglings to wolves. This here misses all major arteries. It's on the left side so the wound doesn't affect the dominant arm.*

The wolf shifted its approach and bit down on Tal's shoulder.

Joshua felt the magic of the Source flood into Tal. It was like holding onto a fire hose. Tal shifted form, becoming a wolf. Tal's wolf was smaller than Joshua expected, nowhere near as big as Seth or Cabot. Its fur was mostly brown colored with hints of red on its muzzle, behind its ears, and the back of its legs. Its bushy tail was tipped with black. It growled and thrashed, pinned in place by Joshua's hold on its shoulder.

"Focus on the person," Seth had told Ewan as they talked about changing younglings. "You want the child, not the wolf. Think of them as you feel around in a darkness and pull them out into the light."

Joshua closed his eyes and focused on Tal. The swagger of self-confidence as he wore the pants made from a trash bag. Tal singing while juggling to distract the aquarium gift store staff. How he offered up his lunch to the wolf without so much as a roll of his eyes.

"I don't want to die!" Tal whispered far away in the darkness. "Please, God! I don't want to die!"

"Tal?" Joshua focused on the whisper. The green forest of the Source took shape around him. The towering trees. The deep shadows. The sunlight dappling through the leaves. The cool air scented by bruised ferns and autumn leaves.

Joshua's wolf caught Tal's scent. Like all the other boys of Blackridge, he wore a blend of hygiene products. Body wash. Acne soap. Deodorant. Hair gel. Tal favored brands with amber and sandalwood. The wolf tracked him through the trees to where a ghostly version of Tal lay among the bracken; so insubstantial, it seemed like a strong wind could tatter him to nothing.

Tal was attempting to sing bravely. His voice cracked and wavered, whisper thin. "Yes, it's really me...I know it's a lot; the hair, the bod! When you're staring at...when you're staring... Who...Who am I?"

"You're Tal!" Joshua knelt beside the boy and cautiously put a hand to the ghostly shoulder. Under his touch, bone, muscle, and skin took solid form. "You're Tal Palfrey. You're president of the drama club, an actor and...and...good in French and an honor student. You're my friend. A good friend! I don't want to lose you!"

"I'm...I'm Tal."

"Yes, Tal Palfrey."

"Am I dead?"

"No, you're not dead. You're going to be fine." Tal was now a werewolf, but not dead. Hopefully Tal was okay with that. Joshua just needed to pull him...someplace. Somehow. He tightened his hold on Tal's shoulder. "Come with me."

He focused back on his own body. He stepped out of the green forest and into the frozen alien cityscape. He was wolf again, giant-sized, with jaws clamped down on Tal's bare human shoulder. At least Tal wasn't a wolf anymore. Nor did he seem on death's door. His wound was healed shut, although freshly scabbed over and red around the edges.

"Oh good, that worked." Joshua let go of Tal.

Tal stared at his hands as if there was something wrong with them. "Is...Is this me?"

"Yes, that is you." Joshua eyed Tal closely to be sure. The boy's shirt and coat had been shredded by his transformation. Hulklike, he'd managed to keep on pants. He seemed as tall and lean as before; maybe a little more muscular, although Joshua had never seen him half naked so maybe not. His brown hair was a lot longer, shaggy and down to his shoulders with no hair gel keeping it neat and orderly. Otherwise, he looked the same as usual. At first glance, there was no way to know that he was now a werewolf—except maybe because he wasn't shivering while half naked in the freezing cold city.

Tal suddenly leapt backward. "Holy shit!"

Joshua looked around frantically and then realized that Tal was staring at him. "Oh! Yeah, I'm a wolf! A good wolf! I'm just really big—at the moment."

He tried to get smaller and less intimidating, but his wolf wasn't having it.

"Is the snake a good snake too?" Tal pointed at Nam-gi coiled in the shadows.

"Yes. A very good snake." Joshua said. "Nam-gi, where's Ji Su?"

The ghost snake flickered out its tongue and slithered away.

✧   ✧   ✧

Ji Su was well hidden down a dead-end alley, quietly weeping. Her dark Goth makeup was running, leaving black streaks down her face.

"Tal!" she cried and flung herself at the boy. "Nam-gi said you were hurt! I wanted to go find you but Nam-gi left so fast, and...and...I was so scared."

Tal gave Joshua a look that said *I have no idea what's going on! Who is this? Why is she hugging me? Are we dating?*

Joshua had no idea if the two were more than just friends. He'd been a little too self-absorbed to pick up clues about anything. Come to think of it, though, they always did end up side by side at the lunch table and on the subway train. He nodded to Tal.

Tal put his arms around Ji Su and did his best to comfort her like a boyfriend would. "It's okay. Anyone would be scared in this place. It's creepy as hell. Where...where exactly are we anyhow?"

"I'll explain later," Joshua said. "We need to find the others."

"There's others?" Tal said.

This got a "what the hell is going on with Tal?" look from Ji Su.

"It's complicated," Joshua said. "We need to hurry and find the others."

Ji Su scrubbed the tears from her face. "Allie was using her ability to backtrack where Danforth has hidden the Mothers' Stone. We ran into this monster and...and...and we scattered. I got lost and then Nam-gi left me. I have no idea where they are."

Who the hell is Danforth? Joshua didn't ask—they would sort everything out later. Nam-gi apparently went to find Joshua. It seemed to be the default response of spirit guides when their medium became endangered: have the badass werewolf deal with it.

"Can Nam-gi find the others?" Joshua asked.

"I think so," Ji Su said as if she wasn't certain. "Spirit guides get their information from the dead—and this place is loaded with dead. When the Dark One was cursed, everyone in the city died all at once. At least that's what Allie said."

"Let's go." Joshua waved toward the mouth of the alley. The sooner they found the others, the sooner he could get everyone safely back to Cambridge.

✧　　✧　　✧

There were dead creatures littering the way. They looked like starfish—if starfish were the size of small dogs with seriously long slender arms covered with thousands of spines. Someone had riddled their pentagon-shaped bodies with arrows.

"Who has the bow?" Joshua said.

"Vijay," Ji Su said. "It's a holy weapon that had been handed down through his family for generations."

Joshua remembered Vijay shooting the bow in gym class, hitting bull's-eye after bull's-eye. It made sense now why he'd been so good at archery.

He heard a weird rapid drumming and loud hiss. *What now?*

"Run!" Ottilie shouted somewhere beyond the tall buildings in front of Joshua. "I'll hold it off!"

The drumming shifted location, as if whatever was making the noise was moving. It seemed to be heading toward Ottilie. There was no clear way, though, for Joshua to head in her direction. The street Joshua was on curved away, doubling back the way they had just come.

Joshua's wolf took over, leaping to the top of the nearest building for a vantage point.

Vijay and Ottilie were penned in to a dead-end corner, their way blocked by a giant beast that was rushing down the street toward them. It looked like a weird cross between a scorpion and a crab. It had eight long segmented legs. The front pair ended in wicked-looking pincers. The other six legs tapered down to hard sharp points—the source of the loud drumming noise. Its long, hard-shelled body had a stinger tail. Darkness gathered about the barbed end, gleaming black with weird motes of purple swirling around it. It hissed again in anger as Vijay's arrows bounced off its shell.

"So foolish was I, and ignorant: I was as a beast before thee!" Ottilie shouted the start of a spell, right hand upraised, blood trailing down from her palm.

Joshua had a sudden premonition that if Ottilie finished her spell, she would die. "Ottilie! Stop!"

"Nevertheless, I am continually with thee: Thou hast holden me by my right hand!" Ottilie continued as if she didn't hear him. "Thou shalt guide me with thy counsel, and afterward receive me to glory. Whom have I in heaven but thee?"

"Ottilie, don't!" Joshua scrambled across the roofs to leap

down in front of the scorpion crab, blocking it from attacking the Goths. "Don't do...it...whatever you're doing, Ottilie! You won't survive!"

"And there is none upon earth that I desire beside—Joshua?" Ottilie cried in surprise and confusion.

"I'll take care of this!" Joshua said with more confidence than he felt. The crab's mouth was a nightmare of parts, bristling with black spikes and moving around in a chewing motion. It was uncomfortably close to his own face.

"No!" Ottilie shouted. "It's too dangerous! I'll open myself to God and become a Power."

"No, you won't!" Joshua shouted back, dodging the black glowing tail. "Trying to be a Power will kill you—if that thing doesn't kill you first!"

"I've got a charm that lets me safely become a..." Ottilie fumbled with the right-hand pocket of her coat. She gasped as she realized that it was torn nearly off. "Oh no! The charm is gone!"

"Watch out!" Vijay shouted. "There's something weird about that tail!"

The tail came stabbing down at him. Joshua dodged it. It slammed into the ground beside him. Everything at the point of contact rippled weirdly. The landscape distorted and twisted. A small dark spot appeared and then grew, becoming a tear in reality with the darkness of the void leaking through.

"Oh shit!" Joshua leapt away from the tear. "What the hell?"

"It's a demigod!" Ottilie shouted. "It can unmake the fabric of this reality!"

Joshua dodged a right swipe of its pincers. He was painfully aware that, once again, he was in a battle without knowing how to fight as a wolf. The crab scorpion had nine limbs that it could bring into play, and he only had his mouth to create leverage. In video games, it was always important to face monsters away from the supporting characters. He jumped aside, forcing the beast to turn.

"Can a demigod be killed?" Joshua shouted.

"I don't know!" Ottilie shouted. "According to legends, they can be killed by other demigods or powerful artifacts! Hercules was poisoned by the blood of the Hydra. Perseus tried to use the Medusa head in battle as an old man and turned himself into stone."

Odd that those demigods were defeated by their greatest victories. No wonder Ottilie thought she needed to be a Power to deal with the beast.

The crab scorpion snapped at him with another right swipe and then a left. Distracted by the discussion, Joshua barely dodged them. Its pincers had jagged edges like sawblades. He couldn't risk letting the monster grab him. If it held him still for even a few seconds, it could hit him with its tail.

Focus! Competition mode: On! Use the enemy's attack against him!

The tail came slashing toward him. He dodged it. It smelled of sea and dead fish and lightning storms as it flashed past him. It hit with a concussion wave on the ground beside him. Instantly, a tear in reality appeared. Fear spiked through him, cold and primal as the void beyond the hole.

Joshua leapt sideways and then dodged the incoming pincers. How was he going to do this? He couldn't take a hit, but he couldn't attack and still duck the blows. The creature's limbs were all long and multi-segmented. He could grab at a leverage point while running, using momentum and weight to create a throw. Would throwing it make any difference with so many legs to right itself?

Wait—what if he threw it into one of the tears that it had just created? Would that do anything? Would it even fit?

What if he got the demigod to make the tear bigger? He shifted until he was as close to the dark hole as he dared.

"Joshua!" Ottilie shouted. "You idiot! Get away from the tear!"

Well, his fake out was working, at least on Ottilie.

The tail came slamming down where he'd been standing. The ground rippled and distorted. The second tear appeared. It grew, merging with the first one.

Now came the scary part. It was like standing at the edge of an impossibly tall cliff, gathering your courage to grab someone and throw them off it.

He ducked a left swipe with the pincer. As the right one came swinging toward him, he caught the limb immediately behind the pincer and threw his weight into its forward momentum.

It worked perfectly. The momentum and the added weight lifted the crab off its feet and tumbled it toward the hole. Its six legs flailed, trying to stop its roll. It went into the hole.

At the last moment, the left pincer caught his right foreleg. Joshua yelped in pain and fear as he was yanked into the void. He was falling through dark nothingness.

He couldn't see the crab, but he could feel it grinding down on his leg. Its six legs jabbed and prodded at him as if trying to grapple him and pull him closer. The image of its horrific mouth flashed through his mind.

Pure panic flashed through him. His wolf took over. He felt himself grow even larger. He bit down on the pincer holding his foreleg. The crab's shell shattered, releasing his leg. His back legs tucked up and kicked the crab away from him. He was free of the monster but still falling.

Falling into nothingness. The hole far above him, a gleam of moonlight, growing smaller.

Shit! Shit! Shit!

Far above him, Ottilie shouted "Joshua! You idiot!"

And suddenly he was standing over Ottilie—only she was tiny.

Oh, yeah! I can teleport! Adrenaline was rushing through him, making his legs weak. The taste of crab still filled his mouth. He used to love crab! He was never going to be able to eat it again without thinking of falling through the void! Soon all seafood was going to be off his "favorite food" list.

"God in heaven!" Ottilie gasped. "You scared me!" And then she hugged his leg, which was kind of like hugging a furry tree trunk.

"I'm sorry," Joshua said.

"Only a rare few of the Grigori can be a Power," Ottilie said quietly, looking equal parts embarrassed and ashamed. "I knew I wasn't strong enough—but I thought I had to try."

Vijay shouldered his bow and came to hug Ottilie and Joshua's leg. He was shaking with fear. "Oh geez, that was scary! I thought it was going to kill us!"

Tal and Ji Su came running down the street.

"Is everyone okay?" Ji Su asked.

"We're fine," Ottilie answered and then a double take at Tal. "What the hell?"

Tal misunderstood the question. "I'm not sure what happened to my shirt."

Ottilie glared at Joshua.

"I'll explain later." He did a head count and came up short. "Where's Allie?"

"We scattered when the crab thing showed up." Vijay pointed at the hole the monster had fallen through. "We thought we lost it, but it caught up to us after the starfish thingies rushed us."

"One of the starfish must have taken the charm," Ottilie said. "Oh, oh, this is bad. If they took it to Danforth . . . We've got to get it back!"

"We should find Allie first," Joshua said. "She could be hurt or in danger. Once we find her, we can figure out how to get the charm back."

"What's that?" Tal pointed toward the mouth of the dead-end street.

They turned with Joshua stepping forward to protect the others. It was Decker and Maisy.

"What are you doing here?" Joshua cried.

"You forgot the obol," Decker said, holding out the small, shielded box. "You'll need it."

It was frustrating that Decker was probably right but still—why did both of them enter the city? Joshua didn't want Maisy anywhere near all these monsters. More than any of them, she was just a normal person with no magical bow handed down through her family or spirit guide or anything.

Maisy was staring at him with huge eyes. Oh, yes, this was the first time she'd seen him as a wolf. In fact, it probably was the first time for all of the Goths.

Joshua silently argued with his wolf, trying to change back into human. As he did, the wolf edged up against Decker.

"There, there." Decker patted the wolf on the shoulder, which was the highest point that Decker could reach.

The wolf tried to tuck its head under Decker's arm, but it was way too big. It shrank down until it could fit.

"Stupid wolf," Joshua muttered. "Decker, we need to find one more person."

"Two," Ji Su said. "If you count Mannie."

Joshua didn't want to count the penguin. The wolf added its opinion with a low grumble of unhappiness. "Does Mannie at least have weapons?"

Ottilie made a face. "Nothing magical and some are totally improvised but I guess they're better than nothing."

"We need to find Allie," Joshua said to Decker. "She's the touch witch I told you about."

"Ah!" Decker continued to pat the wolf on the back. "I remember."

Since Joshua didn't currently have pockets, Decker tucked the shielded box back into his pocket. He pointed off to the left. "She's that way."

The Goths were terrified. It wasn't hard to tell. They clung to each other, squeaking in fear every time something made a noise. Joshua was terrified for them. They were so fragile compared to Decker or himself. He had already seen Tal lying on the ground, a bloody mess and on the edge of death. He'd gotten lucky and had been able to save Tal. Thinking back, he remembered that Tal had mentioned that he didn't know what all was in his bloodline. Maybe one of his ancestors had been a werewolf. Maybe that was why Tal didn't look like any other wolf that Joshua had seen so far.

The Wickers had nearly killed Decker, Cabot, and himself—and they were just a bunch of witches with god complexes. The Dark One and his minions were actual gods and demigods. Joshua wouldn't be able to protect the Goths if things went south.

Thinking about it, though, was only upsetting the wolf, who kept trying to get its head under Decker's arm.

Deep breaths! Focus! Calm!

He really needed to teach meditation to his wolf. He couldn't keep it together on his own.

35: DECKER

He shouldn't have come into the city.

Long ago, when Decker was still new to being a monster, he had had no idea how to control his hunger. He would try not to feed at all—only to lose control. The hunger would start as dark whispers. A murmur to hunt...feed...wallow in blood. Suck on the warm sweetness that was life force—rawer and more potent than rum.

At first, he'd been horrified that he'd apparently become so evil as to "want" to wantonly kill everything around him. Slowly he came to realize that the whispers were not his own subconscious urging him to act.

He'd been young when he'd become a monster but old enough to have let his own weakness talk him into petty crimes. Steal a pie cooling in the window. Raid the neighbor's apple tree. Filch coins from the pockets of sailors lying drunk in the backstreets. His "gift" of dowsing had been a two-edged sword. True, people would pay dearly to find a misplaced tool or the location of a reliable well. The same God-fearing idiots would be quick to turn on him, calling him warlock or devil's worshiper. It meant that at times he was rich as Midas but other times poor as a church mouse. Temptation was a constant friend but one that spoke in his own voice.

The dark whispers were something outside him. Something that he could block out by staying satiated. But if he wasn't careful, the urges slowly built to irresistible levels. It was like being washed away in a dark flood. Only when his hunger was sated would that darkness ebb back, slowly, restoring his sense of self.

It had taken him over two decades, possibly as many as three, to realize that he had to feed to stop the dark whispers. That starving himself made him vulnerable to the voices.

The city was full of the voice, so loud and clear that for the first time he recognized that it had one source. The Dark One.

"Kill them," the Dark One whispered. "Kill them all. Tear them to pieces. Crack their bones. Suck out their marrow."

Worse, Decker was surrounded by innocent children. Joshua's classmates would be helpless if he became overwhelmed by the voice. One had already nearly died. Joshua might be able to stop Decker—the question was if he could do it in time to save the others.

The only good thing was that while he could hear the voice, he did not feel—yet—the compulsion to obey it.

He focused on the missing touch witch. His talent was an imprecise one to start. The city was a maze of winding streets, dead-end alleys, rises and drops in elevation. They wound their way here and there, up and down, forward and back.

Joshua suddenly wrinkled his nose and said. "Ugh, I smell Mannie. I can lead from here."

Round the next bend, they found a swan maiden tied up.

"Mannie must be trying to save all of his people that he can," Joshua murmured. "I'm not sure how he's capturing them alive."

"He's got bolos that he made with paracord and tennis balls," the baby Grigori said. "They look ridiculous, but they must work well enough."

The swan maiden shouted out something in French. Decker had grown up speaking English, Dutch, and German and with a basic understanding of Latin. He even knew a smattering of Welsh from back when colonial Philadelphia considered using it as an official language. French was something he'd never learned.

"Oh spicy!" the new werewolf puppy said. "I only know half those words but they're all very rude. I'm assuming the others are naughty too."

They moved forward, the children all trembling with fear. There were more bird shapeshifters tied up. All of them annoyed and cursing.

"It seems wrong to leave them like that with all the monsters roaming around," the girl with the giant ghost snake said. "If we find the Mothers' Stone, we should free them as we leave."

Joshua had said that his classmates were nice and generous. Decker thought that they might be foolishly kind—as there was no guarantee that the swan maidens would be grateful for their gentleness.

"Kill the birds," the Dark One whispered. "They will taste so sweet. You know how they taste. You consumed one already. They will make you strong."

Out, damn spot, Decker thought. He normally only killed monsters. In certain regards, the firebird at the mall was no more a monster than Joshua or his brother Seth. It probably hadn't really wanted to attack them—but there had been no other way to stop it while it was under control of the Dark One.

He shouldn't have come into this dead city, but Joshua needed him. The children could offer nothing in the way of killing power. They had one bow and a handful of arrows. They would not be anything but a hindrance to his boy. He could not abandon Joshua—even if the voice urged him to violence.

They came to a wide plaza scattered with swan maidens bound like spider-victims. At the center was a massive conch shell on a dais of white coral. Runes were etched into the rough outer edge. Within the smooth interior of the shell sat a smooth, white, fist-sized rock. Decker guessed it was the Mothers' Stone that controlled the swan maidens.

"Kill the children!" the Dark One urged. "Kill them so they can't free the swan maidens."

A young girl with blue dyed hair waved to them in greeting. Joshua's classmates all cried out "Allie!" This must be the missing touch witch.

"Huh, that's one serious ward," the baby Grigori said. What had Joshua said her name was? Ah, yes, Ottilie.

"Multiple *joder* wards!" a male voice from the other side of it. "I can't even get near it!"

That would be the Argentinian rockhopper, Mannie. A young man, barely older than the Blackridge students, came storming around the conch. He was lightly dressed—Decker felt cold just looking at him—in a T-shirt and shorts. While his hair was mostly coal black, he had spiky blond bangs and eyebrows. He glared at Decker with red eyes.

"*Joder!* What's that?" Mannie pointed at Decker.

Joshua shifted between Mannie and Decker. "This is Silas Decker. Be nice. My wolf is already annoyed to hell and back."

Mannie muttered something in Spanish quietly enough that Decker couldn't make out the words. The wolf's keen ears heard enough to growl dangerously.

Decker reached up and caught the wolf by the scruff of his neck. He doubted he could stop Joshua from lunging at Mannie, but he had to try—Joshua would be upset with himself if he hurt the weaker shapeshifter.

Mannie flapped his arms as if they were still short stubby wings. "See, that is what we don't have to deal with—our Source pushing us around, making us do what the Source wants. We swim free."

"According to my elders, their wolves are just an extension of their id," Ottilie said. "It's balanced by their ego and superego— just like a normal human. A newborn wolf is temporarily reduced back to a toddler state where the id can run rampant until the dominant personally can rein it back to what is culturally acceptable behavior."

"Now is not the time for this discussion," Joshua growled.

"Can one of us breach the ward and get the Mothers' Stone?" The ghost-snake girl looked to the baby Grigori.

Ottilie shook her head. Only Virtues and Powers, who were connected to God's strength, could cast the Grigori spells. The "lesser" of the angelic people lacked power to do so without a secondary power source like a candle or lit brazier.

"I tried already," Allie said. "It seems to be warded against humans with divine gifts and swan maidens—"

"And Grigori and werewolves!" Mannie snapped with irritation. "Everyone that could come to our aid!"

Joshua glanced toward Decker with an unasked question. Decker was born with the divine gift of dowsing but that had been overshadowed by becoming a vampire. He might be enough of the Dark One's creature to pierce the ward.

"I can try," Decker said reluctantly. He was already besieged by the Dark One's whispers. Currently he was able to ignore them because the overwhelming urge to feed that normally accompanied them was absent. He wasn't sure how long he could hold out against it if the need set in.

The trip through the werewolf Source had been like a rich

feast of power. He had been drunk on the overwhelming magic influx. Maybe that was why he didn't feel the normal need.

He walked to the giant conch. It loomed over him. It radiated a sense of the otherworldly. He guessed that the shell had never been part of Earth. It came into being in this primal place where chaos reigned. The sea snail had been stained by evil even as it grew to a massive size. Everything about it seemed twisted and wrong.

While the runes of the wards were visible, he could only faintly feel the actual magic shields. They felt like a tangle of barbwire, multiple strands of dangerous spikes to keep out trespassers, harming those who tried to breach them, and trapping the unwary.

Decker braced himself and reached out toward the Mothers' Stone.

The wards were layered thick. His hand hit resistance that slowly gave way. It was like shoving his hand into a thorn bush. Yes, the shielding magic yielded but it tore bloody trails across the back of his hand. His blood scented the air, stirring the first sense of needing to feed.

Decker whispered a curse, struggling not to jerk back his hand from the pain.

"Leave that be!" the Dark One commanded. "Kill the intruders. Feed on their life force!"

I won't listen to you, Decker thought fiercely. He had feasted on the werewolves' Source—this wasn't his true hunger borne from need. This was the Dark One toying with him.

"Kill them!" the Dark One whispered. "Feed!"

Decker growled in anger and frustration. Pushing slowly was only going to extend his torture. He plunged his hand to the core of the wards.

The pain became white-hot daggers stabbing into his hand.

"Feed!"

The need to feed roared through him. He felt his fangs grow long. His eyes went all black.

"Oh, mother of God!" the new puppy breathed, backing away from Decker. "What's gotten into him?"

"No, no, no." Joshua stepped close, looming over him as a massive wolf. "Decker, keep it together."

"Feed!" the Dark One urged.

Decker jerked the Mothers' Stone out of the ward. "I am not your tool!"

He staggered back, gripping the stone tightly.

"Decker?" Joshua kept between him and his classmates. "Are you okay?"

His hands caught hold of the wolf's head and pulled it close. His lips curled back. He could only growl in helpless anger as his body moved by itself.

"No biting!" Joshua cried but didn't attempt to move away.

That's what Decker had promised on the first night they had met. A laugh welled up and forced its way out, past the control of the Dark One. It was like a juggernaut, making a way for his true self to follow and reclaim his body.

"Yes, no biting," Decker laughed. He leaned against the massive wolf's forehead. He glanced down at his right hand. It was bleeding profusely, dripping down onto the white coral pavers. He could see the white of his finger bones in places where his skin had been scraped off. As he gazed at the wounds, though, they healed shut.

"Great!" Joshua breathed in relief. "We can free the swan maidens and get out of here."

Mannie came waddling over. "Give me the Mothers' Stone."

Decker tossed it to him. He felt the ripple of power as Mannie released his people from the Dark One's control. The imprisoned swan maidens stopped their cursing. They murmured "I'm so sorry" as the children freed them.

"We should go," Decker said. "The Dark One knows that we're here."

36: JOSHUA

They hadn't gotten far in the "escape from the lost city" plan when there was a weird loud echoing sound that rang out. The ground shook and the dark water within the tidal pools surged.

"What?" Ji Su cried. "Oh no! Nam-gi says that Danforth has activated some kind of machine."

The swan maidens let out a wail of despair.

"Who?" Joshua asked. "What?"

"The Dark One's Touched." "His servant!" multiple swan maidens cried out. "Danforth has been building a magical device at the center of the city!" "Danforth has powerful artifacts that his family has gathered through the ages." "Danforth found a strong vessel for the Dark One! The Power's driver, Roustabout." "The Dark One comes!" "There's no way to stop him! He will slay the holder of the Mothers' Stone and we'll be enslaved once more!"

Mannie puffed up, trying to look brave, but his voice betrayed his fear. "H-h-he can try."

All of the swan maidens wailed like an entire flock of geese. "All is lost! The world will be swallowed in darkness and the sea will run red with blood."

Joshua couldn't help but agree. Mannie had been a pushover at Blackridge; even Ottilie had been able to kick him around. Joshua scanned the other swan maidens. Most of them were small in build with blond highlights like Mannie. They were probably the missing rockhopper flock. None of the others looked like heavy hitters. There weren't any with the red hair of the firebird. If the swan maidens fell back under the Dark One's control, Joshua wouldn't be able to keep the Goths safe—not while fighting all the birds at once.

He'd fought a demigod and won. Could he fight an actual god?

Yes! Yes! The swan spirit Sioux Zee summoned had said. *It would drive him out of his vessel and send him back to his palace to sleep once more.*

They still had the obol—didn't they? With it, he could at least try. If the god was too hard—he could teleport. Maybe. "Decker, you have the obol?"

Decker gave him a look full of anguish and fear. With a trembling hand, he held out the small shielded box. "I...I won't be able to fight him, Joshua. I might scream at the heavens that I'm not his creature, but I can hear his voice whispering to me to do terrible things. I'm afraid that he can force me into actions that I do not want to take."

"It's okay. It's okay," Joshua repeated, unsure of what else to say. After seeing Tal torn apart and dying, Joshua didn't want the Goths anywhere near the bad guys. If he could get to this Danforth before the Dark One was fully awake and present, it might be a simple fight. Throw Danforth to the other side of the city, smash the device he made, rescue that Roustabout guy so Danforth couldn't use him for anything—and then run. "Get everyone out of the city. I've got this."

"You don't have to do this," Decker said. "We can run, and call Elise, and Francis could—"

"There isn't time," Joshua growled with sudden certainty. "I have to go now, or I'll be too late."

Joshua snatched the box from Decker's hand with his teeth. He leapt to the nearest rooftop and worked his way higher and higher until he could see over the maze of twisting streets. At the heart of the city was a gleaming plaza made of mother-of-pearl. It glistened in a rainbow of color. It should have been stunningly beautiful, but there were just too many creepy elements added to it. At the center of the plaza was a wading pool full of blood. The dank coppery smell of it hung thick in the air. Roustabout was chained in the pool. He struggled against his bonds, shouting. Poised over him like some kind of cyberpunk spider in a web of wire and gleaming electronics and glowing spell runes was a weird contraption that radiated "mad scientist evil world domination device."

Danforth stood on an upraised podium/altar. Half a dozen of those giant starfish were swarming toward the man. Joshua did not want to get into a grappling fight with them. Nor could he tell which one was carrying the talisman that they'd taken from Ottilie, or even if one of them actually had it. The one that snagged the talisman could be lying dead from one of Vijay's arrows.

"The Lord is my shepherd; I shall not want!" Roustabout shouted at the top of his lungs. "He maketh me to lie down in green pastures: He leadeth me beside the still waters!"

"Your God does not listen to prayers," Danforth shouted back. "He never answers them. He leaves humans to muddle on."

Roustabout shook his head. "You hover over toddlers. But as children grow, you step back and give them freedom to learn from their mistakes. Why else would He make heaven a place to enter once we've grown to be enlightened? If He didn't want us to have freedom to worship Him however we wanted, He'd write His rules in the sky where all could read them."

"Shut up, you stupid sheep!" Danforth flipped a big switch. "He never came for me! He'll never come for you!"

Roustabout screamed as the blood surged up his body. "He... He restoreth...my...soul! He leadeth...me..."

Joshua raced toward the man. He had to act now, or he'd lose the fight even before it began. At the edge of the pool, he dropped the shielded box onto the ground. "I need to be human now!" Amazingly, his wolf cooperated. He changed to human and scooped up the box to fumble out the ancient coin. He forced himself to hold it firmly as the power within it crawled across his flesh. It felt angry and impatient.

Joshua leapt down into the pool of blood. The blood surged around him, grabbing hold of him like the tentacles of the monster at the aquarium. His wolf growled, wanting to shift form.

"Not. Yet." Joshua forced his way forward to Roustabout.

"Damn wolf!" Danforth shouted. "Get away from him!"

The blood had surged up to Roustabout's torso and then climbed to his neck. All the muscles in the man's body were taut as he forced the words "I. Will. Fear. No. Evil."

Joshua shoved the obol in Roustabout's mouth. The man's eyes went wide. From his mouth and nose and ear and eyes, a thick black liquid oozed out. As the black liquid seeped downward, bristling in anger, the blood fled before it.

Was that it? Did we win? Something felt off—like they were still far from winning. Joshua grabbed the chains that were holding Roustabout. He jerked them free from their anchors.

The black liquid clung like tar to Roustabout, not draining down into the pool. The blood, however, moved like a shapeless creature. It surged toward Danforth on the altar, flowing up the steps.

"No!" Danforth shouted. "No! Don't take me! Him! Use him!"

The blood washed up onto the altar and surrounded Danforth.

"I'll find another!" Danforth cried as he was enveloped. "Please! Spare me!"

Danforth screamed as the blood covered him completely. For a few seconds, the red mass was easily identifiable as a man. Then the red mass grew and changed as it writhed. Huge tentacles stretched out of the blood, darkening to pure black even as they took form. A massive fish head formed with a gaping mouth and rows of ragged teeth.

"Oh, shit," Joshua whispered. How was he supposed to fight that? If he didn't, who would?

One of the massive tentacles reached for him. He shifted into a massive wolf—the largest he'd ever been. It was growling with the anger and fear. His wolf charged the creature without a plan.

"This is not a good idea," Joshua growled, dodging slaps by the massive tentacles. The god-monster was growing larger and larger, sprouting more tentacles.

A tentacle smashed Joshua across the plaza. He landed hard, rolling to dodge a second hit.

He came to his feet just short of Enyo, who was hidden in a small alcove and eating a tub of popcorn.

"Good college try!" Enyo cried. "Give it another go! You still have some time before the Dark One grows a new body that can fully contain his power. Not much, but some."

"Don't you care what happens to the world?" Joshua snarled.

"It's fate!" Enyo said. "It doesn't matter if I care or not. All that changes is the body count in the end. And being dead is just a state of mind. Give it another try! You might succeed. See the bright glimmer on its forehead? That's the soul talisman that your little Grigori friend lost. Good for her, she would have gone up in flames, but bad for you as it's making Danforth's body able to withstand the Dark One's power. You have about ninety seconds to get it off the Dark One before he becomes invincible, even to a Power. If not... well, it will still be entertaining to watch."

His wolf roared and lunged forward. It caught her by her coat and flung her as hard as it could. She went soaring through the sky like an awkward bird.

"Oh, that was not cool!" Joshua chided his wolf. Distracted, he barely dodged the incoming tentacle.

In the center of the god-monster's forehead, dangling from a bony spike, was Ottilie's soul talisman. Joshua raced toward the god-monster, dodging slaps by the massive tentacles. He leapt, aiming to snag the talisman with his teeth. A tentacle smashed him out of the air. He landed hard, rolling to dodge a second hit.

One of the tentacles caught hold of him. It wrapped tight around his midsection and snatched him off the ground. He struggled to wriggle free, biting savagely at the tentacle that held him. Even as he tore chunks of flesh from the limb, the wounds healed close. The god-monster smashed him against the ground again and again. He yelped in pain.

Roustabout came to his rescue, using the chains that had bound his wrists as a flail. He beat on the tentacle until it dropped Joshua in favor of trying to grab the human. The black coating, however, bristled. The tentacles shied back as if afraid.

The moment of distraction gave Joshua an opening. He charged and leapt high over the monster. As he fell, he transformed back to human. He landed on the god-monster's head. Plucking the talisman from the spike, he shoved it into his pants pocket and shifted back to wolf. It sent the amulet to the werewolf's Source.

The god-monster howled. The sound was deafening. All of the tentacles reached for him in a desperate scramble to retrieve the amulet.

"It's gone! You'll never get it back!" Joshua shouted.

Cracks formed in the god-monster's skin. They become fissures through which darkness seemed to leak out. The monster flailed and howled. It seemed to be shrinking.

Suddenly, there was another massive being in the plaza. It was glowing white with multiple wings. It hovered in the air, blazing like a white star.

"Francis!" Roustabout shouted.

"That's Francis?" Joshua said.

Roustabout nodded. "We should run! Don't look back! Just run!"

37: SETH

"The king is awake," Thane Mandeville had said as he handed a replacement phone to Seth. "He wants to see you and Isaiah immediately. I'm heading up to Westchester."

The Retreat was a seven-bedroom house surrounded by national park in Westchester County. The king rarely used it as it was too small for more than a dozen of the Thanes. The basement had a reinforced cage, strong enough to hold even a prince.

Seth took the stairs up to the king's penthouse suite, feeling queasy. He was afraid that he knew what was coming and what it could mean for the future.

He expected to find the king as a man dressed in his normal suit or at least his old-fashioned nightclothes. Instead, Alexander was a white wolf lying in front of the roaring fire in his ancient hearth. Bishop was the only elder Thane in the room. The others probably were off, seeing to things that had gone undone while the king slept.

There were so many questions that Seth wanted to ask, but Isaiah had beaten him to the suite.

"Here." Bishop handed a paper to Isaiah.

"What is this?" Isaiah asked.

Alexander indicated the list of names on the paper. "Choose a dozen of my Thanes to make up your pack."

"What?" Isaiah said, not understanding what it meant.

Seth stepped back, feeling like he'd been punched hard in the stomach. At the moment, Isaiah couldn't stand up to Seth. If he became Prince of New York, Isaiah would be stronger than Seth.

Joshua wouldn't be safe in New York, nor Jack or even Seth himself.

New York City was about to become hell on Earth.

Seth took a second step backward, feeling panic set in.

"You're to choose which of the Thanes will be yours," Alexander said.

"What?" Isaiah said again.

"I am making you Prince of New York," Alexander said.

"Now?" Isaiah cried.

"Preparations need to be made." Alexander snapped. Hundreds of years in New York and yet Alexander retained a rough accent from some ancient language; Seth was never sure if it was Latin or Greek or something older. The first sign of his annoyance was that the accent grew stronger. "Until I am sure you will not go feral, you will need to be isolated with those who are part of your pack close at hand."

"I'm getting New York?" Isaiah looked stunned. "I'm getting New York!" He threw his fists up in the air. "Yes! Finally!"

Isaiah bounced in place as excitement filled him. For a moment, he looked like he would fling himself at his father to hug, but then he obviously thought better of it. He gave Seth a measuring look, rejected him as a possible celebrant, and hugged Bishop instead.

"Go, talk to the ones you pick, explain what is about to happen. Make sure that they wish to follow you to a new pack."

Isaiah bounded toward the door but stopped short to turn and ask, "What about my wife? Who is she?"

"Go." Alexander motioned him away without giving any sign that there would be a wife.

Isaiah's brow furrowed with jealous anger as he glanced toward Seth. The old Marquis of Albany had claimed that Isaiah would never be made prince because the king had never given him a wife. What did it mean that Alexander had given him just half of his promised birthright?

"You are going to give me a wife? Right? I'm nearly thirty! I should have a half dozen kids by now. You promised . . ."

"I promised nothing." Alexander didn't move but his anger filled the room. Bishop and Isaiah knelt instantly. Seth decided that it would be advantageous to allow the weight of the power push him to the ground. "If you go feral, your mate would be the first to follow you unless her breeding somehow managed to save her. I have no unwed females who could bear the weight of New York."

Isaiah stabbed a finger toward Seth. "His wife! They've only seen each other once. He's still too young to father children. She could—"

"She is mine!" Seth snapped even though he knew that he should be silent. He would be damned if he allowed Kate to be married to someone as childish and petty as Isaiah.

Alexander glanced at Seth to silence him. "She belongs to herself. She is not a thing to be passed around."

"You shuffle people around like chess pieces." Isaiah whispered the rebellious words, probably unable to summon the power to state them louder. "You gave her to him."

"I offered her Boston; Seth is part and parcel of all that is Boston. I offered to make her a princess of a ruined city and a shattered pack. I laid out the risks and the rewards as much as she could understand it at her age. My people are not my slaves. They are my children as much as you are my child. If you do not want to be Prince of New York, say so now. Know that if you go feral, I'll be forced to put you down."

"I. Want. It," Isaiah whispered fiercely as if the alpha was air itself.

"Prepare yourself." Alexander flicked a paw toward the door.

Isaiah staggered to his feet. "What of the Thanes?"

"What of them?" Alexander said.

"If I go feral, don't they run the same risk as my wife?" Isaiah said.

"Yes," Alexander said.

"Why?" Isaiah whispered with confusion and anger. "Why not wait to move them until afterward?"

"Because you cannot bear the alpha alone. You are not Seth. You could never stand against Boston with only a wife and one Thane. Without a dozen Thanes supporting you, New York would crush you instantly."

Isaiah gave Seth a look filled with hatred.

"Go," the king said. "Talk to your wolves. Prepare them."

Isaiah stalked out of the room. Bishop bowed to the king and left to follow some unspoken order.

Seth remained kneeling, trying to stay in control of his wolf. He needed to keep the conversation from shifting to why he lost his temper at school. He had to keep Joshua in Boston. When he was thirteen and his family had been killed, he'd only suffered the loss through the nebulous connection that all pack members had for each other. Each of his little brothers dying had been like a dim, distant light being snuffed out. As prince, though, he would feel his older brother's death as if it were his own body. Joshua was a powerful wolf; he might be able to hold his own against Isaiah if the older man were just a Thane. When Isaiah became the Prince of New York, though, there wasn't anyone on the planet other than Alexander who could stand against him.

"Isaiah isn't strong enough to hold New York," Seth said. "If he was, you would have given it to him long ago."

Alexander sighed deeply. "He will hold long enough."

How long was 'long enough'? Seth's grandfather had only lasted twenty years with a strong wife and elderly aunts and uncles who burned out with him. By the time Seth's father had become prince, the pack was only his grandfather's children. It meant that all the Thanes who joined Isaiah would also die young.

Seth's mother had been a hasty substitute for his father's murdered first wife. The funeral was barely done when she'd arrived in Boston with orders to provide an heir as soon as possible. It was why Seth was less than a year younger than Joshua. Everyone had said—in whispers—that while she was a strong wolf, she didn't compare to the powerhouse that had been Anastasia.

Until recently, Seth hadn't considered how he was bearing Boston without strain. Kate had to be as strong a wolf as he was. It would explain how he could carry the power with Jack as his only other support. It would also explain why the king had yanked her family across the country in a matter of hours for the emergency wedding.

"I will not give him my wife, Kate," Seth said. "But a strong female could save him. Is there really no female that could support him enough to make him able to safely hold New York?"

"It might seem as if I'm heartlessly moving my people like chess pieces, but it is not by choice nor without great grief. We are magical beasts. We are constrained by fate. Your marriage at such a young age was forced upon me by the breach that killed your family. Without your bride, you would have gone feral and taken Boston with you. Luckily, you two were already fated to be mates. It was only a matter of speeding up the process. Among our people, there is a female who could save Isaiah—but it is not her fate. I cannot offer her to Isaiah—nor would I want to, for she is much too young and far too headstrong. The two would tear the territory apart in their disputes."

"For the sake of Boston," Seth's mother used to say, "I will not argue this point."

While his parents' marriage had not been affectionate, they were both deeply committed to protecting their territory.

The old Marquis of Albany had claimed that the king had planned for Isaiah. Did even he guess how ruthless that plan was?

"When you grow as old as I am, while the future is fraught with surprises, you come to be able to guess what lies ahead. I knew that I would need a strong prince to whom I could pass my wisdom. I thought it would be your father. I am sorry that I needed to allow Isaiah to ride roughshod over you, but I needed you two to come to an understanding that he cannot push you around. I thought too that you would need that inner tenacity to deal with your older brother. I was afraid that he would be twisted by a long captivity among the Wickers. I am glad that he is as straightforward as he is—despite the troubles that it will bring you."

"He cannot be here where Isaiah can reach him."

"I know." Alexander considered Seth for several minutes. He broke his silence by starting out slowly, as if carefully picking out his words. "Once upon a time, I took years to train my princes, teaching them all that I knew before setting them in place. The world has grown too large. We have spread too wide. Cruel fate, though, has brought you to me to be trained as those of times long gone by."

"Yes, I'm aware that you've been training me, but I don't understand—why didn't you train your son at the same time?"

"The Court of Saint Petersburg is very isolated in comparison to almost any other Court in the world. Raisa had never dealt with outsiders. Her eye strayed to another and her heart followed. I'd hoped that by simply removing the temptation, she would come back to me—but she killed herself instead. I should have known—wolves mate for life."

Seth reeled under the unsaid implications. Isaiah wasn't the Wolf King's son? That would explain why he wasn't strong enough to hold New York. Isaiah looked so much like his mother that no one had ever questioned who his father was.

"I cannot, in good conscience, allow Isaiah to have children," Alexander said. "He would make them part of his pack and when he dies, one by one, they would be crushed by New York. Nor—if they were anything like their father—could they peacefully step aside if I managed to find someone to take Isaiah's place. There is no good end for him having heirs.

"If I had any other choice, I would simply keep him from taking New York," he continued. "I'm afraid that fate has pushed me to accept what I cannot change. For good or evil, he will be Prince of New York."

"I . . . I cannot stay here if he's Prince of New York," Seth said. "Not if you don't give him a wife. He'll remain deadly jealous of me until he has all that I have."

"You're to pack all your belongings and return to Boston," Alexander said. "And call your wife. I will not ask for an heir for Boston immediately. You will need her close in the days to come."

As recently as last week, Alexander had refused to consider allowing Seth to return to Boston. Had something happened beyond an entire day of deep sleep?

"Why now?" Seth said.

Alexander narrowed his eyes. His power surged over Seth, overwhelming, forcing Seth to bow his head against his will.

Seth growled softly, hating it when the king used his dominance on him.

"Of all my wolves," Alexander said, "only you can stand against my power. Fate forces my hand. Isaiah must hold New York for as long as he is able. I need you in Boston, ready for the worst. I give you leave to open your pack to any who wish to change alliances. Gather to you anyone who can be trusted."

Seth had been dragged from Boston, angry and defiant, ignorant of so many things. He hadn't known that the king had wanted him in New York City to save his life. He hadn't known until recently that the king had wanted all his little brothers to accompany Seth and that their father had refused the king's orders. Alexander had known that disaster was about to fall on Boston. He had tried to save the bloodline while leaving enough wolves behind to protect the city. Seth's father had accidentally doomed his youngest children because he didn't trust the king.

It was terrifying to think that it was now Seth's turn to stand and face the enemy. What if he failed as badly as his father had?

38: ELISE

Elise and Cabot were almost to Bog Hollow when Cabot suddenly snarled in anger.

Elise tightened her hands on the wheel, bracing for an attack. Francis's SUV was two hundred feet ahead of her Jeep. The bright yellow of the Escalade made it easy to follow despite the strangely dark night. There was nothing dangerous in any of Elise's mirrors, except the angry wounded Thane in her backseat. "What is it?"

Cabot growled. "The king is making Isaiah the Prince of New York!" His phone dinged again. He'd been updating the frantic Seth, so the news was probably from him. "Oh! Good! The king has ordered Seth and his wife to Boston!"

"Oh!" Elise echoed his surprise. "That's great!"

Boston really needed Seth and Cabot to be present, not in New York, hours away. It had only been a few weeks since Joshua moved into the city, but the number of monsters was way down. She and Cabot worked well together. Hopefully the boys would stay safe in school. Theo didn't like werewolves because she was constantly having to negotiate jurisdiction with them. That could be just Theo being Theo and the Viscount of Burlington being a middle-aged wolf set in his ways. Elise simply didn't want to put Seth at risk, and Joshua was a sweet, clumsy dork who was easy to push around.

Cabot's phone dinged again. "Oh! Seth is already packing to move up! If he can get a truck, he plans to drive up tomorrow with everything." He murmured a curse while typing. "I need to get a place for us to rent."

"You might be better off buying a condo than trying to rent. I had Central buy my condo with cash after not being able to cough up all the paperwork that the rental places wanted. All the apartments I looked at had some weird math calculations that they did based on monthly salary—something like 'you need to show that you earn three times the monthly rent.' We Virtues don't handle money like that: Central covers all our expenses. It means that our electricity won't be turned off because we're off saving the world instead of paying bills."

"We do the same," Cabot said. "I think I found a nice place. The size and location are perfect. I was going to see it this weekend. I'm asking the real estate agent if I can take it sight unseen. If it's not good, we can always find someplace better later. I've given her our bank reference—she seemed to accept that."

By "bank reference," Cabot probably meant confirmation that his family owned the bank. The Tatterskeins had spent centuries building wealth in Boston. The real estate agent probably rolled over and accepted that "money is not a concern" with Cabot.

"Where is this apartment?" Elise asked.

"Cambridge, a few blocks from Blackridge. We wanted our wolves to be able to walk to Harvard or Boston University or MIT if they came for school."

A few blocks from her condo.

"Wow." Her mind went to a naughty place where she and Cabot didn't have to worry about underage boys in the adjacent bedroom. She blushed, glad that the inside of the Jeep was dark. "That's...that's great!"

His phone dinged again. "Oh, good. She's willing to do it now. I just need to transfer the money and electronically sign the leases."

The yellow Escalade suddenly slammed on its brakes. Elise slowed down and then stopped behind it. She couldn't see anything wrong. She flipped on her emergency flashers to warn any oncoming cars.

"What's wrong?" Cabot asked.

"I don't know." Elise's phone rang. She hit the ANSWER button on her steering wheel.

"Francis vanished!" Theo shouted over the phone. "God fucking moved him again!"

"I'm searching for his phone," Clarice said in fake calm mode. Theo must have conferenced her in. "It will take a few minutes until it pings off a tower."

"He could be anywhere on the freaking planet!" Theo snapped. The SUV started to move again. "I'm continuing to Bog Hollow."

Elise followed, turning off her flashers.

"New update on the kids," Clarice said. Her initial report was what started Elise and the others toward Bog Hollow. "All but Joshua are out of the Dark One's city. They've freed the swan maidens, so you don't need to worry about fighting that army. Ottilie says that Joshua went to stop Danforth at the center of the city. She says he needs backup but that she doesn't have any magical weapons."

"Keep her out of this," Theo growled. "Chances are good that's where Francis went. If he's in there, then the biggest danger is friendly fire."

"I agree with that," Elise said.

Chaos reigned at Bog Hollow. The driveway was blocked by a big van with BOUNCE CIRCUS! CASTLE AND WATER SLIDE! written on its side. A weird assortment of birds milled about. There were an entire flock of penguins, dozens of big white swans, and smaller black penguins with bright red bills, some tall Japanese cranes, and doves looking tiny in comparison to the other birds. The birds squawked and wailed and trumpeted and roared and shouted in a dozen different languages. They made a deafening cacophony.

Theo had somehow muscled Francis's Escalade past the van. Elise pulled in far enough to get her rear bumper off the road. Cabot whimpered in pain as he half fell out of the back to join her in the snow.

Behind the van and the milling birds lay the cranberry bog, frozen over with winter. A ghostly city rose from the ice, its towers soaring hundreds of feet up, reaching for the dark night sky. Its towers and spires looked alien in design. The odd whistling sound of a Dissonance was unmistakably loud.

Cabot pointed. "That's bad, isn't it?"

"Possibly," Elise said. "It depends if Francis is actually here or not."

Cabot cocked his head. "Do you hear that?"

"That" was a sound like a thousand voices vocalizing in harmony. It started softly but grew in volume until it drowned out the birds. She sensed that the voices were singing words, but they were ones that she couldn't understand. Not just the language but the concepts behind the words beyond that God was great. It demanded worship. It washed over her, forcing her to kneel. All around her, the birds knelt in reverence.

"What is that?" Cabot growled as he was forced to the ground.

"Francis," Elise whispered. "This is what he's like when he's going full out. This is God's power, pure and simple."

A gleaming figure appeared over the city. It was a mass of too many wings to be anything natural. Its light grew brighter and brighter.

"Look away!" she shouted to all in hearing range. "Close your eyes and cover them!"

Warmth like a summer breeze washed over them with the smell of spring. For a moment, she thought she felt something brush over her head, like an adult's hand when she was a child. *Well done*, it seemed to say to her. Tears welled up in her eyes.

She realized that she'd been afraid that by dating a werewolf, God would be disappointed in her. She'd been comforting herself with the fact that none of the rules put down by God had included who the Grigori could fall in love with. Her mother and grandfather had slept with Decker, but she'd been secretly afraid that they were repeating the sins of their angelic founders.

Even with her eyes closed and covered, the light leaked in as the warmth washed over her. It was like staring up at the sun on a clear summer day. The brilliance grew until it seemed as if she didn't have her eyes protected at all.

And then the light faded.

Elise cautiously opened her eyes. The city was gone. The ice was melted, and steam rose up to create a mist over the bog. Francis was drifting down out of the sky, nearly human except for the glow of holiness that still surrounded him. It made him more beautiful than she'd ever seen him.

"The king always warned us that Powers were impossibly strong and not to be messed with," Cabot murmured. "I didn't know how understated that warning was until now."

"Theo! Elise!" Francis called as he alighted, gently as a feather.

"I found Roustabout! Well... actually... not exactly. He's here somewhere. He knew what was coming and took off running."

"Francis!" a male voice called.

"There he is!" Francis bounded away as if gravity barely pertained to him.

The tall man was handing a battered Joshua over to Decker. It wasn't clear who had rescued whom. Roustabout threw wide his arms just as Francis flung himself at the man.

"You came for me," Roustabout said as Francis bawled with guilt. "That's all that matters. I had faith that you would find me. It kept me strong, knowing that you would not stop until you found me."

With a thunder of wings, all the swan maidens that were capable of flight took off. They wheeled in the dark skies as flocks and headed off in different directions by species. The swans headed north to Boston proper, probably to catch planes out of Logan International. The doves and the cranes went southwest, heading toward New York. While the penguins couldn't fly away, many of their kind were in human form and making phone calls—seemingly trying to arrange for transportation.

"Looks like we missed all the fun," Theo grumbled as she came up beside Elise. "I suppose all's well that ends well."

Elise was just glad that she hadn't needed to fight all the various shapeshifters, nor figure out how to get them all home. What to do with monster bodies was among the most hated aspects of her job.

"Let's grab our people and get out of here before something triggers Francis," Elise said.

39: DECKER

Something was wrong with him.

Gloriously wrong.

It was three hours to sunset and Decker was sitting at the kitchen counter, drinking tea, watching the sunlight move through the house like a long-lost lover. Joshua had replaced all the sun-rotted drapes with sheers, which let light pour in through the big windows. It was marvelous.

Decker hadn't drunk any liquid for two centuries or more when he gave up trying to social drink. He'd woken up—in the middle of the day—oddly thirsty and found a box of tea called English Breakfast in the kitchen. Apparently, the Boston wolves had kept their British habit of being tea drinkers. Seth and Cabot had had tea every morning of their visit. Joshua had this marvelous contraption—an electric kettle that could boil water in mere minutes—but sadly, he hadn't bought any tea strainers or teapots. It seemed something like sacrilege to pour the hot water on the teabag. The resulting liquid had a wonderful taste that spread warmth through him. It might make him sick later, but the tea was splendid.

The question was, why? After three hundred years, he thought he'd fully understood the limits of his existence. Why was he suddenly awake so early and feeling alive? Why was he thirsty for water and could drink this tea without feeling ill? Was it because Francis had killed the Dark One that controlled Decker for so long? Or was it from being dragged through the werewolf Source?

Considering he started to wake up early prior to the fight in the lost city, it would seem as if the trigger hadn't been the death of the Dark One. It must have been his repeated exposure to the werewolf Source. He had been feeding on it exclusively for almost a month. It never occurred to him that changing the type of magic he existed on would change him.

Maybe he should have Joshua drag him through his Source a few more times.

As he considered the possible dangers, someone stomped their way up the front steps and rang the doorbell.

Who in the world was at his front door? He went to the hall and peered down the dark passage to the leaded glass front door. Whoever it was, they were surprisingly short. A child or a dwarf. Maybe a tall penguin—considering life for the last few days. The problem was that the hallway was drenched in sunlight. Would he burn if he answered the door?

He moved to the very edge of the sunlight and put out his left pinkie on the theory that it would be the least annoying body part to lose. The light danced on his fingernail. He couldn't feel any burning. He pushed more and more of his left hand into the sunlight. Nothing.

He slowly and cautiously walked to the door. The leaded glass distorted his view, but he could see that one of Joshua's classmates stood on the front porch. The little Dominion in training. What was her name? Ottilie.

He opened the door and instantly regretted it. He'd forgotten how bitterly cold it had been the last few days. Thankfully, the furnace kicked on and he retreated to the air duct to get warm again.

"Come in! Come in!" he called from the warmth of the duct. "I'm sorry but Joshua isn't here. He was going to go straight from school to some apartment that Thane Cabot rented this morning."

Ottilie stood in the open doorway a moment, looking unsure. "I-I-I didn't expect you to be awake," she said, but she did step into the house and shut the door. "I did come to see you, so I guess that's a good thing."

"You came to see me?" Decker repeated in surprise.

She nodded, undoing her silk scarf of burnt red and orange and yellow that beautifully framed her dark curls. She was going to be a stunning woman when she grew up. "I thought Joshua would be home and I could ask him if you would mind...talking."

"Talking?" Decker echoed, still surprised and now confused as he realized that Joshua wouldn't have given his home address to a classmate, not even a Grigori one. "How did you know where we lived?"

She blushed and fidgeted shyly. "When I got the charms for the mediums at the Watertown Depot, there was this old bill in the sign-out catalog with your name on it. Based on the post-mark, Virtue Saul started to use it as a bookmark shortly after you moved to Boston and never threw it away."

That sounded like Saul.

It had been years since he'd had a visitor. Centuries, if one didn't count Elsie introducing her cousins to the family's pet monster.

"Would you like some tea? Coffee?" He wasn't sure how to make it, but he knew that both Seth and Elise had been drink-ing some over the Thanksgiving holiday. "I think we have hot chocolate."

"Tea would be nice." Ottilie undid the toggle closures on her black duffle coat. Underneath she had on her school uniform. She must have come straight from Blackridge. Joshua had gone straight to his brother's new apartment to help him move in.

Decker hung her coat in the closet and led the way back to the kitchen. She took a perch on one of the tall chairs at the island while Decker set out the tea makings of cups, bags, sugar, and milk. He refilled the marvelous electric kettle contraption. While the machine came up to a boil, he rummaged through the kitchen and found a vast store of cookies. Joshua must have had them delivered because Decker would remember carrying this many containers home.

"Oh! You have a cat!" Ottilie said as Trouble introduced himself by leaping into her lap.

"He belongs to Joshua," Decker said. "Or perhaps more correctly, Joshua belongs to him. He has no fear nor sense of propriety."

"I always wanted a cat." Ottilie endeared herself to Trouble by pouring milk into her saucer for him. "Dogs always seem that they can't help but like anyone who fills their food dish, but cats...you need to work to earn their love."

"I suppose people are the same," Decker said. "Some will love you no matter what you do, and others require constant proof that you love them back."

In those terms, Saul had been a dog and Lauretta had been a cat. They had been very different lovers.

Decker considered the state of his body as he poured the hot water. He still felt fine despite drinking the earlier cup of plain tea. How far did this feeling of being alive extend? Could he stomach milk and sugar? He scooped in the sugar, stirred his tea with a spoon until the sugar dissolved, and then topped off the cup with a generous pour of milk. It was heavenly tasting.

"I'm studying to be a Dominion," Ottilie said. "I see no point in trying to be a Virtue. I like to research and find answers for people. If I wasn't a Grigori, I think I would be a librarian. I'd be happy if I never had to leave the school library. It's really wonderful."

Joshua had told Decker about the secret section of the Blackridge library. It sounded like it might surpass what the Grigori had in Philadelphia—but then the Tatterskeins always were very wealthy. The Grigori had a great deal of generational wealth, but it was spread thin.

"One thing I noticed while looking for mystical sites here in Boston, I thought the Blackridge library was missing books. Not in the way that someone had taken them out and not returned them, but never collected them in the first place. All of the old-world stuff was there—covered in detail. I could find plenty of information on swan maidens and selkies and such—all written before the 1600s. There was nothing about the penguins. Barely anything about the witch trials of Salem and known local Dissonances. And the Monkshood Wickers? There's just like one footnote in the overview of the establishment of the Tatterskeins in Boston which gives the name of the coven that Barnabas chased out of New England. When I spoke to Central Office, they— Clarice—said that those kinds of books had never been written. We're not sure if it was the Salem witch trials making those who knew about the supernatural afraid to share their information, or the weird general populace losing awareness of monsters, or maybe the Dark One's Touched suppressing information, but it's a huge hole in our knowledge base: what has happened on our own doorstep since the arrival of the Europeans."

"I see." But really Decker didn't—not at least why she was here now, talking to him.

"You've been alive during all that time!" Ottilie cried. "You know a lot of what happened! What no one else has written down!"

"I . . . I was . . . present." Decker couldn't say he was "alive" during that period of time. He spent much of the time dead to the world when such events tend to happen. "In Philadelphia, mind you, until the 1950s."

"That's more than what anyone else can say! I want to write down everything you lived through! It would be a history of the East Coast!"

"I-I-I . . . What I mean . . . I-I-I . . . All three hundred years?"

"Yes, all three hundred years. I figure that we could use a normal history of the United States as a guideline and reminder of what happened. We would step forward year by year and write down everything that you remember. It has to be thorough to be effective."

"I'm not sure if you understand the scope," Decker said. "It would take days, weeks even, maybe even months to cover everything."

"I fully expect it to take years to do it properly!" Ottilie said.

He remembered then that Grigori were always zealots of one type or another. Yet, he had to admit that he'd already noticed that Elise was ignorant of things that her forefathers knew. Even Lauretta and Saul had holes in what had been common knowledge when Decker first fell under Grigori protection.

But truthfully, what else was he going to do with these new waking hours?

It would be good to expand his circle of people. Thanksgiving had been joyous with Joshua, Seth, Cabot, Elise, and Bethy. He'd been so happy.

One more person in his life would be good.

40: SETH

"How is that even possible?" Kate asked after Seth tried to update her the next morning. She'd called him to ask about their new puppy, Tal Palfrey. Seth hadn't talked to Joshua directly yet because he was afraid that Joshua would end up in New York City again. He'd gotten a rough sketch of what had happened from Jack.

"I don't know," Seth said. The conversation had started in relative privacy at the last service station on the Massachusetts Turnpike as Thane Mandeville filled up the U-Haul truck that they'd driven up from New York City. Now the elder Thane sat beside him in the cab, guiding them through Boston on their way to the Cambridge apartments that Cabot had rented. The Thane's presence had cut short his explanation. Seth didn't want to talk about all the insanely impossible things that his brother was doing. Not with Mandeville sitting beside him to overhear every word.

"The king has given me permission to move back to Boston," Seth said instead. "I'm heading to our temporary Bachelor House now. It's a set of rented apartments, side by side, one for males, the other for females."

He felt Kate reach out to check where he was. "Wow! Cool! So . . . what about me?"

"The king wants you to come to Boston," Seth said.

"Really? That's amazing! I'll have to start packing." She gave a slight laugh. "That's why I was so mad back when we got married. I have this hope chest filled with stuff that my *abuela* Marrón

441

gave me. I was her only granddaughter, so she left me this very cool music box, these fancy lace shawls, all her jewelry, and a collection of these kaleidoscopes. My other grandmother sent me this beautiful quilt that she made for my first communion. I also have a ton of books and things. I thought I was going to be stuck in New York without being able to go home and pack up my stuff. I thought my brothers would go through my room and take anything that they wanted before my parents could ship my hope chest to me. I knew that my parents wouldn't bother to pack up my books. And yeah, everything that I was mad about probably would have all happened if I hadn't gone home after we got married."

"After we got married" still felt weird when he heard it. He'd spent the last three years married but never really thinking about it. He still felt vaguely guilty about not reaching out to her earlier, but he couldn't change the past. He needed to focus on their future, making things strong enough to survive whatever was coming. If Kate really needed all her stuff to be happy with a move across the country, then he should make sure she could get it all to Boston easily.

He knew from his experience last night, trying to arrange getting his own stuff to Boston, that U-Haul wouldn't let anyone under eighteen rent their trucks. He and Kate were both just sixteen. While professional movers would take a small load any distance, they were booked solid for weeks in advance—at least the New York City ones had been. He needed to recruit Mandeville to rent the truck and drive it to Boston.

How could he help Kate move?

"I could see if the king could send his jet to San Diego to pick you up," Seth said.

"I've got the minivan! I'm not giving that up! I can just pack everything into there and drive to Boston."

He'd forgotten about her new car. "Oh, yeah, that works."

"This is so great! I'm so excited! I can't wait!"

He spotted their next turn. "Take a right here," he told Mandeville. "We're almost there. I need to go. I'll call you later on, fill in the holes."

Joshua was waiting in the parking lot, bouncing up and down with nervousness. He greeted Seth with: "I know I wasn't supposed to bite anyone, but he was dying, Seth, and I had to do something. I'm sorry, but I couldn't just let him die without trying to save him." Joshua's wolf, however, was grumbling and projecting that he'd protect his new puppy, regardless of what Seth planned.

"It's fine," Seth said, rubbing his temple. "I understand. He's a werewolf now—part of our pack. We'll take care of him. Okay? The important thing is to keep him under watch until we can be sure he's got his wolf under control."

"He's doing better than me," Joshua said. That was not saying much considering how little control Joshua had. "Cabot took him to his—"

He suddenly sprang past Seth and bowled over Thane Mandeville, who'd come around the back of the truck.

"Joshua! No!" Seth shouted. "Down! Bad boy!"

"He's a wolf!" Joshua said. "I looked at him and I could tell!"

"Yes, he's a wolf. Get off him." Seth hauled his brother off the old man. "I'm sorry. He's still a puppy."

"Yes, I see." Mandeville got to his feet. "I should have been more careful around him."

"This is Thane Mandeville," Seth told Joshua as he brushed the man off.

"Everyone always knows I'm a werewolf as soon as they see me." Joshua ignored personal space to examine Mandeville extremely closely, nearly nose to nose—or more accurately nose to chin, since Joshua was half a head shorter than Mandeville. "You really can tell immediately, can't you?"

Mandeville took a step back. "Yes. With experience, you'll be able to judge how strong they are."

Seth grabbed Joshua by his collar and pulled him back. "Give the man some space."

"Is he staying?" Joshua asked.

"No, he's not staying. Where are Tal and Jack?" Seth could tell that they were together off to the northeast but not why or where.

"Cabot took Tal to his mom's. He's going to get his clothes and whatever else he might need. His mom and little sister aren't home, so we figured now was the best time to pick it up."

"Okay, let's unload. Jack said the place was unfurnished so I brought everything I thought we might need to get up and running. Beds. Pillows. Sheets. Blankets. I stripped both Jack's room and mine and then grabbed some stuff out of a spare bedroom. Cook even gave us some old plates and silverware."

It had taken hours to gather boxes, pack them, seal them shut, ferry them to the truck, and negotiate taking what furniture and linens that he needed. Unloading took only a few minutes with three werewolves. Everything just went into a pile in the sprawling living room on the first floor since he hadn't labeled any of the boxes or decided who got what bedroom.

"Wow, this place is bigger than my mom and dad's house!" Joshua called from somewhere upstairs, his voice echoing. "Like, maybe, twice its size!"

"I should be going," Thane Mandeville said. "The king will be shifting the Thanes that are staying with him to another territory. He'll wait for me to return before giving Isaiah New York."

"Thank you for your help," Seth said.

"It's been a pleasure watching you grow into your power," Thane Mandeville said. "And a comfort to know our future is in good hands. Have a merry Christmas and may God be with you."

Seth didn't know how to respond to all that, especially knowing that the Thane was returning to possible disaster in New York. He settled on, "May God be with you too."

Tal had been two grades ahead of Seth when they both attended Blackridge.

This mattered much in terms of knowing him since he often was in a different section of Blackridge through most of the six years that Seth attended. He was aware of the boy because all his female cousins had had a crush on him, due to frequent appearances in the school plays. Because of this, he knew a weird amount about a boy that he never really interacted with. Tal's mother and father had met while both their families were working in a circus run by his mother's distant relative. His mother had traded up from the family's high wire act to study ballet at Juilliard and then joined the Boston Ballet troop. His father, the source of the spiritual bloodline, had trailed behind his wife's ambition, doing odd jobs, until the stress of the uneven lifestyle broke apart the marriage. Tal had a little sister who also attended Blackridge. She was years behind Seth and a bit of an unknown except for the fact that she had run roughshod over Seth's brothers—which was an amazing feat considering younglings were often stronger than a normal human child.

Tal returned with Cabot, loaded down with his life's belongings. He was taller than when Seth last saw him and had picked up a polished style that even being a newborn werewolf didn't ruffle. He wore a leather coat that looked like something out of *Assassin's Creed*, a pair of calf-high boots, and a knitted slouch hat. He grinned in greeting to Seth.

"This is great! The thing is my mom's place is really small. When me and my sister were little, we shared the second bedroom. After I started high school, though, I had to move onto the three-season porch. It's really sweet in the summer, but most of winter I have to sleep on the couch. I really wanted to move into the dorms at Blackridge, but with us living right in Watertown, I didn't qualify for that part of the scholarship."

"Sorry about that," Jack said as he came to hug Seth in greeting. It had only been a few days, but Jack had nearly died in the interim. "We're back!"

He meant back in Boston to stay. Back home—or at least as close as to home as they could get.

The way things were going, they needed to hit the ground running. They needed to be as strong as possible if the king was going to continue to grow weaker. If Isaiah failed to hold New York. If the Dark One wasn't the last of their worries.

41: JOSHUA

"Hark, the herald angels sing!" Joshua sang, struggling to remember the words. "Glory to the newborn king!"

Elise groaned on the couch. Cabot lay beside her, half asleep in a food coma, his head in her lap. "Oh, God, please, no!"

"Sorry, it just feels like there should be music," Joshua said. "And that seemed...I don't know...appropriate."

"I'll find something festive," Ottilie said, taking out her phone.

It had been less than two weeks since Seth had moved into the Bachelor House. It had been a frantic ten days, doing everything from buying four new cars, having Joshua get his actual driver's license, teaching Tal how to be a proper werewolf, enrolling Seth at Blackridge, calling the surrounding packs to let them know that Boston was accepting young wolves, and buying everything needed to live in the two apartments. Appliances to vacuum cleaners. With all that was going on, getting a tree had been pushed to Christmas Eve.

Because of Decker's high ceilings, they could get a seven-foot-tall fir tree that filled the house with the smell of pine. After feasting on Chinese takeout, they settled in to decorate the tree.

They were an odd bunch: four werewolves, a vampire, two angels, and Bethy. The Blackridge dorms had closed for the holiday break and Ottilie hadn't wanted to go home.

"My family doesn't celebrate the Winter Solstice or Christmas or Hanukkah," Ottilie had said. "Going home is fairly pointless.

My brothers and sisters are all in Greece, training. There's a good chance my parents will be out hunting. I'll be sitting at home, alone, eating Chinese takeout and trying to find something on television that isn't related to Christmas."

Joshua supposed it was like having all the kids in your class going to a giant birthday party that you weren't invited to. Somehow, Ottilie ended up staying at Decker's for the entire holiday break. Joshua wasn't sure how that came about.

The idea of Chinese food, though, sounded like a great idea to everyone. They'd gotten more food than even four werewolves could eat. Some of the dishes Joshua recognized, like orange chicken, and fried rice and beef with garlic sauce, but a ton of others that he'd never had before. Scallion Pancakes. Drunken Chicken. Five-Spice Beef Shin. Dumplings. Buns. Noodles.

Ottilie found "Last Christmas" on some music app and started to play it.

Joshua wasn't sure if it was "festive" but at least it was bouncy.

Joshua scanned the many boxes of ornaments laid out on the coffee table. They had raided all the local stores for decorations to counter expected and unexpected losses. Joshua had only broken two so far. Tal was winning at six shattered ornaments, but Joshua's kitten Trouble wasn't far behind. Said kitten lay under the Christmas tree, gazing upward as if mesmerized by the twinkling lights and gleaming decorations above him.

Joshua spotted the gift that Mannie had given him when the shapeshifter showed up at Blackridge to say goodbye. It was a ceramic penguin ornament with a wide grin, holding a banner with the year written on it.

"I couldn't find a rockhopper." Mannie had been in his human form, dressed for cold weather. It meant that he had been getting curious stares from students who hadn't been able to see him the first time he visited the school. Mannie held out the unwrapped box showing a grinning penguin that looked nothing like his bird shape. "Think of this as our emperor. I'm told he's quite... cheeky. He'd probably thank you himself, if he was anywhere north of the equator. We all want to thank you... you saved all of our people. We're indebted to you... and Decker... so... this is wildly insufficient to what we owe you two—but hopefully it will be a reminder that we penguins are grateful for all that you've done for us."

"Oh!" Joshua hadn't known what to say as he accepted the ornament. He'd never saved an entire race of people before. "Okay. Thank you."

"We're heading back home now." Mannie had pointed vaguely toward the airport. "I doubt we'll ever see each other again—what with me living nearly in the Antarctic and whatnot. Have a good life."

"You too." Joshua had stopped himself from saying "see you" since he wouldn't. "Goodbye."

Joshua picked the ceramic penguin off the coffee table, wondering if Mannie had gotten home safely. Was Mannie celebrating Christmas with a tree and decorations or just swimming in the ocean, catching fish and swallowing them whole?

Joshua really hoped his life would get back to being normal soon.

Another glass ornament exploded in Tal's hand. He was still getting used to his werewolf strength.

"Ouch!" Tal peered at his hand to see if any of the glass had embedded in his palm. "I really thought that I'd be better at this since I juggle and such."

"It's a matter of controlling the wolf, not hand/eye coordination." Seth studied the tree, a deep red ornament in hand. He'd always been the quiet, serious type but the last week or so, it had seemed like he had the weight of the world on his shoulders. "You're doing very well. My dad had me moving eggs from one carton to the other for a month when I was first changed. But I think he was being extra careful with me because of my little brothers and my family's history."

Seth found a bare spot to hang the red glass ball.

"Oh, yeah, we want to be careful." Tal paused and then added, "I just remembered. I talked to my mom last night. She and my sister got to Oklahoma fine. Her whole family is there and it's one big literal circus. Flying trapeze and clown cars!"

It was one of the reasons that Seth had insisted that Tal stay in Boston.

"I'm sorry," Joshua said.

"It's okay. It's just that one of my cousins is an internet You-Tube influencer. Her channel is about growing up 'under the big top.' She makes insane amounts of money and is in the middle of talks with Hollywood to have her own television shows. She went big on genealogy recently, so she got everyone in the family one of those DNA tests kits. That made Grandma pull my mom aside and confess that she'd fooled around and got pregnant before she married Grandpa, and my mom isn't his kid. She wanted to tell Mom before all the DNA profiles came back with proof that Mom isn't a full sibling to my aunts and uncles. Grandma told her that her real dad was a guy she met in New Orleans during Mardi Gras by the name of Adelard Domengeaux."

Seth stared at Tal. "Earl Adelard of the New Orleans pack?"

Tal shrugged. "Possibly. Domengeaux is a common name in those parts."

"Well, if it was, it would explain your little sister," Seth said.

"Truth. I swear she growls in her sleep."

The timer in the kitchen went off, signaling that the fifth pie of the day was done. They'd eaten a blueberry, an apple, a cherry, and a pumpkin pie already. This was a pecan pie. Joshua hung the penguin on the tree and headed into the kitchen.

Bethy had beaten him to the oven. She took out the pie. "I can't believe how much food you're putting away and not getting fat."

"Yeah, my wolf is a bottomless pit, it seems." Joshua caught himself taking a plate out of the cabinet. "We're not eating it until it cools down!"

"Thanks for the gift cards," Bethy said. "I really wasn't expecting that much but it's going to go a long way toward keeping me mobile."

"Let me know if you need anything." Joshua distracted his wolf from the pie by opening up the boxes of fancy cookies. One of the Tatterskein Christmas traditions that Seth recreated was an extensive order of cookies from a North End bakery called Bova. They bought pounds of snowflake-shaped pizzelle, sugar-dusted Italian wedding cookies, coconut macaroons, red-and-white butter cookies, and lemon-powdered sugar cookies. With the endless pies, the boxes had sat mostly untouched.

"I need to take a doggie bag with me." Bethy pointed at the cookie boxes but was careful to keep out of snapping distance. She had been taught werewolf precautions at Thanksgiving. "Those are amazing."

"Tell me what you want, and I'll make it for you." He found a quart-size plastic storage container that he'd bought thinking that he could meal prep lunches like his mom did for her and his dad at the garage. The last two weeks had proved it was futile to plan meals ahead; his wolf ate everything long before lunchtime rolled around.

"Three or four of each of them." She picked up the electric teakettle and filled it with water. "I told Mom and Dad that my team was having a holiday party, and the coach strongly suggested that I show up. I promised to be home tonight. I said I was going to be late, but I really need to get going."

"Thanks for coming all this way to see me," Joshua said, knowing that she had a three-hour drive back to their parents' home. The weather, at least, was clear for the next two days.

"I have something for you." She flipped on the kettle and then picked up her backpack to dig through it.

It was a plastic gallon freezer bag holding the holiday card that he'd mailed to his parents before Thanksgiving.

"Oh shit!" He took the bag. "How did you get that?"

"When I went home after my last final, I stopped at the garage. Mom and Dad were super busy and didn't notice me. I snooped through Mom's desk and found this. I figured that I'd never have a better chance of grabbing it and not get caught. From what I could put together without asking any direct questions, she was going to drive up to Grandpa's a week ago and drop it off and get the money. Great Aunt Ginny, though, called and said that her spiritualist had gone missing."

"Missing?" Joshua echoed. Ewan must have had his "talk" with the con man who was scamming Great Aunt Ginny. "That's good—maybe."

Hopefully "missing" didn't mean "dead."

"Between that and your Christmas presents, they stopped talking about you being dead."

Bethy had been against Joshua sending anything, but he had a weird feeling that silence would be worse. He didn't want his mom thinking he'd been tortured, brutally murdered, and buried in some unmarked grave. He figured gifts that could have only come from him would reassure his folks that he was alive and well—even if he was a little "delusional" about being kidnapped as a baby.

Part of the mass ornament-buying spree he'd done with Seth had included a local antique store that stocked retired Hallmark decorations. It had been another Tatterskein Christmas tradition that each kid was allowed to buy one ornament for the year. That way, each child would have a small collection of sentimental decorations when they married and moved out.

Seth had gone to the store to find replacements for beloved ornaments that been lost in the fire. Joshua had tagged along and found two that were perfect for his parents. He'd gotten his dad a model of a 1936 GMC pickup truck that had been released in 2013. He'd added a note, explaining that he remembered all the stories about how his dad had helped his grandfather refurbish the truck when he was a boy. For his mom, it was a 1968 Chevrolet Corvette—which had been the car that made her fall in love with Dad. The ornaments were small, easy to ship, relatively inexpensive, and yet suited their taste.

Bethy took a large travel mug out of her bag. "I don't know if this solves the problem of Grandpa telling the police that you're adopted, but at least now the police can't do shit like check the postmark or analyze the card for DNA."

The important thing was that the police didn't find out that he'd been kidnapped as a baby. Since none of his relatives believed his kidnapping story, it was quite possible that they wouldn't think of mentioning everything that he wrote in the card. Still, it was also possible that his grandfather would bulldoze ahead without any evidence—sure that he was right. It was a family trait, one their dad shared. It was the reason Joshua didn't dare try to contact his parents until he was legally an adult and able to refuse to go back to his old school.

The water had come to a loud boil. The kettle clicked off. She put tea bags in her travel mug and poured the hot water into it.

"I thought about just telling Mom and Dad that you called me," Bethy said as she waited for her tea to brew. "When I ran the scenario in my head, I realized they would probably try to give my phone to the police. Even if I could talk them out of physically taking it, the police could just pull my phone records with a warrant—and possibly charge me with obstruction of justice. I mean, if you were just a runaway—no, they probably wouldn't bother but we're looking at more than two dozen people torn to pieces. The police *will* want to track you down and have *looong* conversations with you."

Another reason why not to go home. There was no way he could explain all the weirdness that had happened to him since he'd fled his parents' house. Even stripping away the werewolves, the vampires, the witches, the shapeshifting penguins, and the evil god, he'd be left with the shooting of his birth mother that would implicate his parents in murder and kidnapping.

"Best thing to do now is sit tight and be quiet until Mom and Dad see the logic of leaving you in Boston," Bethy said.

"April," he said firmly. His real birthday was in March. April would put him firmly into eighteen years old.

"April," Bethy echoed. "Maybe June—after you graduate. That's the big problem. You can't go back to our old high school. Those idiots never stopped bullying you, even after you started judo. They're not going to stop."

"Yeah, I know."

She checked her watch. "I've got to go if I'm going to be home by midnight."

"Drive safe," he said. "And you're welcome to come back anytime."

She surprised him by hugging him tightly. "You be safe! You're the one fighting gods. Be more careful! Stop being so weird."

"I'm trying!" he said.

She said goodbye to the others and headed home. It felt weird to close the door behind her. Somehow, he felt adrift in the world, cut off from the life that he used to know. June seemed like years in the future.

Decker came ghost-quiet down the hall. Joshua's wolf leaned into him. Lately, Decker smelled of the green forest of Joshua's Source—it had something to do with him being awake a good part of the day and actually eating real food. And the fact that Decker now wanted to teleport when they went out despite the fact that it made him drunk.

"Now, now." Decker patted him on the head. "I know three months seems like forever, but it will go quickly. Meanwhile, you have your new family here."

"I know," Joshua said. Unlike Seth, Joshua's parents were still alive. There would be other Christmases. He wasn't even the only one who had parents they weren't seeing during the holiday season. Both Tal and Ottilie were going to be spending the school break with Joshua instead of their parents.

"Hey, Joshua! We're done!" Seth called from the living room. "We're out of decorations. It's movie time!"

The tree looked like Seth had spent over a thousand dollars on ornaments and lights. It was the most amazing Christmas tree that Joshua had ever seen.

"Photo time!" Cabot announced, pulling out his phone. "Brothers' first Christmas together!"

This triggered everyone into taking out their phones and taking pictures. They posed in groups in front of the tree. Brothers. Werewolves. Angels. Goths. Vampires with house pets (which is what Decker said with his apologetic "I can't help it, I find it funny" grin).

After all possible groupings and individual photos were exhausted, they settled in to watch the movie. Seth had a full range of old comedies that Joshua had never seen. The adults sat on the big leather couches. The kids all sprawled on the floor in a non-furry puppy pile. They laughed until it hurt and, for a while, all was right with the world.